HELLSING ⑥

ヘルシング

平野耕太
KOHTA HIRANO

translation
DUANE JOHNSON

lettering
WILBERT LACUNA

DARK
HORSE
MANGA

DMP
Digital Manga
Publishing

publishers
MIKE RICHARDSON and HIKARU SASAHARA

editors
TIM ERVIN and FRED LUI

collection designer
DAVID NESTELLE

English-language version produced by
DARK HORSE COMICS and DIGITAL MANGA PUBLISHING

HELLSING VOL. 6

T 251339

Dark Horse Manga
A division of Dark Horse Comics, Inc.
10956 S.E. Main Street
Milwaukie OR 97222

darkhorse.com

Digital Manga Publishing
1487 West 178th Street, Suite 300
Gardena CA 90248

dmpbooks.com

To find a comics shop in your area, call the
Comic Shop Locator Service toll-free at 1-888-266-4226

First edition: March 2005
ISBN-10: 1-59307-302-X
ISBN-13: 978-1-59307-302-2

3 5 7 9 10 8 6 4 2

Printed in Canada

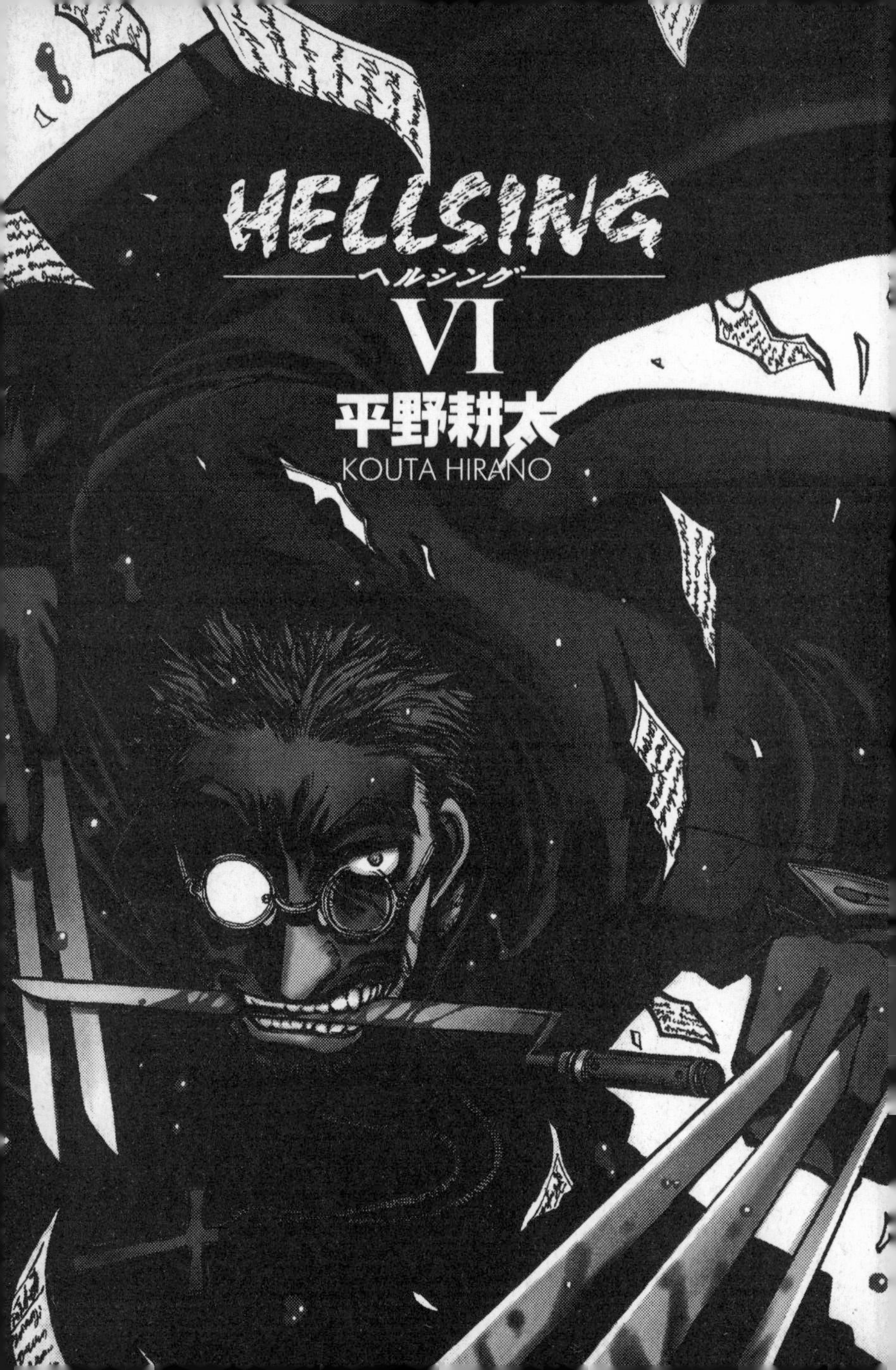
HELLSING
ヘルシング
VI
平野耕太
KOUTA HIRANO

HELLSING ⑥

ORDER 1

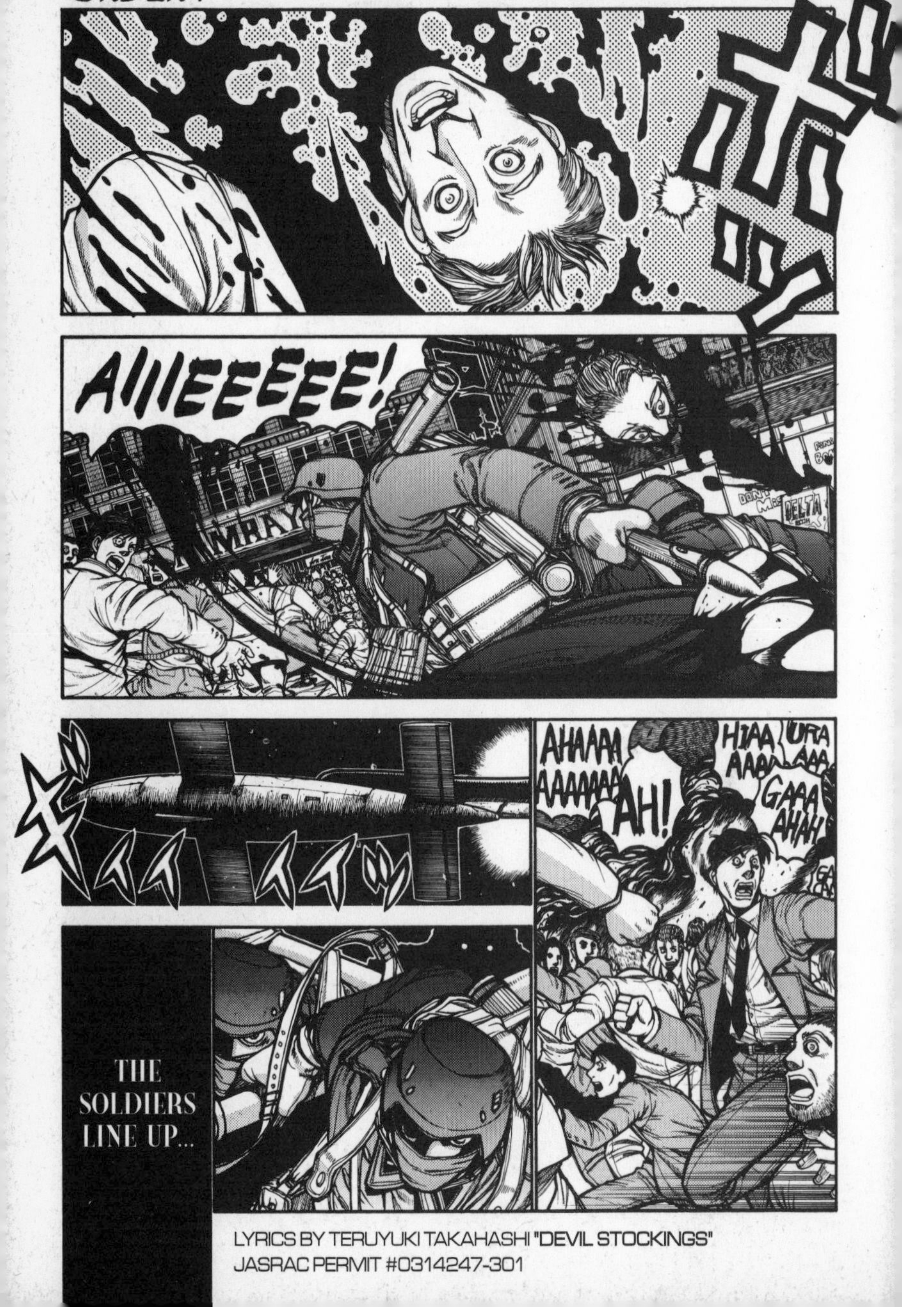
AIIIEEEEEE!
URA AAA
HIAA AAA
AHAAAA AAAAAAAAAH!
GAAA AHAH
THE SOLDIERS LINE UP...

LYRICS BY TERUYUKI TAKAHASHI "DEVIL STOCKINGS"
JASRAC PERMIT #0314247-301

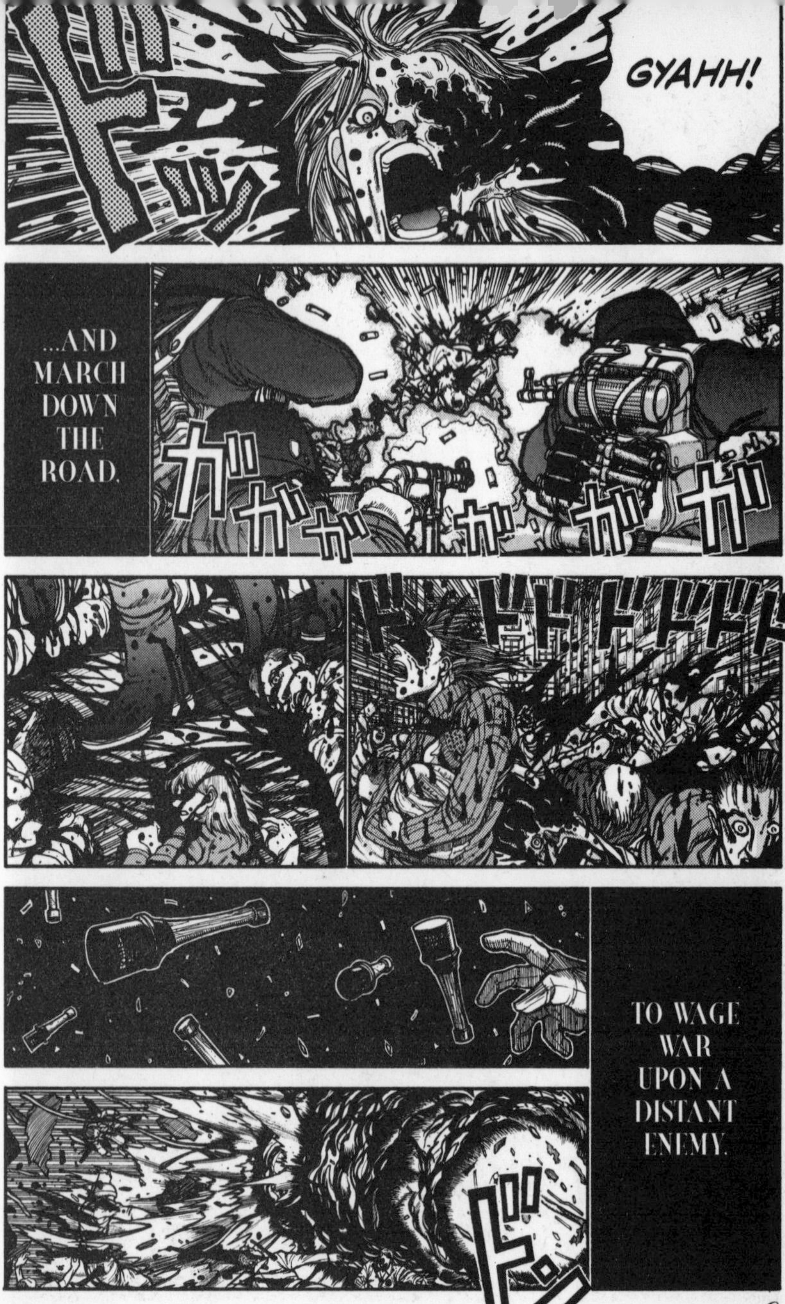
GYAHH!
...AND MARCH DOWN THE ROAD.
TO WAGE WAR UPON A DISTANT ENEMY.

THEY KEEP
MARCHING
ON.

JUST SO
THEY
CAN DIE...

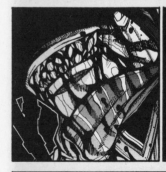

...IN THIS TIME GONE MAD.

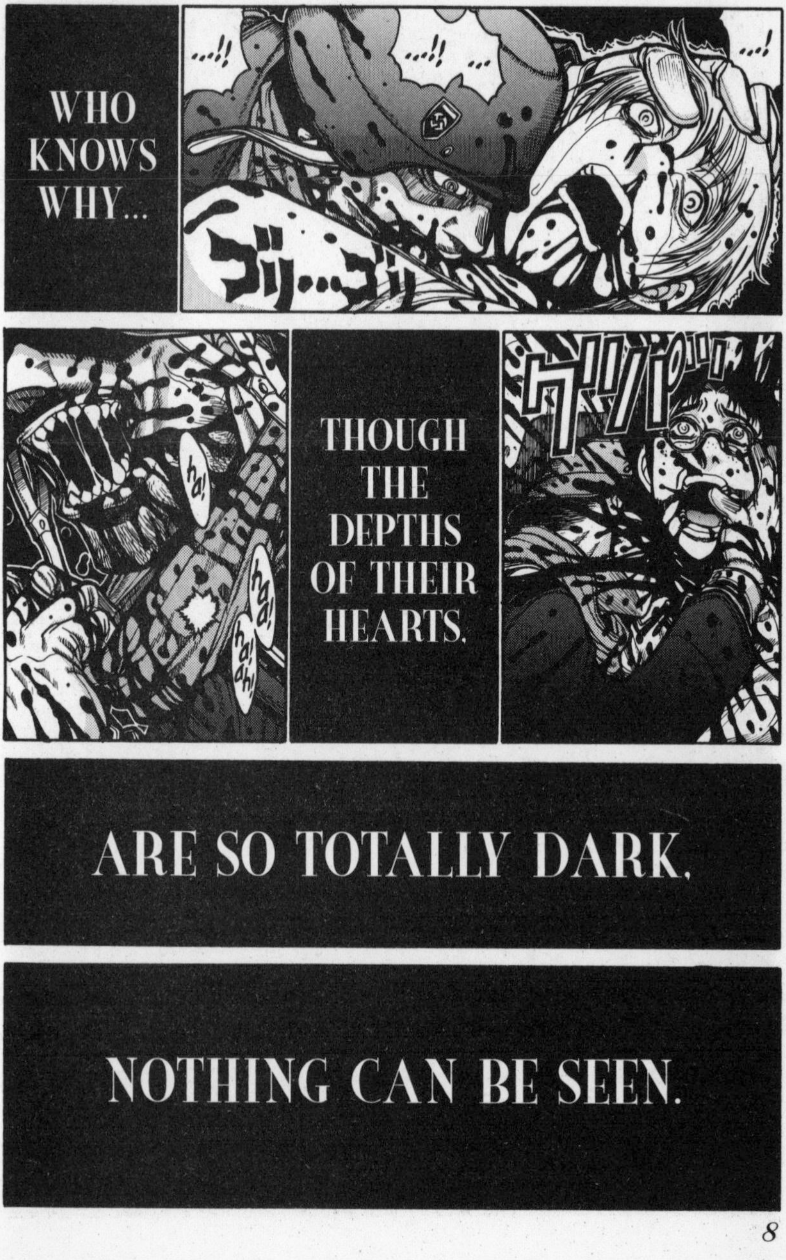
...!
...!!
...
...!!
ゴリ…ゴリ
WHO KNOWS WHY...
THOUGH THE DEPTHS OF THEIR HEARTS.
ha!
ha!
ha!
ha!
ah!
ARE SO TOTALLY DARK,
NOTHING CAN BE SEEN.

THEY STAND IN A WIND-BLOWN FIELD.

COUNTING THE NUMBER OF CORPSES.

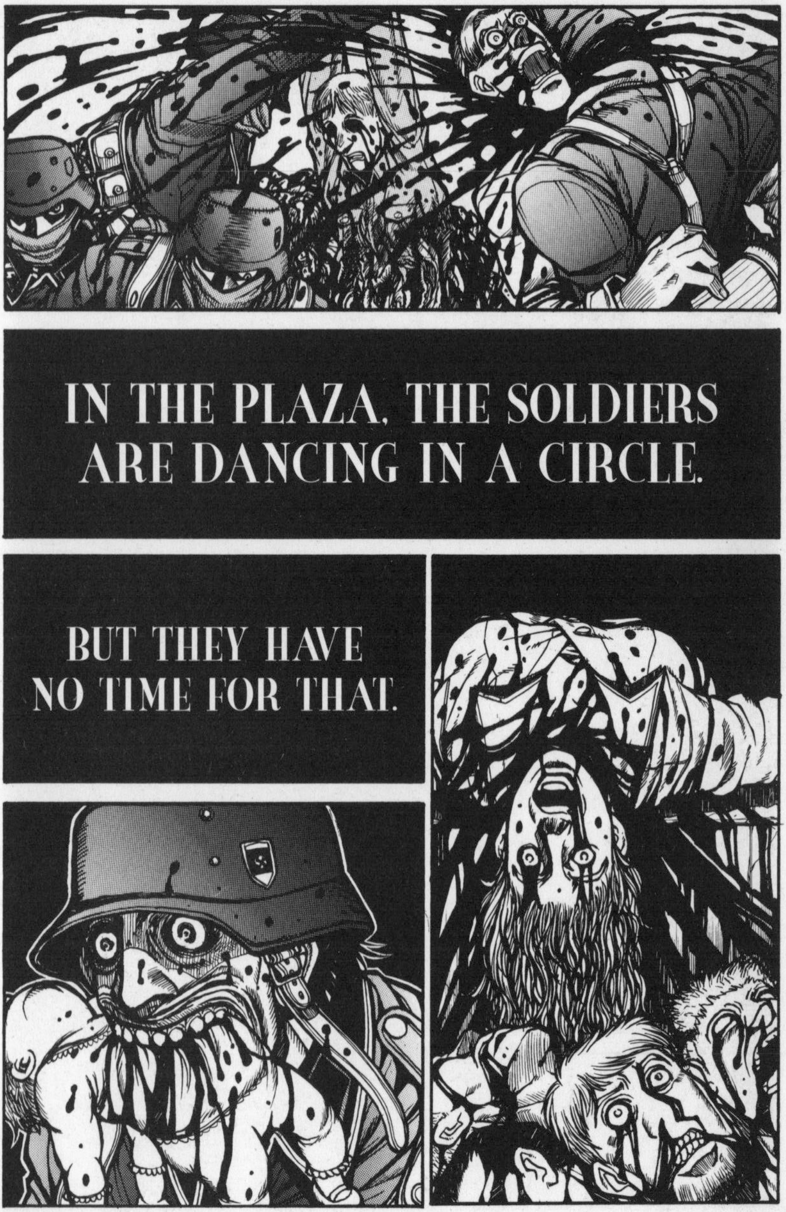
IN THE PLAZA, THE SOLDIERS ARE DANCING IN A CIRCLE.
BUT THEY HAVE NO TIME FOR THAT.

TO MAKE
THEIR
ESCAPE,

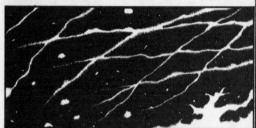

TO PROLONG...

THE
LENGTH
OF
THEIR
LIVES.

THEY WATCH HOW THE
ROTTEN SHADOW

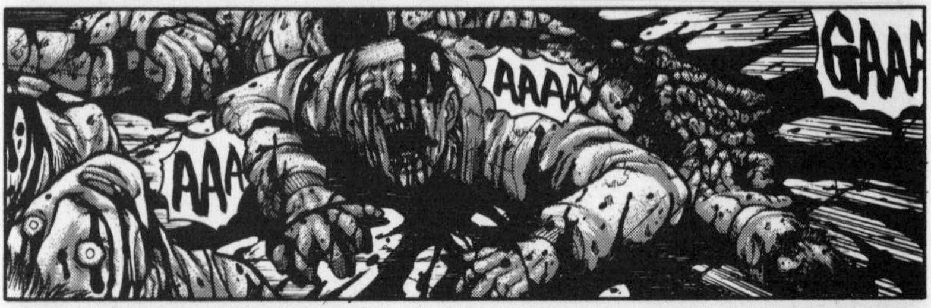
GAA
AAAA
AAA

FROM THE CLOCKTOWER AT
THE END OF THE WORLD

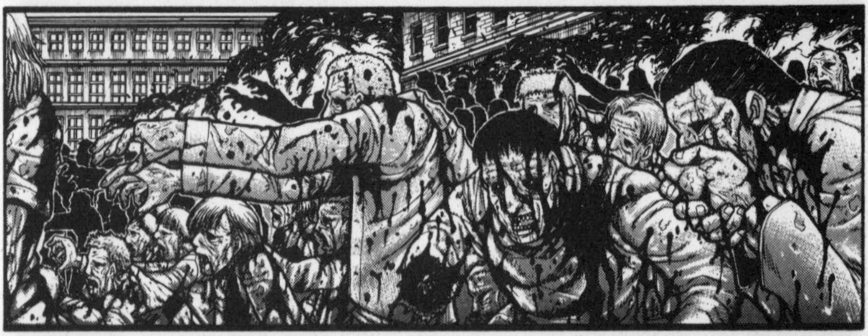

FALLS ACROSS THE RED FIELD.

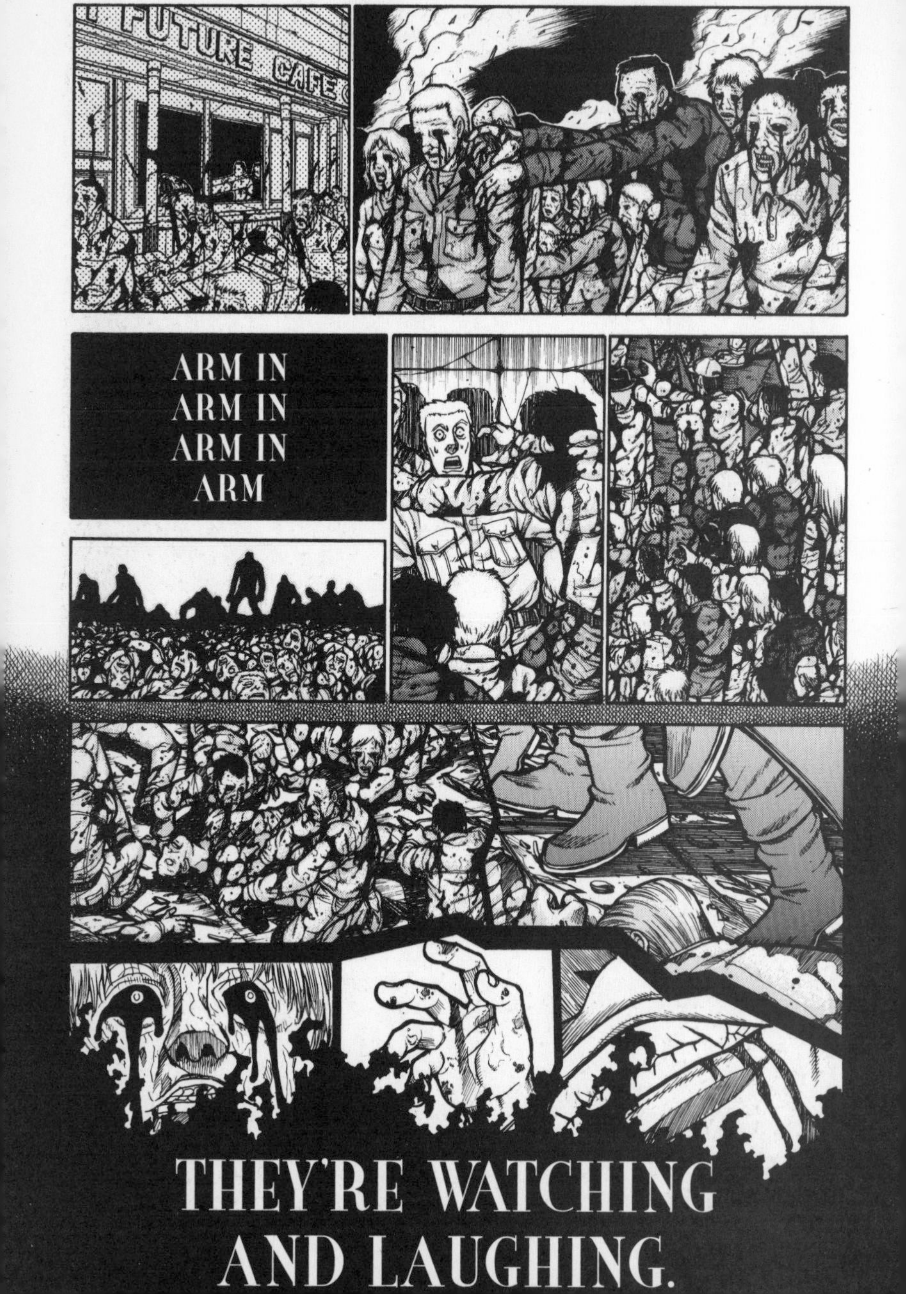
FUTURE CAFE
ARM IN ARM IN ARM IN ARM
THEY'RE WATCHING AND LAUGHING.

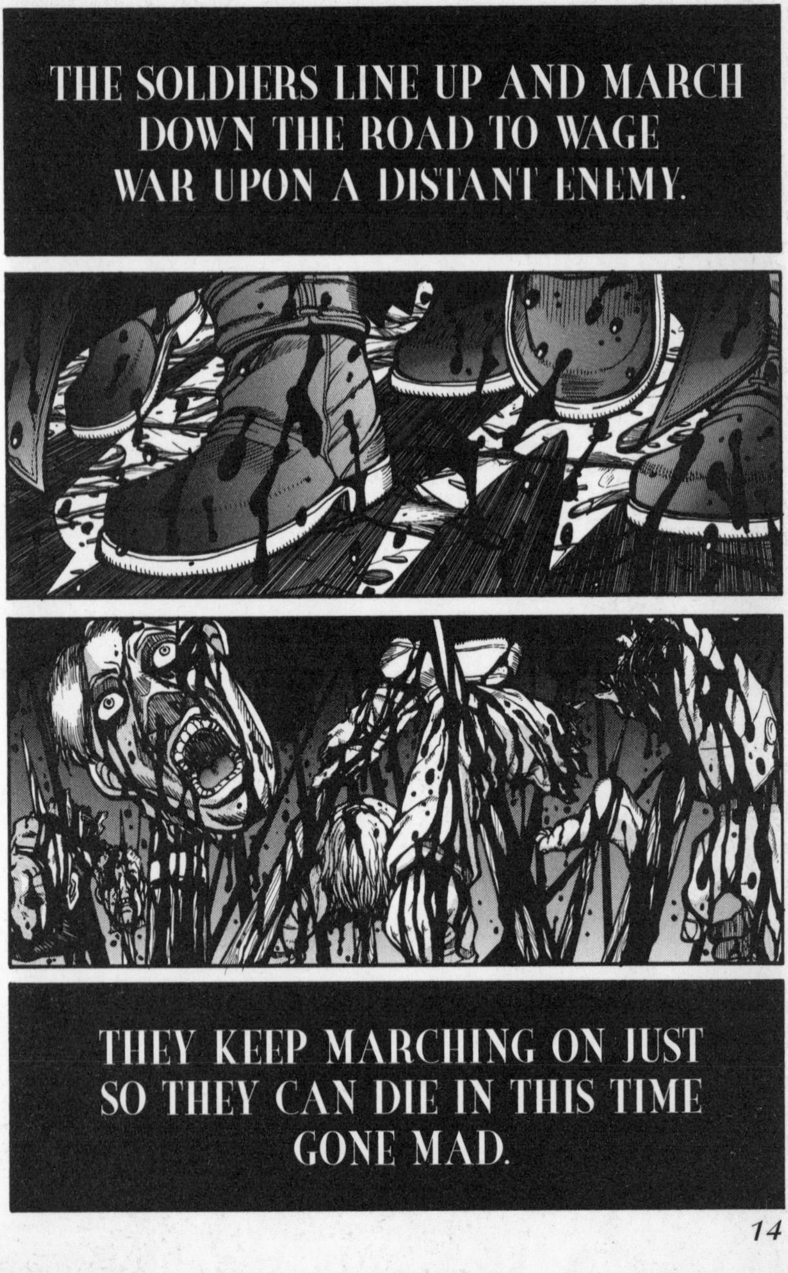
THE SOLDIERS LINE UP AND MARCH DOWN THE ROAD TO WAGE WAR UPON A DISTANT ENEMY.
THEY KEEP MARCHING ON JUST SO THEY CAN DIE IN THIS TIME GONE MAD.

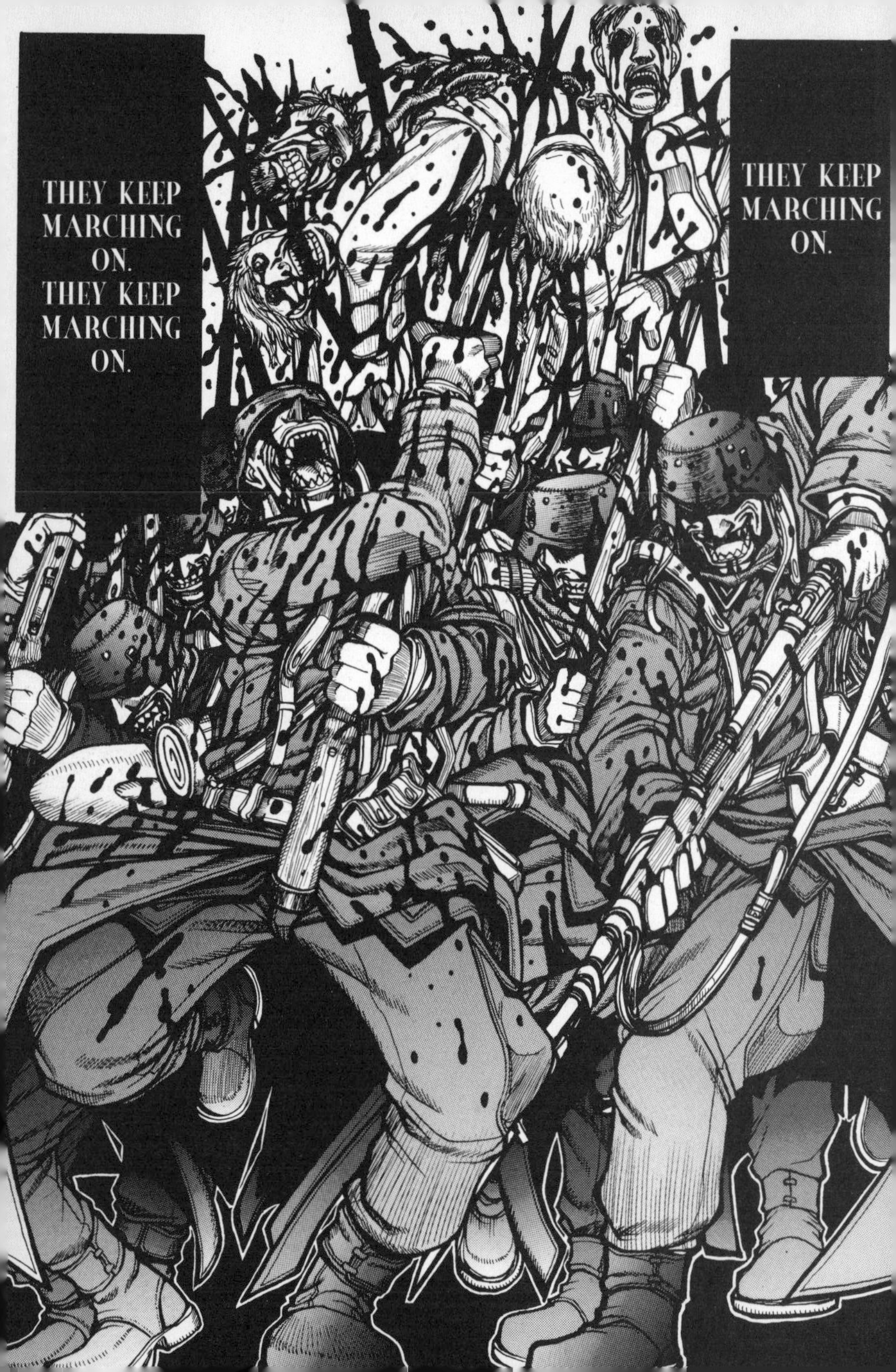
THEY KEEP MARCHING ON.
THEY KEEP MARCHING ON. THEY KEEP MARCHING ON.

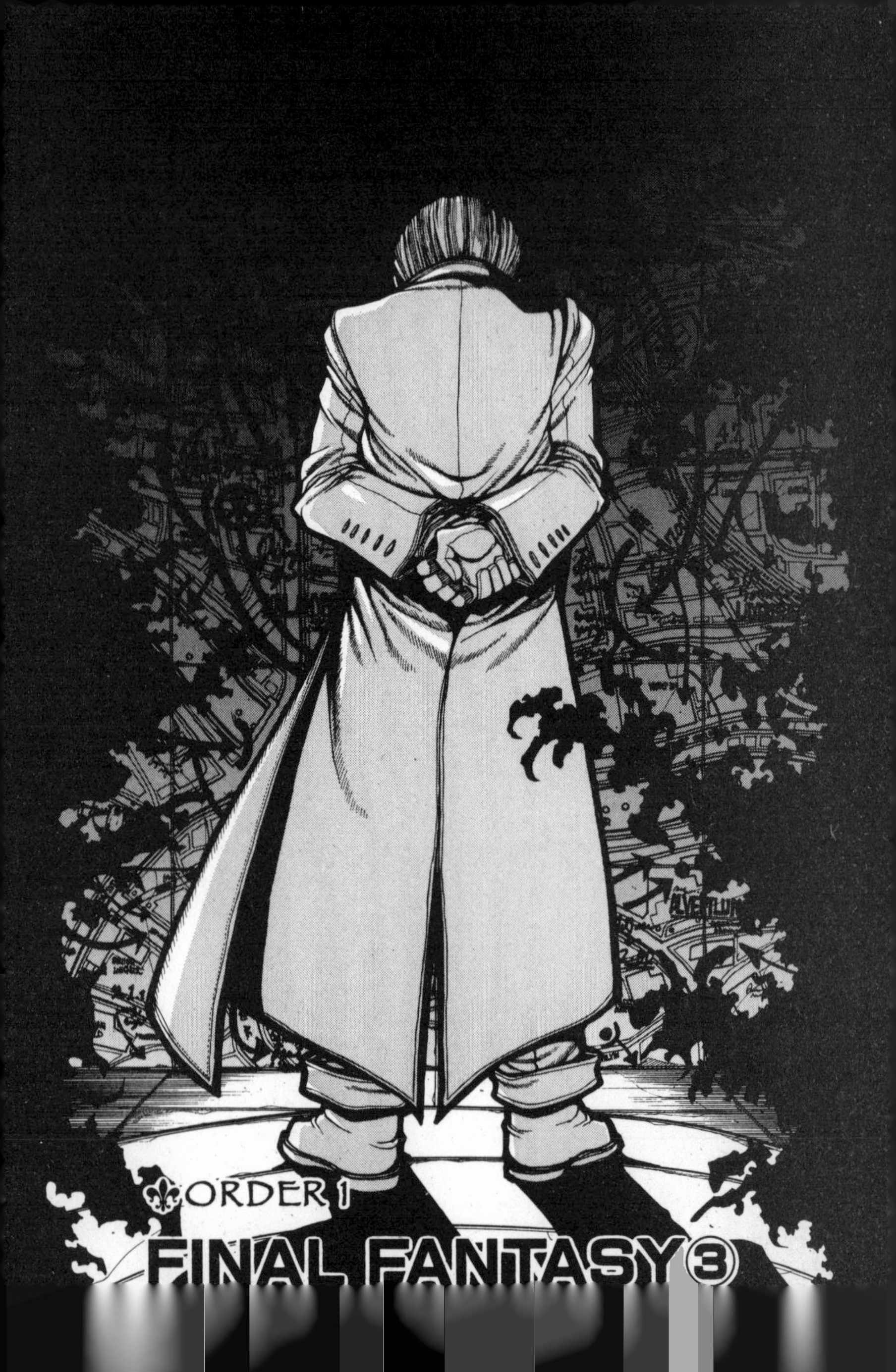
ORDER 1
FINAL FANTASY 3

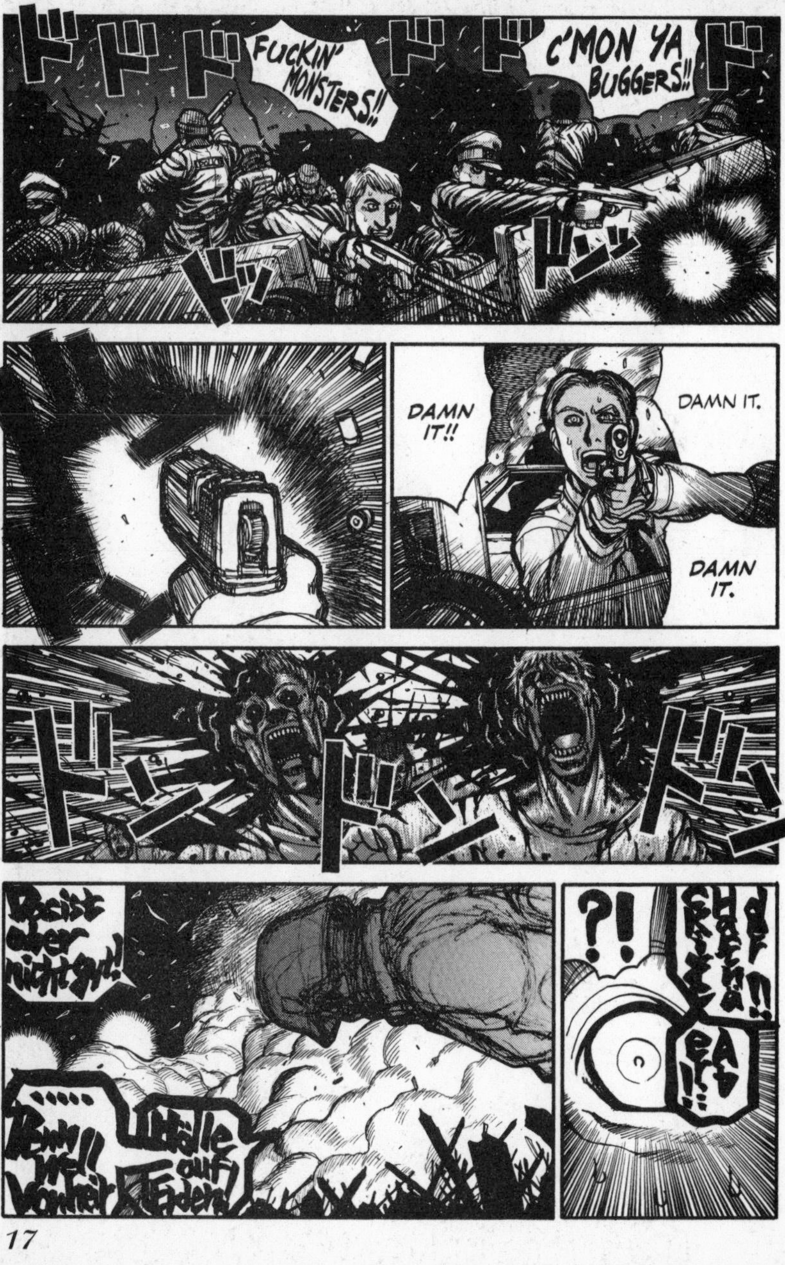
C'MON YA BUGGERS!!
FUCKIN' MONSTERS!!
DAMN IT.
DAMN IT!!
DAMN IT.
?!
Dasist aber nicht gut!
Hölle auf Erden!

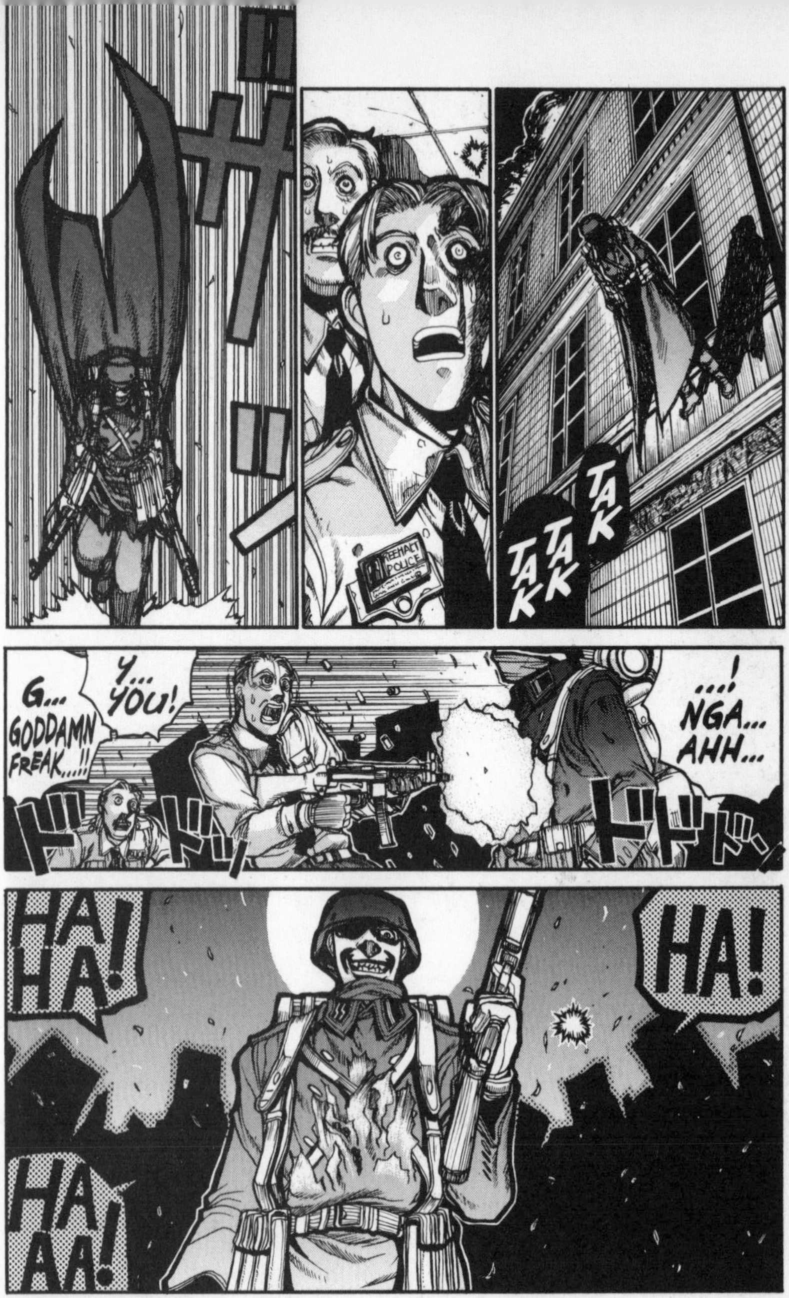
TAK TAK TAK
...! NGA... AHH...
ドドドド...
Y... YOU!
G... GODDAMN FREAK...!!!
ドドド
HA!
HA HA!
HA HA!

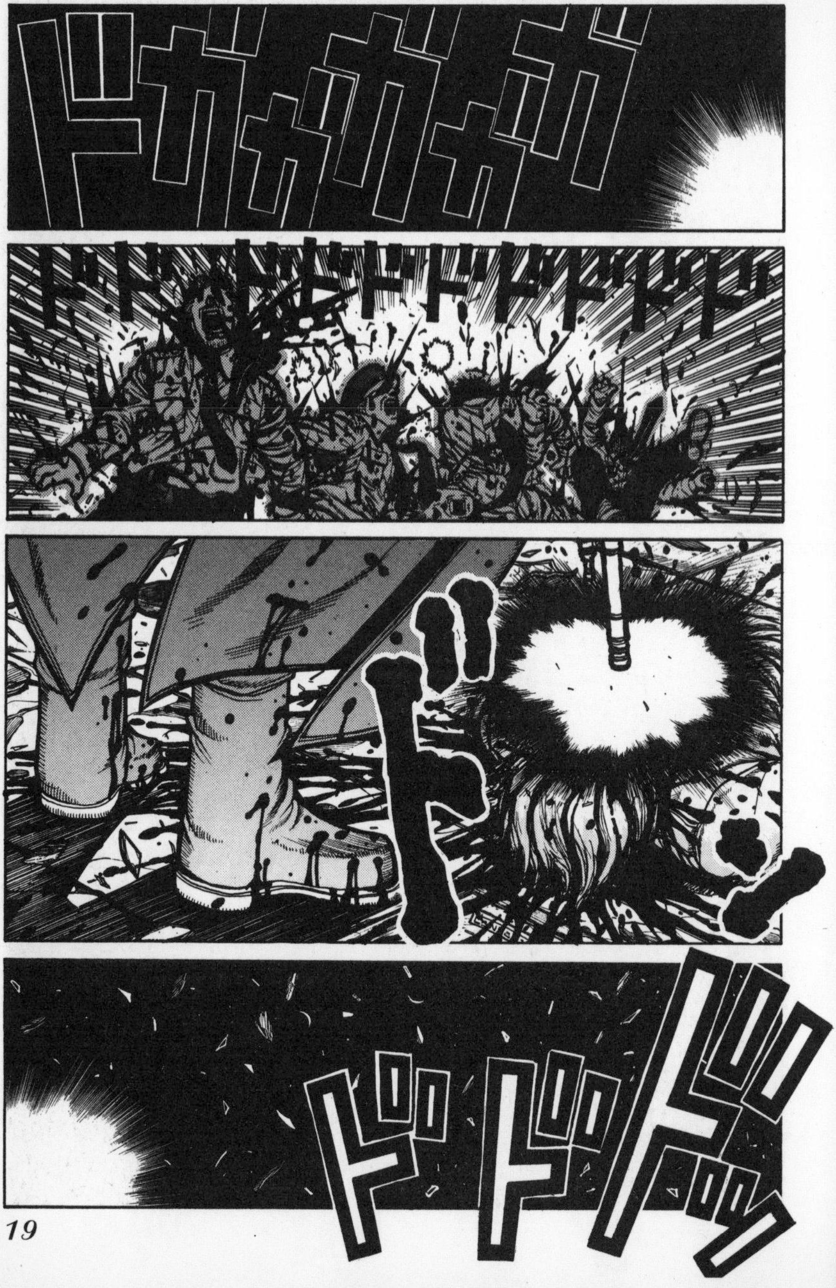

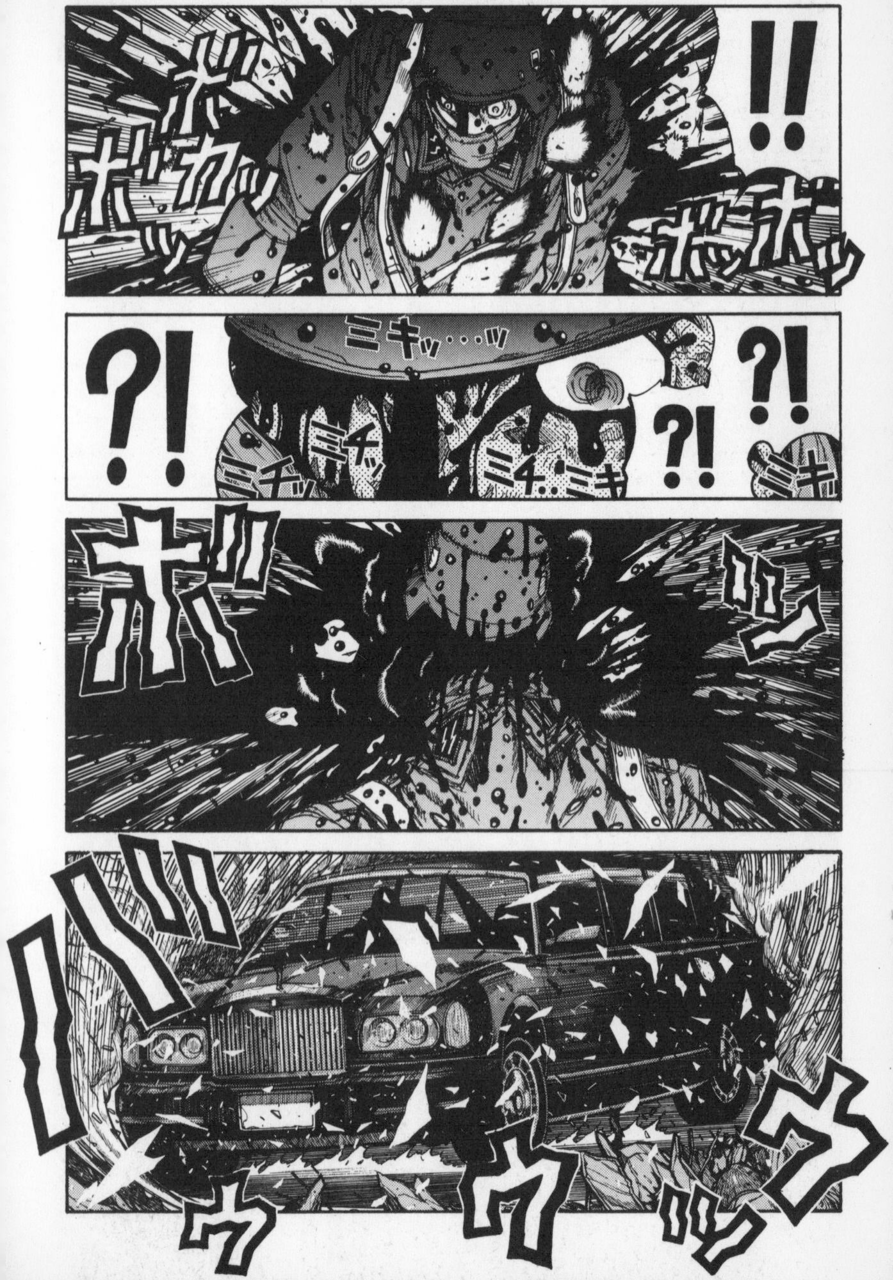
!!
ボッボッ
?!
ミキッ・・・ッ
?!
?!
ミキ
ミキ・・・ミキ
ミヂッ
ボゴン

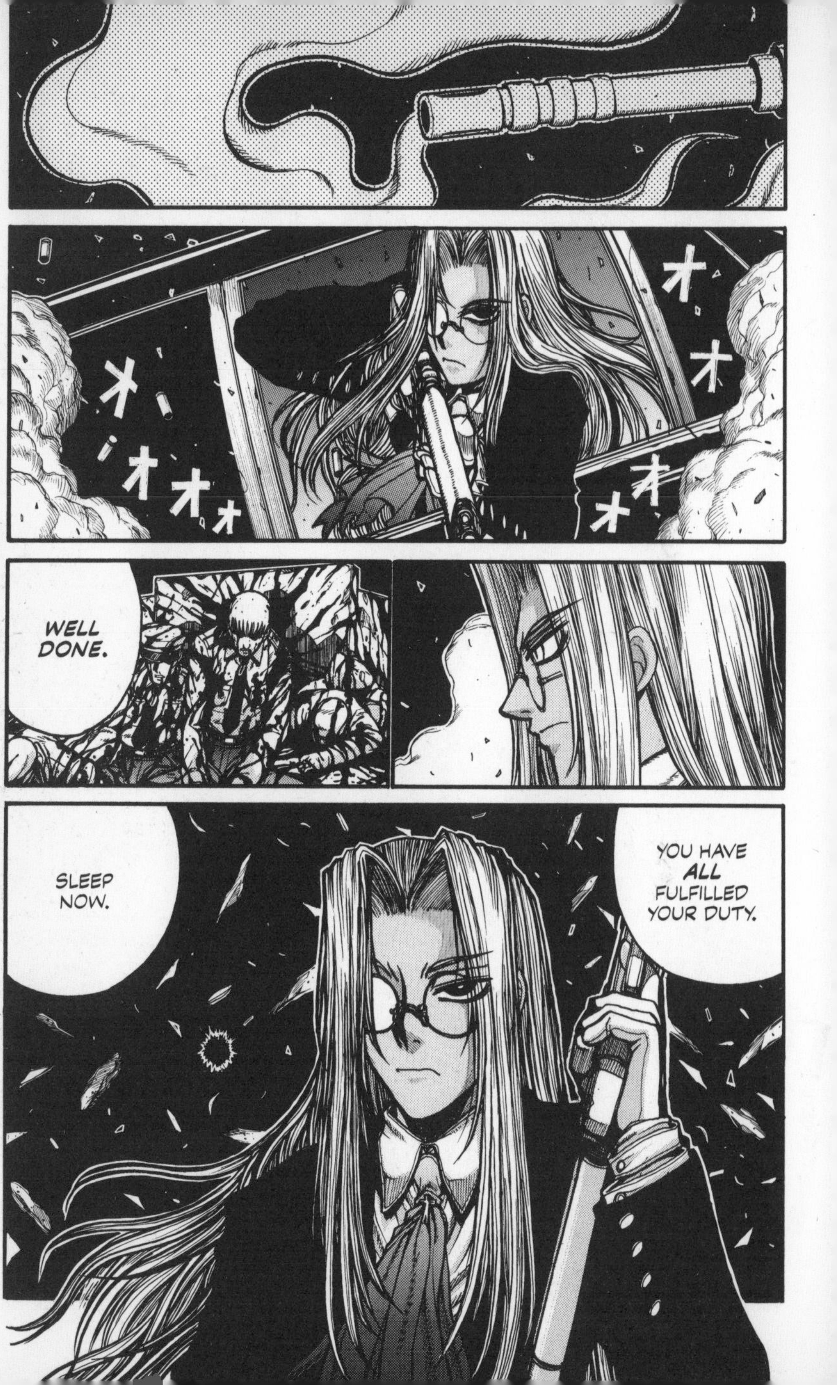
WELL DONE.
YOU HAVE *ALL* FULFILLED YOUR DUTY.
SLEEP NOW.

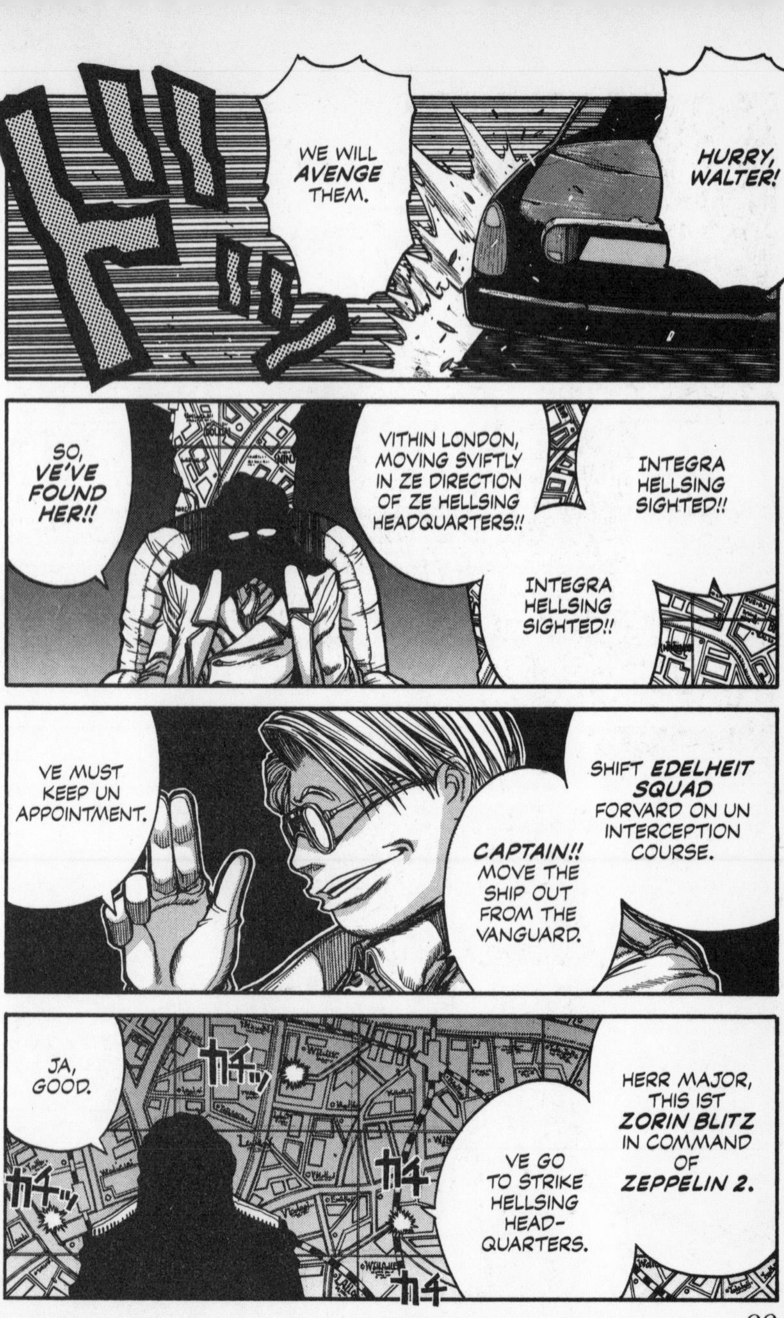
HURRY, WALTER!
WE WILL AVENGE THEM.
INTEGRA HELLSING SIGHTED!!
VITHIN LONDON, MOVING SVIFTLY IN ZE DIRECTION OF ZE HELLSING HEADQUARTERS!!
INTEGRA HELLSING SIGHTED!!
SO, VE'VE FOUND HER!!
SHIFT EDELHEIT SQUAD FORVARD ON UN INTERCEPTION COURSE.
CAPTAIN!! MOVE THE SHIP OUT FROM THE VANGUARD.
VE MUST KEEP UN APPOINTMENT.
HERR MAJOR, THIS IST ZORIN BLITZ IN COMMAND OF ZEPPELIN 2.
VE GO TO STRIKE HELLSING HEAD-QUARTERS.
JA, GOOD.

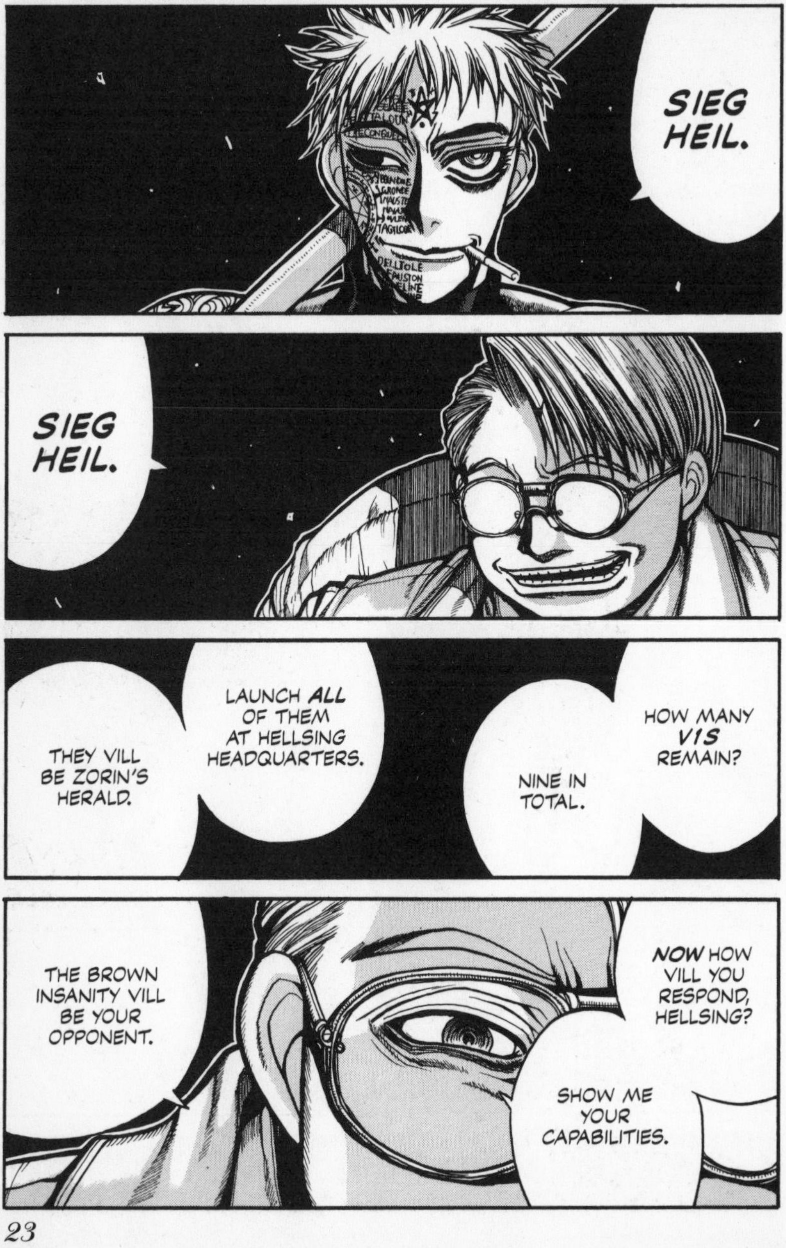
SIEG HEIL.
SIEG HEIL.
HOW MANY VIS REMAIN?
NINE IN TOTAL.
LAUNCH ALL OF THEM AT HELLSING HEADQUARTERS.
THEY VILL BE ZORIN'S HERALD.
NOW HOW VILL YOU RESPOND, HELLSING?
SHOW ME YOUR CAPABILITIES.
THE BROWN INSANITY VILL BE YOUR OPPONENT.

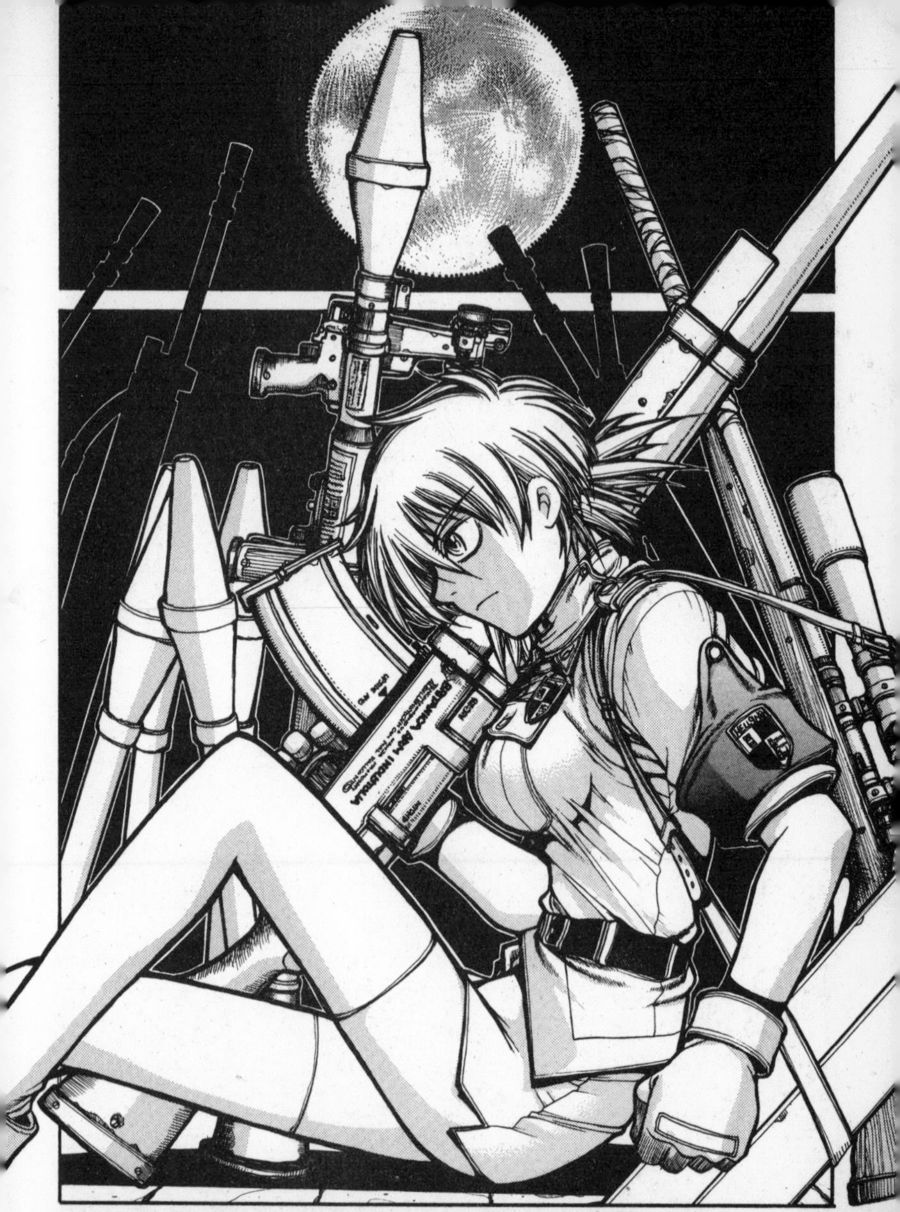

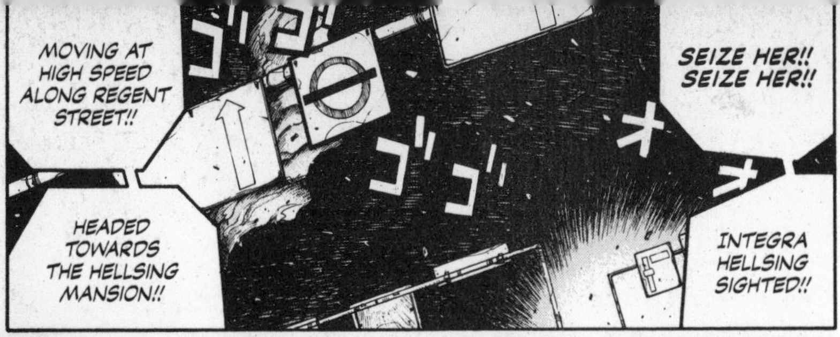
SEIZE HER!! SEIZE HER!!
MOVING AT HIGH SPEED ALONG REGENT STREET!!
INTEGRA HELLSING SIGHTED!!
HEADED TOWARDS THE HELLSING MANSION!!

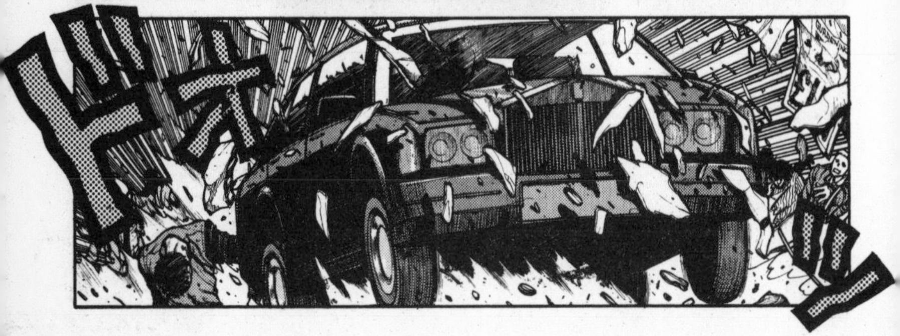

⚜ORDER 2

FINAL FANTASY④

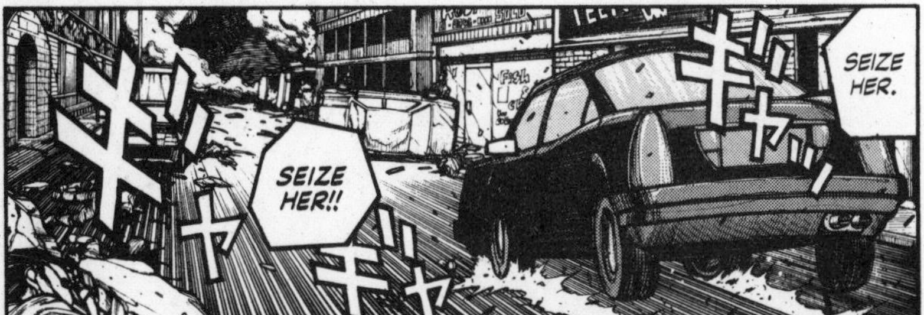
SEIZE HER.
SEIZE HER!!

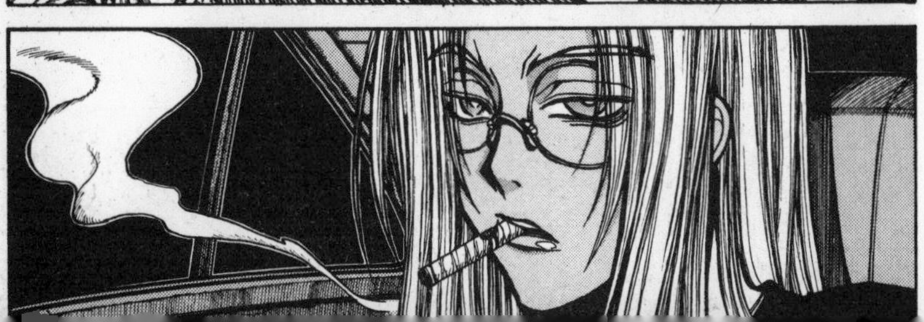

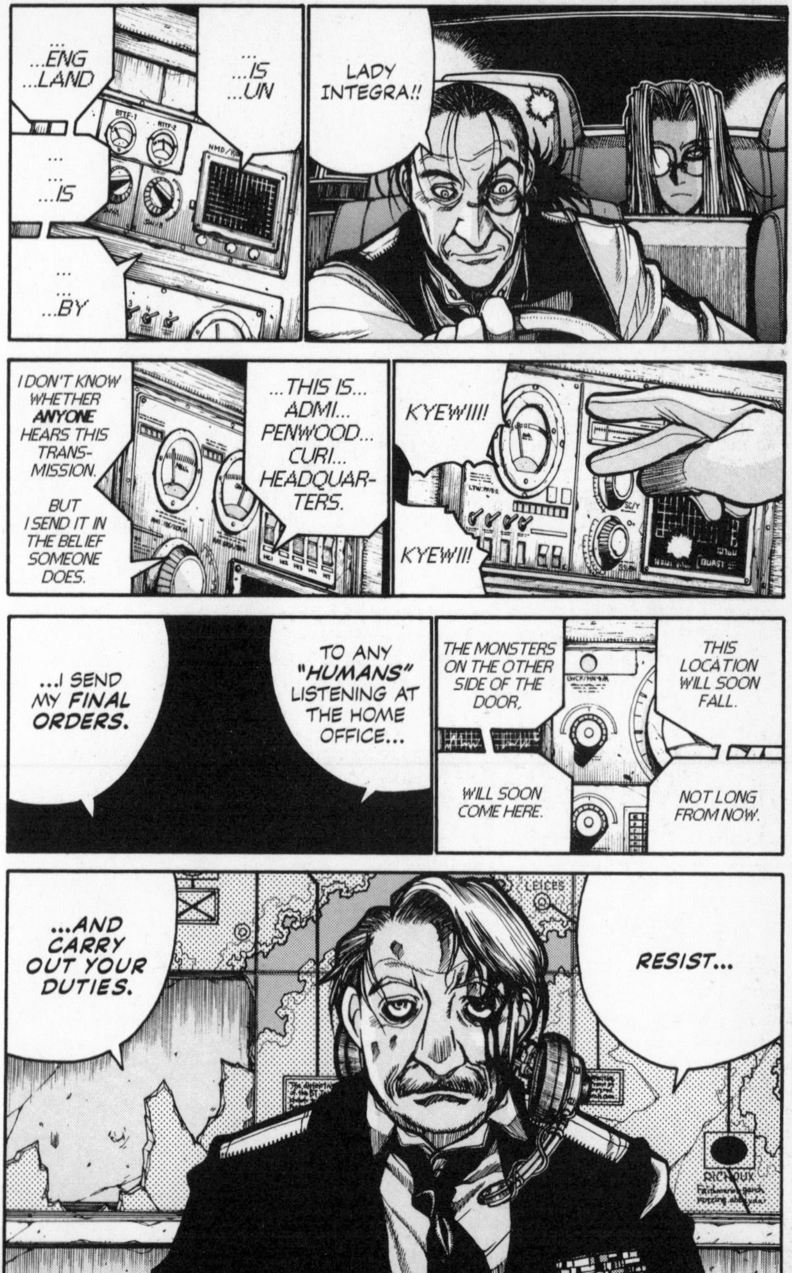
LADY INTEGRA!!
... ...IS ...UN
... ...ENG ...LAND
... ...IS
... ...BY
KYEWIII!
KYEWIII!
...THIS IS... ADMI... PENWOOD... CURI... HEADQUAR-TERS.
I DON'T KNOW WHETHER **ANYONE** HEARS THIS TRANS-MISSION.
BUT I SEND IT IN THE BELIEF SOMEONE DOES.
THIS LOCATION WILL SOON FALL.
THE MONSTERS ON THE OTHER SIDE OF THE DOOR,
NOT LONG FROM NOW.
WILL SOON COME HERE.
TO ANY "*HUMANS*" LISTENING AT THE HOME OFFICE...
...I SEND MY **FINAL ORDERS.**
RESIST...
...AND CARRY OUT YOUR DUTIES.

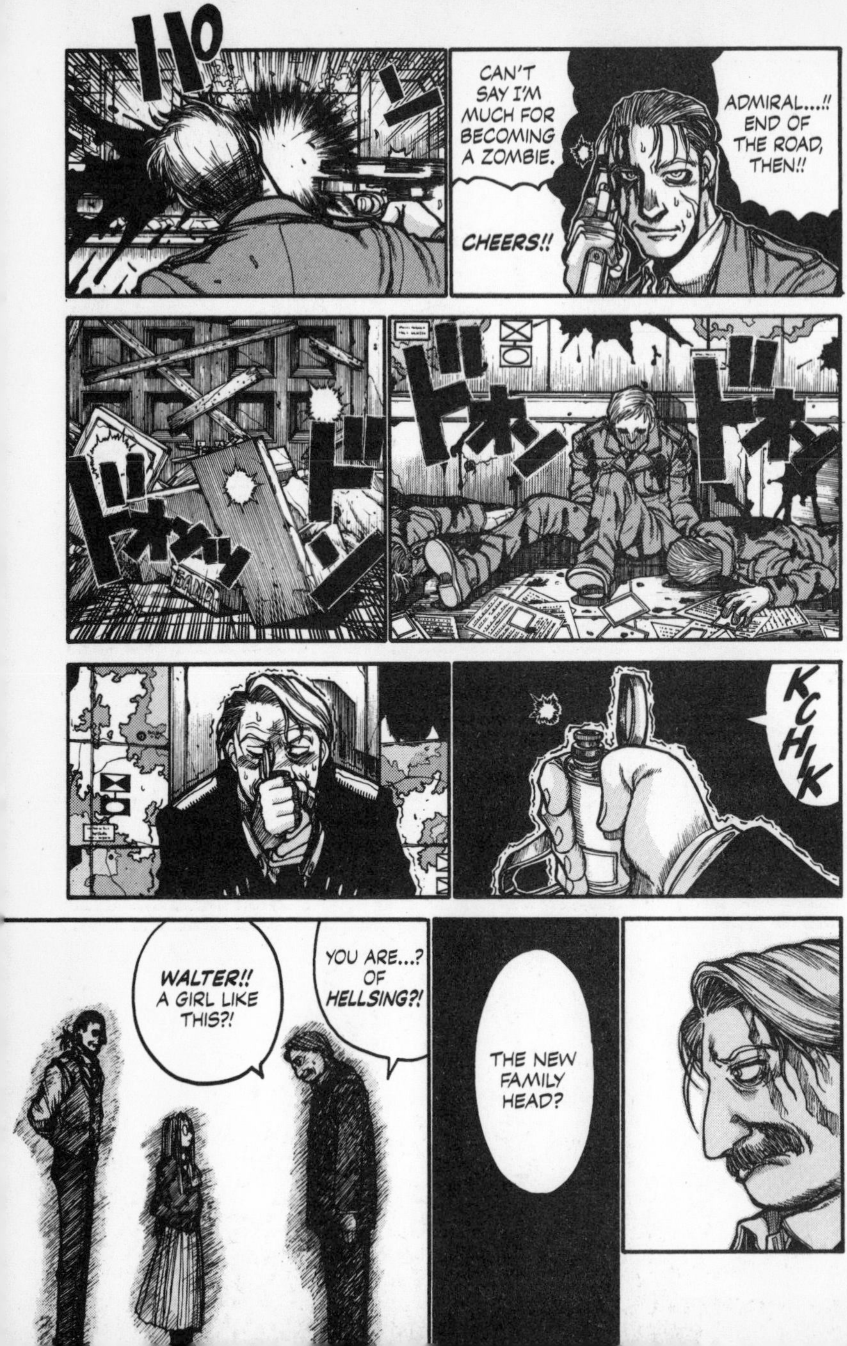
ADMIRAL...!! END OF THE ROAD, THEN!!
CAN'T SAY I'M MUCH FOR BECOMING A ZOMBIE.
CHEERS!!
KCHIK
THE NEW FAMILY HEAD?
YOU ARE...? OF HELLSING?!
WALTER!! A GIRL LIKE THIS?!

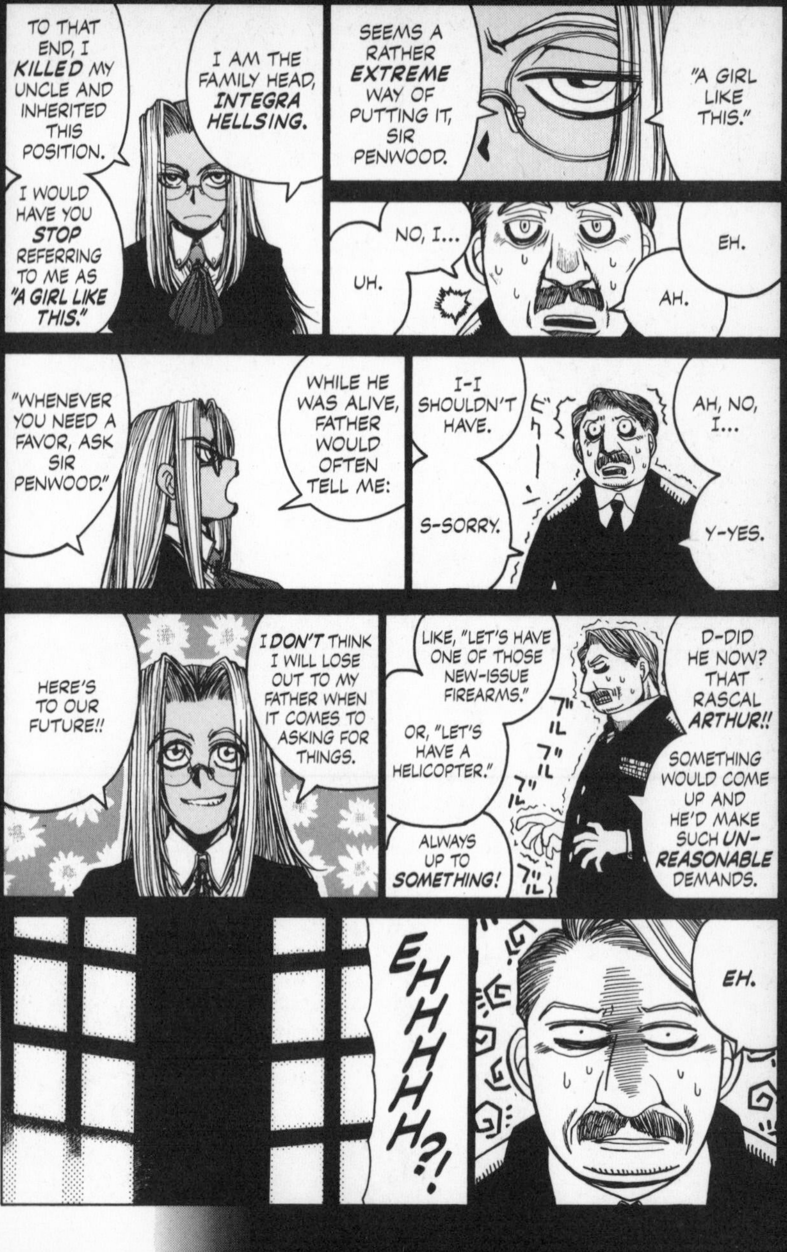
"A GIRL LIKE THIS."
SEEMS A RATHER EXTREME WAY OF PUTTING IT, SIR PENWOOD.
EH.
AH.
NO, I...
UH.
I AM THE FAMILY HEAD, INTEGRA HELLSING.
TO THAT END, I KILLED MY UNCLE AND INHERITED THIS POSITION.
I WOULD HAVE YOU STOP REFERRING TO ME AS "A GIRL LIKE THIS."
AH, NO, I...
Y-YES.
I-I SHOULDN'T HAVE.
S-SORRY.
WHILE HE WAS ALIVE, FATHER WOULD OFTEN TELL ME:
"WHENEVER YOU NEED A FAVOR, ASK SIR PENWOOD."
D-DID HE NOW? THAT RASCAL ARTHUR!!
SOMETHING WOULD COME UP AND HE'D MAKE SUCH UNREASONABLE DEMANDS.
LIKE, "LET'S HAVE ONE OF THOSE NEW-ISSUE FIREARMS."
OR, "LET'S HAVE A HELICOPTER."
ALWAYS UP TO SOMETHING!
I DON'T THINK I WILL LOSE OUT TO MY FATHER WHEN IT COMES TO ASKING FOR THINGS.
HERE'S TO OUR FUTURE!!
EH.
EHHHHHH?!

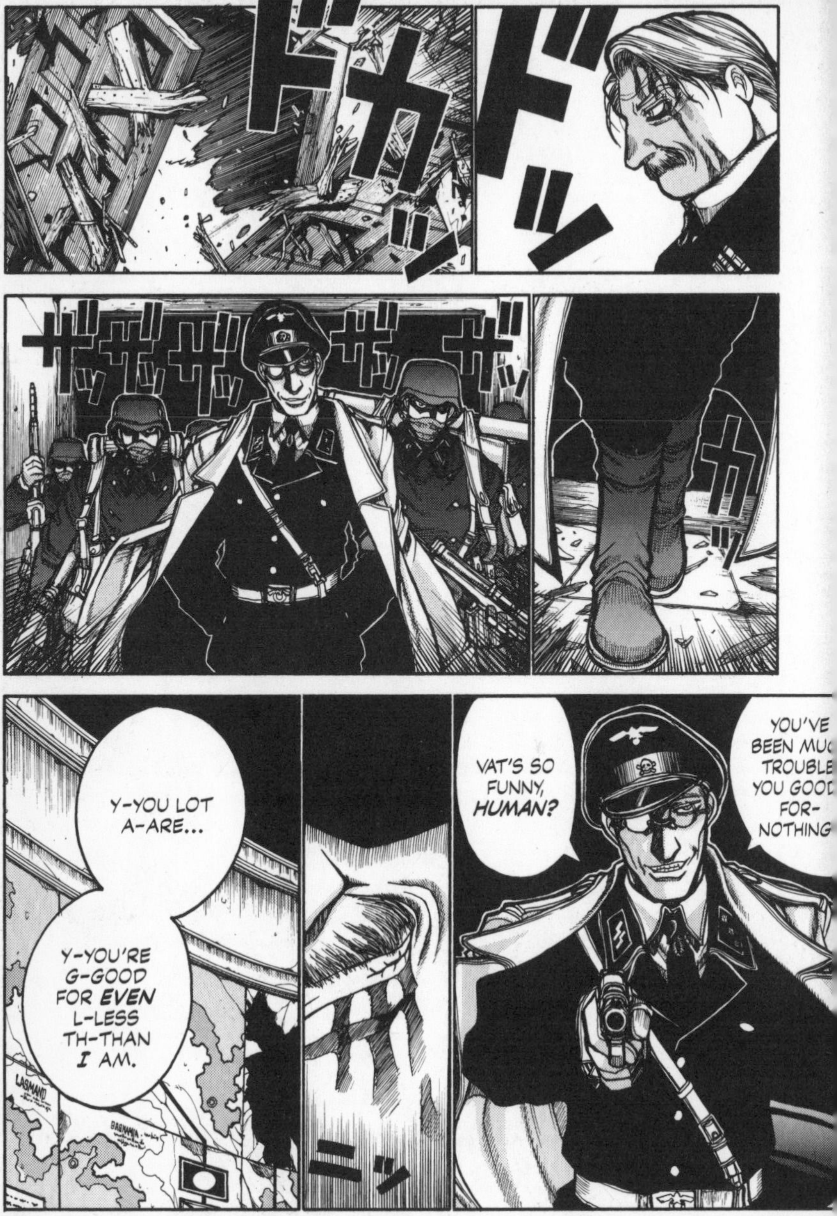
ドッ
ドガッ
カッ
ザッ ザッ ザッ ザッ ザッ
YOU'VE BEEN MUC TROUBLE YOU GOOD FOR- NOTHING
VAT'S SO FUNNY, **HUMAN?**
ニッ
Y-YOU LOT A-ARE...
Y-YOU'RE G-GOOD FOR **EVEN** L-LESS TH-THAN **I** AM.

I-IT'S BEEN *FUN* FOR ME, *TOO.*

G-GOD, *GODSPEED,* I-INTEGRA.

SWOOOP!!

S--!

THAT'S ONE FAVOR I *WON'T* GRANT!!

NO!!

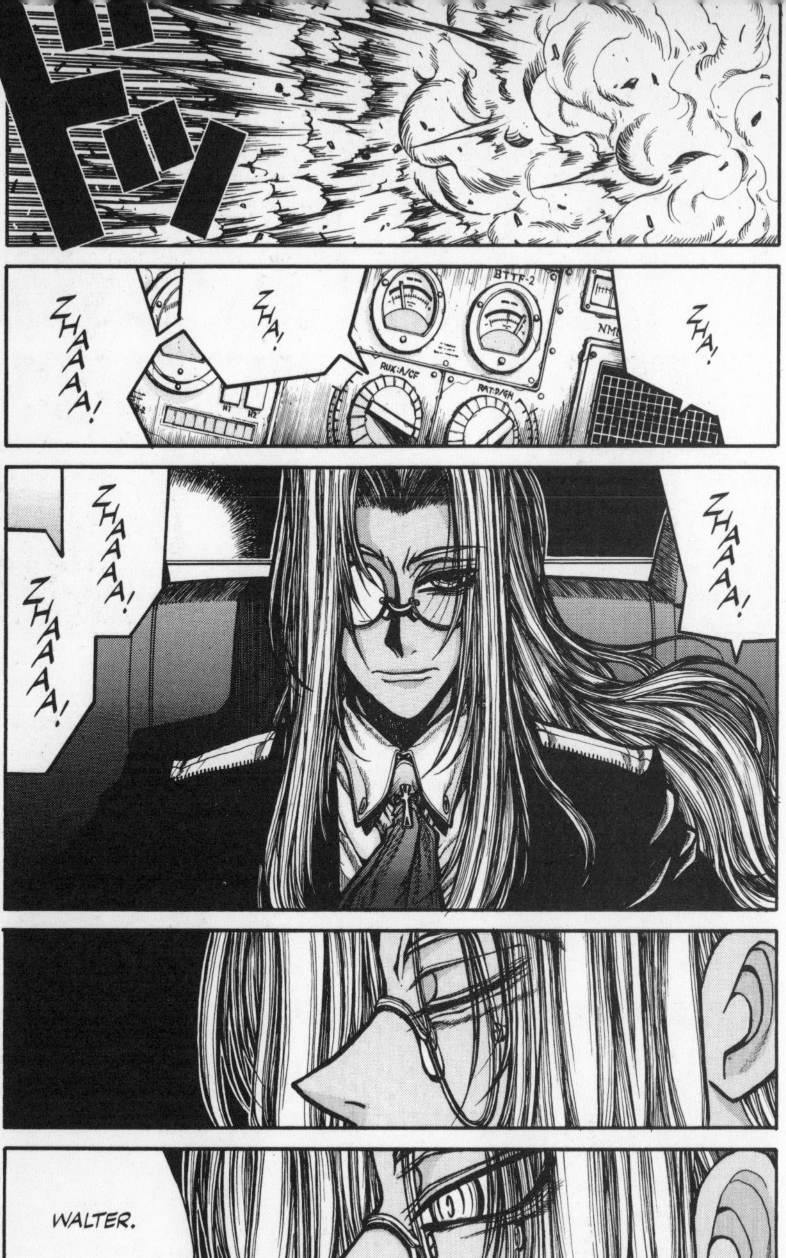
ドッ
ZHA!
ZHA!
ZHAAAAA!
ZHAAAAA!
ZHAAAAA!
ZHAAAAA!
WALTER.

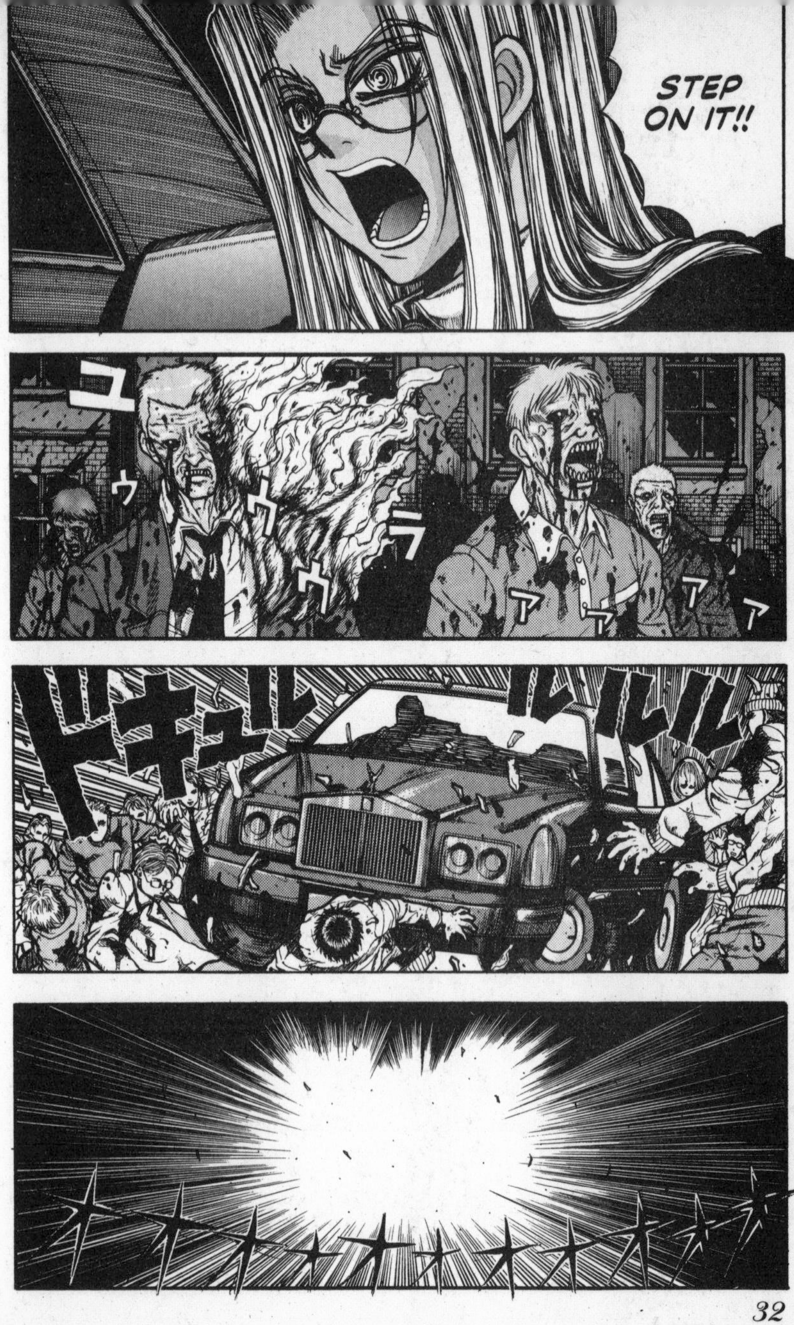
STEP ON IT!!

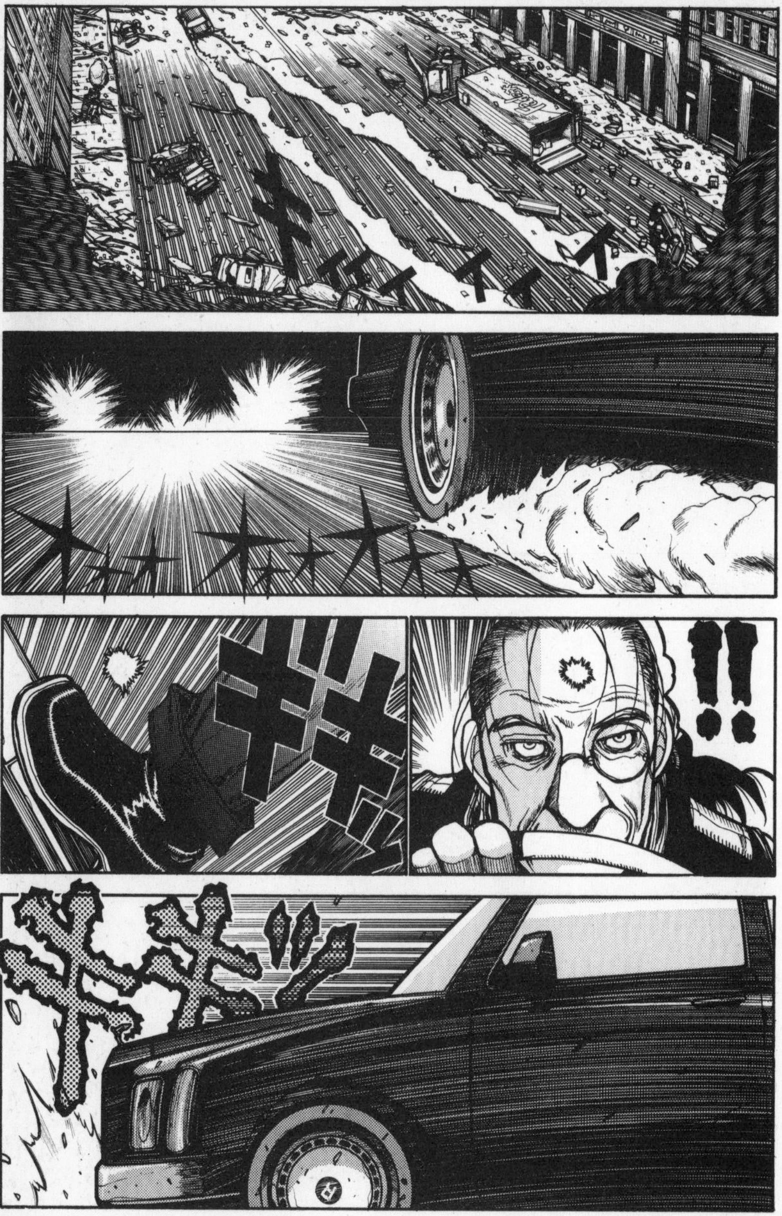
!!

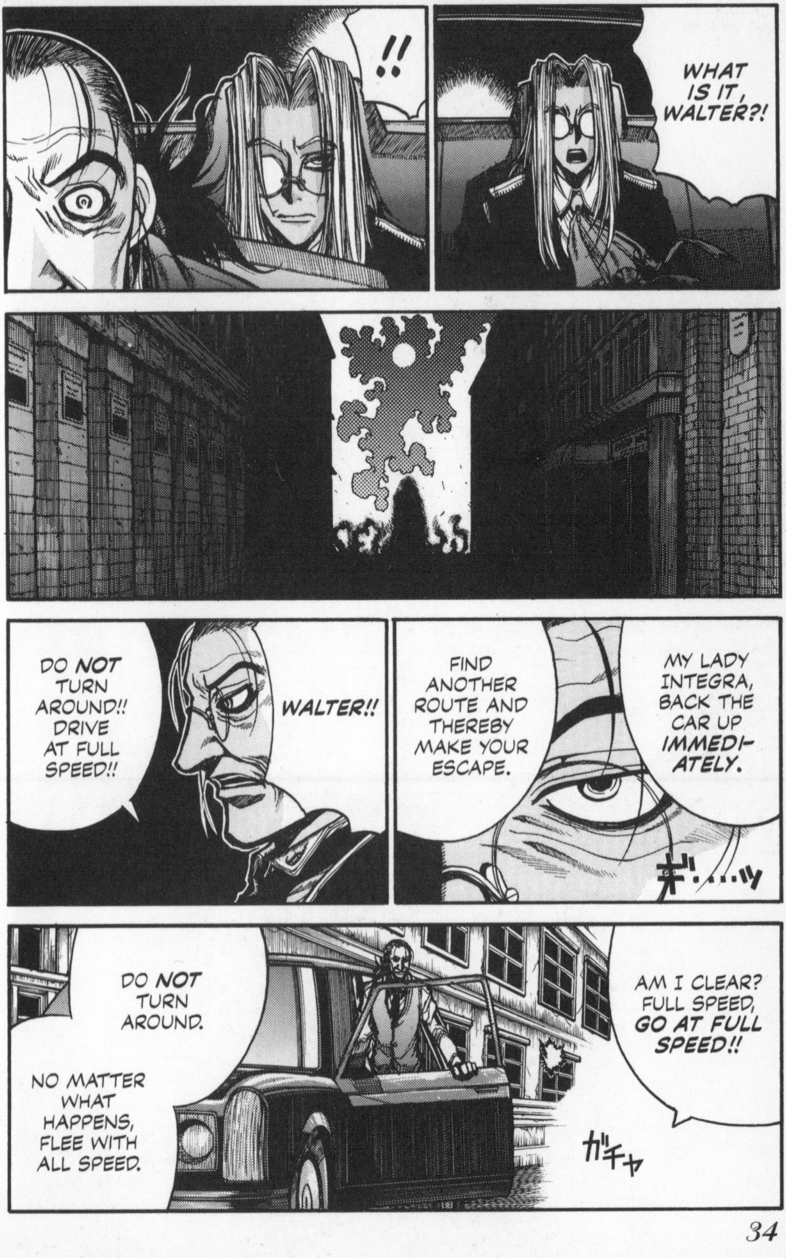
WHAT IS IT, WALTER?!
!!
MY LADY INTEGRA, BACK THE CAR UP IMMEDIATELY.
FIND ANOTHER ROUTE AND THEREBY MAKE YOUR ESCAPE.
ギ....ッ
WALTER!!
DO NOT TURN AROUND!! DRIVE AT FULL SPEED!!
AM I CLEAR? FULL SPEED, GO AT FULL SPEED!!
ガチャ
DO NOT TURN AROUND.
NO MATTER WHAT HAPPENS, FLEE WITH ALL SPEED.

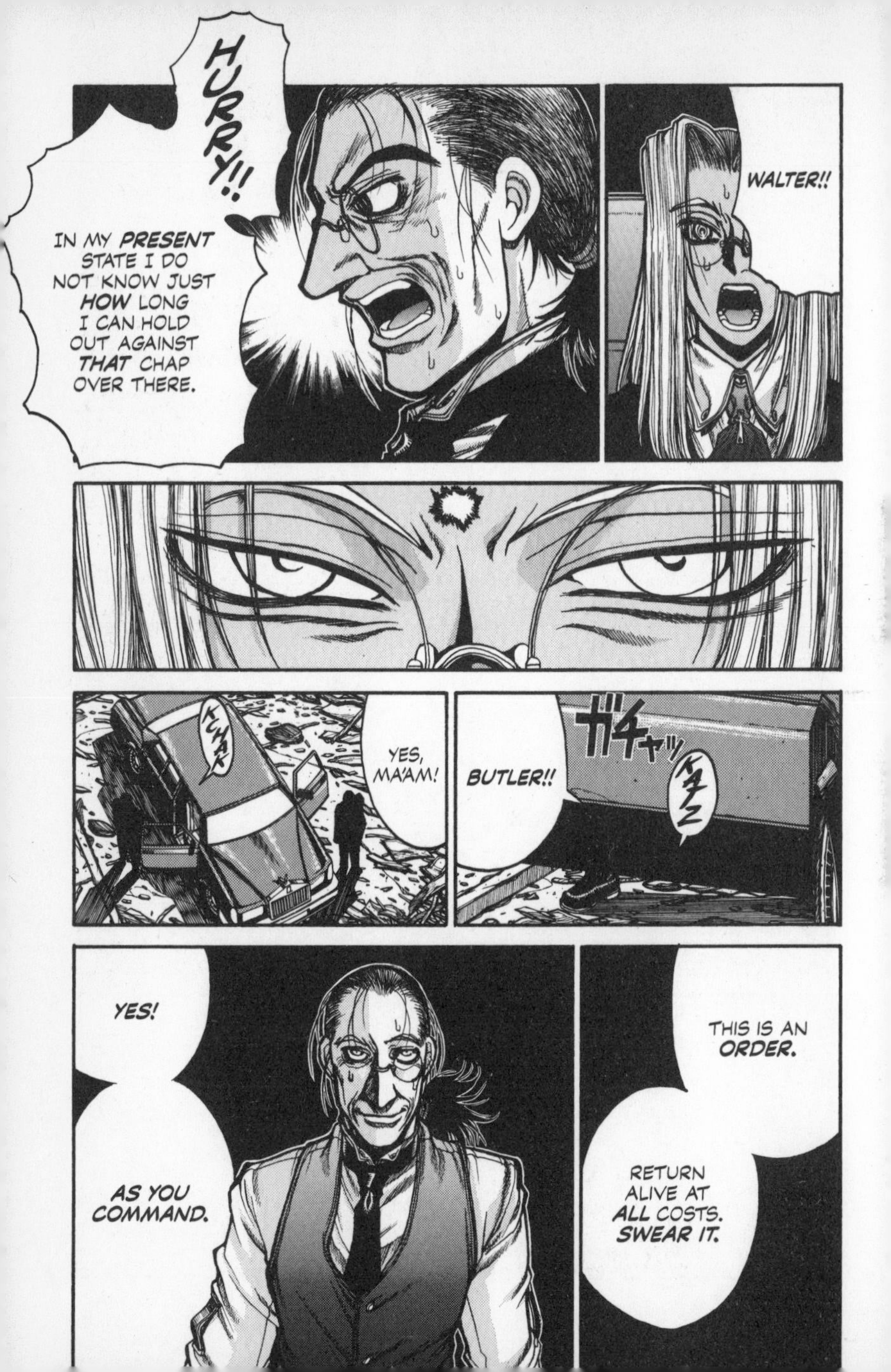
WALTER!!
HURRY!!
IN MY PRESENT STATE I DO NOT KNOW JUST HOW LONG I CAN HOLD OUT AGAINST THAT CHAP OVER THERE.
BUTLER!!
ガチャッ
KAZZ
YES, MA'AM!
KCHAK
THIS IS AN ORDER.
RETURN ALIVE AT ALL COSTS. SWEAR IT.
YES!
AS YOU COMMAND.

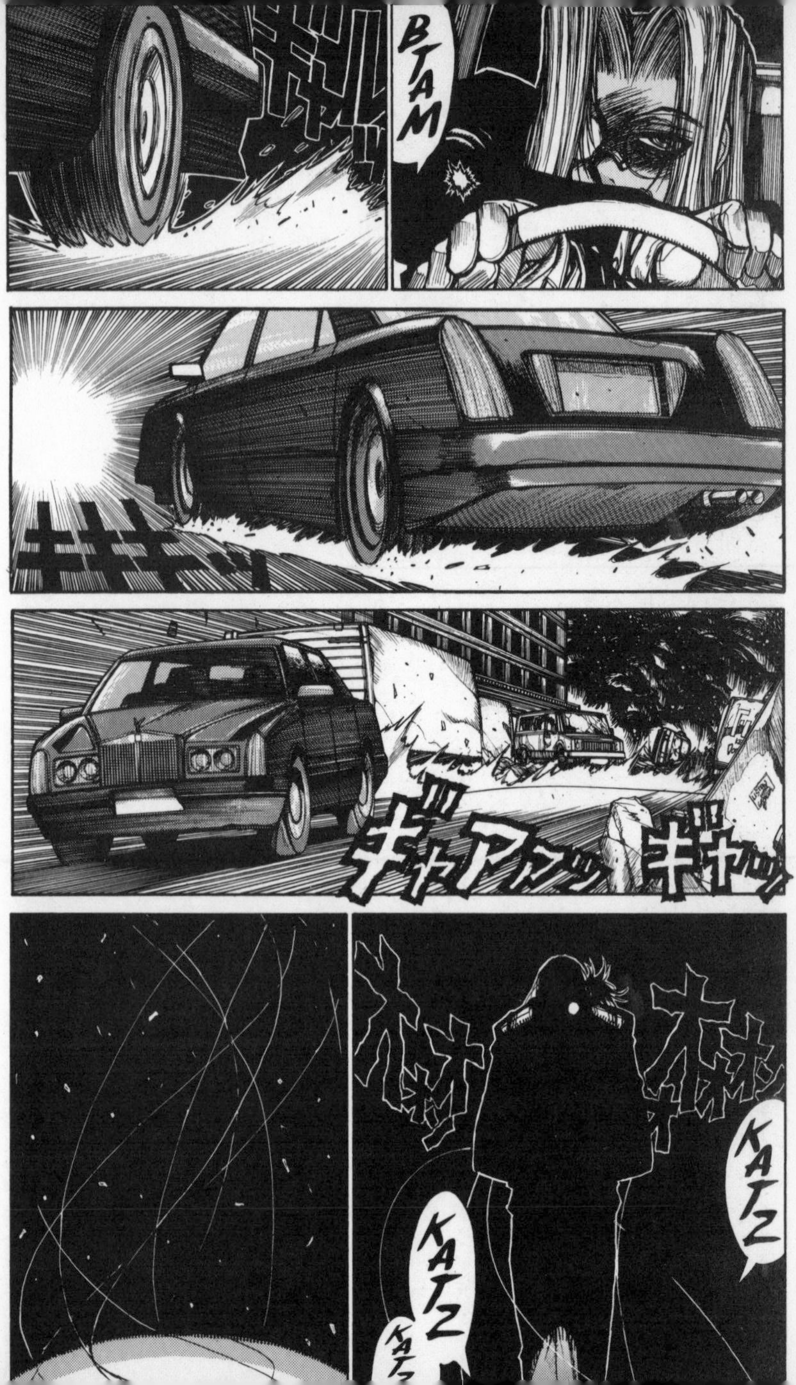
BTAM
KATZ
KATZ

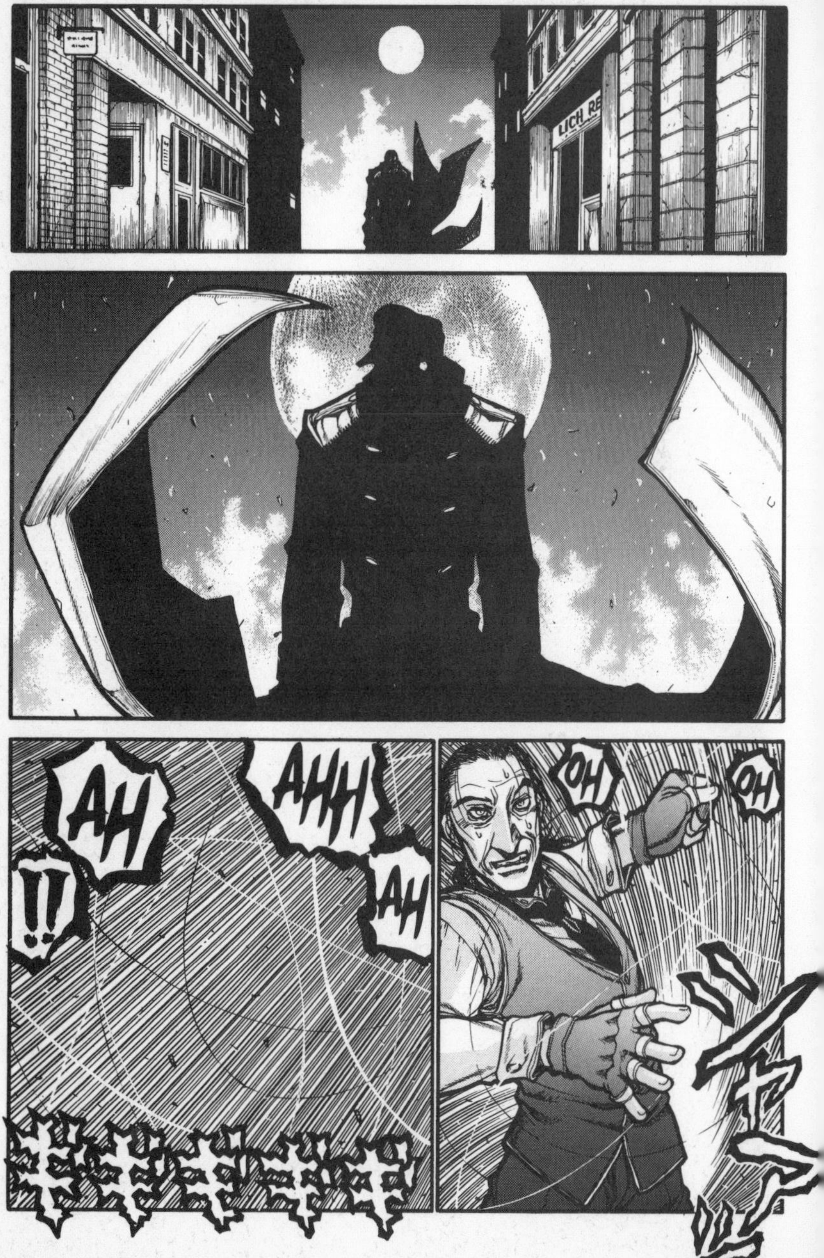
LICH RE
OH
OH
AHH
AH
AH
!!

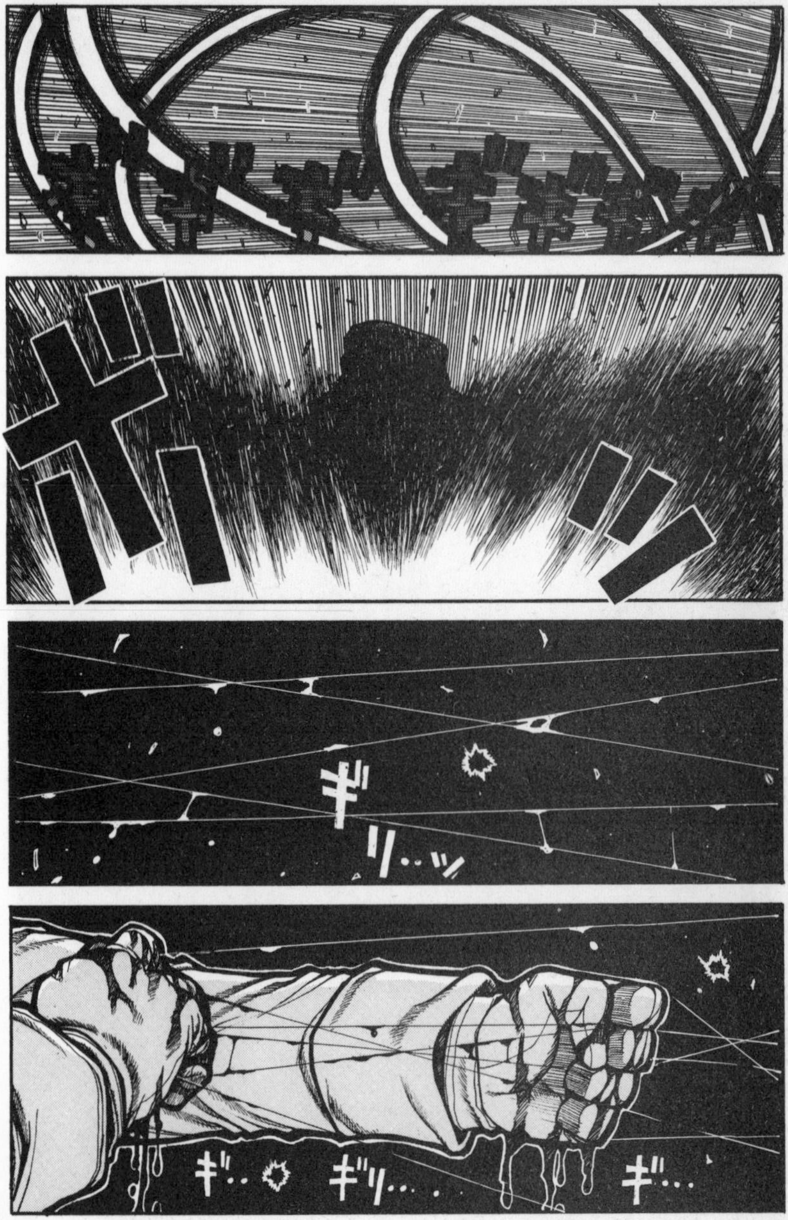
ギギギギギギギ
ギッ
ギリ…ッ
ギ…
ギリ……
ギ…

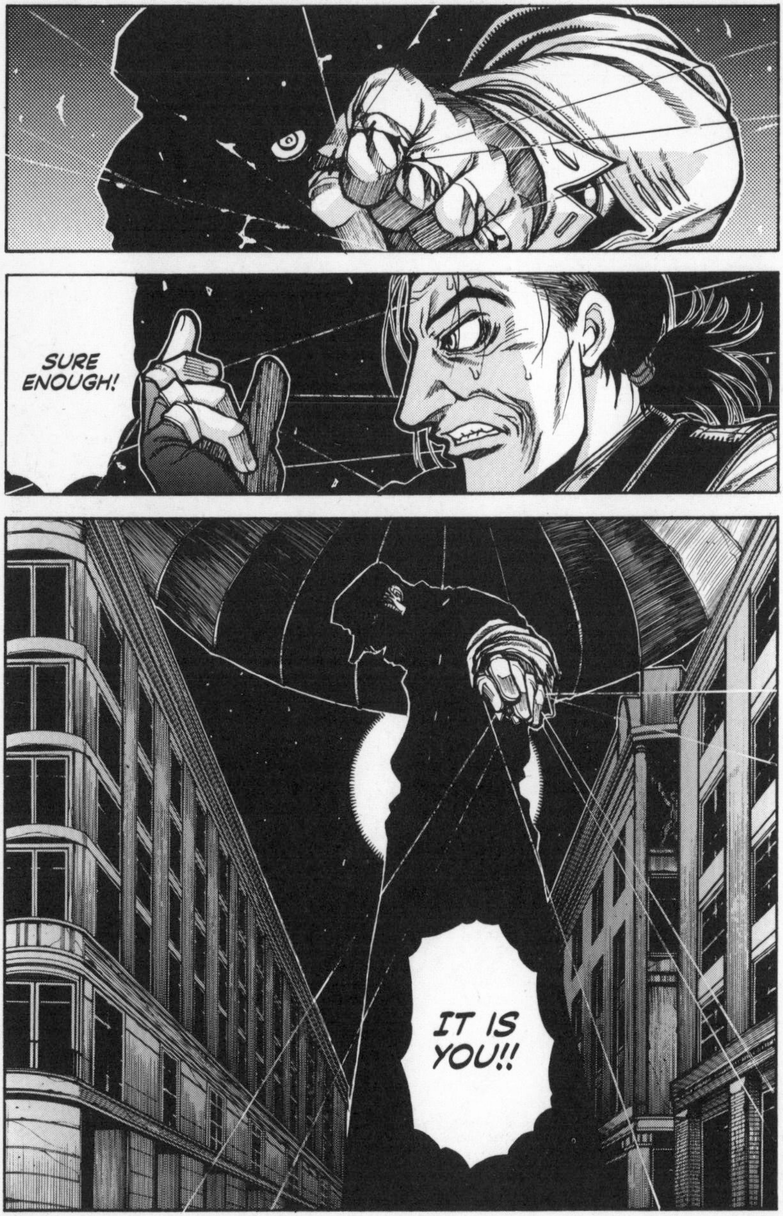
SURE ENOUGH!
IT IS YOU!!

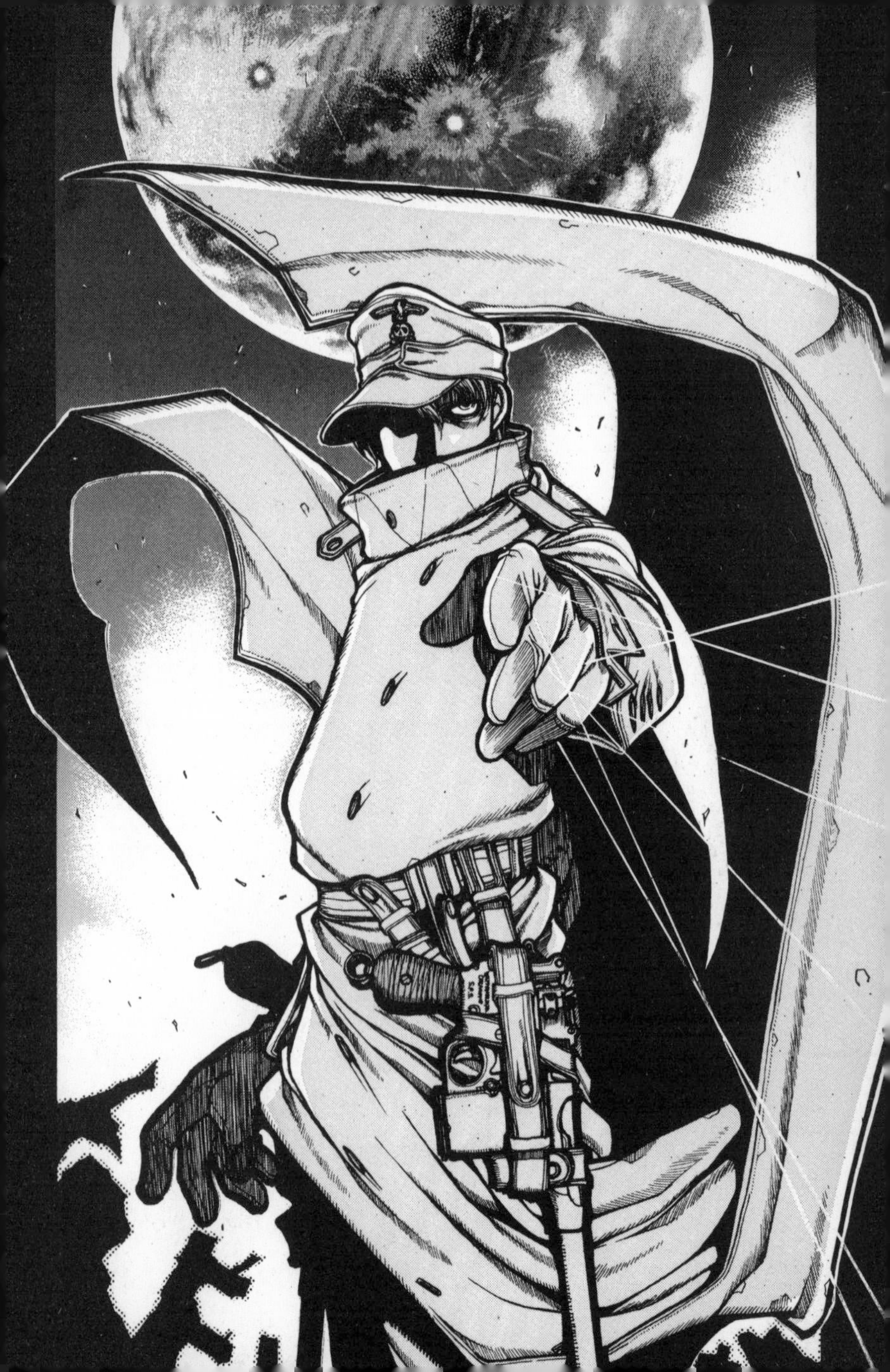

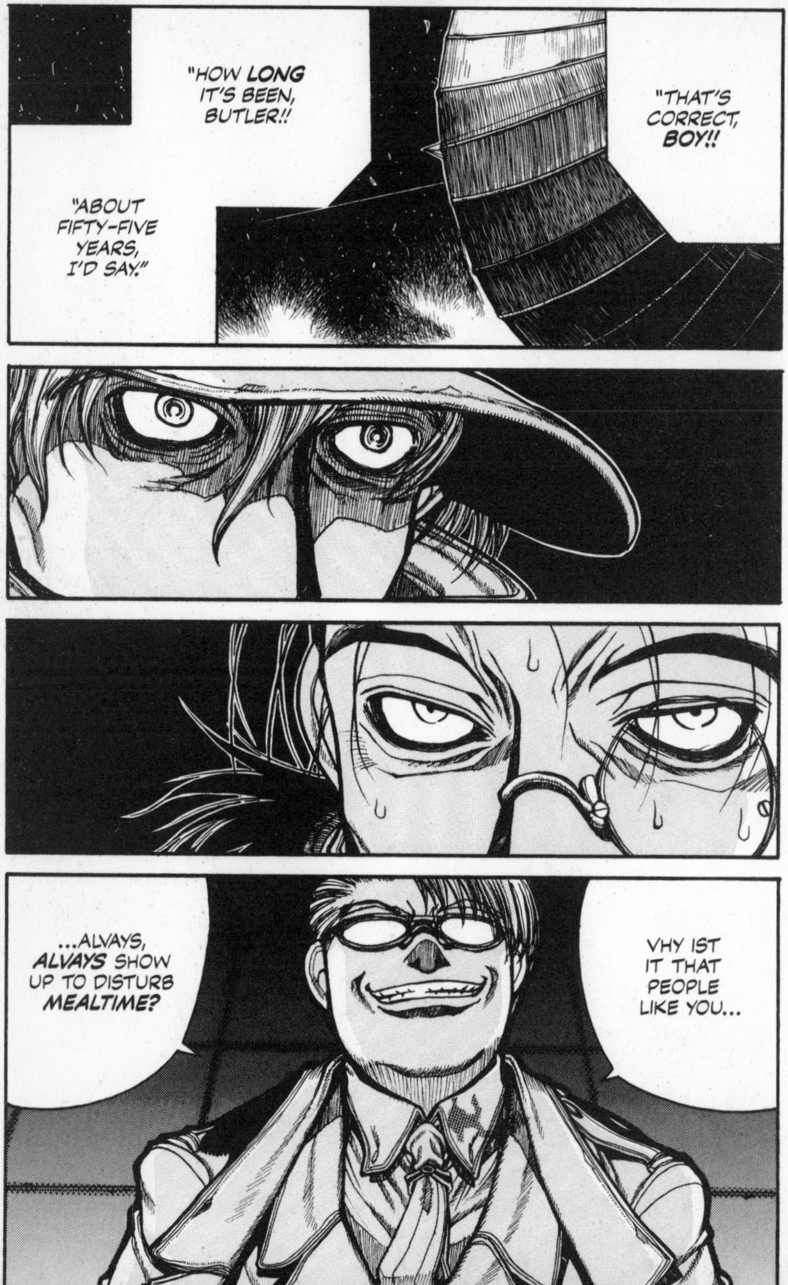
"THAT'S CORRECT, BOY!!
"HOW LONG IT'S BEEN, BUTLER!!
"ABOUT FIFTY-FIVE YEARS, I'D SAY."
VHY IST IT THAT PEOPLE LIKE YOU...
...ALVAYS, ALVAYS SHOW UP TO DISTURB MEALTIME?

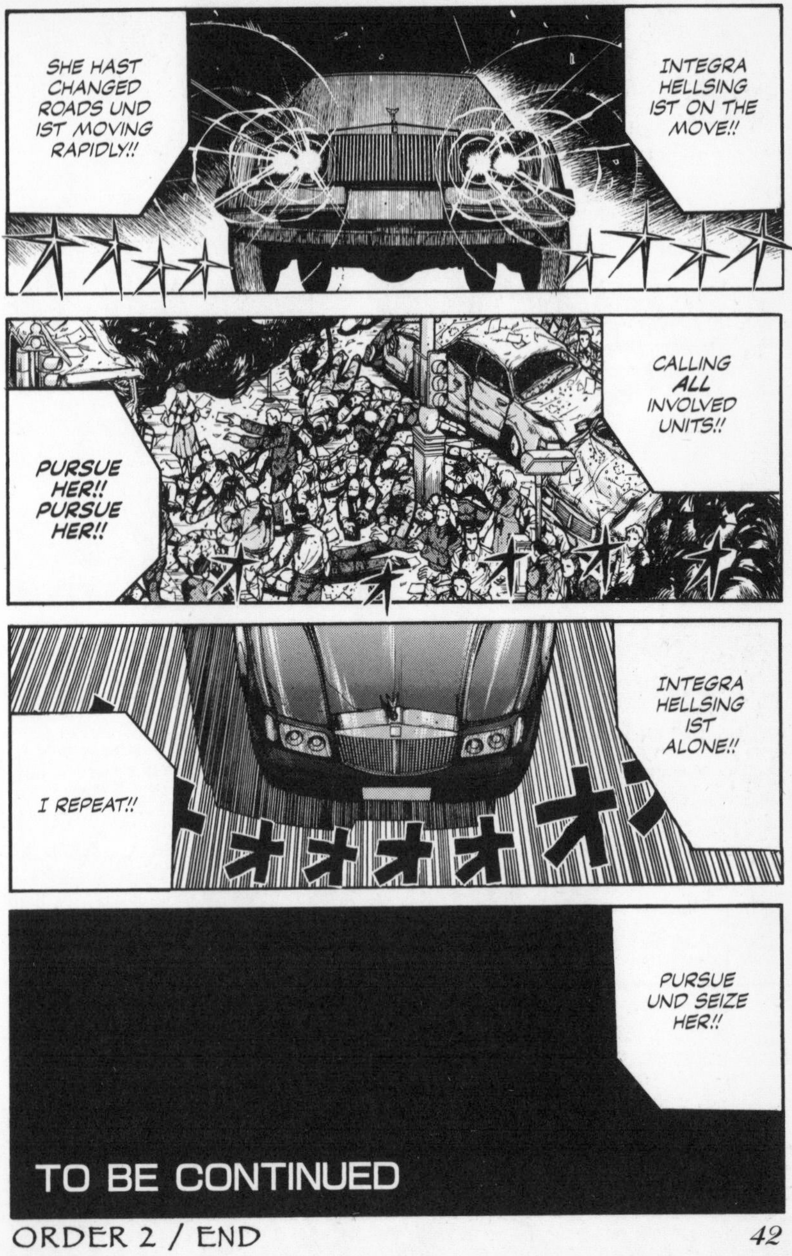
INTEGRA HELLSING IST ON THE MOVE!!
SHE HAST CHANGED ROADS UND IST MOVING RAPIDLY!!
CALLING **ALL** INVOLVED UNITS!!
PURSUE HER!! PURSUE HER!!
INTEGRA HELLSING IST ALONE!!
I REPEAT!!
PURSUE UND SEIZE HER!!
TO BE CONTINUED

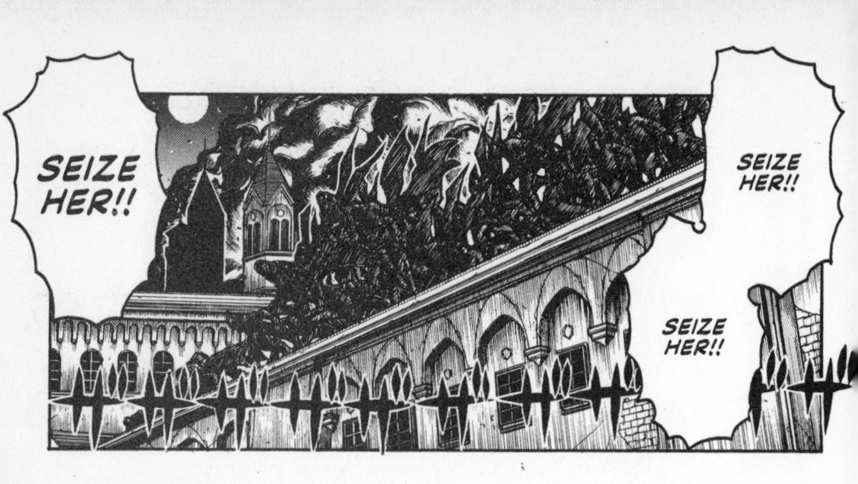
SEIZE HER!!
SEIZE HER!!
SEIZE HER!!

ORDER 3

FINAL FANTASY⑤

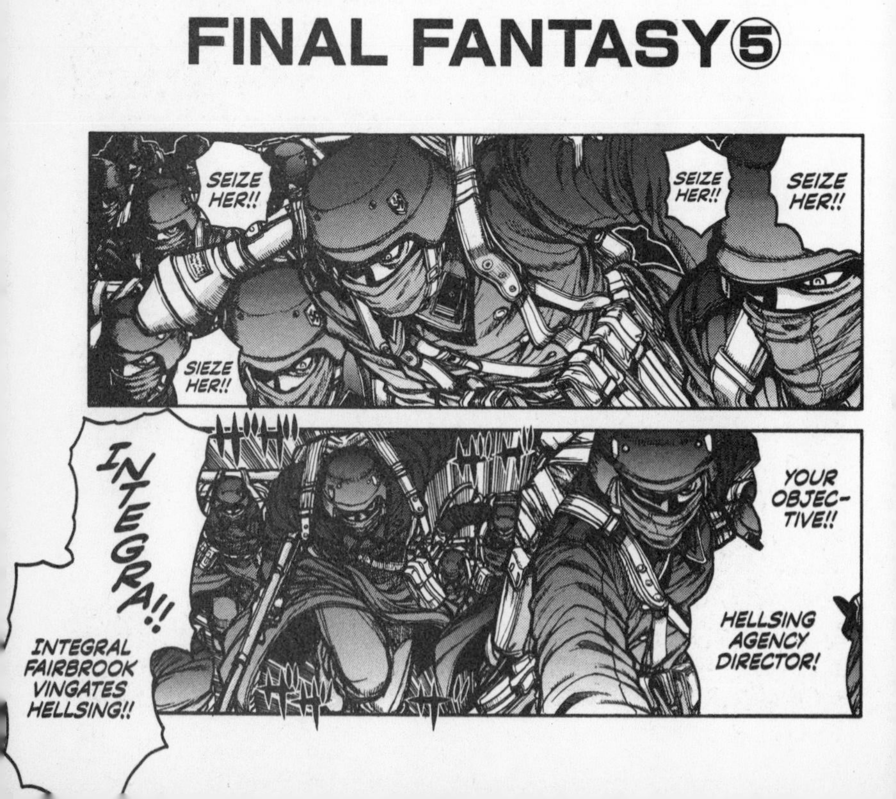
SEIZE HER!!
SEIZE HER!!
SEIZE HER!!
SIEZE HER!!
YOUR OBJEC-TIVE!!
HELLSING AGENCY DIRECTOR!
INTEGRA!!
INTEGRAL FAIRBROOK VINGATES HELLSING!!

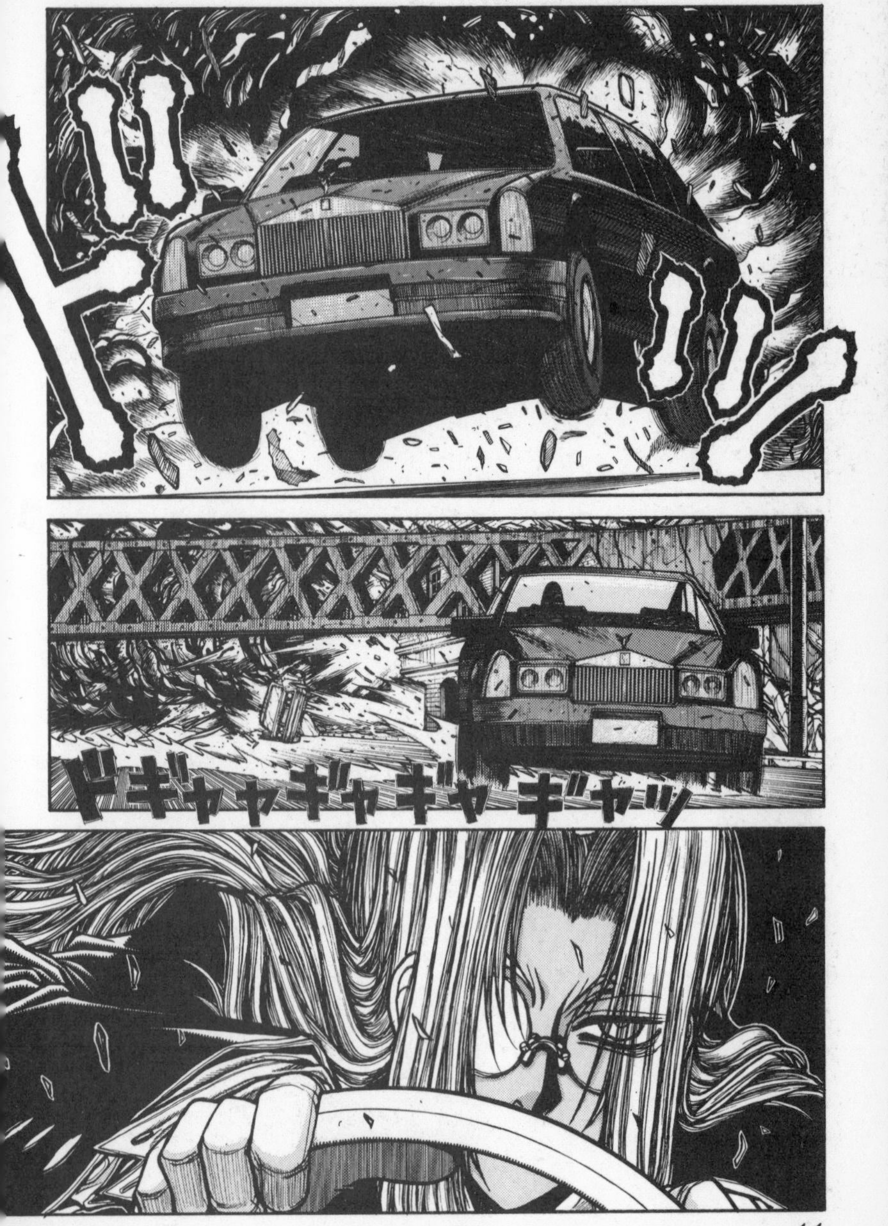
ドギャャギャギャギャッ

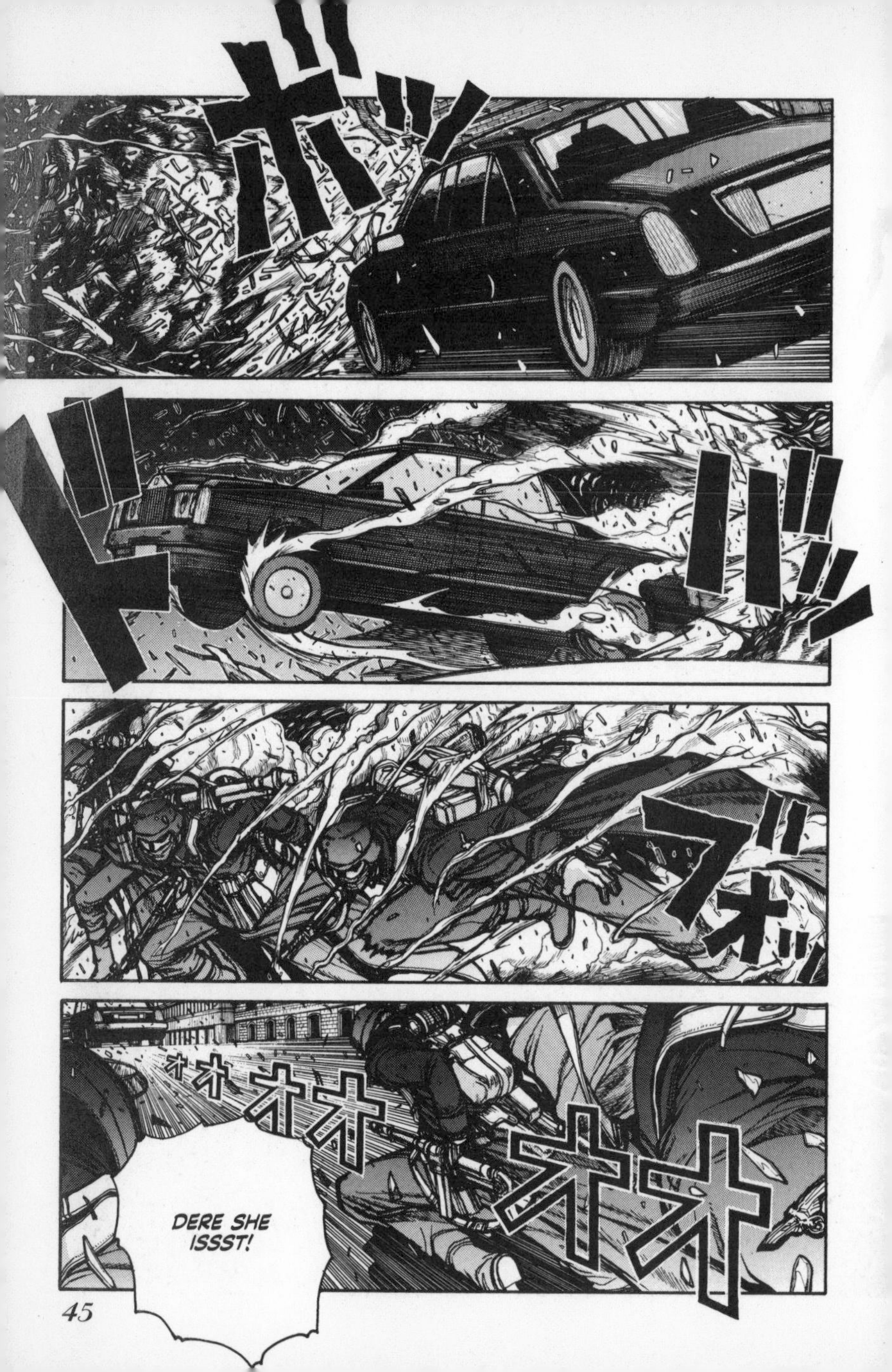
DERE SHE
ISSST!

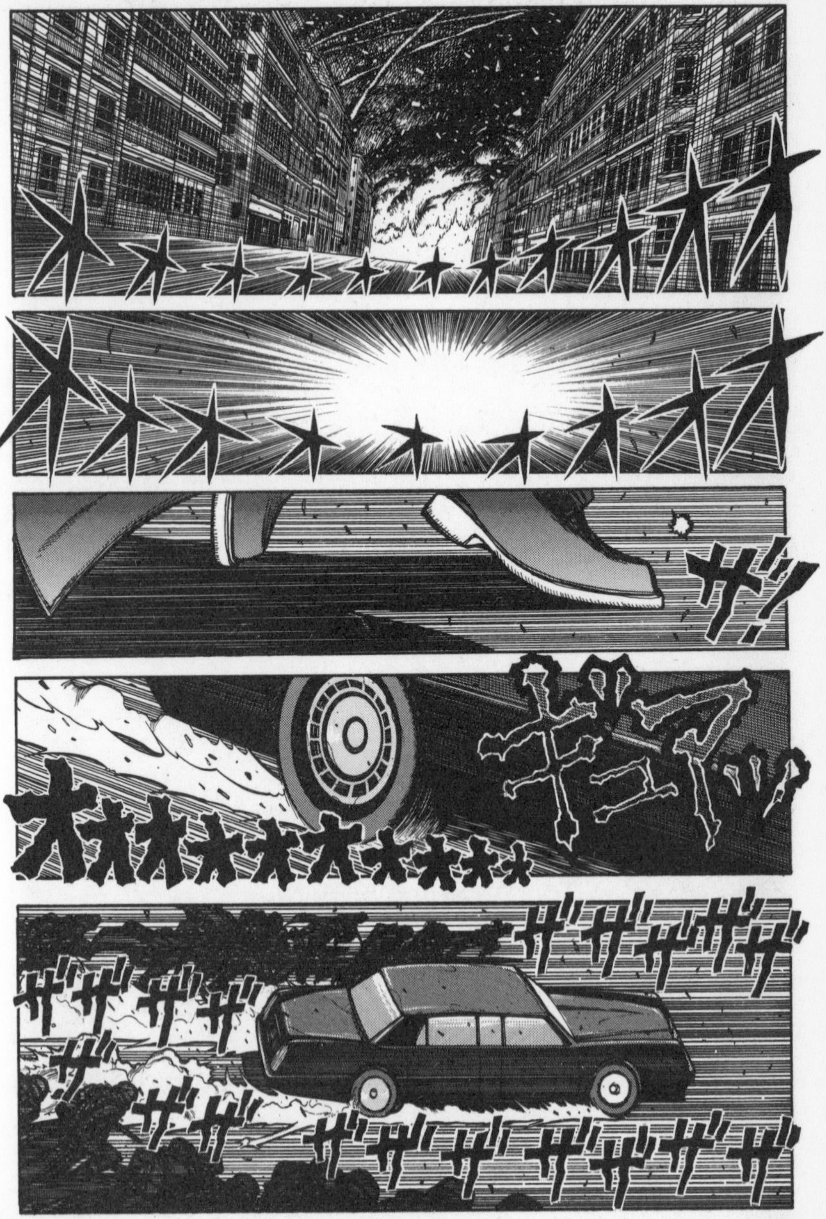

ォォォォォォォォォォォォ
ォォォォォォォォォォォォ
ザッ
キュアッ
オオオォォォォォォォォ
ザザザザザ
ザザザザ
ザ
ザザ
ザザザ ザザザザ

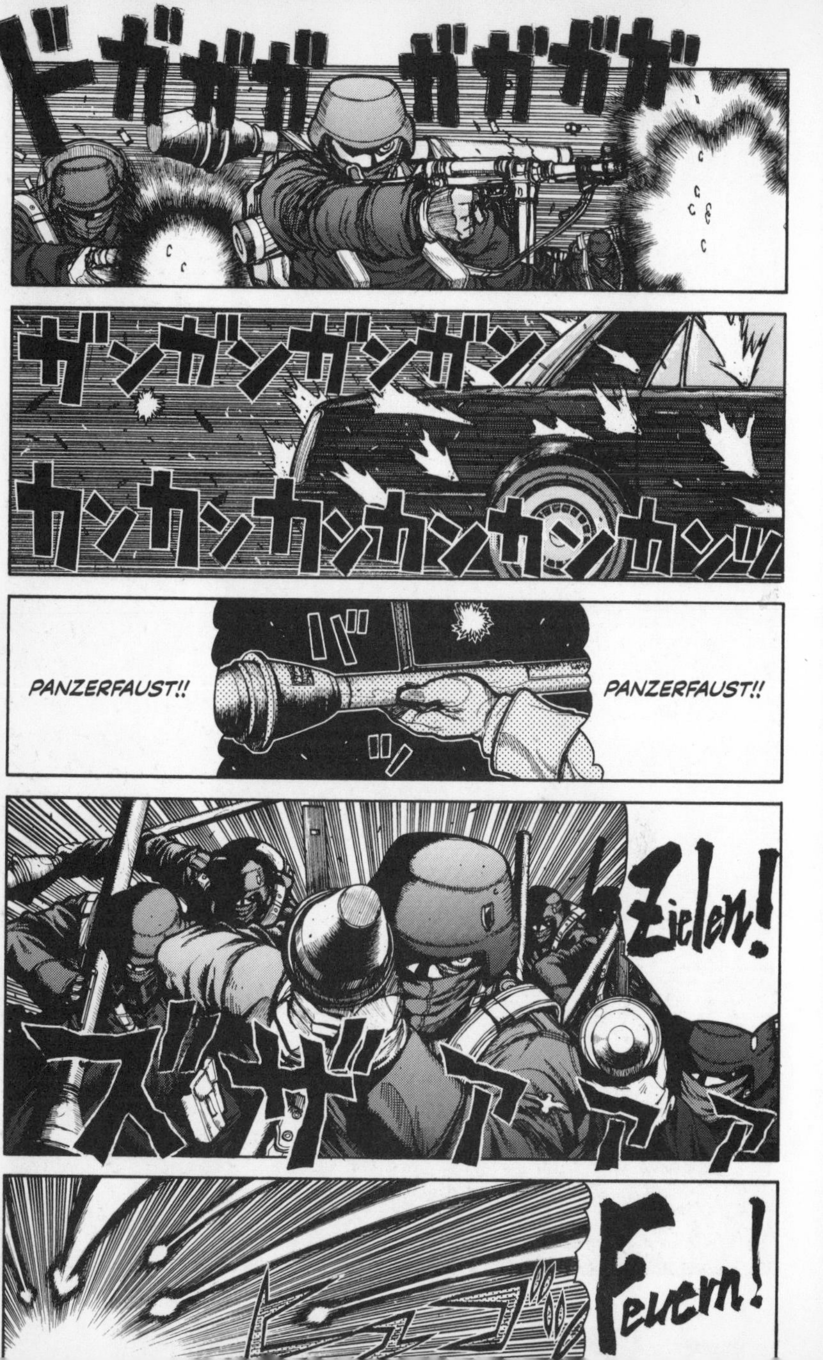
ドガガガ ガガガガ
ザンガンザンガン
カンカンカンカンカンカンッ
PANZERFAUST!!
バ
PANZERFAUST!!
Zielen!
ズガァァァ
Feuern!

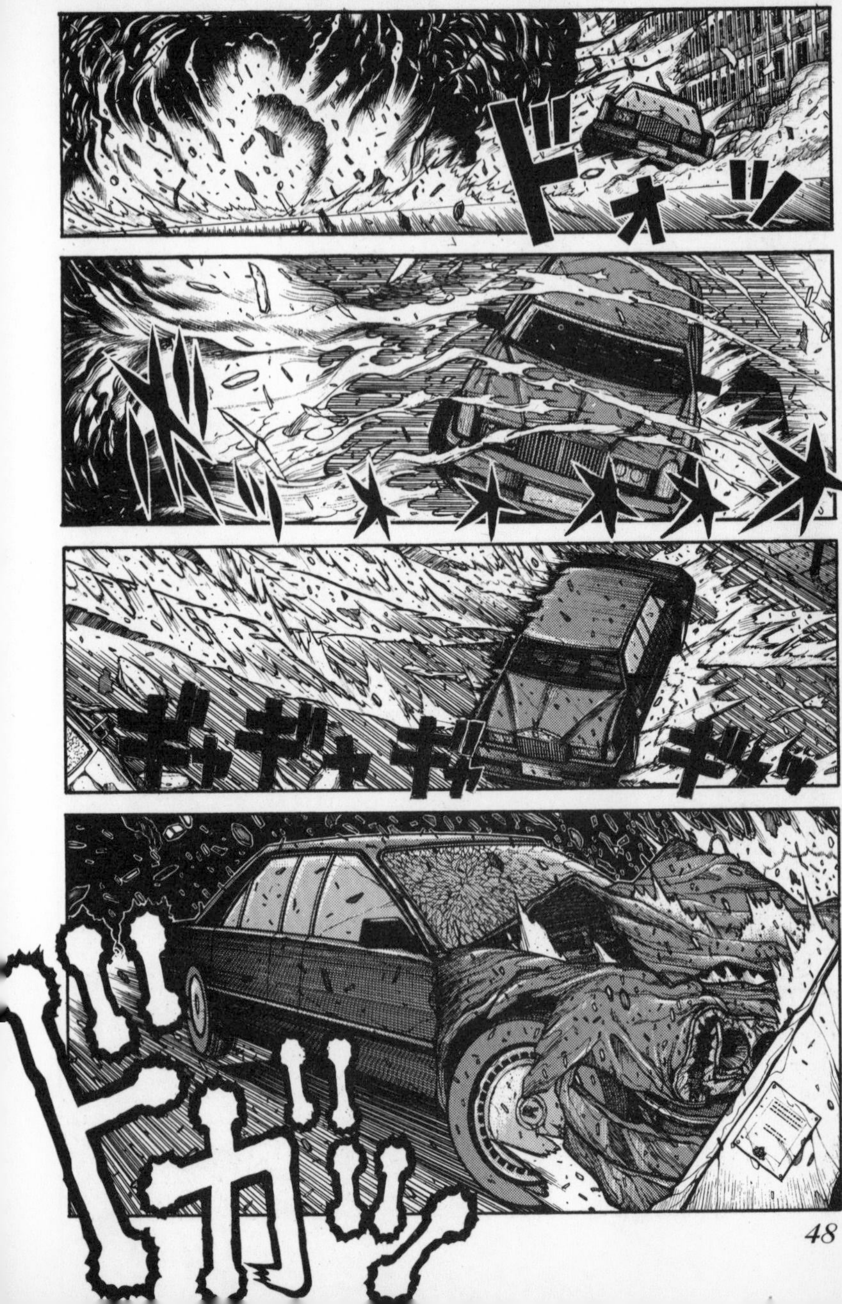
ドォッ!!
ズッ
ギャギャギャギャ
ドカッ!!

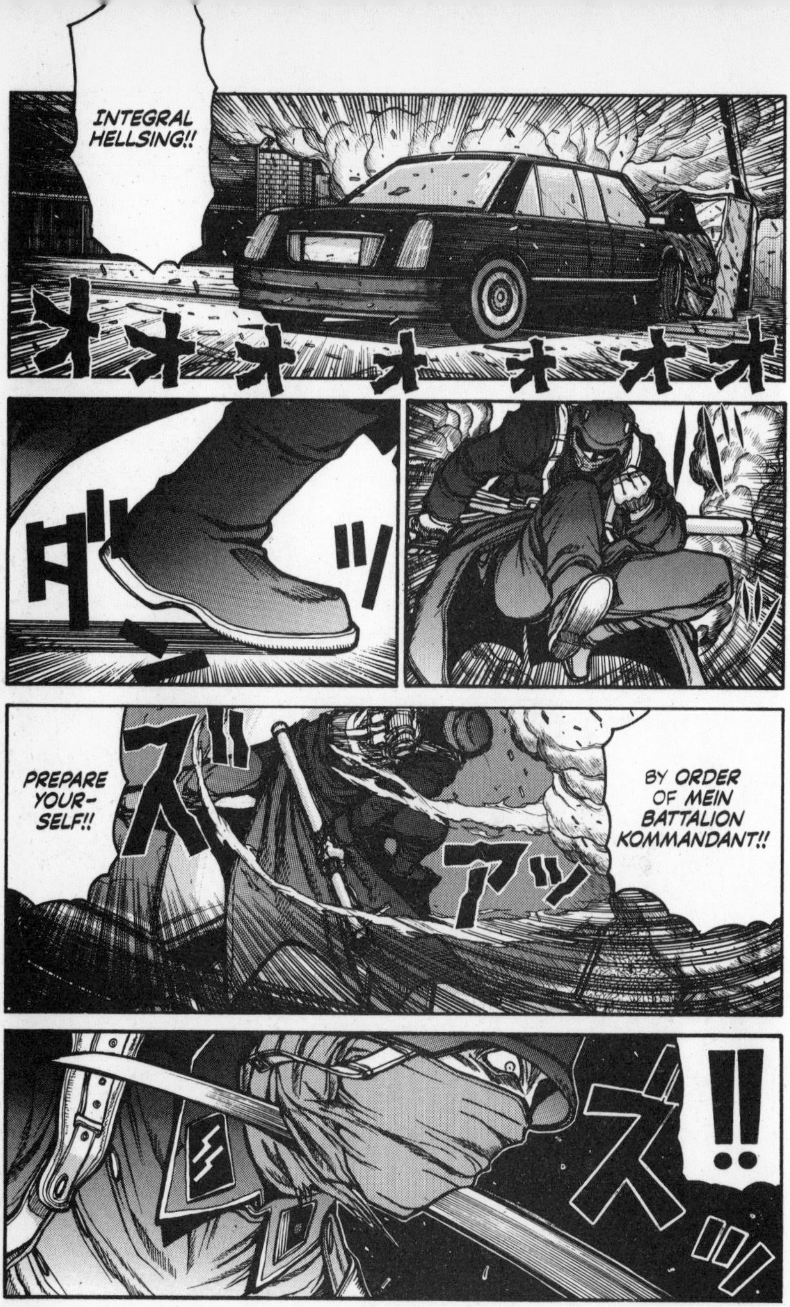
INTEGRAL HELLSING!!
オオオオオオオ
ダッ
BY ORDER OF MEIN BATTALION KOMMANDANT!!
PREPARE YOURSELF!!
ズアッ
ズッ!!

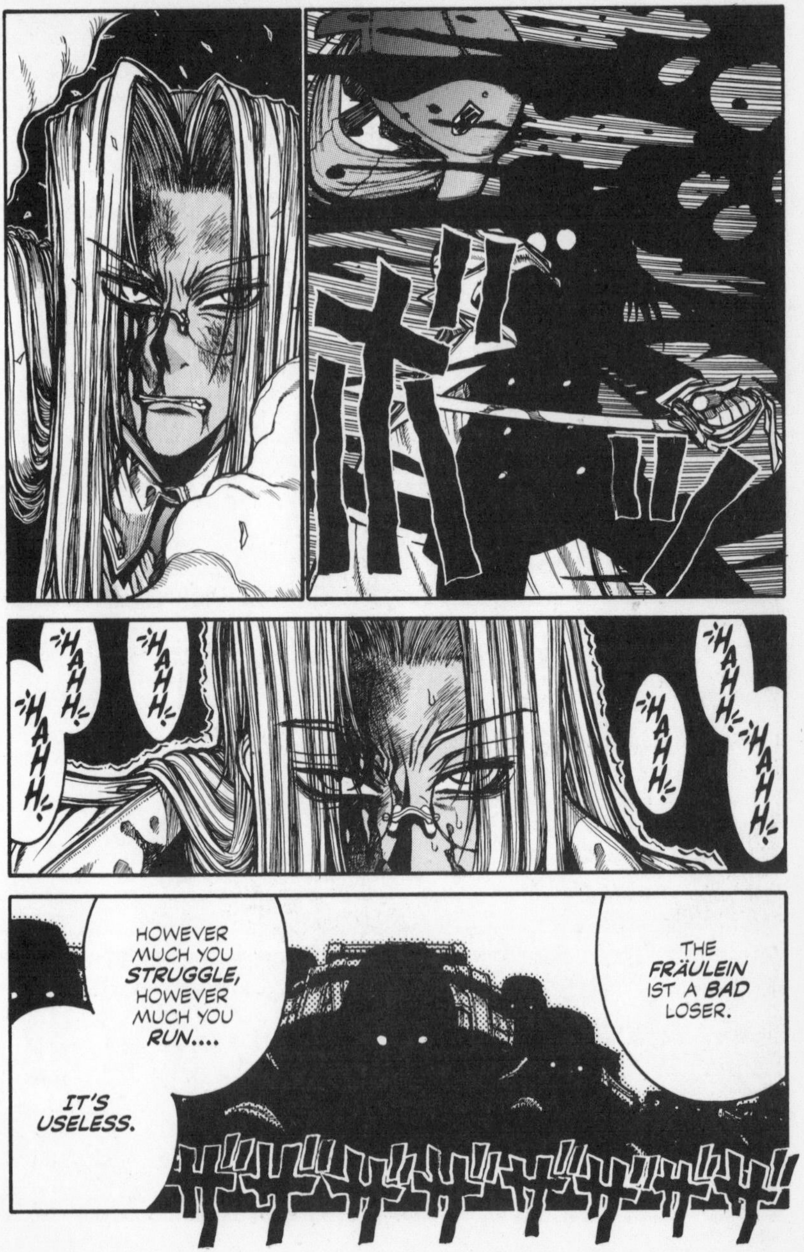
HAHH. HAHH
HAHH
HAHH
HAHH
HAHH
THE FRÄULEIN IST A BAD LOSER.
HOWEVER MUCH YOU STRUGGLE, HOWEVER MUCH YOU RUN....
IT'S USELESS.

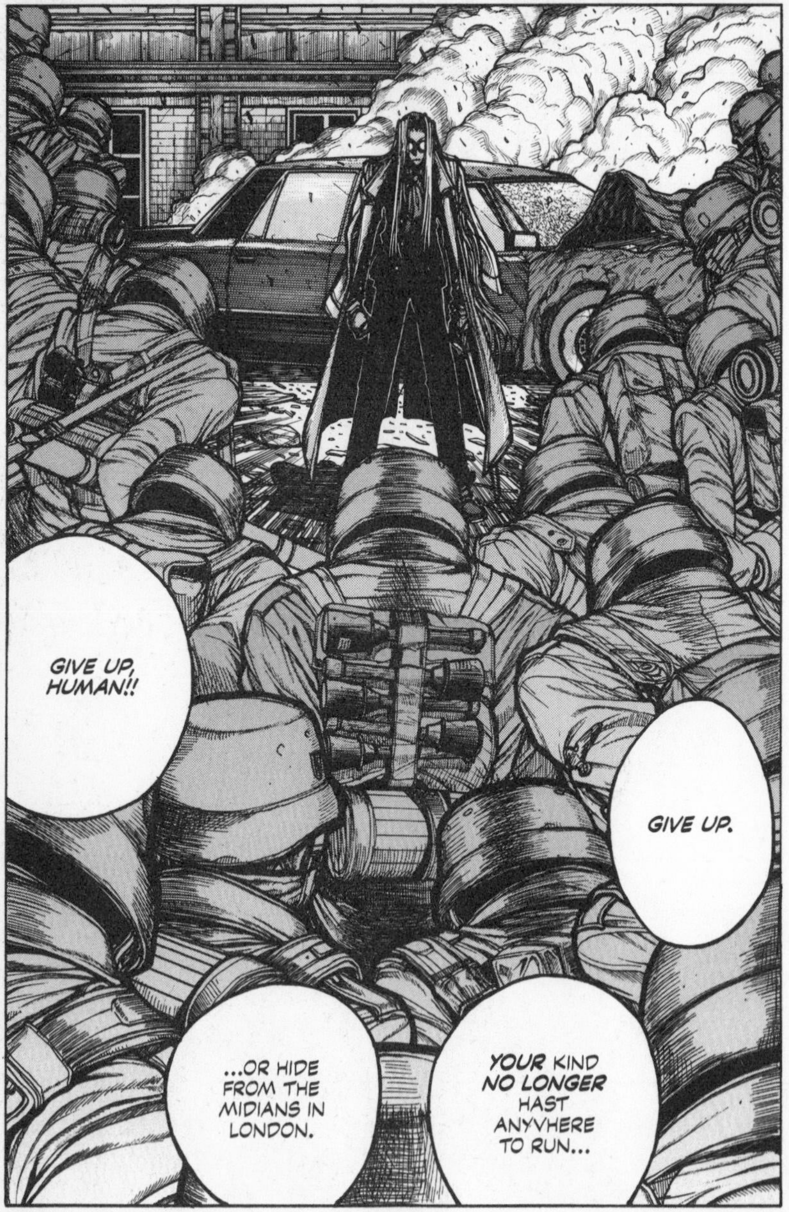
GIVE UP, HUMAN!!
GIVE UP.
YOUR KIND NO LONGER HAST ANYVHERE TO RUN...
...OR HIDE FROM THE MIDIANS IN LONDON.

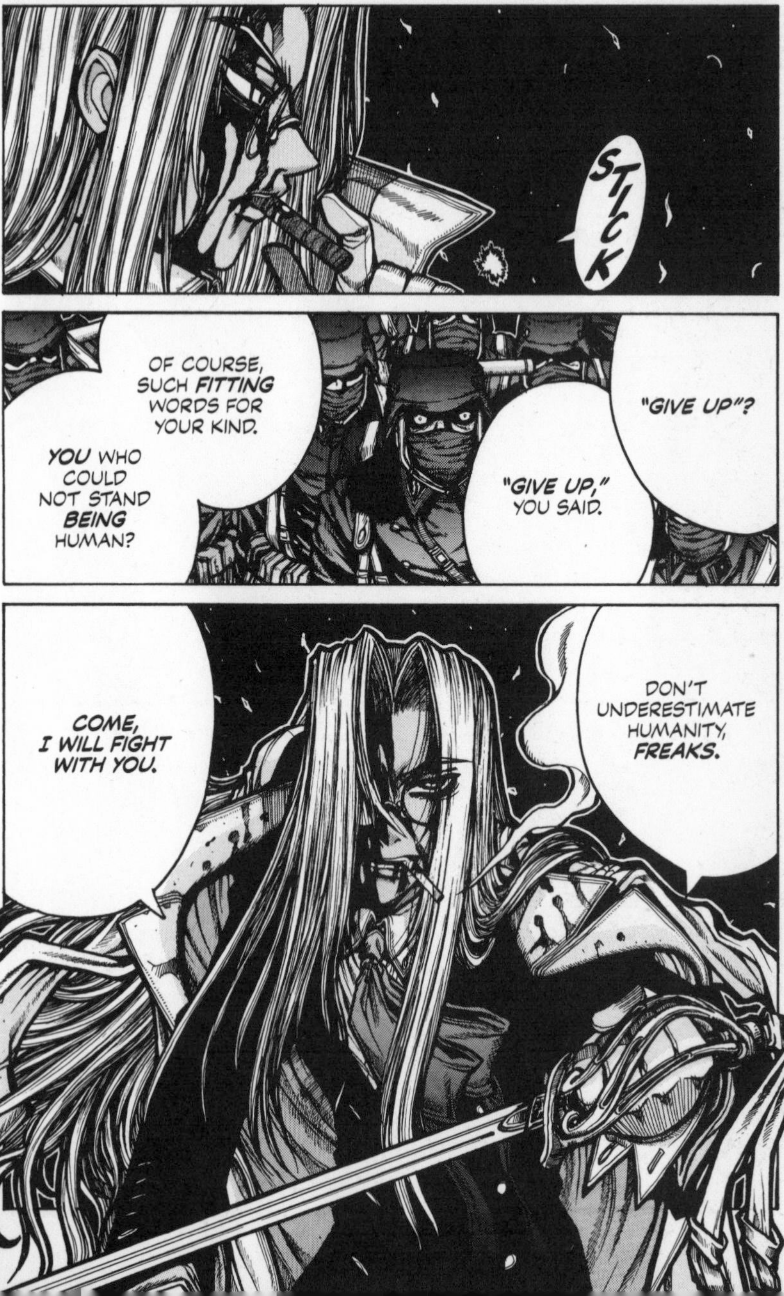
STICK
"GIVE UP"?
"GIVE UP," YOU SAID.
OF COURSE, SUCH FITTING WORDS FOR YOUR KIND.
YOU WHO COULD NOT STAND BEING HUMAN?
DON'T UNDERESTIMATE HUMANITY, FREAKS.
COME, I WILL FIGHT WITH YOU.

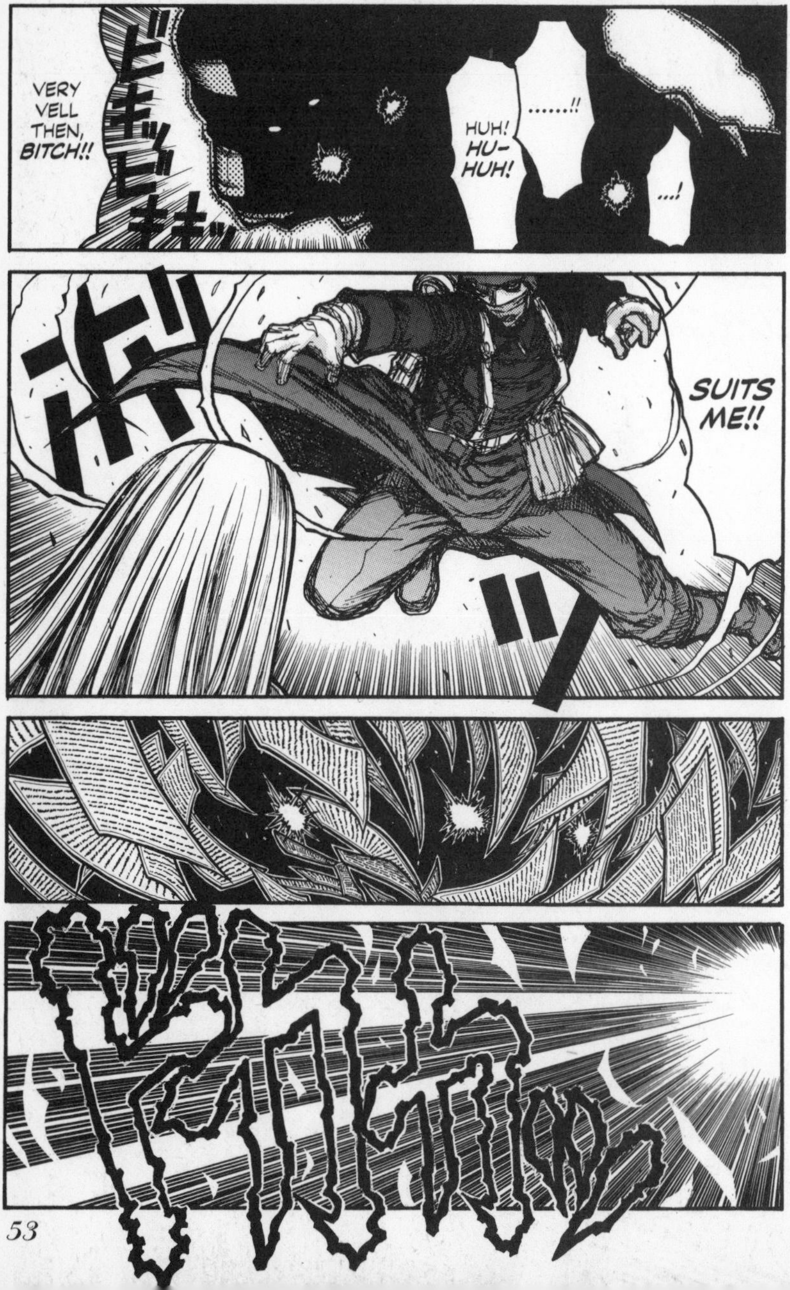
.......!!
...!
HUH! HU-HUH!
VERY VELL THEN, BITCH!!
SUITS ME!!

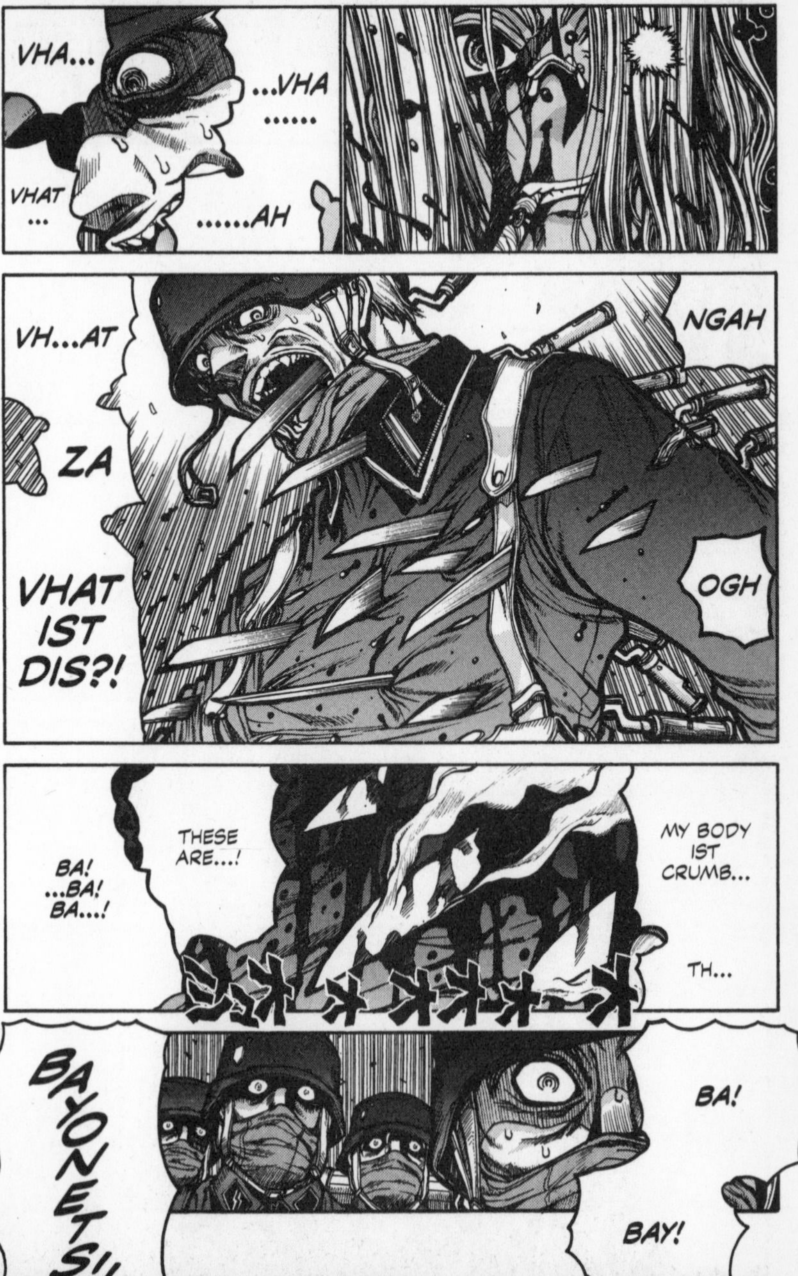
VHA...
...VHA ......
VHAT ...
......AH
NGAH
VH...AT
ZA
OGH
VHAT IST DIS?!
MY BODY IST CRUMB...
THESE ARE...!
BA! ...BA! BA...!
TH...
BA!
BAY!
BAYONETS!!

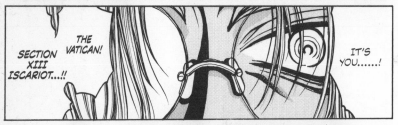

THE VATICAN!

SECTION XIII ISCARIOT...!!

IT'S YOU......!

BAYONET.

ANGEL DUST.

REGENE-RATOR.

HIT MAN.

KILLING JUDGE.

FATHER

SSSS!

SSSSSSSSS

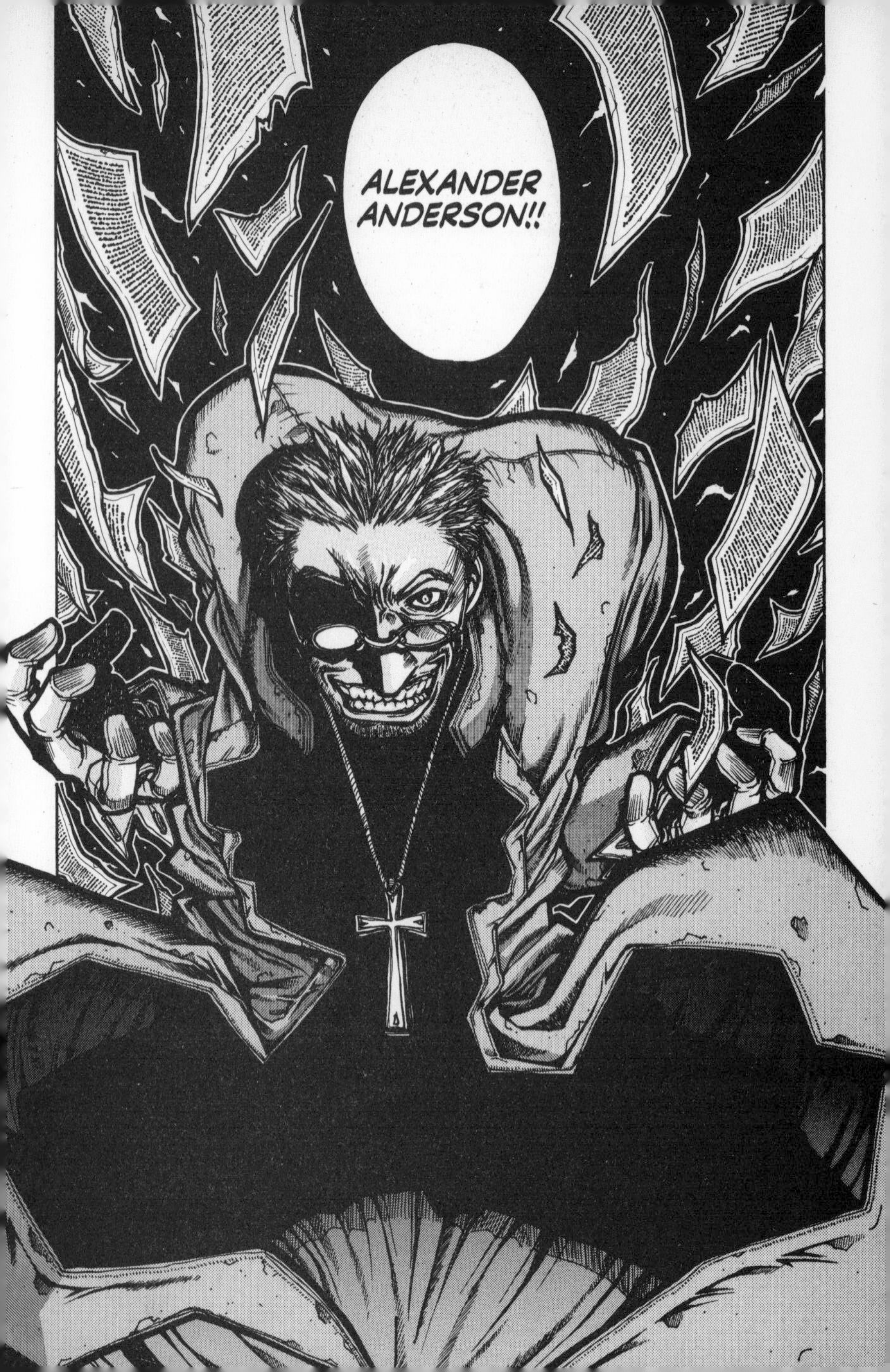
ALEXANDER ANDERSON!!

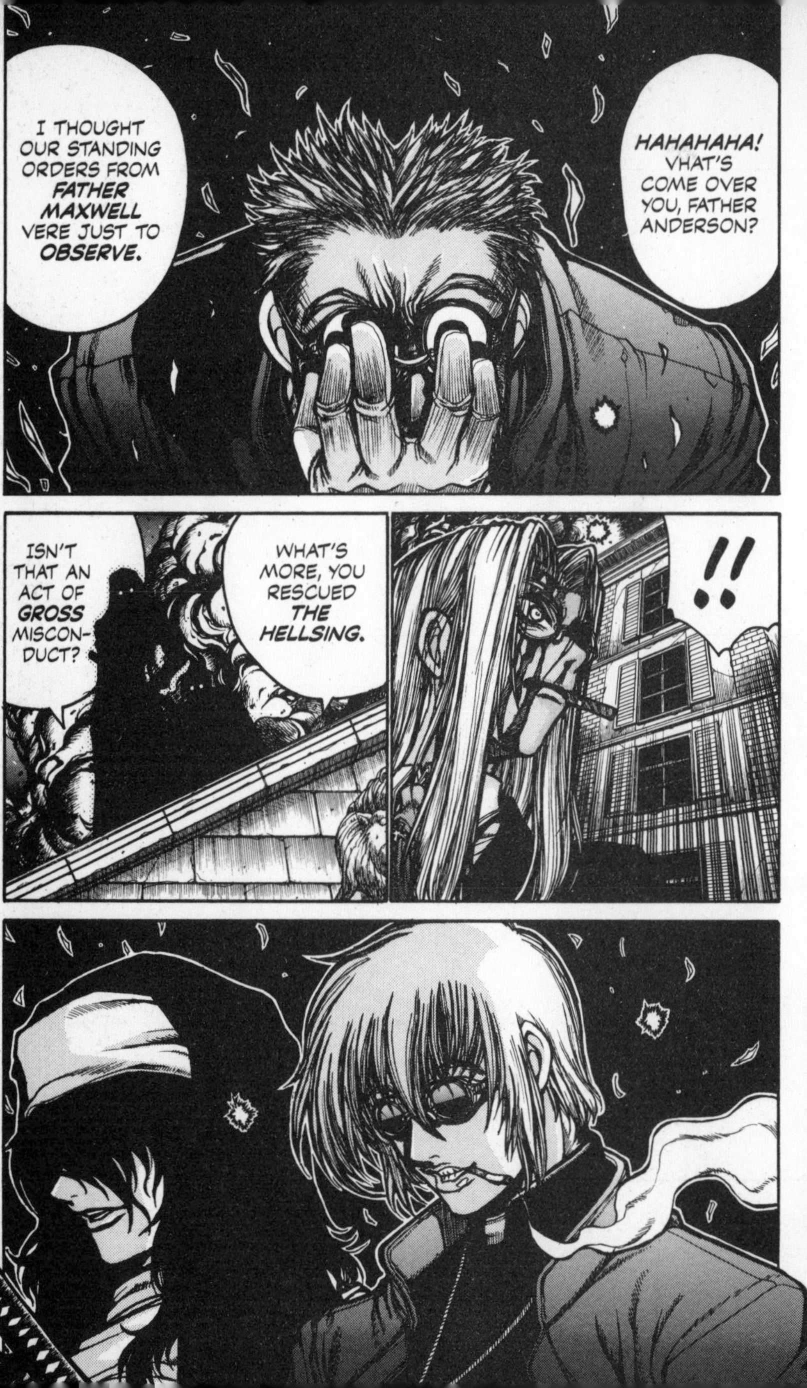
HAHAHAHA! VHAT'S COME OVER YOU, FATHER ANDERSON?
I THOUGHT OUR STANDING ORDERS FROM FATHER MAXWELL VERE JUST TO OBSERVE.
!!
WHAT'S MORE, YOU RESCUED THE HELLSING.
ISN'T THAT AN ACT OF GROSS MISCON-DUCT?

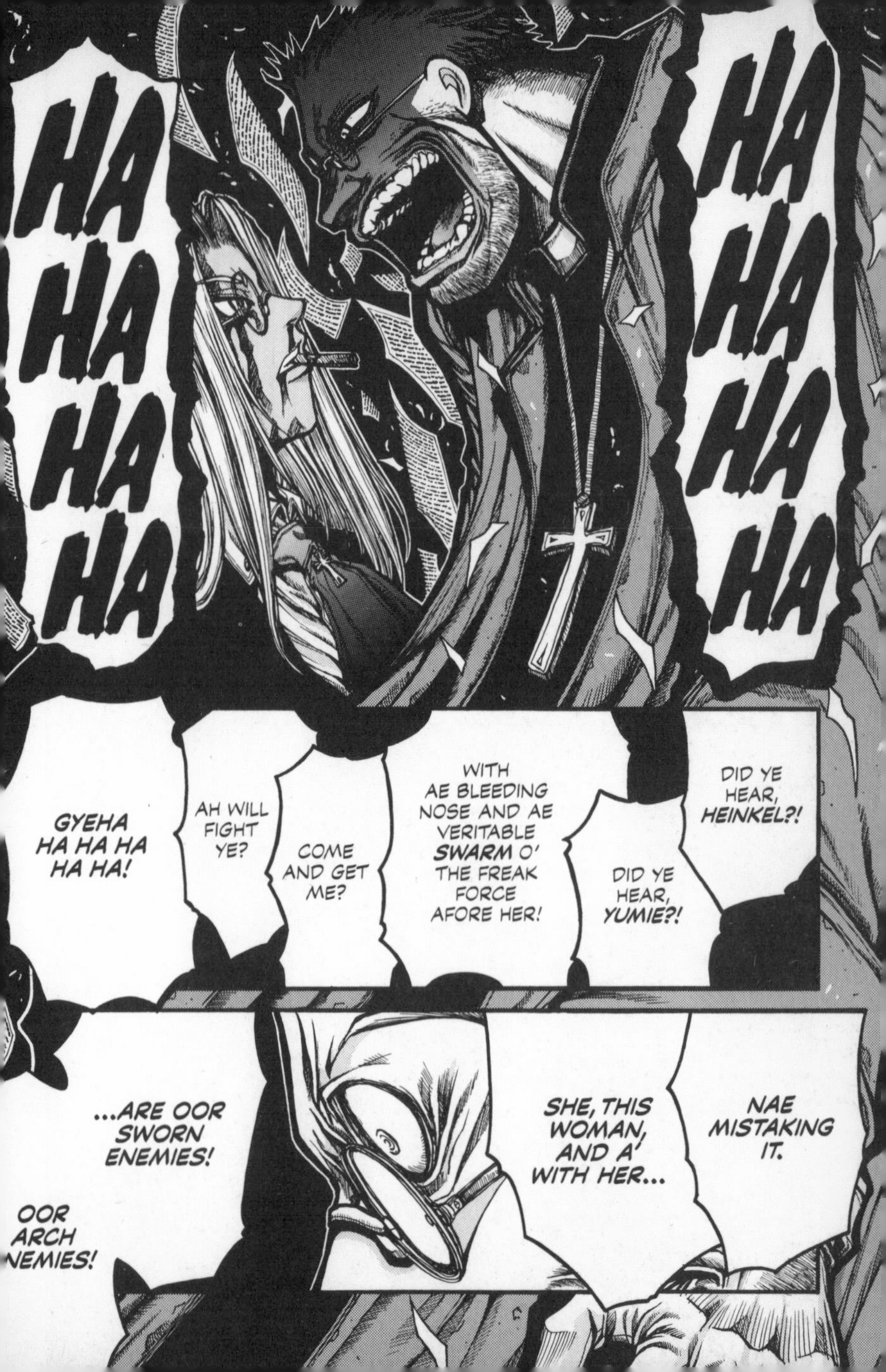
HA HA HA HA HA HA HA HA HA
HA HA HA HA HA HA HA HA
DID YE HEAR, HEINKEL?!
DID YE HEAR, YUMIE?!
WITH AE BLEEDING NOSE AND AE VERITABLE SWARM O' THE FREAK FORCE AFORE HER!
COME AND GET ME?
AH WILL FIGHT YE?
GYEHA HA HA HA HA HA!
NAE MISTAKING IT.
SHE, THIS WOMAN, AND A' WITH HER...
...ARE OOR SWORN ENEMIES!
OOR ARCH NEMIES!

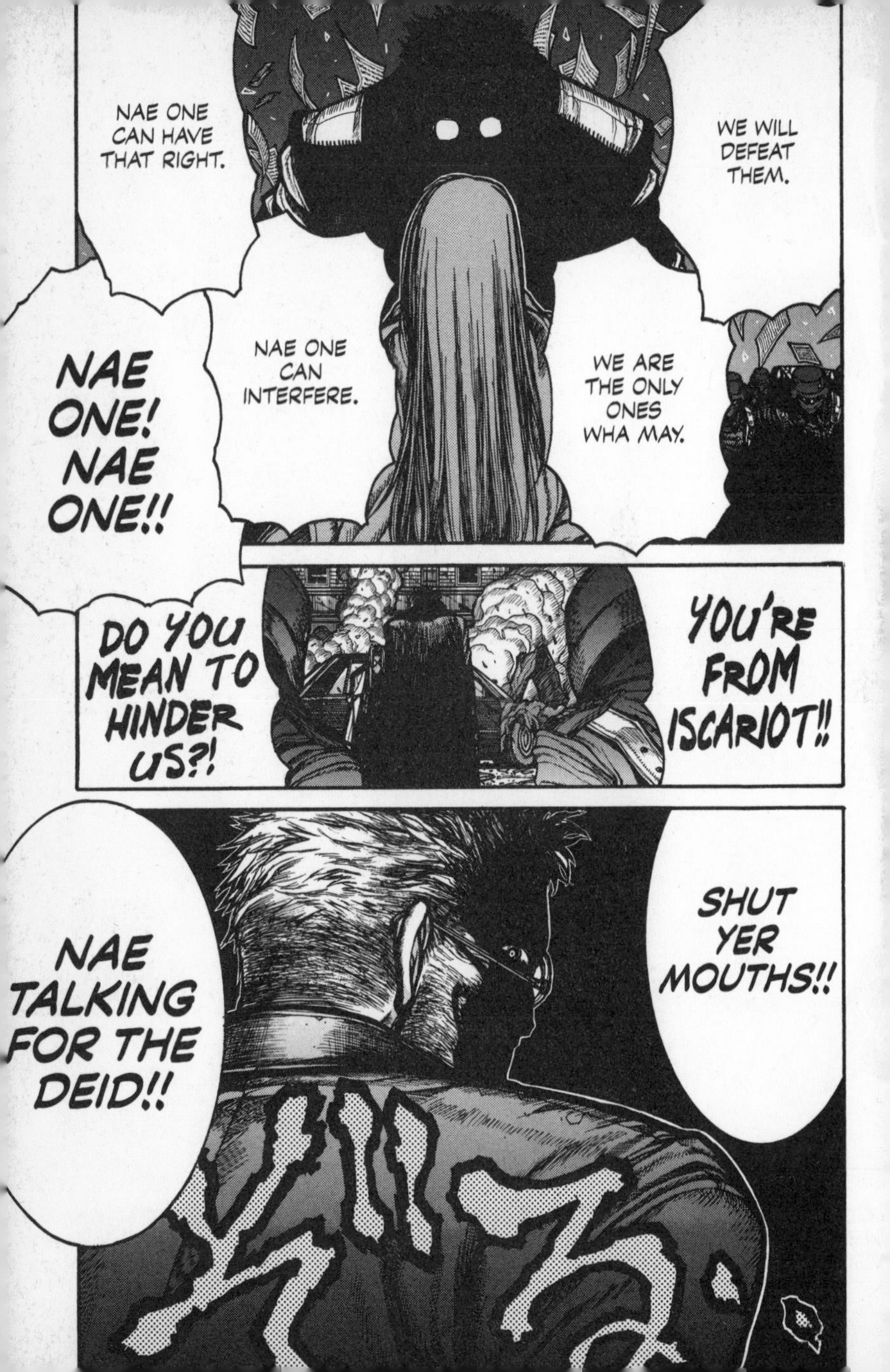
WE WILL DEFEAT THEM.
NAE ONE CAN HAVE THAT RIGHT.
WE ARE THE ONLY ONES WHA MAY.
NAE ONE CAN INTERFERE.
NAE ONE! NAE ONE!!
YOU'RE FROM ISCARIOT!!
DO YOU MEAN TO HINDER US?!
SHUT YER MOUTHS!!
NAE TALKING FOR THE DEID!!

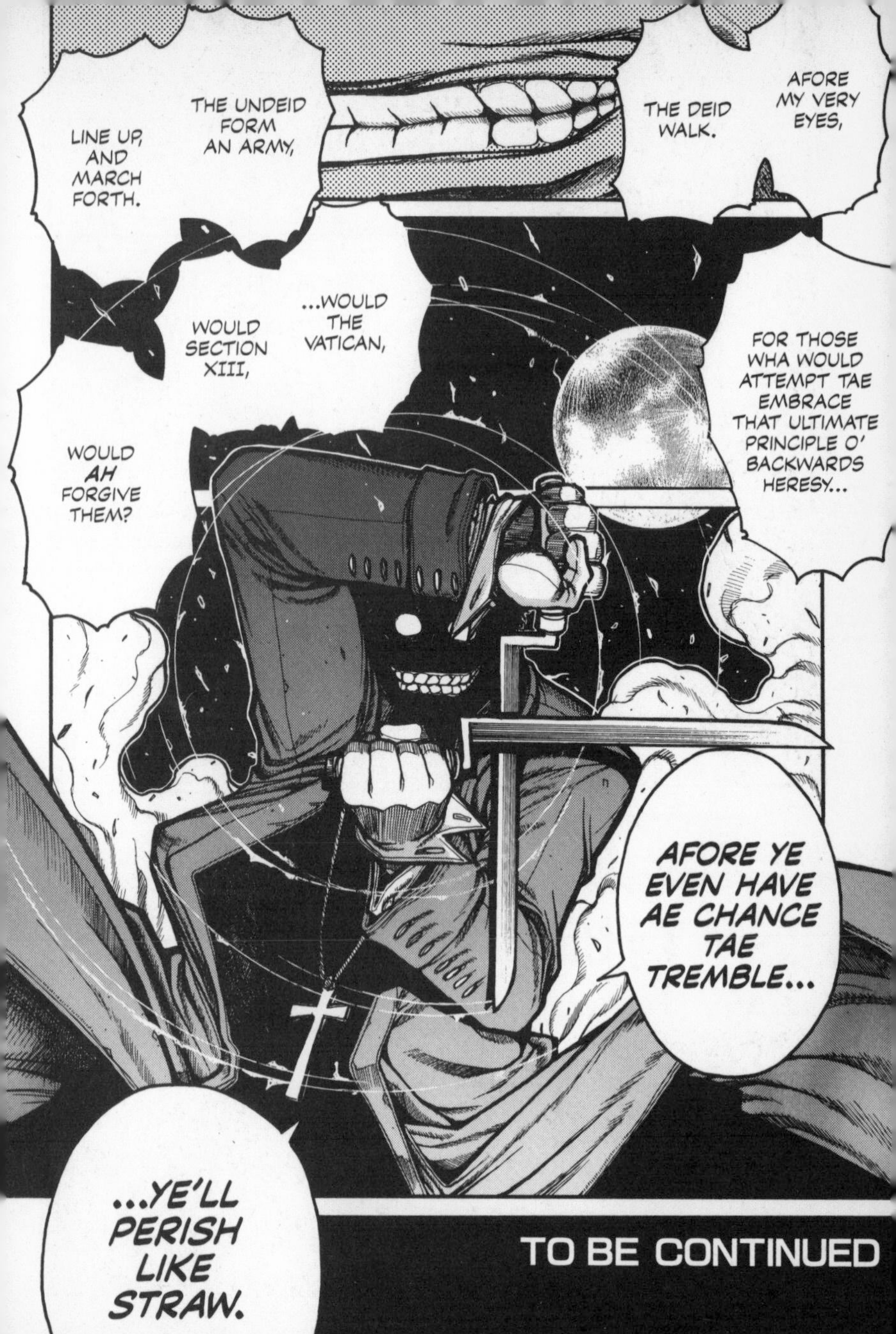
AFORE MY VERY EYES,
THE DEID WALK.
THE UNDEID FORM AN ARMY,
LINE UP, AND MARCH FORTH.
FOR THOSE WHA WOULD ATTEMPT TAE EMBRACE THAT ULTIMATE PRINCIPLE O' BACKWARDS HERESY...
...WOULD THE VATICAN,
WOULD SECTION XIII,
WOULD AH FORGIVE THEM?
AFORE YE EVEN HAVE AE CHANCE TAE TREMBLE...
...YE'LL PERISH LIKE STRAW.
TO BE CONTINUED

ORDER 3 / END

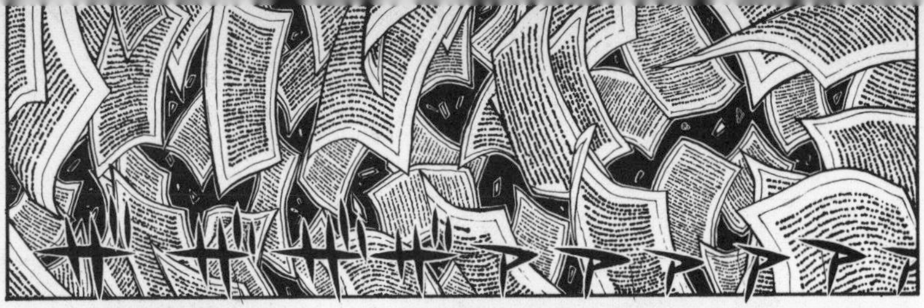

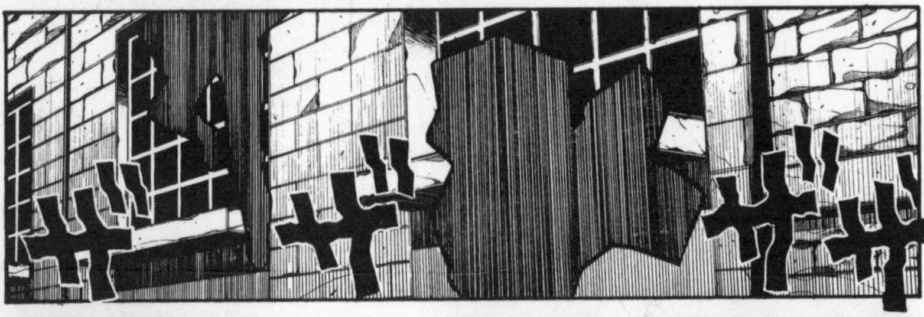

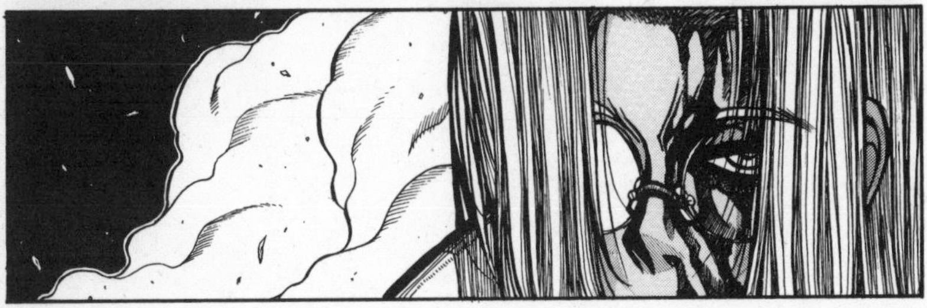

⚜ ORDER 4

THE SCREAMER

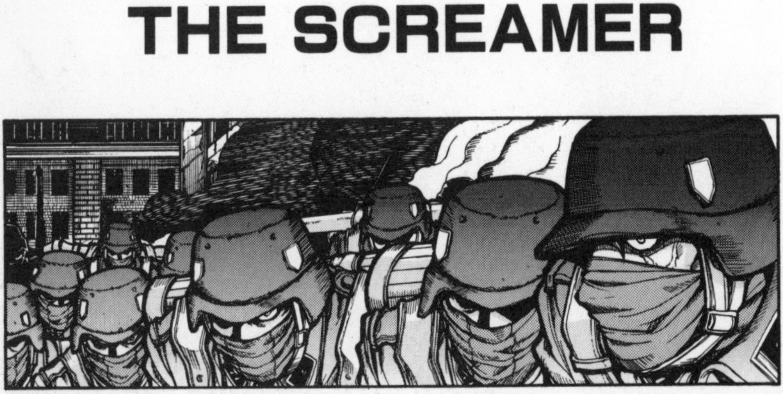

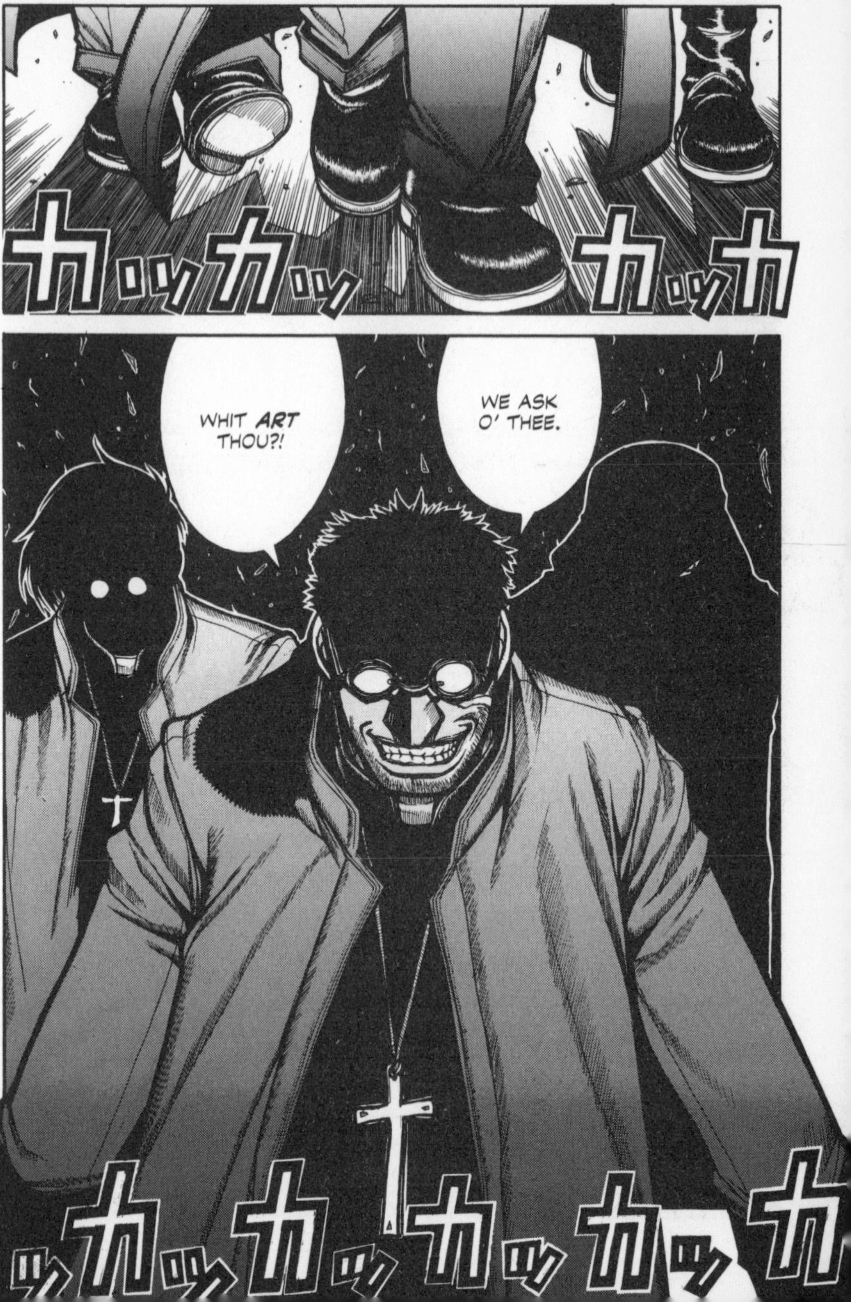
カッカッ
カッカ
WE ASK O' THEE.
WHIT *ART* THOU?!
ッカッカッカッカッカッカ

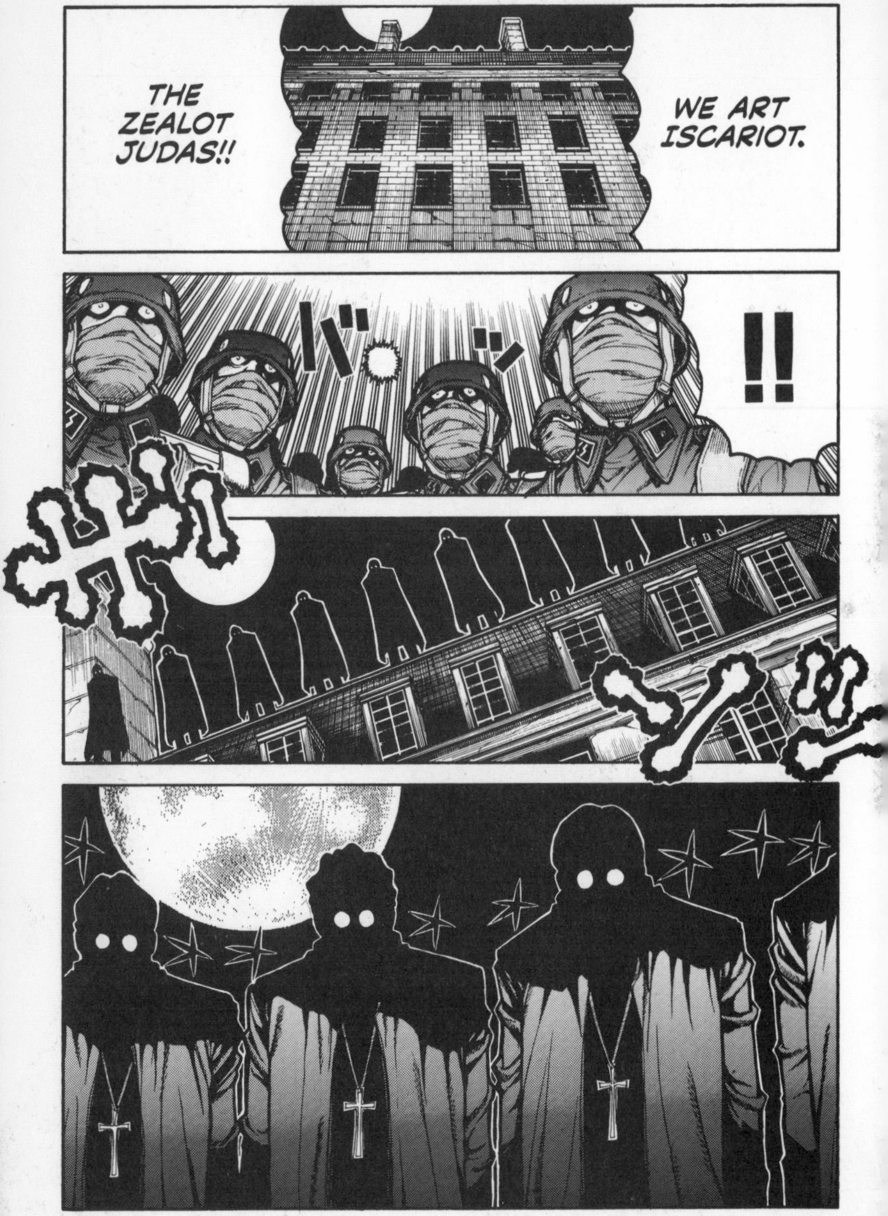
WE ART ISCARIOT.
THE ZEALOT JUDAS!!
!!
バッ

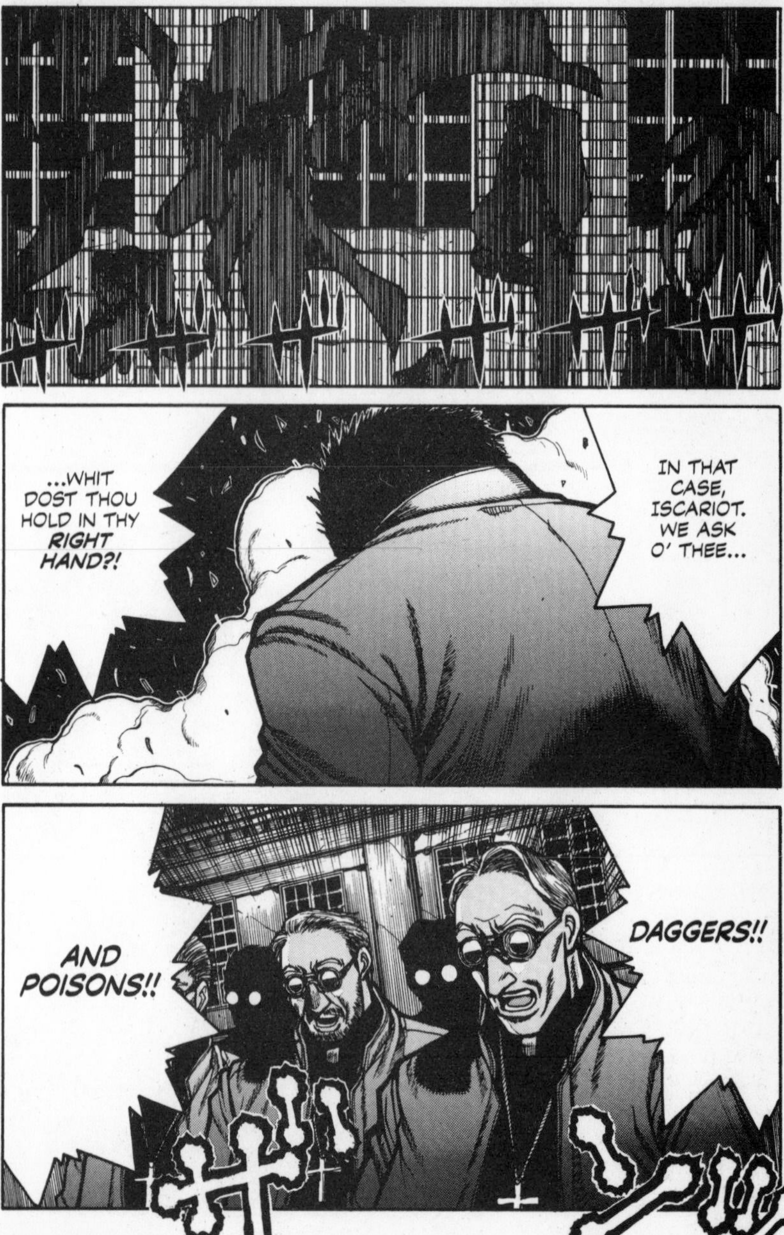
IN THAT CASE, ISCARIOT. WE ASK O' THEE...
...WHIT DOST THOU HOLD IN THY *RIGHT HAND?!*
DAGGERS!!
AND POISONS!!

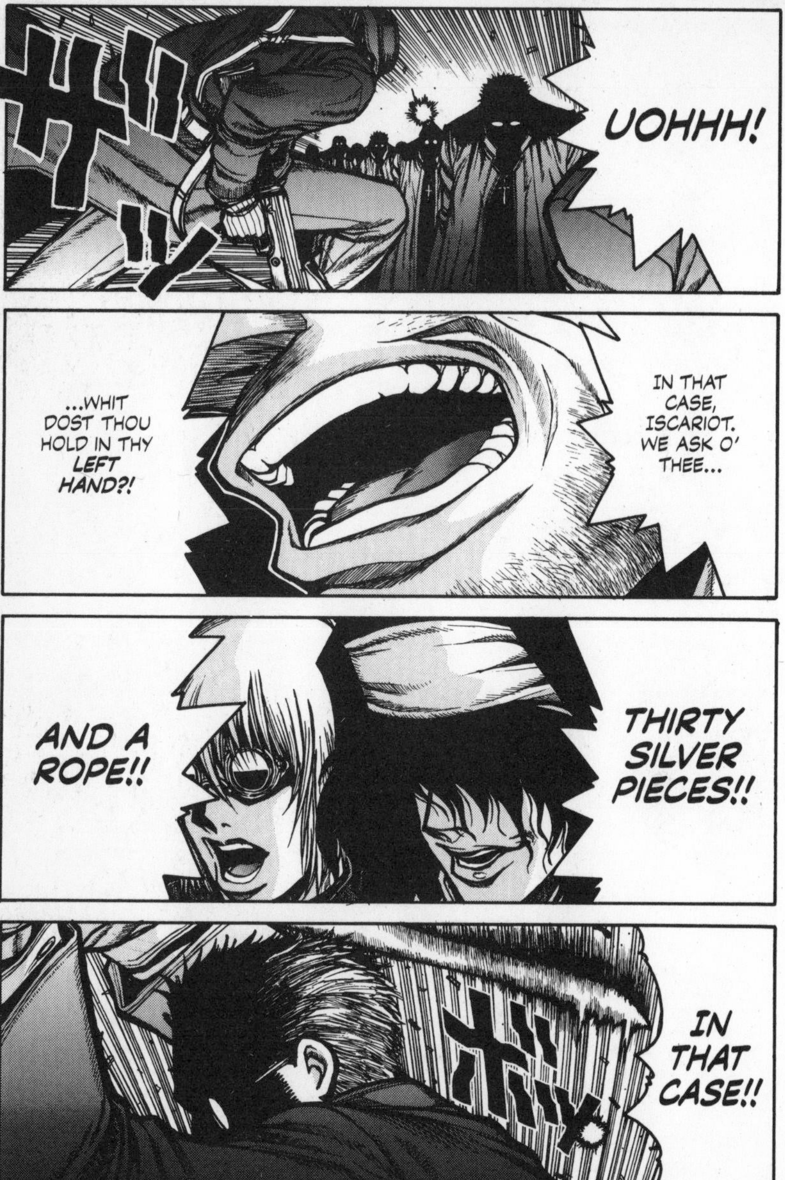
UOHHH!
IN THAT CASE, ISCARIOT. WE ASK O' THEE...
...WHIT DOST THOU HOLD IN THY LEFT HAND?!
THIRTY SILVER PIECES!!
AND A ROPE!!
IN THAT CASE!!

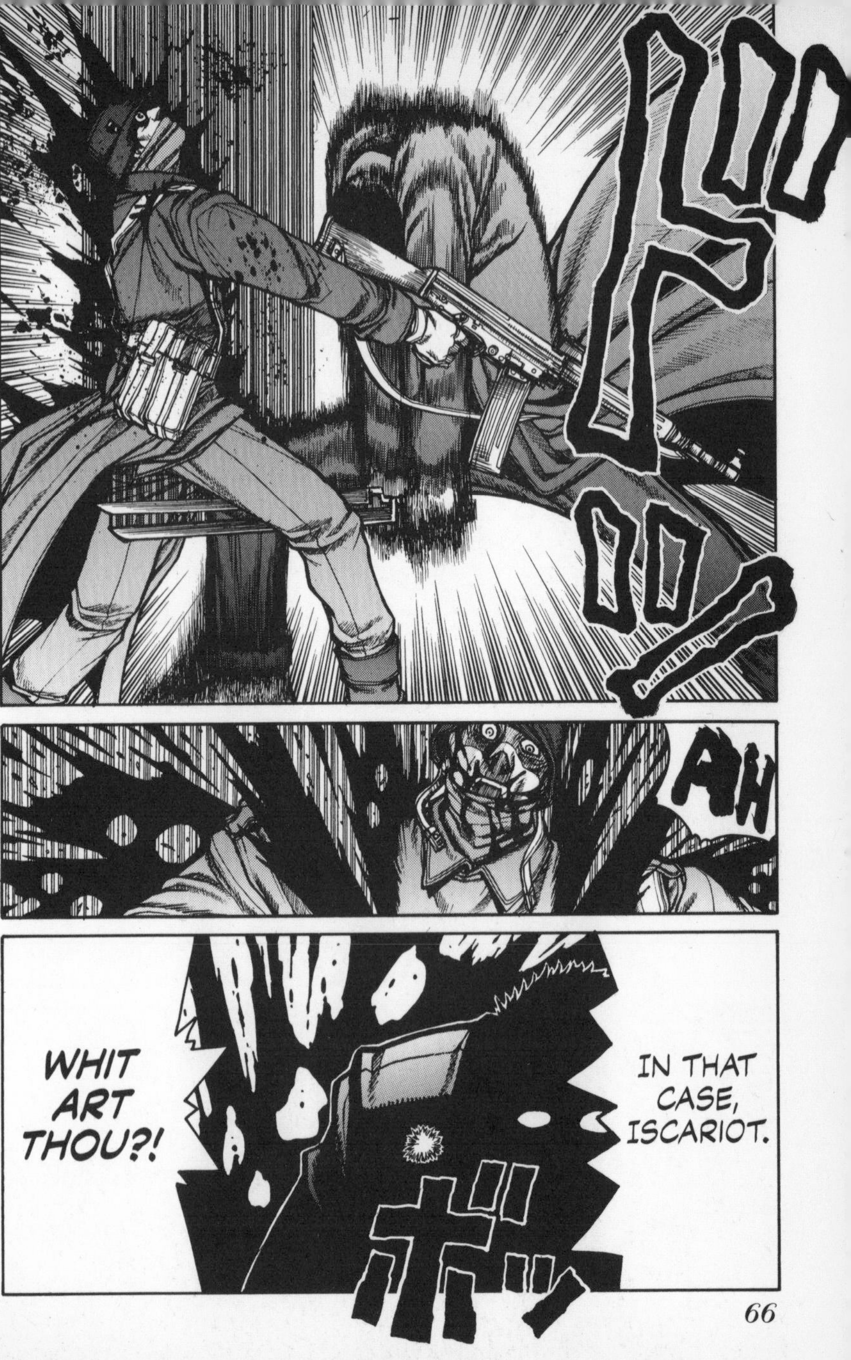
DOOOO!
AH
IN THAT CASE, ISCARIOT.
WHIT ART THOU?!
ボッ!

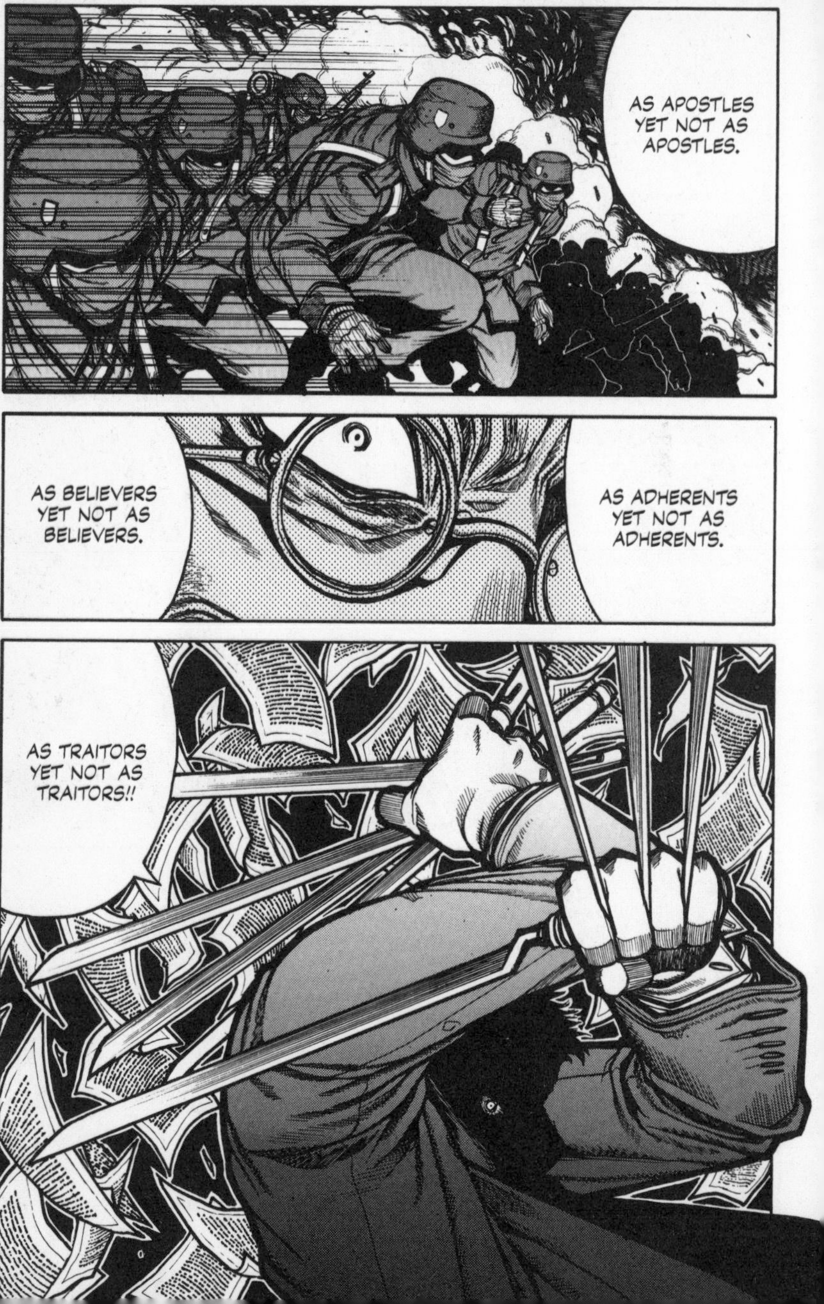
AS APOSTLES YET NOT AS APOSTLES.
AS ADHERENTS YET NOT AS ADHERENTS.
AS BELIEVERS YET NOT AS BELIEVERS.
AS TRAITORS YET NOT AS TRAITORS!!

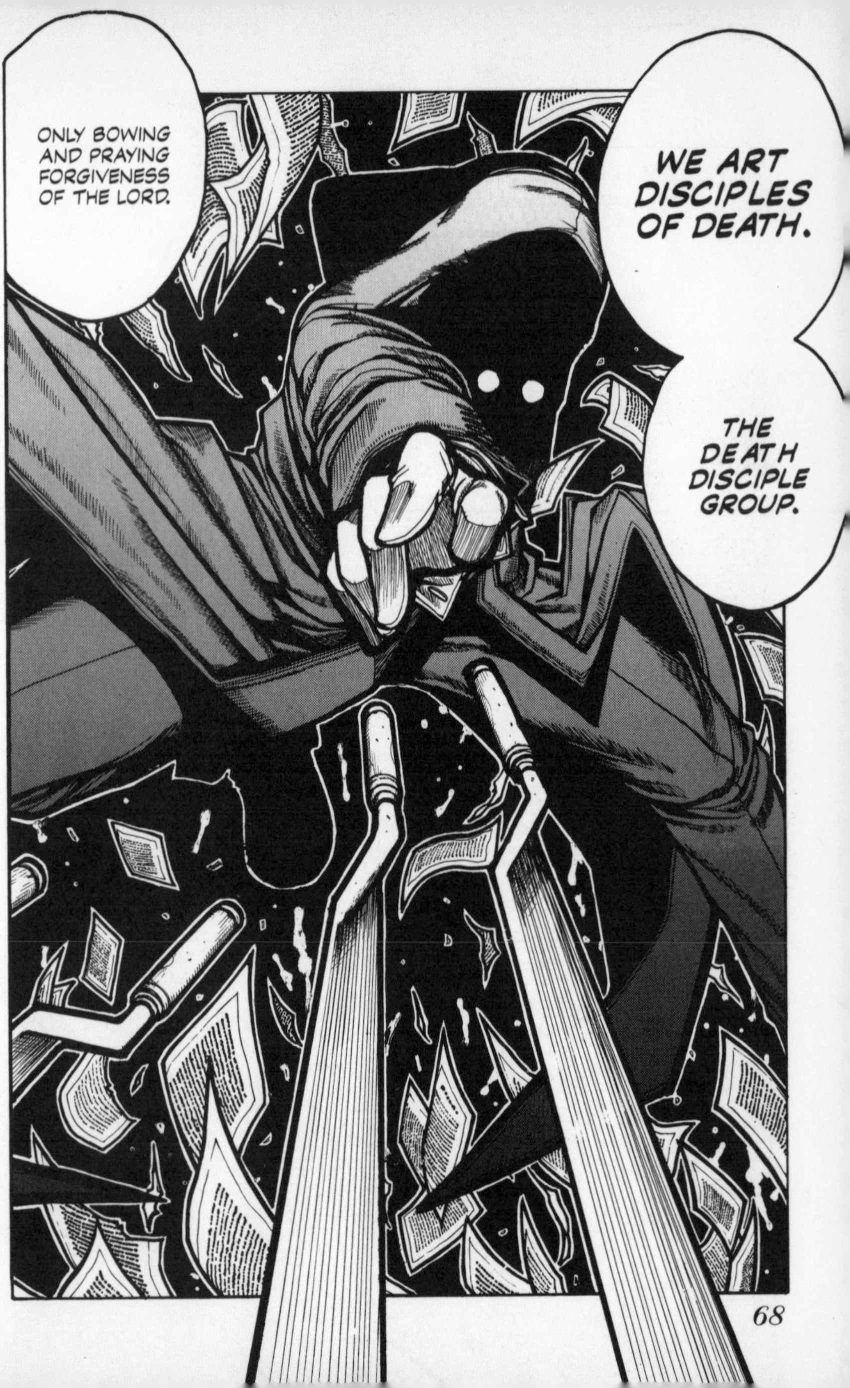
WE ART DISCIPLES OF DEATH.
THE DEATH DISCIPLE GROUP.
ONLY BOWING AND PRAYING FORGIVENESS OF THE LORD.

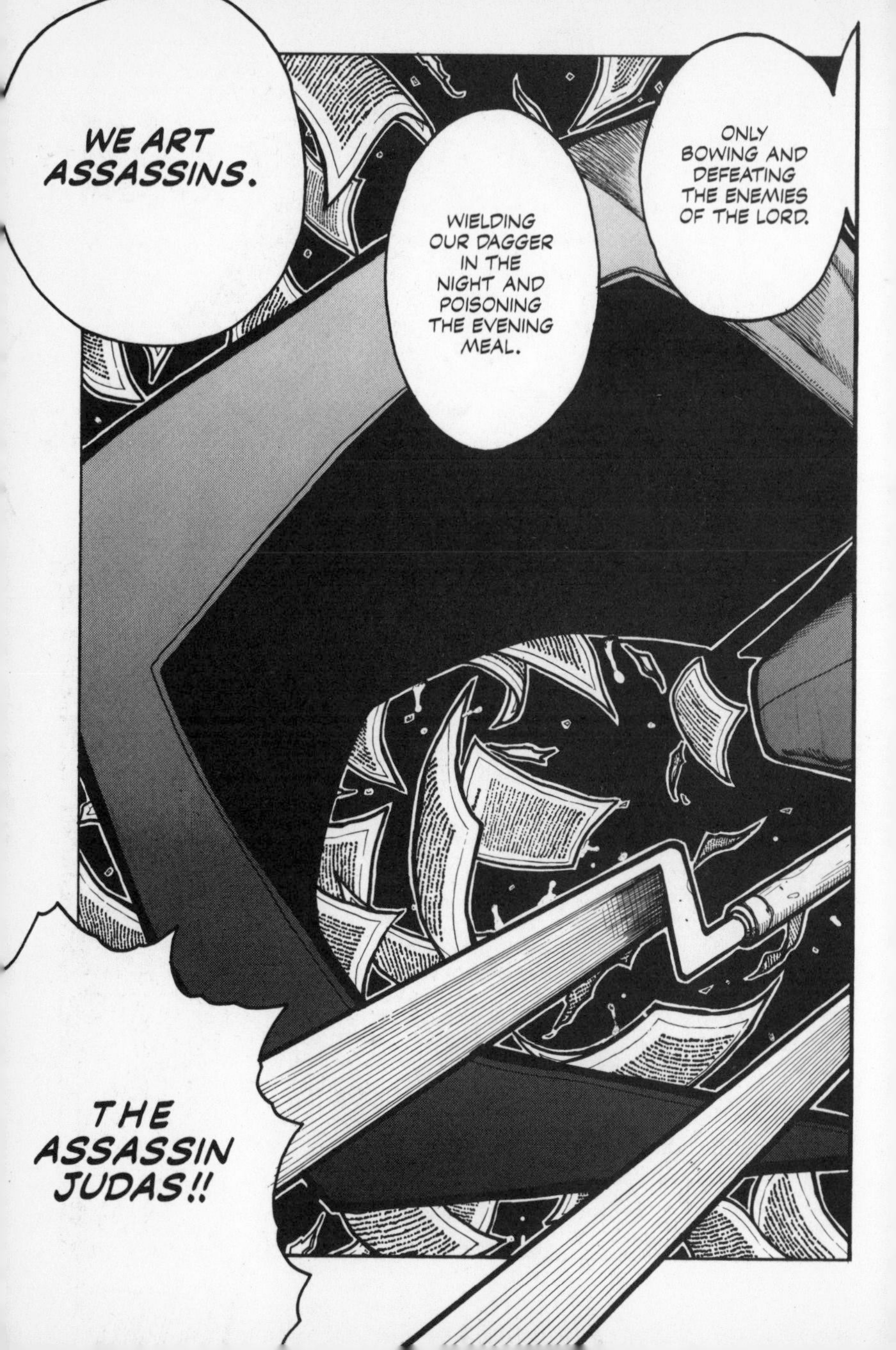
ONLY BOWING AND DEFEATING THE ENEMIES OF THE LORD.
WIELDING OUR DAGGER IN THE NIGHT AND POISONING THE EVENING MEAL.
WE ART ASSASSINS.
THE ASSASSIN JUDAS!!

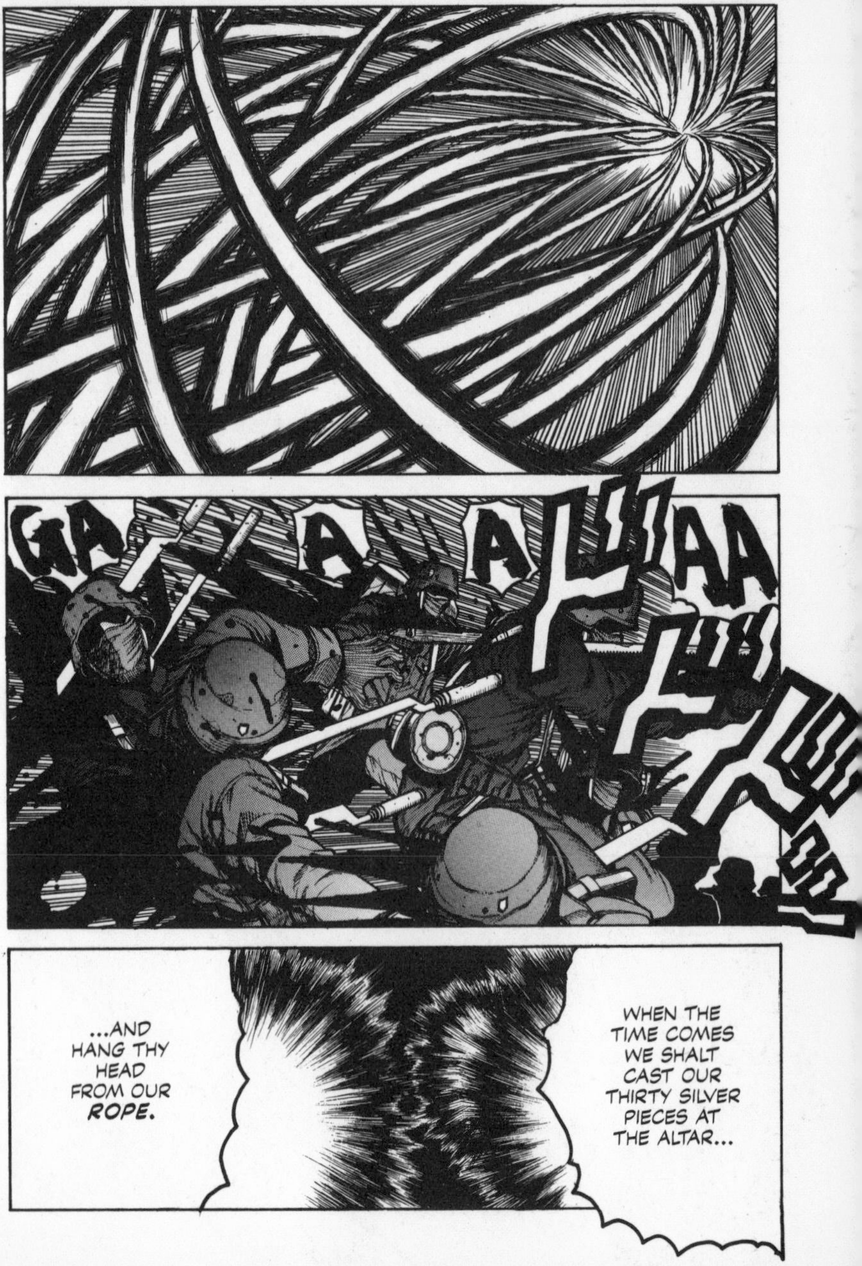
WHEN THE TIME COMES WE SHALT CAST OUR THIRTY SILVER PIECES AT THE ALTAR...
...AND HANG THY HEAD FROM OUR *ROPE*.

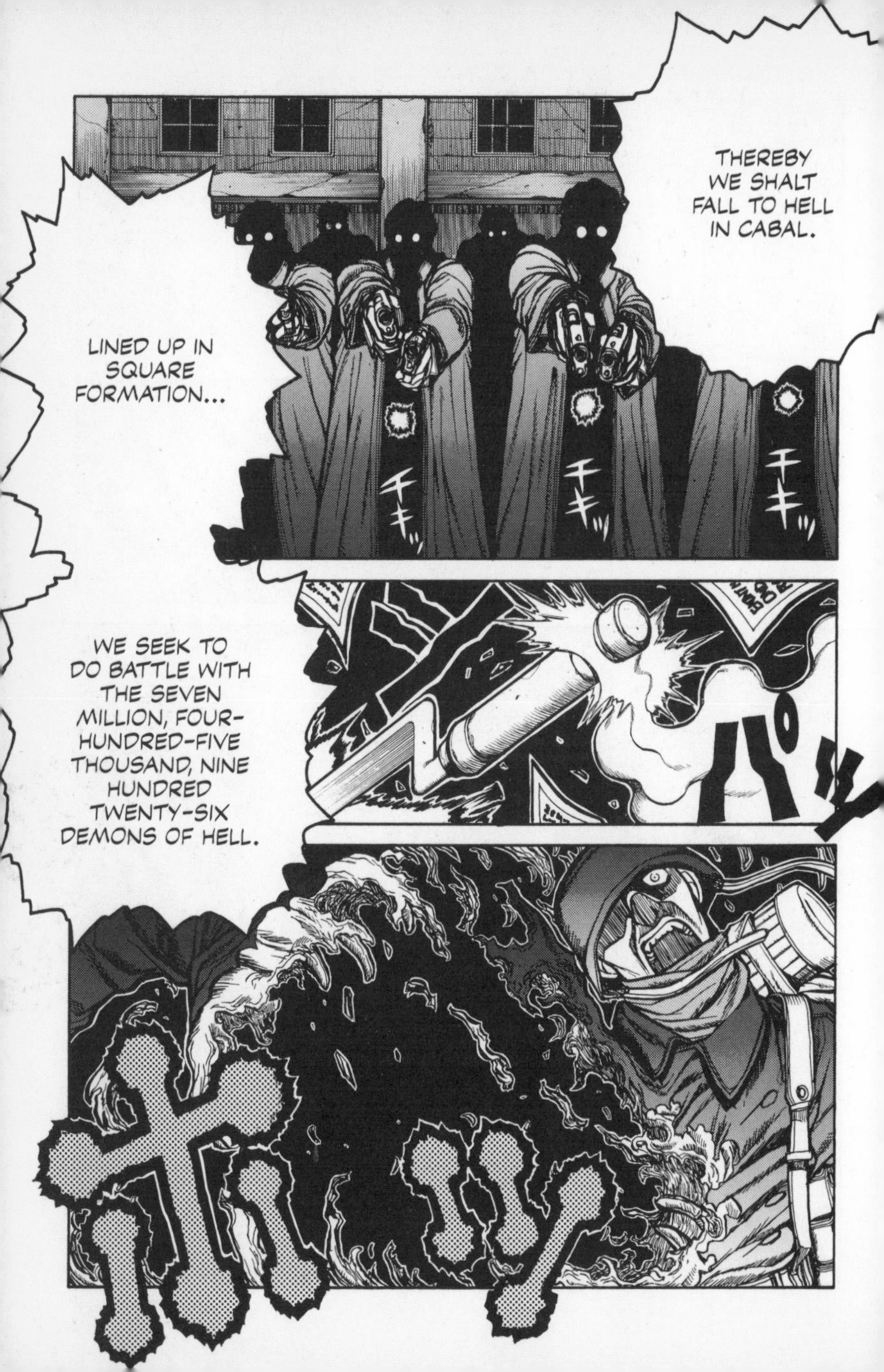
THEREBY WE SHALT FALL TO HELL IN CABAL.
LINED UP IN SQUARE FORMATION...
チキッ
チキッ
チキッ
WE SEEK TO DO BATTLE WITH THE SEVEN MILLION, FOUR-HUNDRED-FIVE THOUSAND, NINE HUNDRED TWENTY-SIX DEMONS OF HELL.

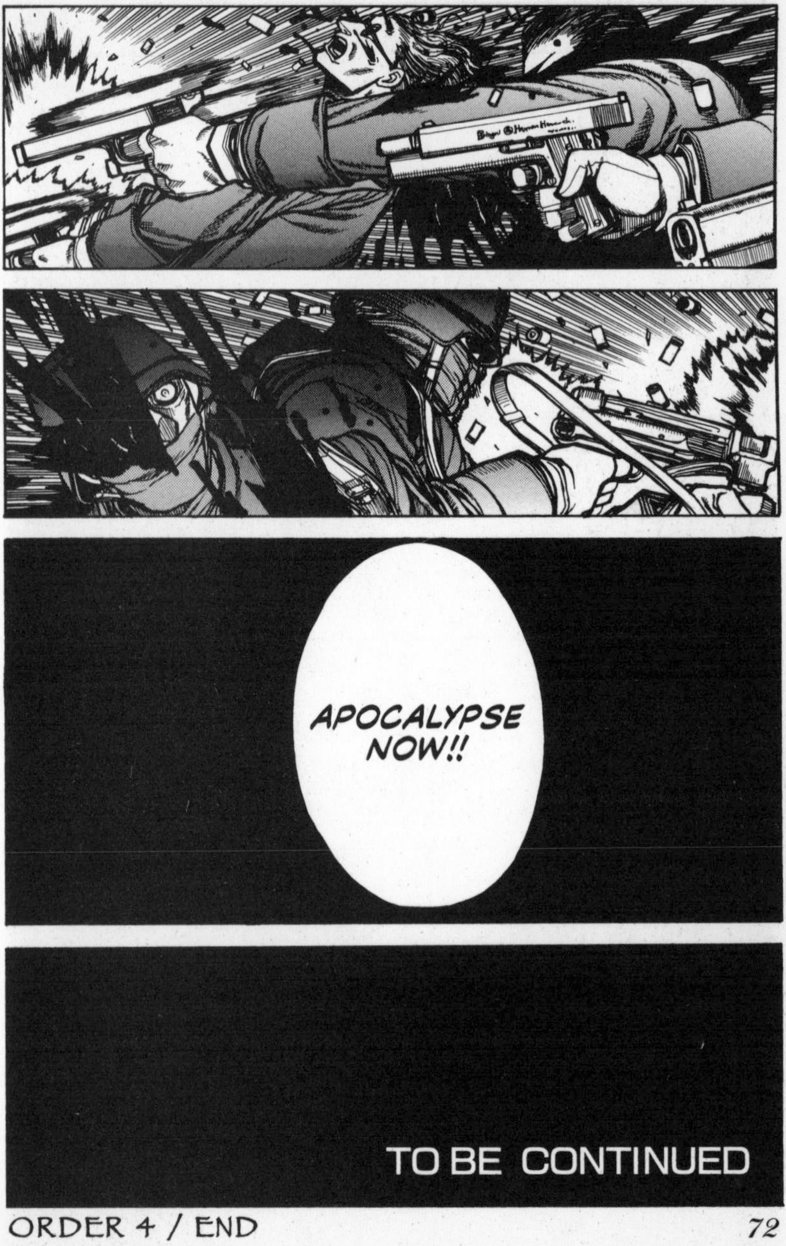
APOCALYPSE NOW!!
TO BE CONTINUED

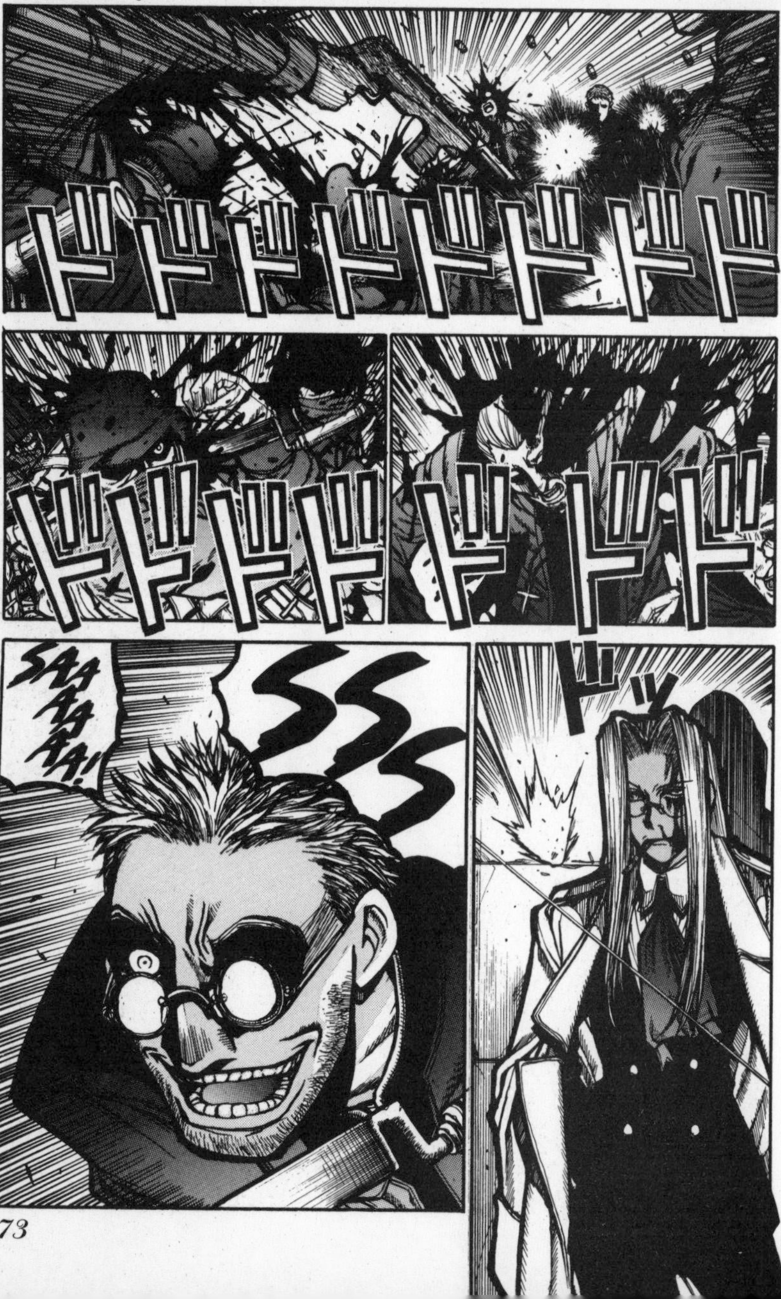
ドドドドドドドド
ドドドド
ドドドド
ドッ
SAAAAAAAA!
SSS

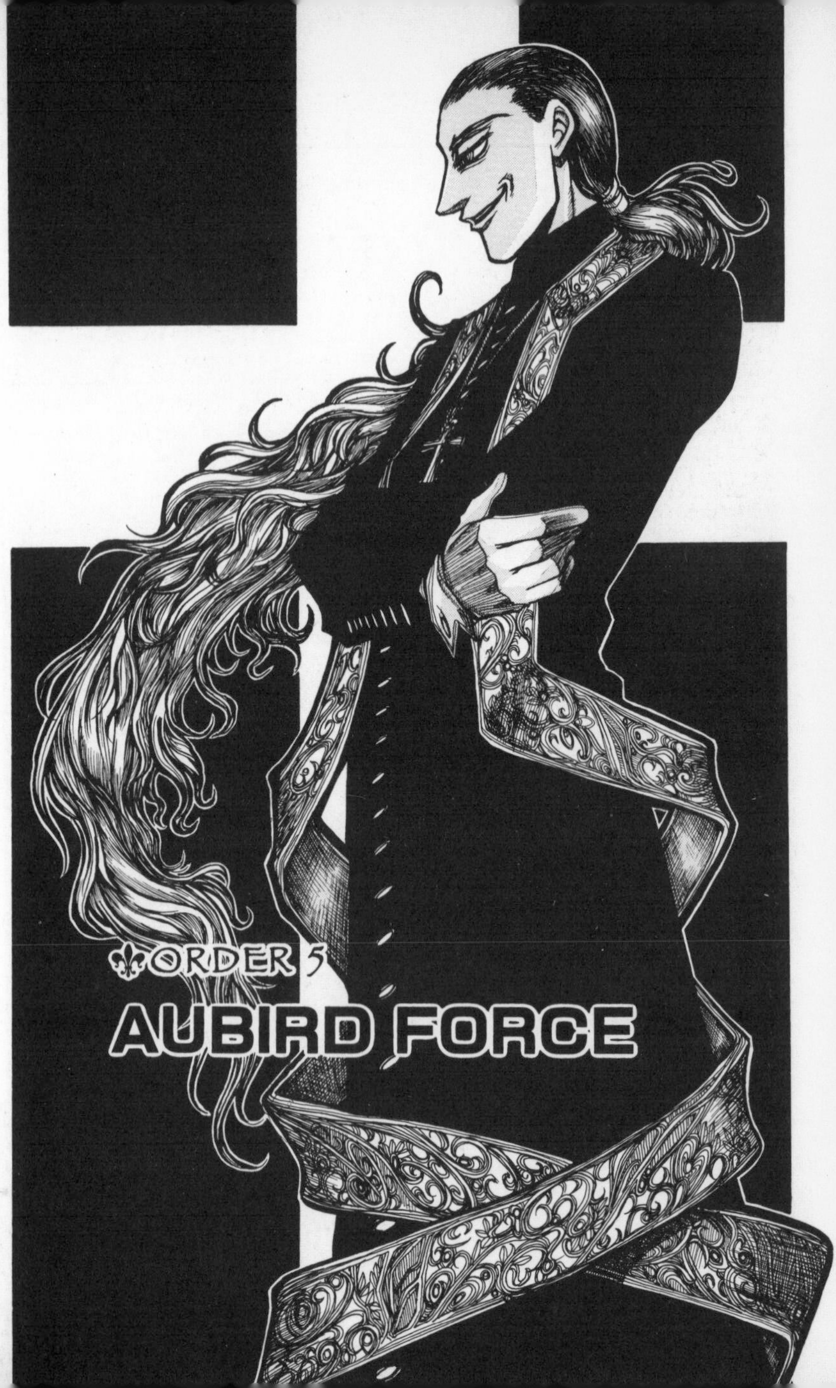
ORDER 5
AUBIRD FORCE

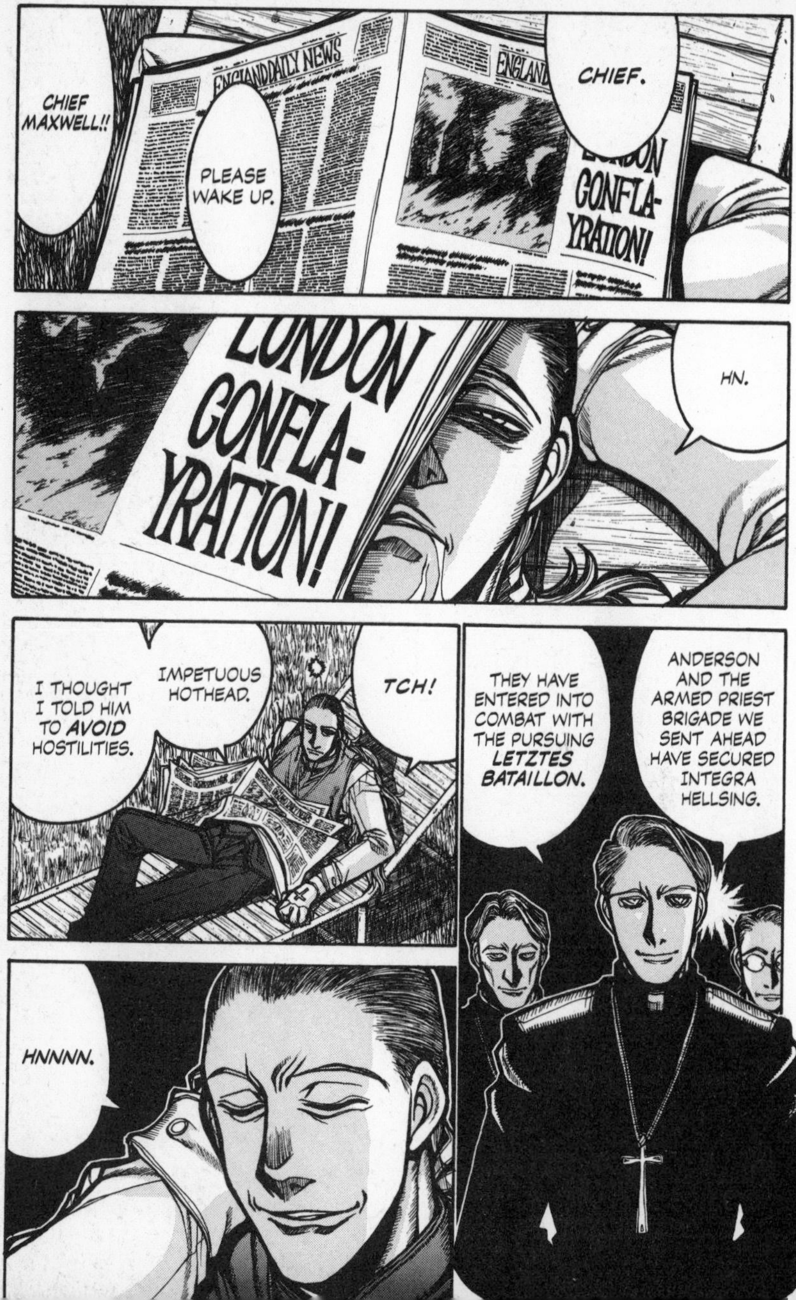
CHIEF.
PLEASE WAKE UP.
CHIEF MAXWELL!!
ENGLAND DAILY NEWS
LONDON CONFLA-YRATION!
LONDON CONFLA-YRATION!
HN.
ANDERSON AND THE ARMED PRIEST BRIGADE WE SENT AHEAD HAVE SECURED INTEGRA HELLSING.
THEY HAVE ENTERED INTO COMBAT WITH THE PURSUING *LETZTES BATAILLON.*
TCH!
IMPETUOUS HOTHEAD.
I THOUGHT I TOLD HIM TO *AVOID* HOSTILITIES.
HNNNN.

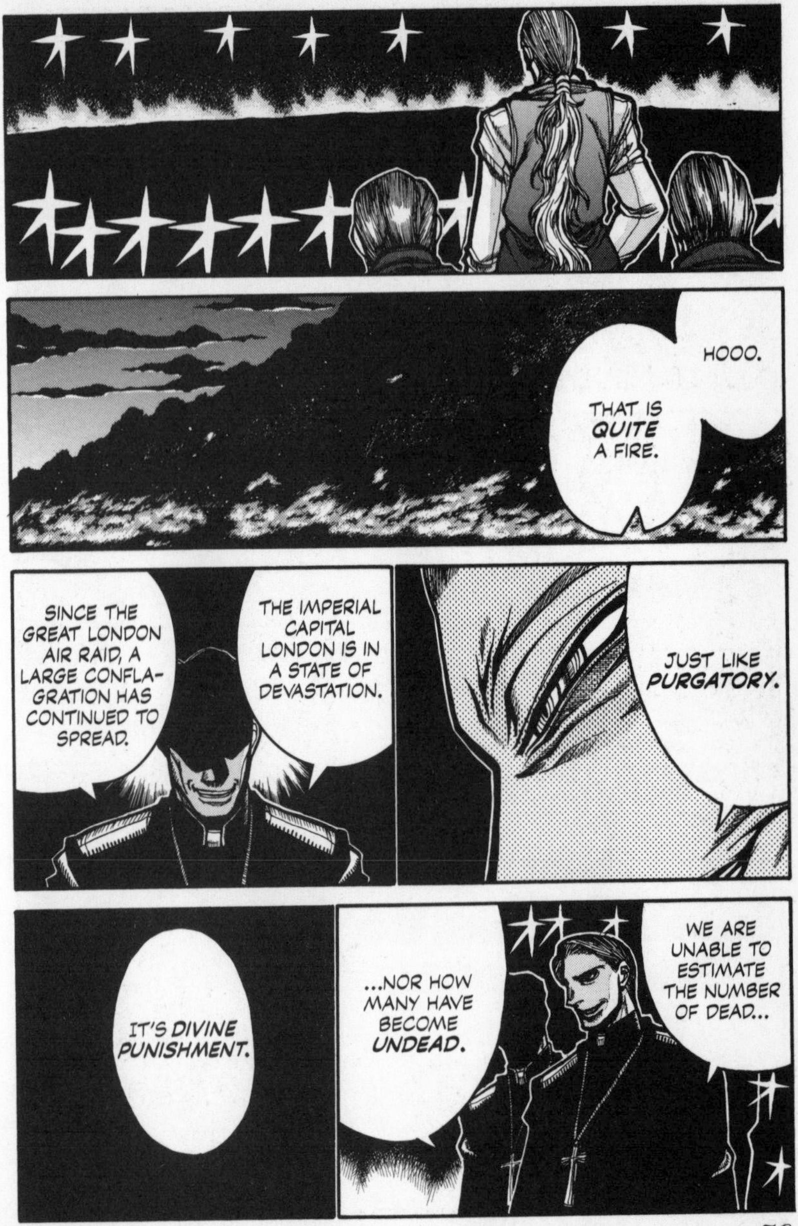
HOOO.
THAT IS *QUITE* A FIRE.
JUST LIKE *PURGATORY*.
THE IMPERIAL CAPITAL LONDON IS IN A STATE OF DEVASTATION.
SINCE THE GREAT LONDON AIR RAID, A LARGE CONFLA-GRATION HAS CONTINUED TO SPREAD.
WE ARE UNABLE TO ESTIMATE THE NUMBER OF DEAD...
...NOR HOW MANY HAVE BECOME *UNDEAD*.
IT'S *DIVINE PUNISHMENT*.

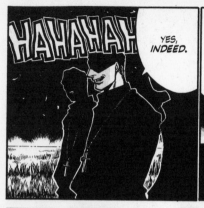

BECAUSE THE FOOLS OVEREXTENDED THEMSELVES, FELL INTO HERESY, AND REJOICED OVER IT, THIS HAPPENS.
WHAT A GOOD FEELING.
YES, *INDEED.*
HAHAHAH
ザッ
ザッ
ザッ
ザッ
AND THE *U.S.A.?*
MAJOR CHAOS.
AS OF NOW THE *WHITE HOUSE* IS IN FLAMES...
...AND SOMEHOW IT SEEMS THAT THIRTEEN CABINET MEMBERS BENEATH THE PRESIDENT *DIED* ALL AT ONCE.
WELL, WHEN A PRESIDENTIAL AIDE BECOMES A VAMPIRE IN THE MIDST OF PROCEEDINGS,
I *SUPPOSE* THAT *WOULD* HAPPEN.

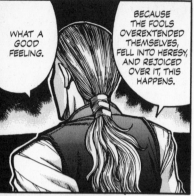

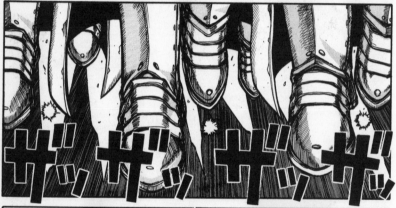

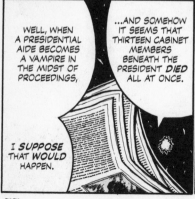

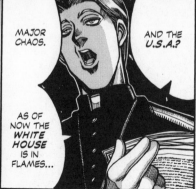

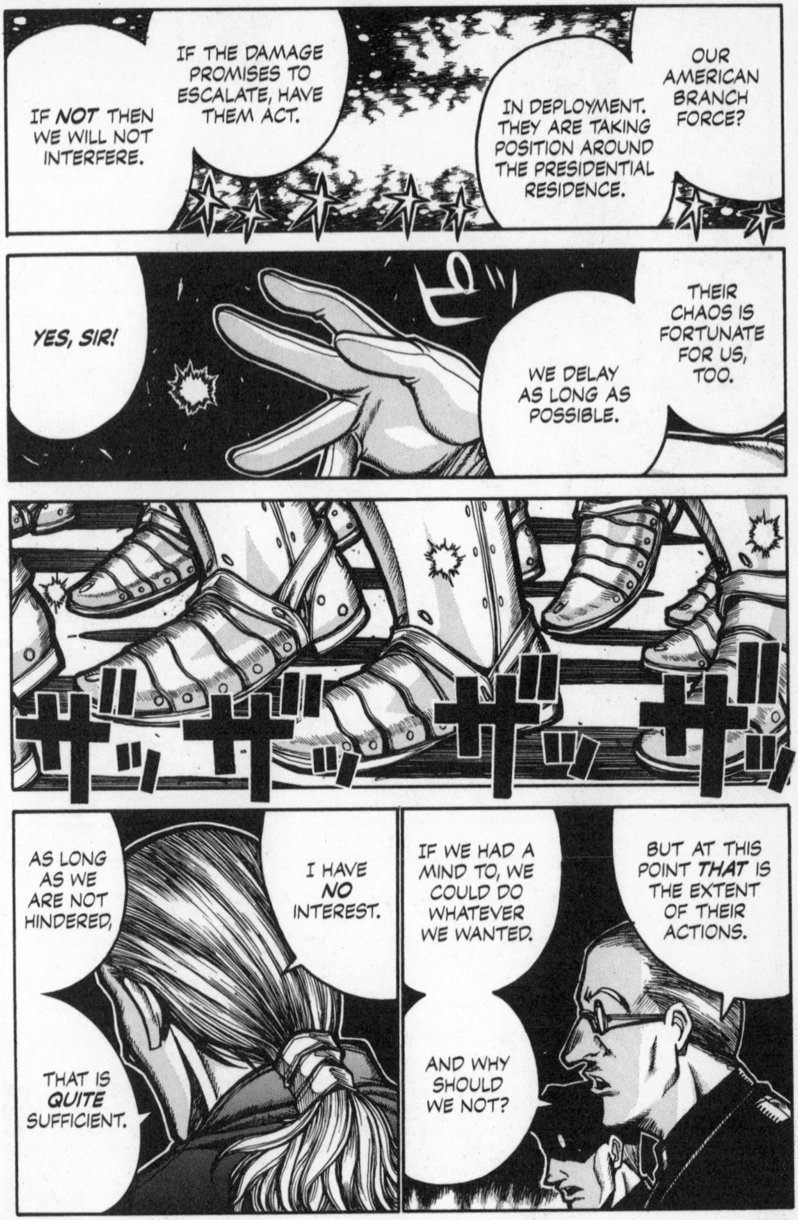
OUR AMERICAN BRANCH FORCE?
IN DEPLOYMENT. THEY ARE TAKING POSITION AROUND THE PRESIDENTIAL RESIDENCE.
IF THE DAMAGE PROMISES TO ESCALATE, HAVE THEM ACT.
IF *NOT* THEN WE WILL NOT INTERFERE.
THEIR CHAOS IS FORTUNATE FOR US, TOO.
WE DELAY AS LONG AS POSSIBLE.
YES, SIR!
ザッ
ザッ
ザッ
ザッ
BUT AT THIS POINT *THAT* IS THE EXTENT OF THEIR ACTIONS.
IF WE HAD A MIND TO, WE COULD DO WHATEVER WE WANTED.
AND WHY SHOULD WE NOT?
I HAVE *NO* INTEREST.
AS LONG AS WE ARE NOT HINDERED,
THAT IS *QUITE* SUFFICIENT.

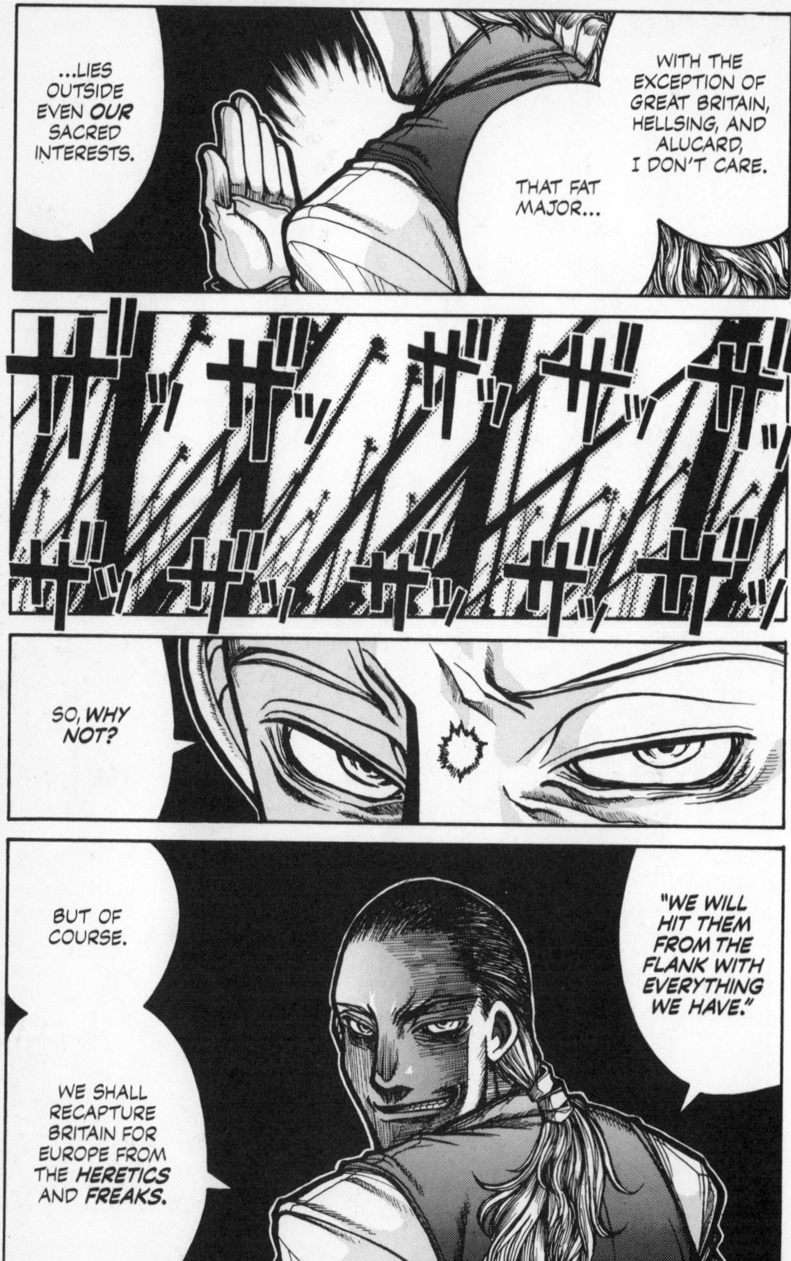
WITH THE EXCEPTION OF GREAT BRITAIN, HELLSING, AND ALUCARD, I DON'T CARE.
THAT FAT MAJOR...
...LIES OUTSIDE EVEN **OUR** SACRED INTERESTS.
ザッ ザッ ザッ ザッ ザッ
ザッ ザッ ザッ ザッ ザッ
SO, ***WHY NOT?***
"WE WILL HIT THEM FROM THE FLANK WITH EVERYTHING WE HAVE."
BUT OF COURSE.
WE SHALL RECAPTURE BRITAIN FOR EUROPE FROM THE ***HERETICS*** AND ***FREAKS.***

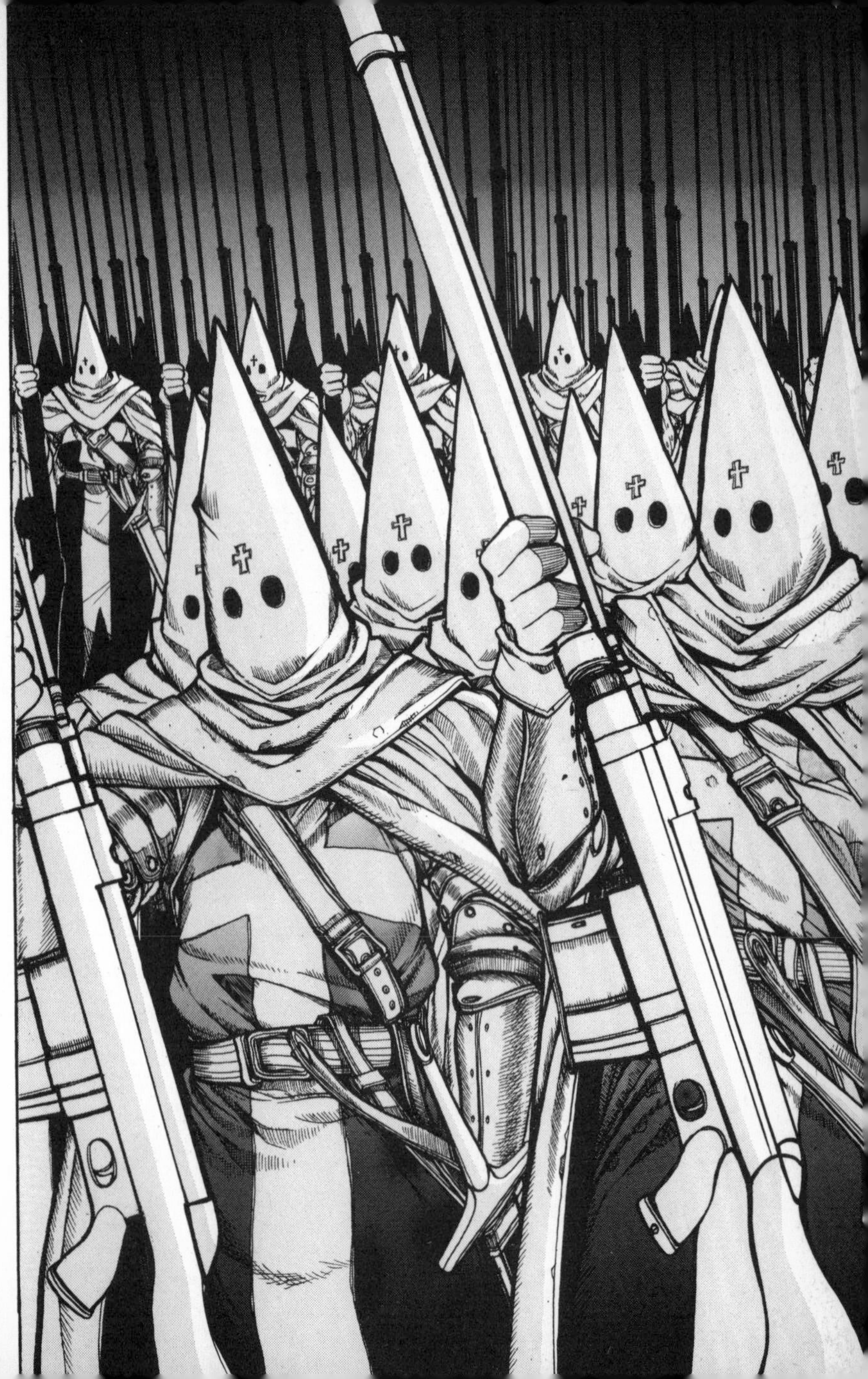

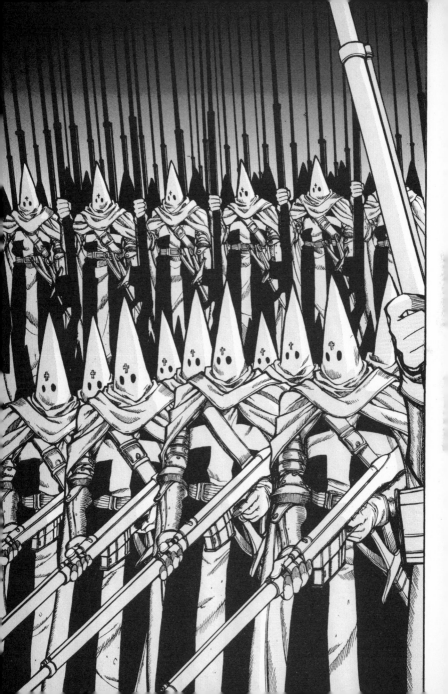

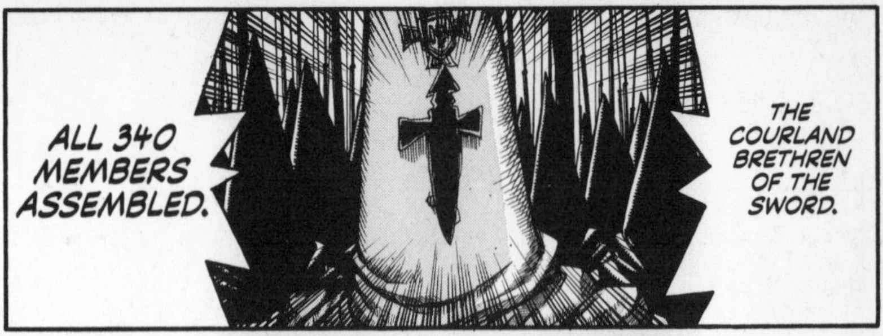
THE COURLAND BRETHREN OF THE SWORD.
ALL 340 MEMBERS ASSEMBLED.

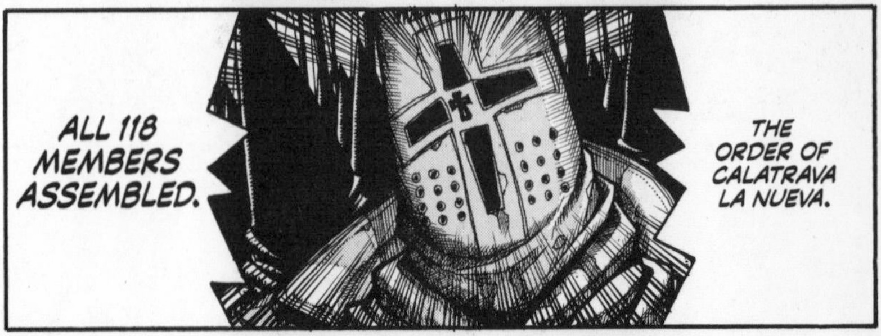
THE ORDER OF CALATRAVA LA NUEVA.
ALL 118 MEMBERS ASSEMBLED.

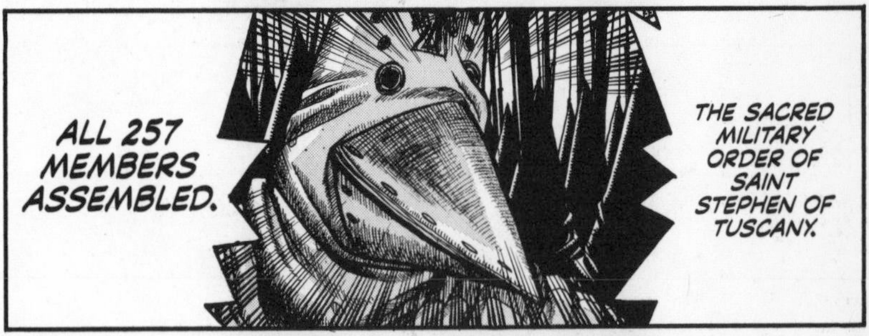
THE SACRED MILITARY ORDER OF SAINT STEPHEN OF TUSCANY.
ALL 257 MEMBERS ASSEMBLED.

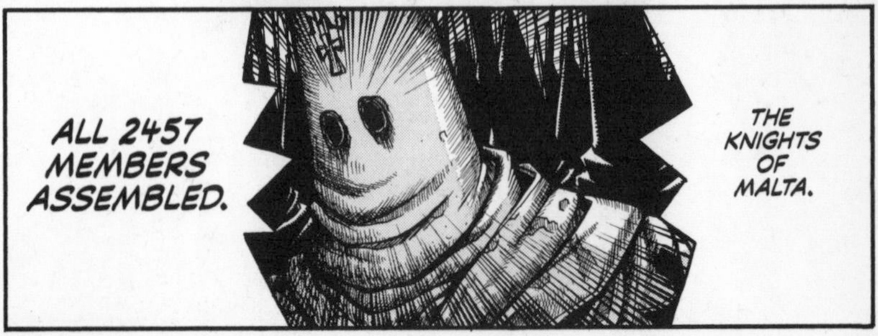
THE KNIGHTS OF MALTA.
ALL 2457 MEMBERS ASSEMBLED.

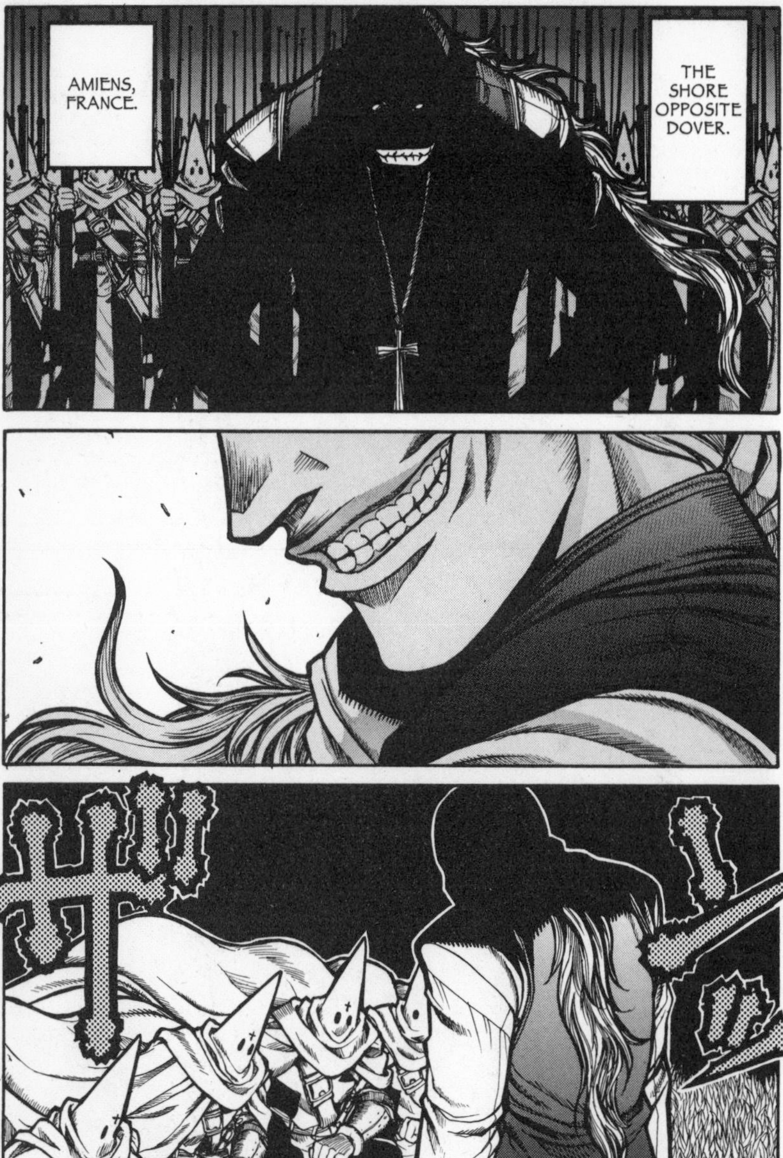
THE SHORE OPPOSITE DOVER.
AMIENS, FRANCE.

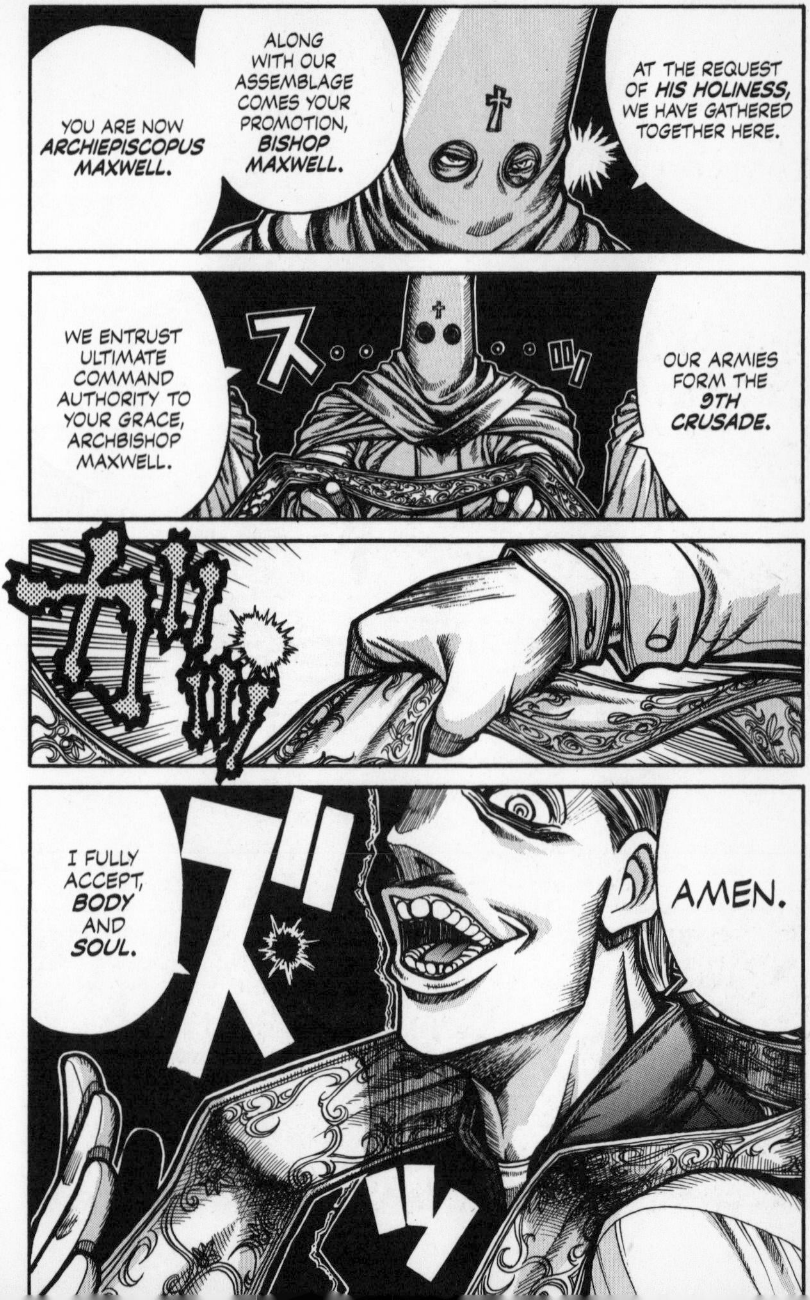
AT THE REQUEST OF *HIS HOLINESS,* WE HAVE GATHERED TOGETHER HERE.
ALONG WITH OUR ASSEMBLAGE COMES YOUR PROMOTION, *BISHOP MAXWELL.*
YOU ARE NOW *ARCHIEPISCOPUS MAXWELL.*
OUR ARMIES FORM THE *9TH CRUSADE.*
ス
WE ENTRUST ULTIMATE COMMAND AUTHORITY TO YOUR GRACE, ARCHBISHOP MAXWELL.
カッ
AMEN.
ズッ
I FULLY ACCEPT, *BODY* AND *SOUL.*

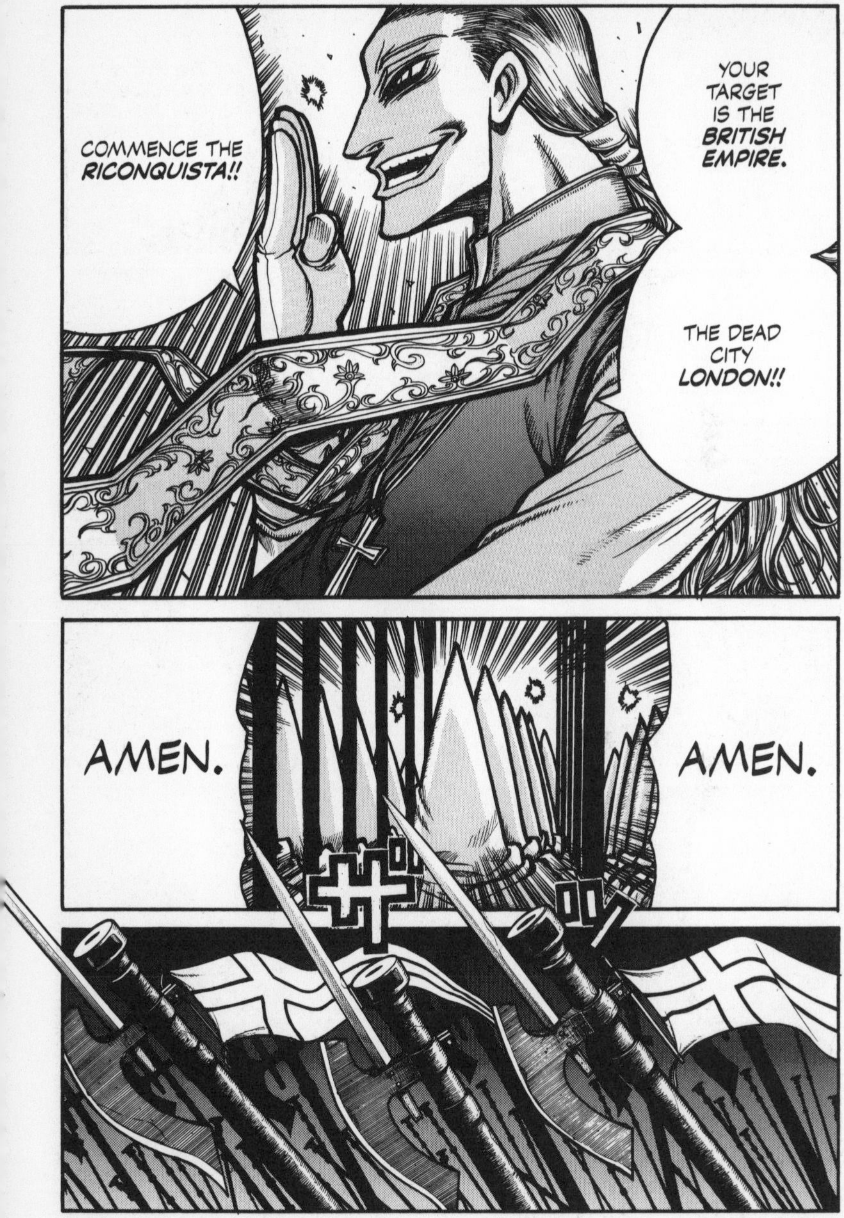
YOUR TARGET IS THE *BRITISH EMPIRE.*
THE DEAD CITY *LONDON!!*
COMMENCE THE *RICONQUISTA!!*
AMEN.
AMEN.

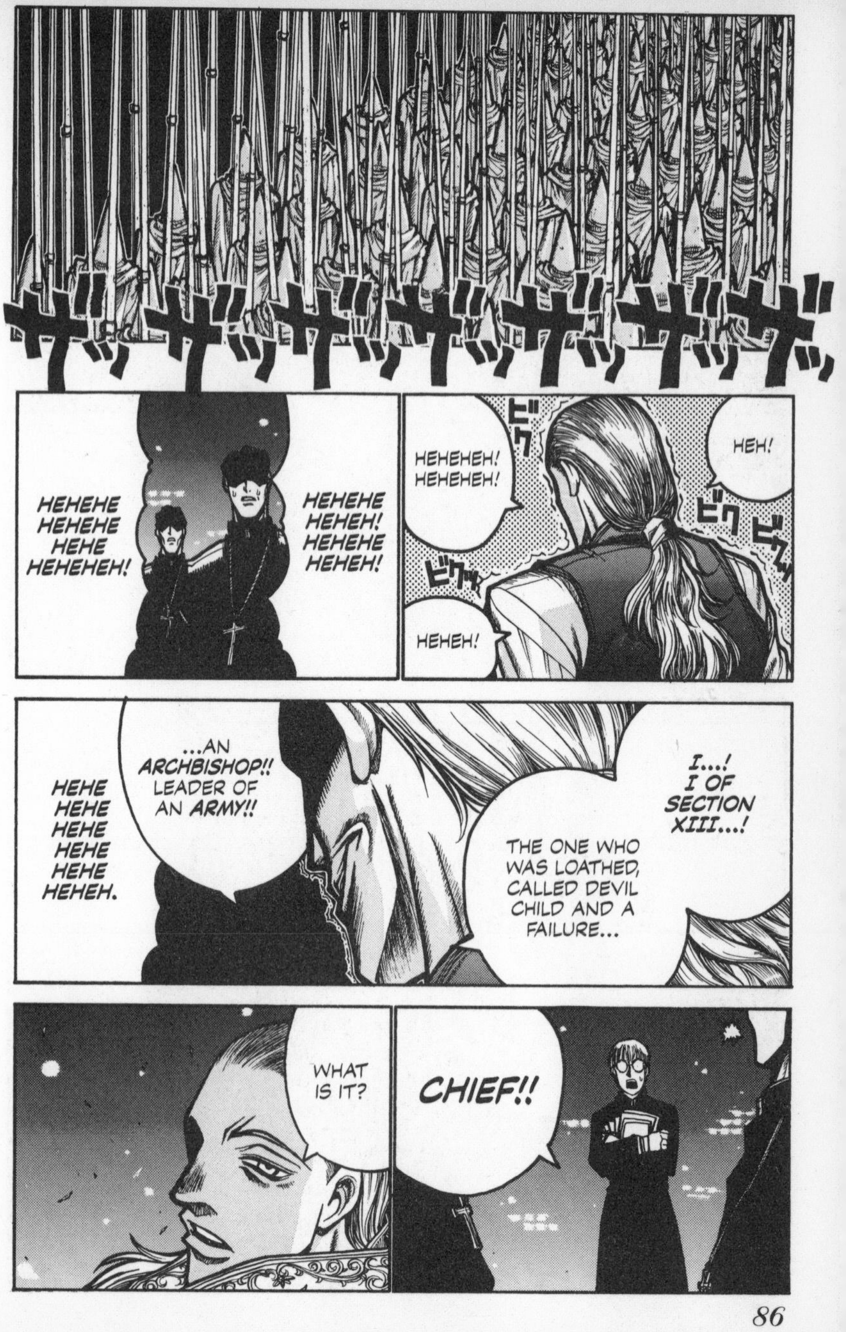
ザッザッザッザッザッザッ
HEH!
HEHEHEH! HEHEHEH!
ビク
ビク ビクッ
ビクッ
HEHEH!
HEHEHE HEHEH! HEHEHE HEHEH!
HEHEHE HEHEHE HEHE HEHEHEH!
I...! I OF SECTION XIII...!
THE ONE WHO WAS LOATHED, CALLED DEVIL CHILD AND A FAILURE...
...AN ARCHBISHOP!! LEADER OF AN ARMY!!
HEHE HEHE HEHE HEHE HEHE HEHEH.
CHIEF!!
WHAT IS IT?

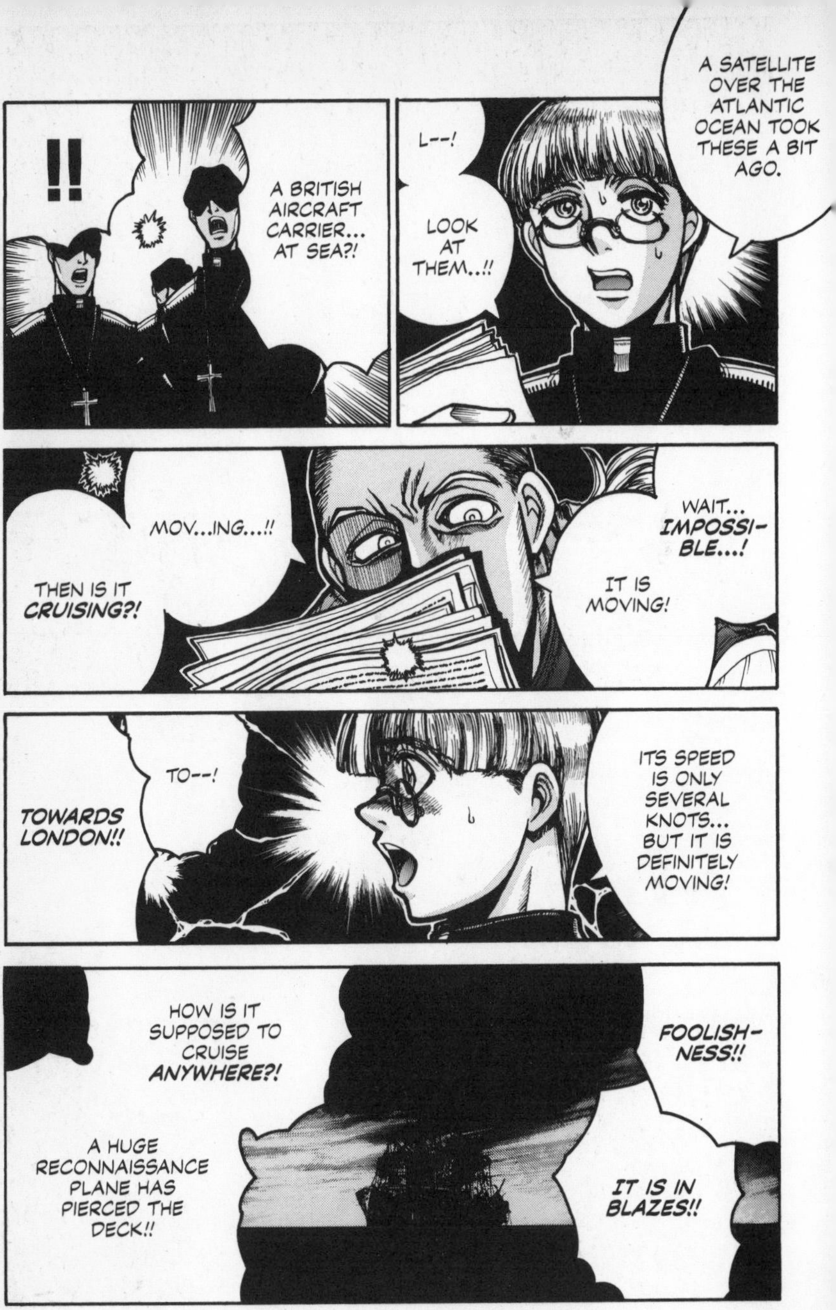
A SATELLITE OVER THE ATLANTIC OCEAN TOOK THESE A BIT AGO.
L--!
LOOK AT THEM..!!
!!
A BRITISH AIRCRAFT CARRIER... AT SEA?!
WAIT... *IMPOSSIBLE...!*
IT IS MOVING!
MOV...ING...!!
THEN IS IT *CRUISING?!*
ITS SPEED IS ONLY SEVERAL KNOTS... BUT IT IS DEFINITELY MOVING!
TO--!
TOWARDS LONDON!!
FOOLISHNESS!!
HOW IS IT SUPPOSED TO CRUISE *ANYWHERE?!*
IT IS IN BLAZES!!
A HUGE RECONNAISSANCE PLANE HAS PIERCED THE DECK!!

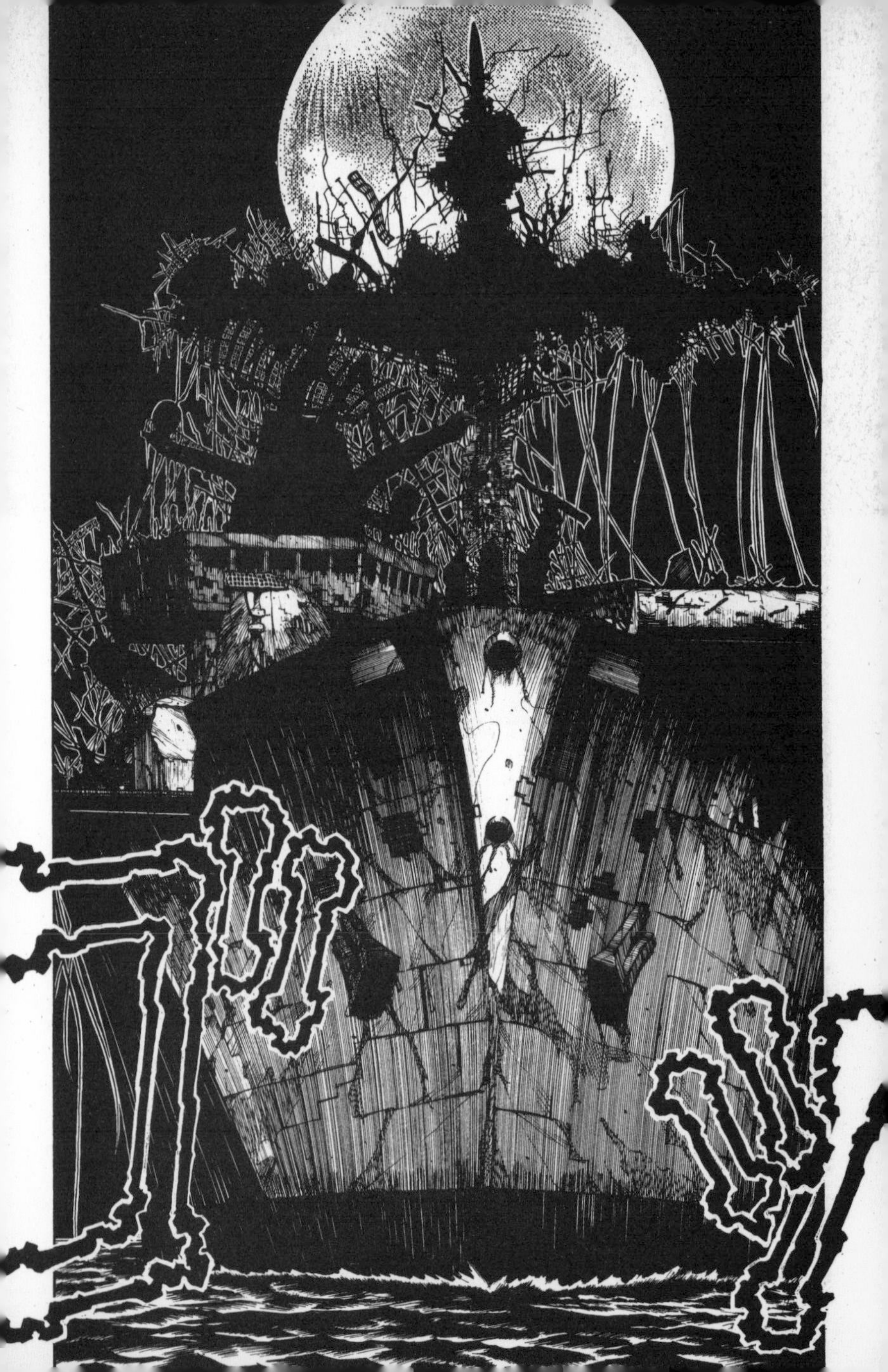

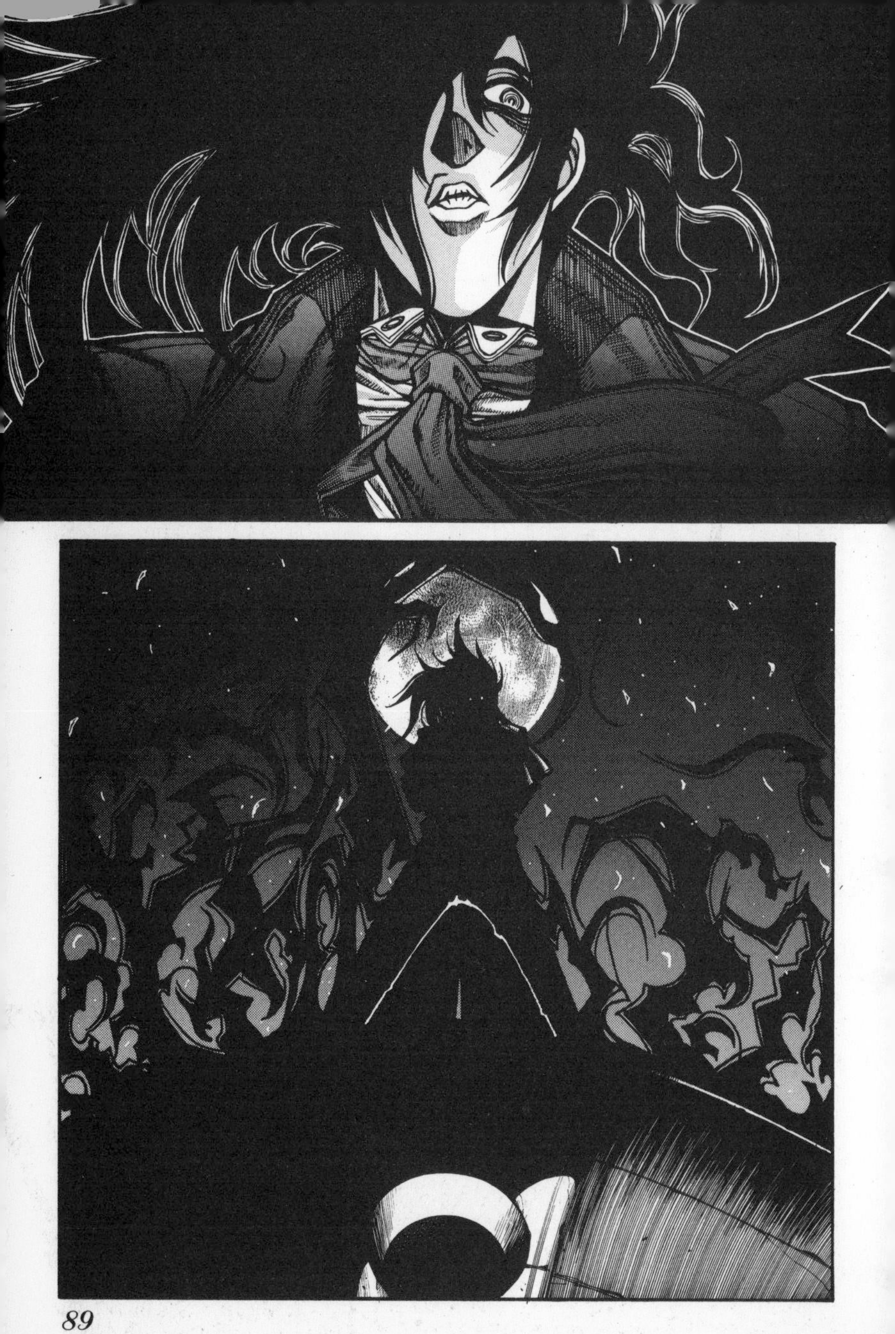

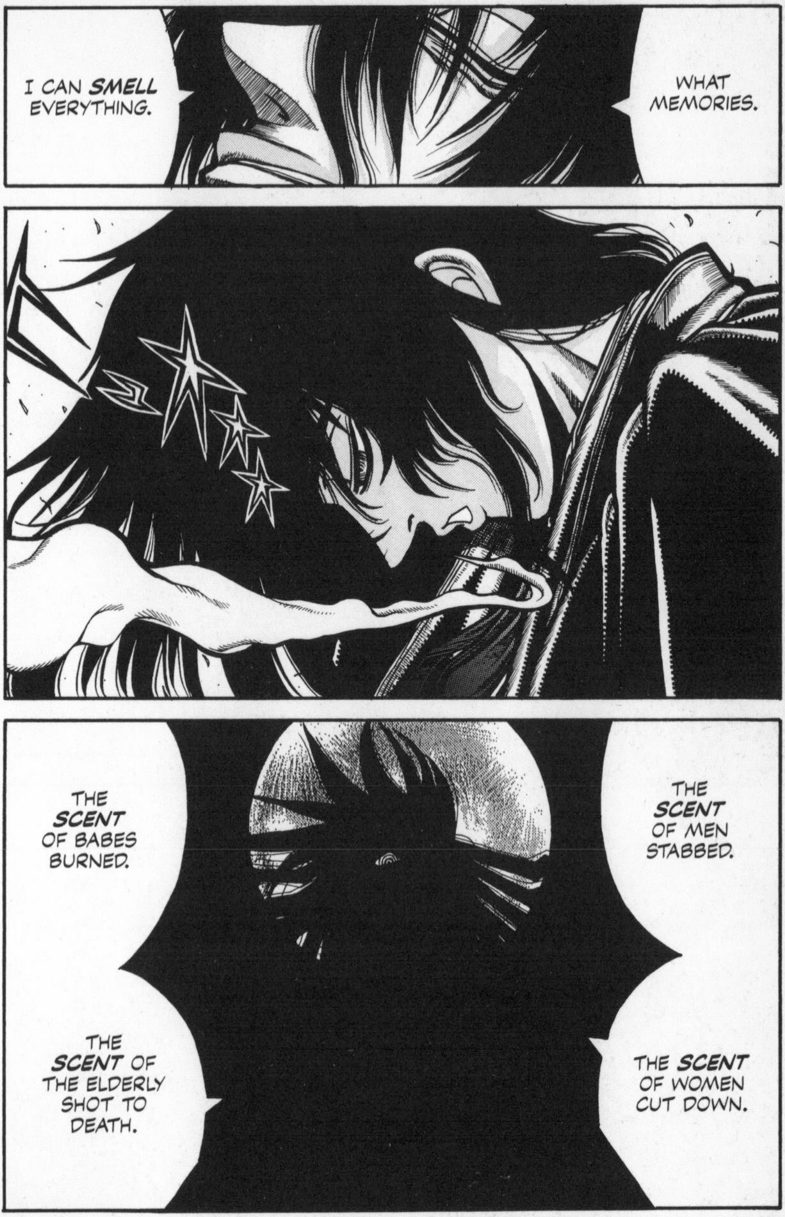
WHAT MEMORIES.
I CAN SMELL EVERYTHING.
THE SCENT OF MEN STABBED.
THE SCENT OF BABES BURNED.
THE SCENT OF WOMEN CUT DOWN.
THE SCENT OF THE ELDERLY SHOT TO DEATH.

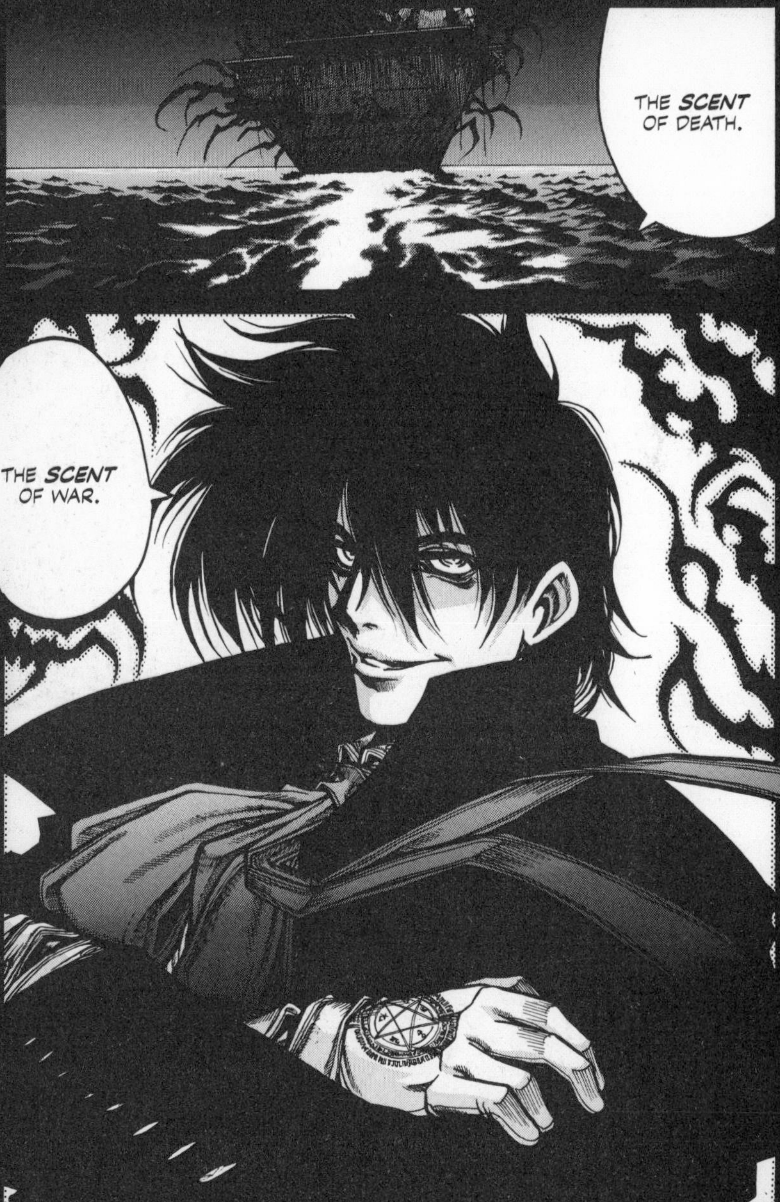
THE SCENT OF DEATH.
THE SCENT OF WAR.

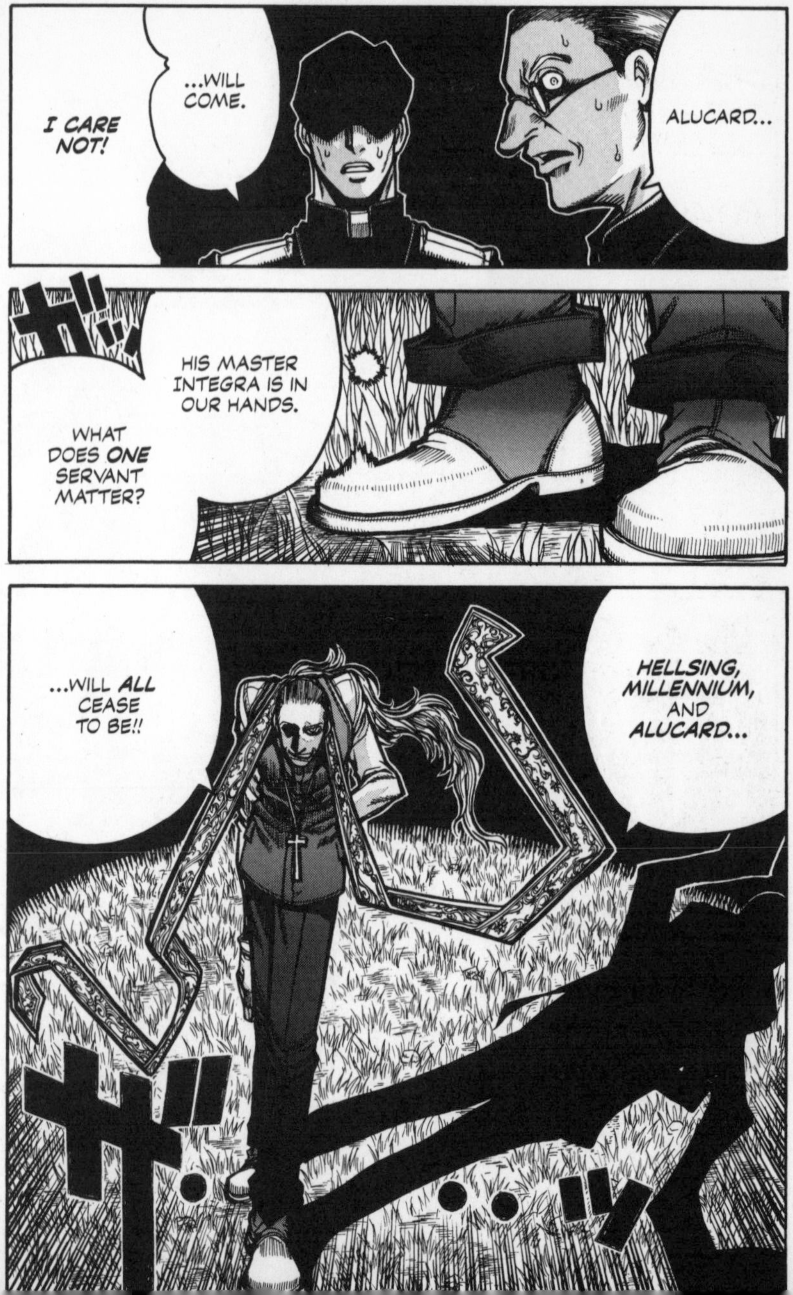
ALUCARD...
...WILL COME.
I CARE NOT!
ザッ
HIS MASTER INTEGRA IS IN OUR HANDS.
WHAT DOES ONE SERVANT MATTER?
HELLSING, MILLENNIUM, AND ALUCARD...
...WILL ALL CEASE TO BE!!
ザ・・・ッ

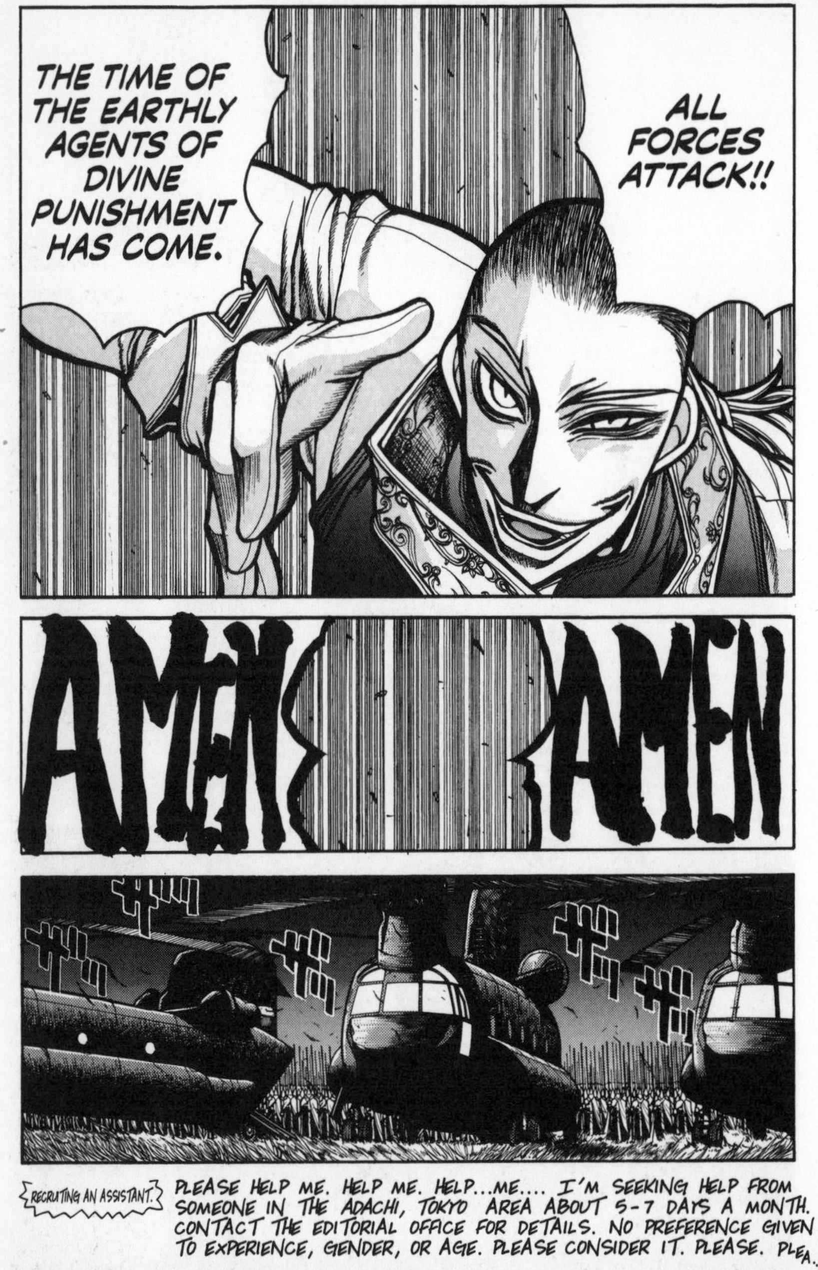
THE TIME OF THE EARTHLY AGENTS OF DIVINE PUNISHMENT HAS COME.
ALL FORCES ATTACK!!
AMEN
AMEN

RECRUITING AN ASSISTANT.

PLEASE HELP ME. HELP ME. HELP...ME.... I'M SEEKING HELP FROM SOMEONE IN THE ADACHI, TOKYO AREA ABOUT 5-7 DAYS A MONTH. CONTACT THE EDITORIAL OFFICE FOR DETAILS. NO PREFERENCE GIVEN TO EXPERIENCE, GENDER, OR AGE. PLEASE CONSIDER IT. PLEASE. PLEA..

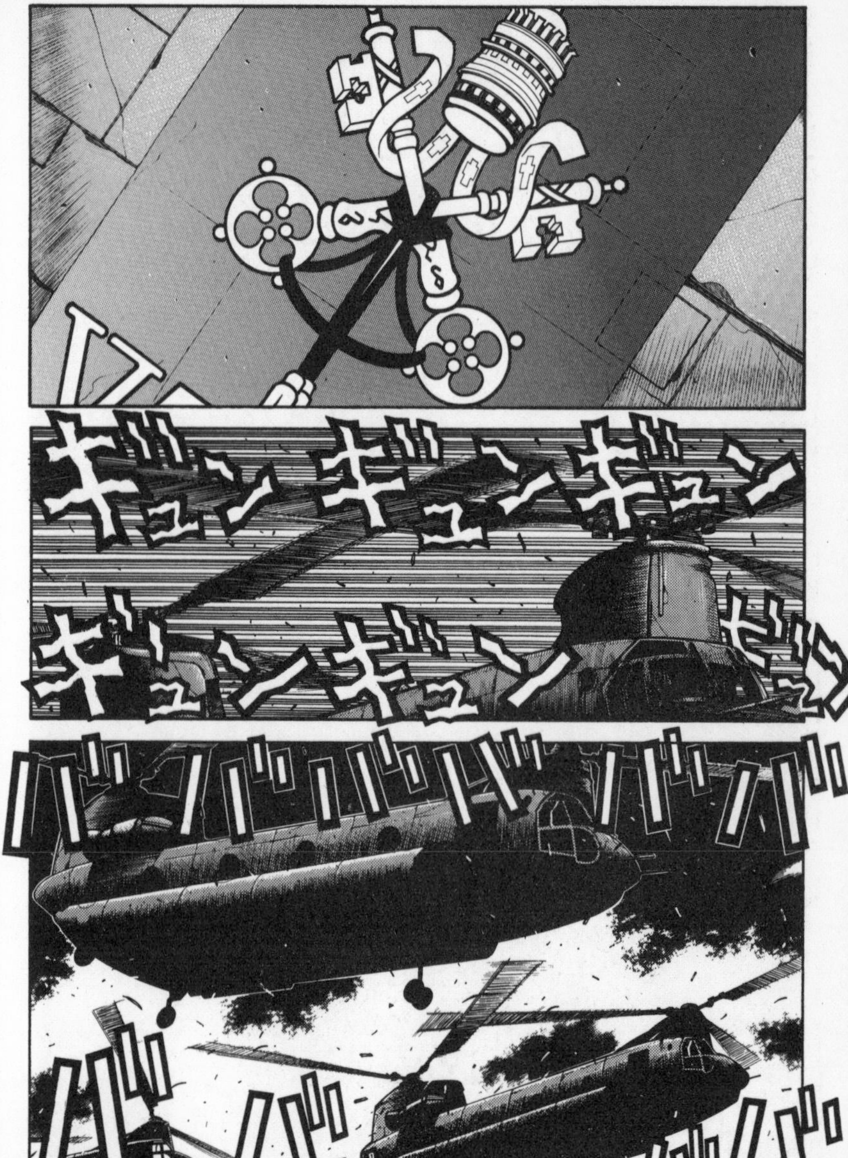
ギュンギュンギュン
ギュンギュンギュン
バババババババ
ババババ

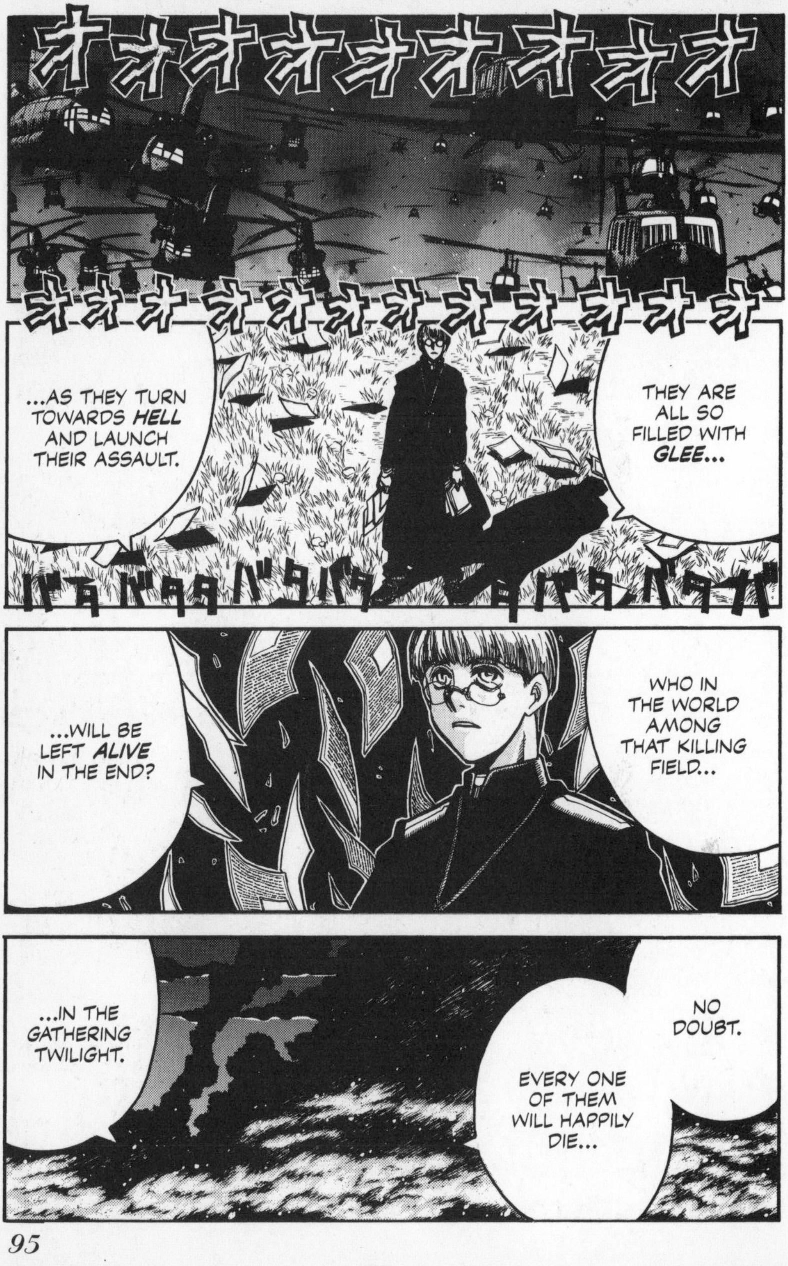
THEY ARE ALL SO FILLED WITH **GLEE...**
...AS THEY TURN TOWARDS **HELL** AND LAUNCH THEIR ASSAULT.
WHO IN THE WORLD AMONG THAT KILLING FIELD...
...WILL BE LEFT ***ALIVE*** IN THE END?
NO DOUBT.
EVERY ONE OF THEM WILL HAPPILY DIE...
...IN THE GATHERING TWILIGHT.

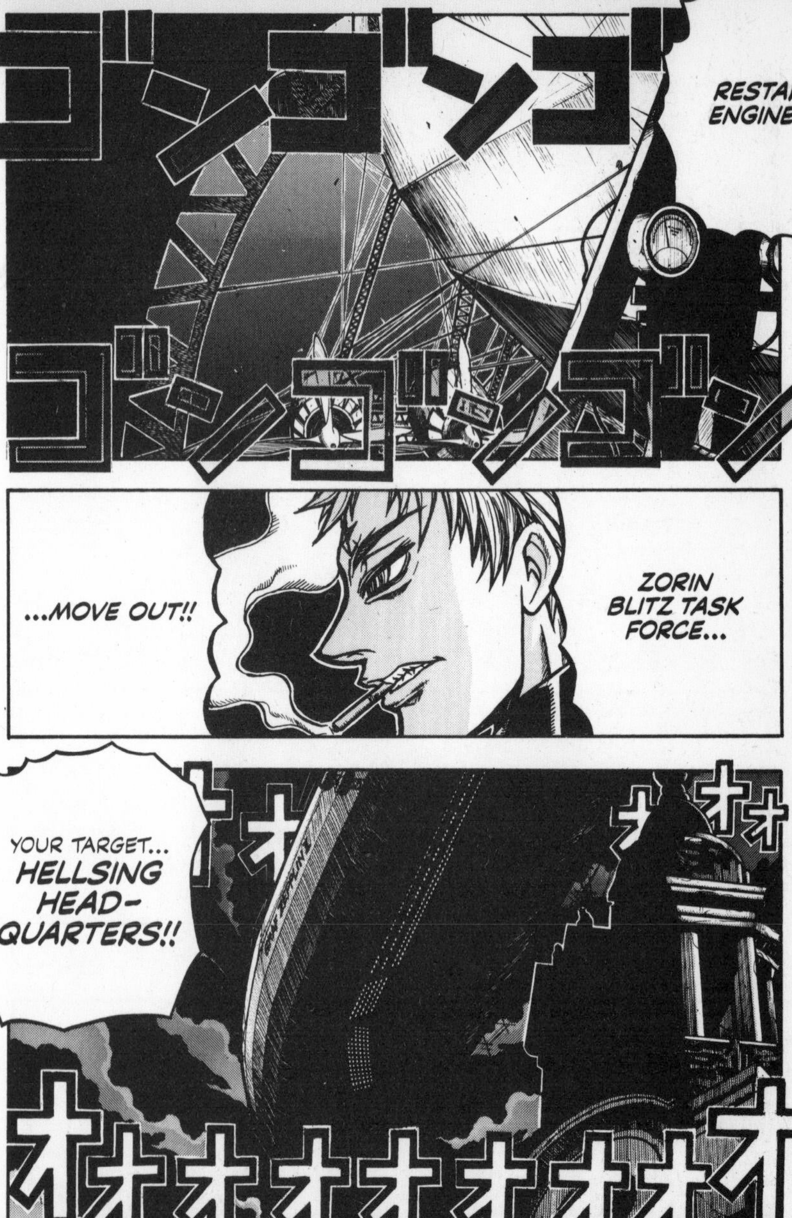
RESTART ENGINES!!
ゴンゴンゴ
ゴンゴンゴンゴン
ZORIN BLITZ TASK FORCE...
...MOVE OUT!!
YOUR TARGET... HELLSING HEAD-QUARTERS!!
オオオオオオオオオオ

TO BE CONTINUED

ORDER 5 / END

ORDER 6

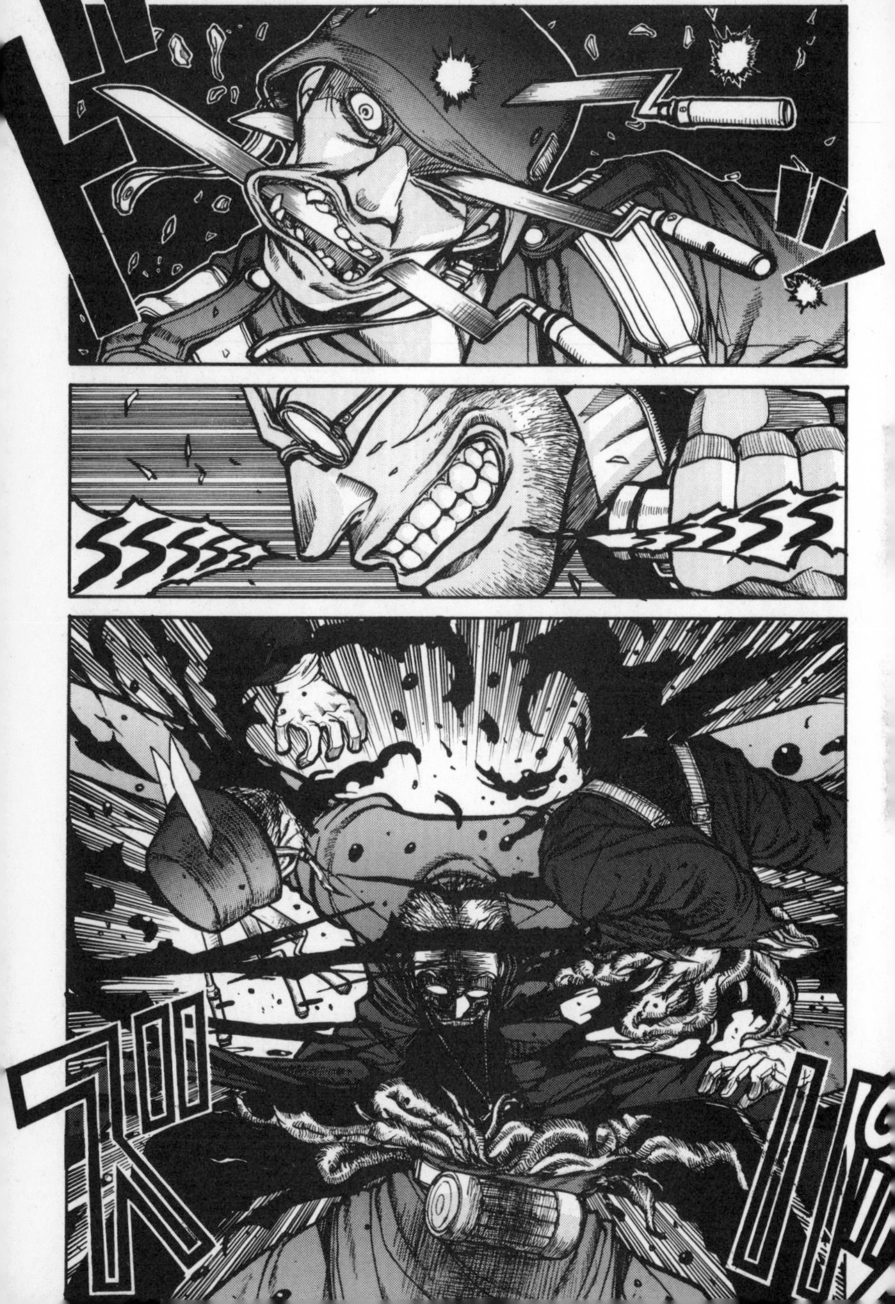

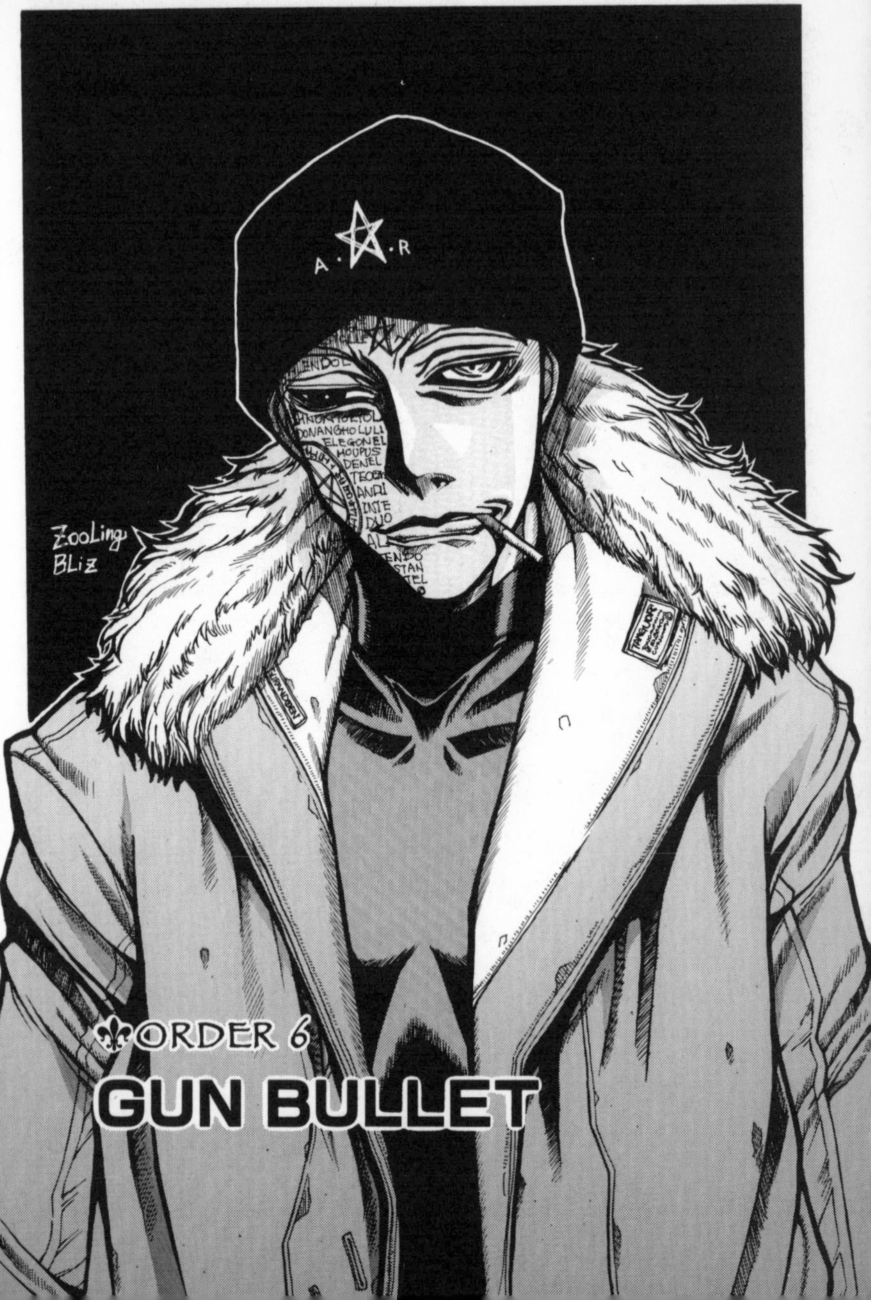
ORDER 6
GUN BULLET
A·R
ZooLing
BLiz

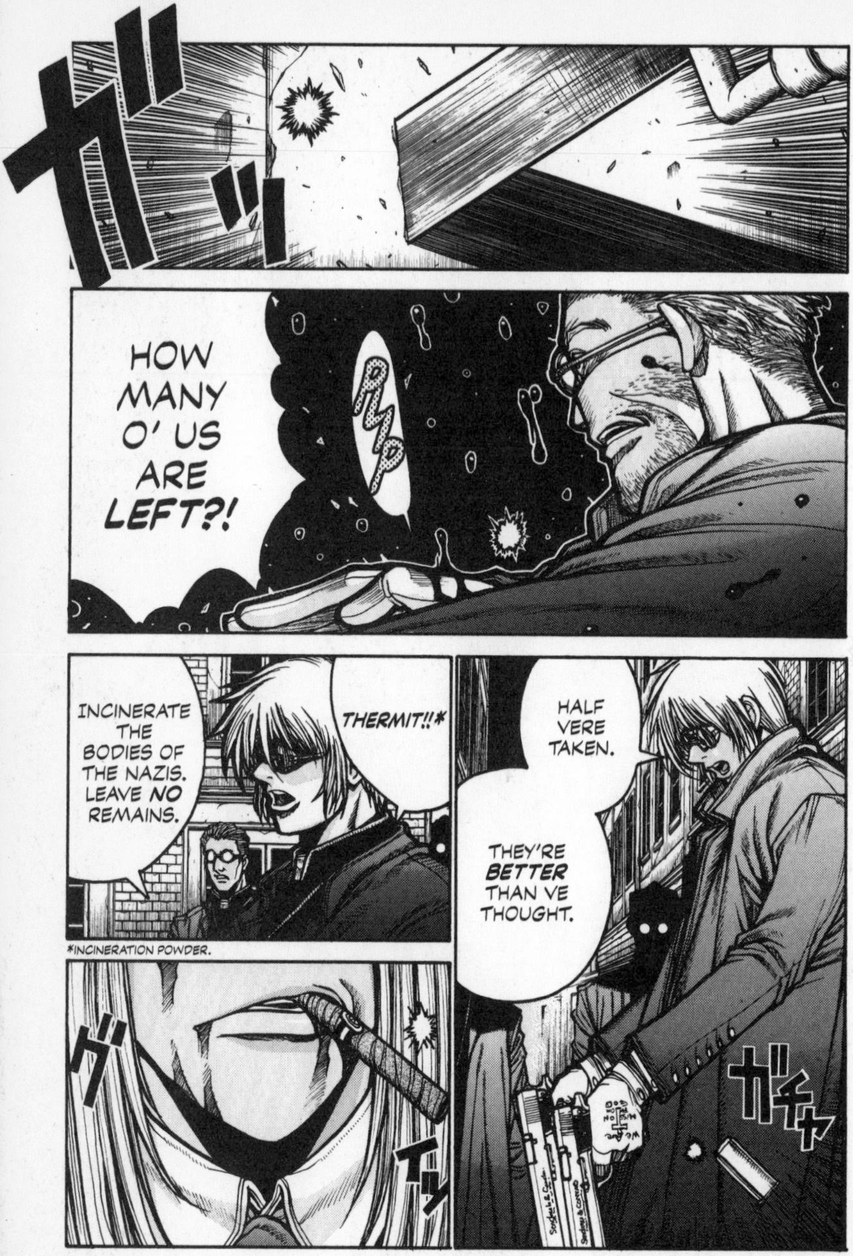
HOW MANY O' US ARE LEFT?!
HALF VERE TAKEN.
THEY'RE BETTER THAN VE THOUGHT.
THERMIT!!*
INCINERATE THE BODIES OF THE NAZIS. LEAVE NO REMAINS.

*INCINERATION POWDER.

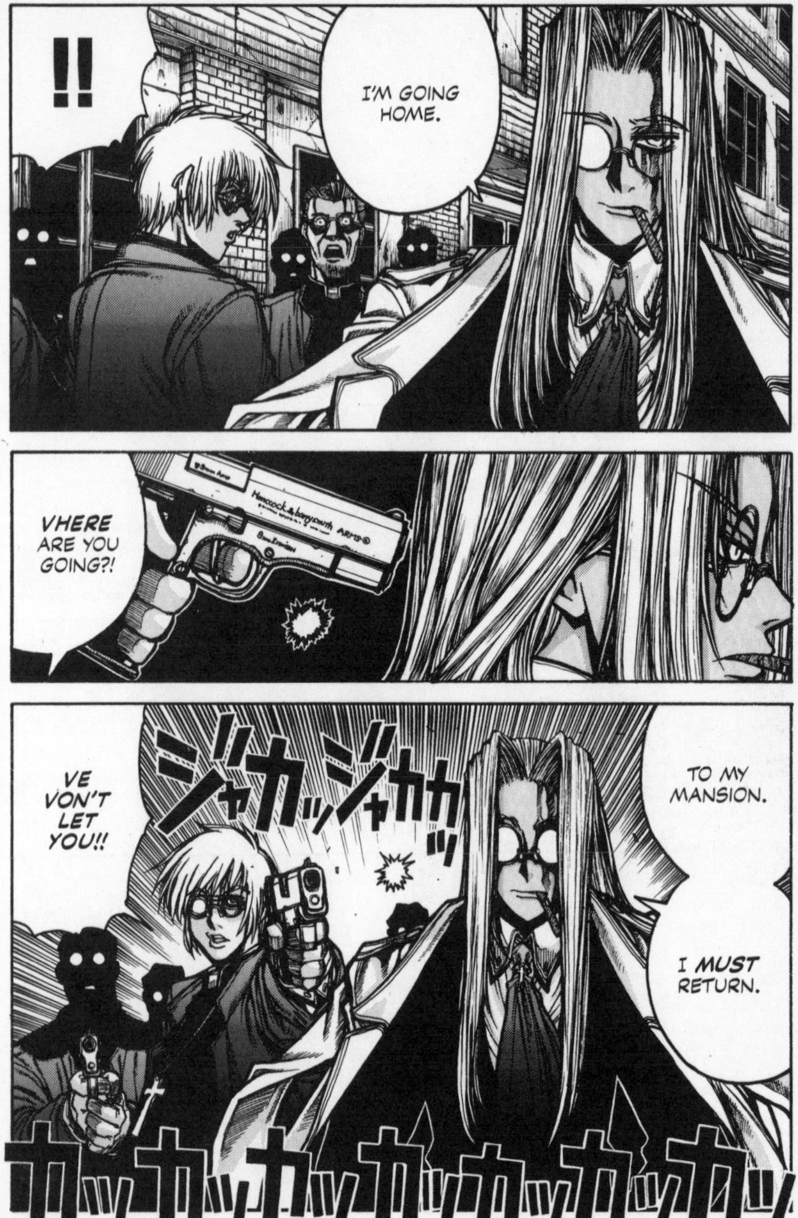
I'M GOING HOME.
!!
VHERE ARE YOU GOING?!
TO MY MANSION.
I MUST RETURN.
ジャカッジャカカッ
VE VON'T LET YOU!!
カッカッカッカッカッカッカッ

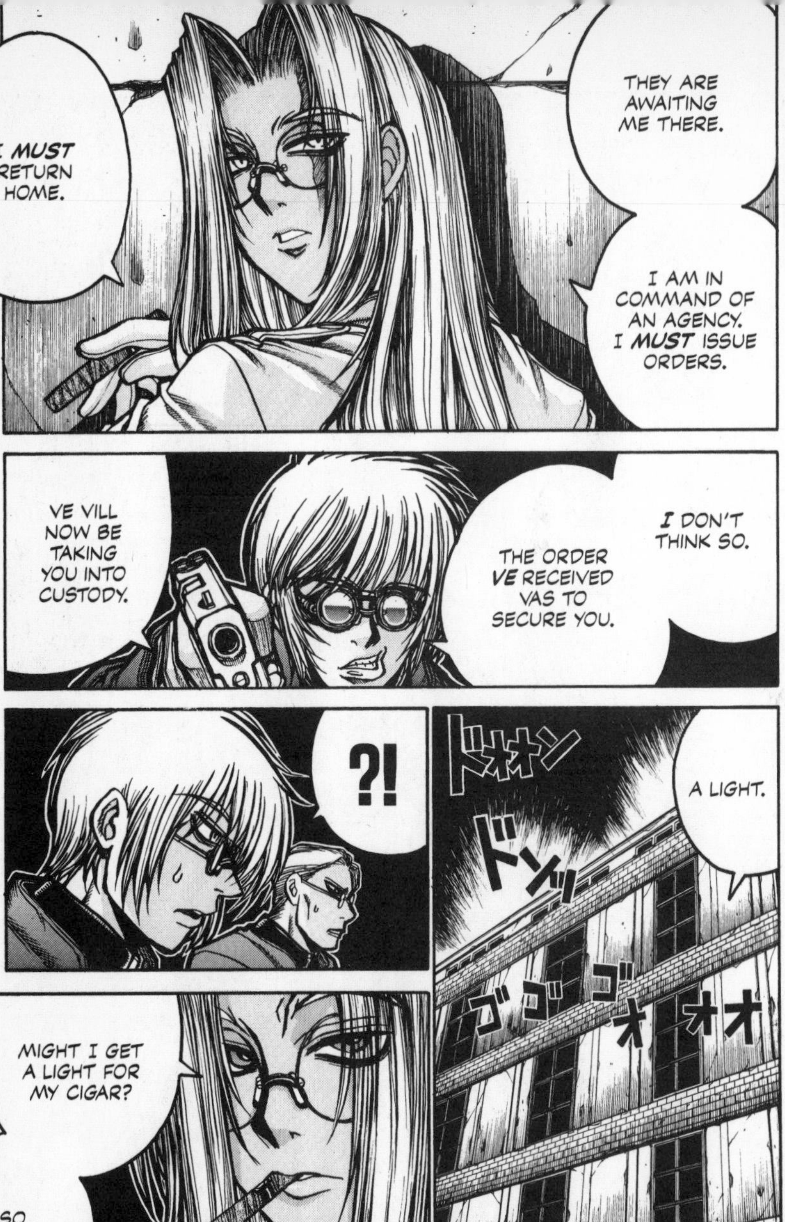
THEY ARE AWAITING ME THERE.
I AM IN COMMAND OF AN AGENCY. I *MUST* ISSUE ORDERS.
I *MUST* RETURN HOME.
I DON'T THINK SO.
THE ORDER *VE* RECEIVED VAS TO SECURE YOU.
VE VILL NOW BE TAKING YOU INTO CUSTODY.
ドオオン
A LIGHT.
ドンッ
ゴゴゴオオオ
?!
MIGHT I GET A LIGHT FOR MY CIGAR?
SO THOUGHTLESS OF YOU.

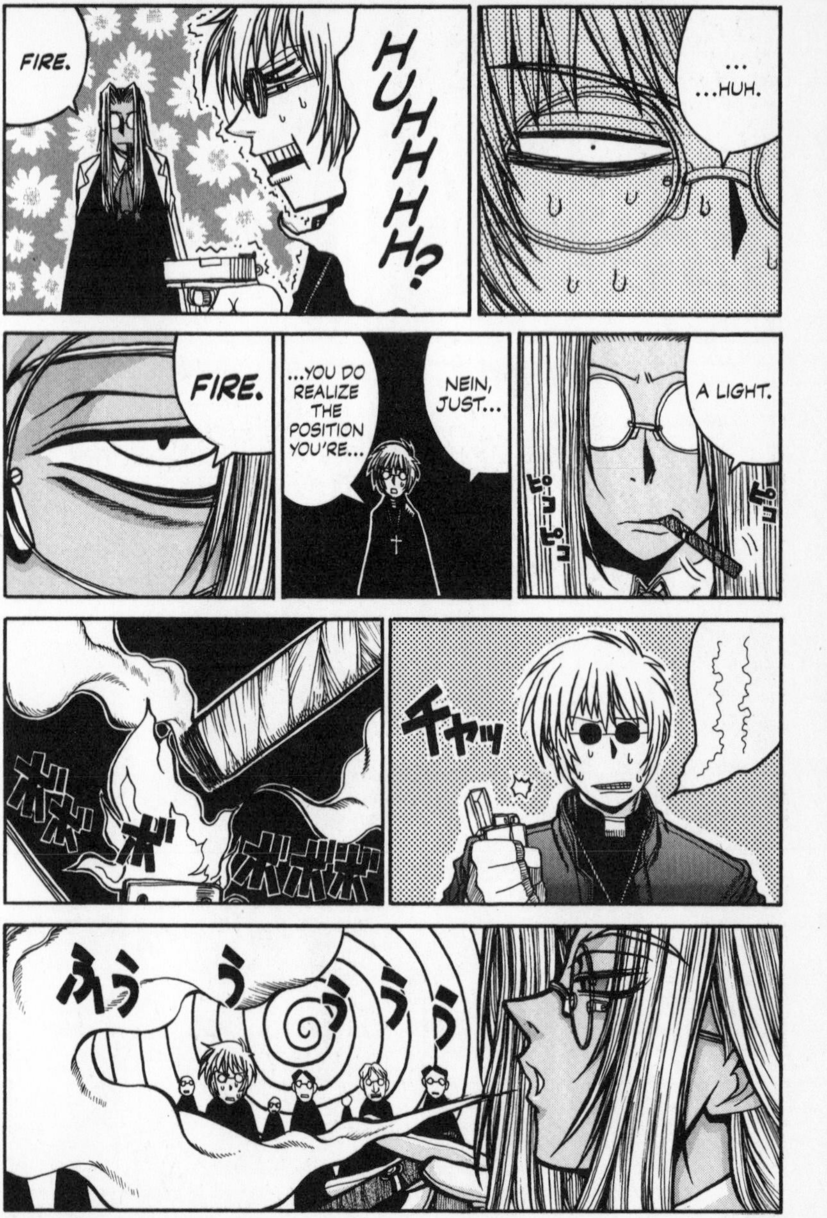
...
...HUH.
FIRE.
HUHHHHH?
A LIGHT.
ピコ
ピコ ピコ
NEIN, JUST...
...YOU DO REALIZE THE POSITION YOU'RE...
FIRE.
チャッ
ボボ ボ ボボボ
ふうううう

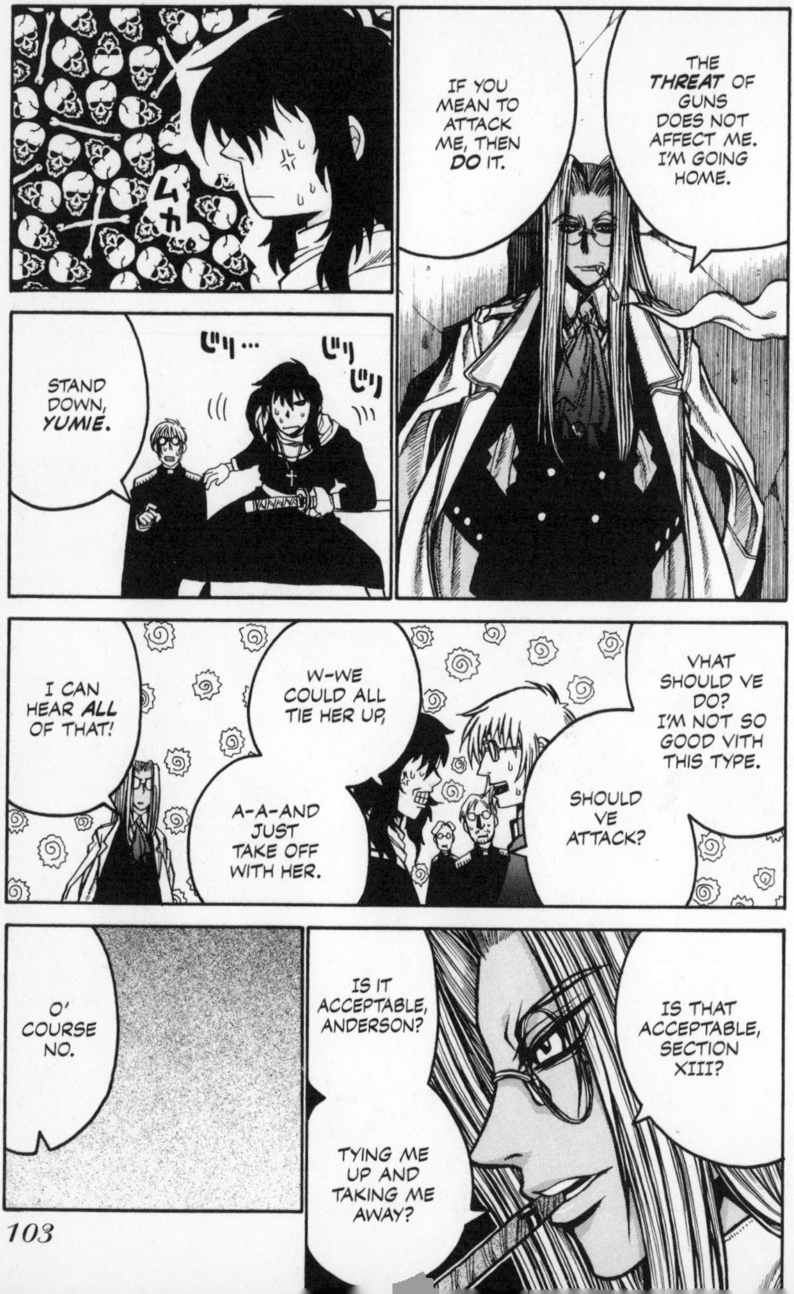
THE THREAT OF GUNS DOES NOT AFFECT ME. I'M GOING HOME.
IF YOU MEAN TO ATTACK ME, THEN DO IT.
ムカ
ジリ…
ジリ ジリ
STAND DOWN, YUMIE.
VHAT SHOULD VE DO? I'M NOT SO GOOD VITH THIS TYPE.
SHOULD VE ATTACK?
W-WE COULD ALL TIE HER UP,
A-A-AND JUST TAKE OFF WITH HER.
I CAN HEAR ALL OF THAT!
IS THAT ACCEPTABLE, SECTION XIII?
IS IT ACCEPTABLE, ANDERSON?
TYING ME UP AND TAKING ME AWAY?
O' COURSE NO.

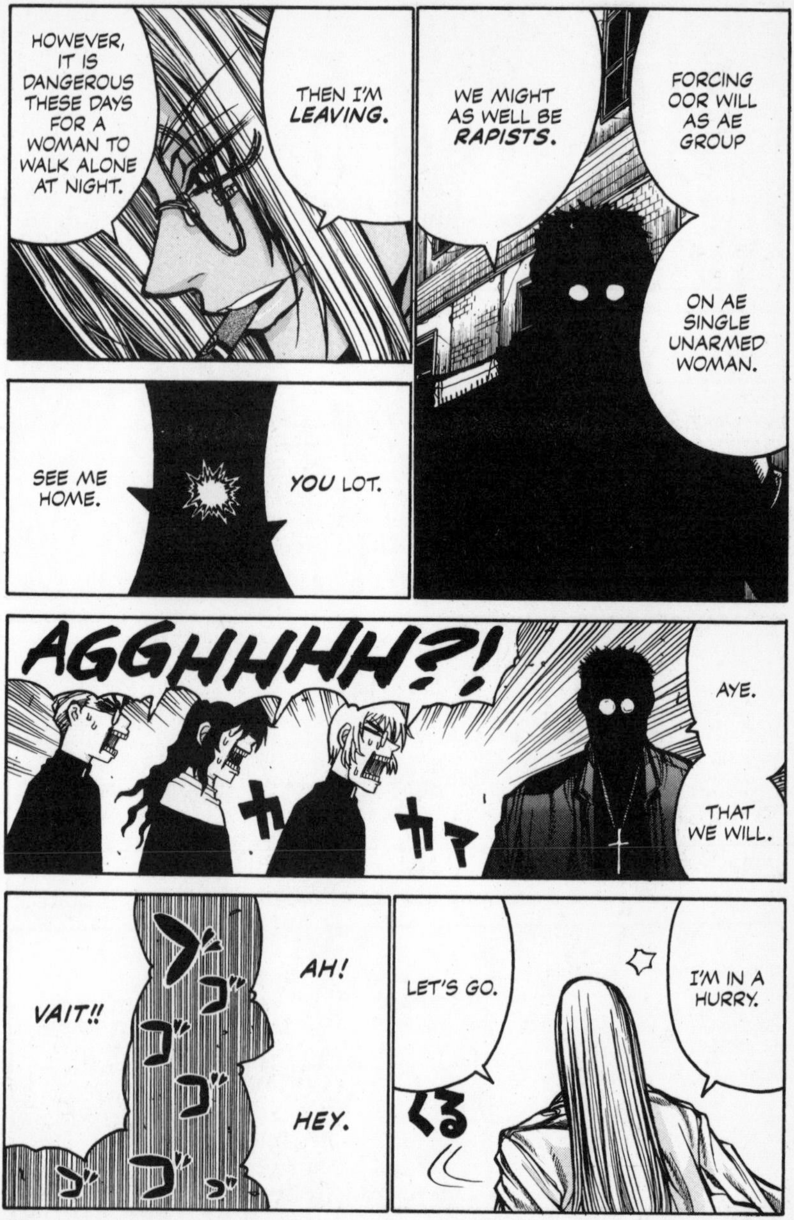
FORCING OOR WILL AS AE GROUP
ON AE SINGLE UNARMED WOMAN.
WE MIGHT AS WELL BE RAPISTS.
THEN I'M LEAVING.
HOWEVER, IT IS DANGEROUS THESE DAYS FOR A WOMAN TO WALK ALONE AT NIGHT.
YOU LOT.
SEE ME HOME.
AYE.
THAT WE WILL.
AGGHHHH?!
I'M IN A HURRY.
LET'S GO.
くる
AH!
HEY.
VAIT!!

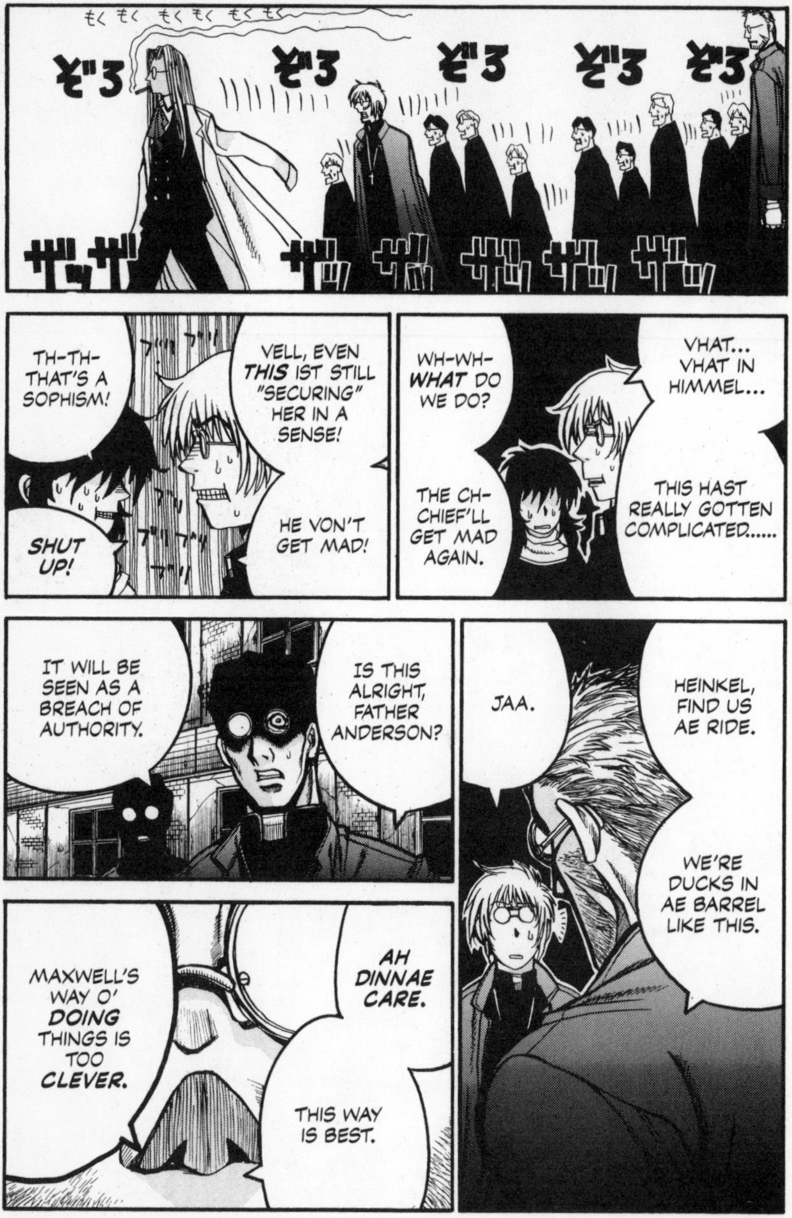

もくもく もくもく もくもく
ぞろ ぞろ ぞろ ぞろ ぞろ
ザッザ
ザッ ザッ ザッ ザッ ザッ
VHAT... VHAT IN HIMMEL...
THIS HAST REALLY GOTTEN COMPLICATED......
WH-WH-**WHAT** DO WE DO?
THE CH-CHIEF'LL GET MAD AGAIN.
VELL, EVEN **THIS** IST STILL "SECURING" HER IN A SENSE!
HE VON'T GET MAD!
TH-TH-THAT'S A SOPHISM!
SHUT UP!
HEINKEL, FIND US AE RIDE.
JAA.
WE'RE DUCKS IN AE BARREL LIKE THIS.
IS THIS ALRIGHT, FATHER ANDERSON?
IT WILL BE SEEN AS A BREACH OF AUTHORITY.
AH DINNAE CARE.
THIS WAY IS BEST.
MAXWELL'S WAY O' ***DOING*** THINGS IS TOO ***CLEVER.***

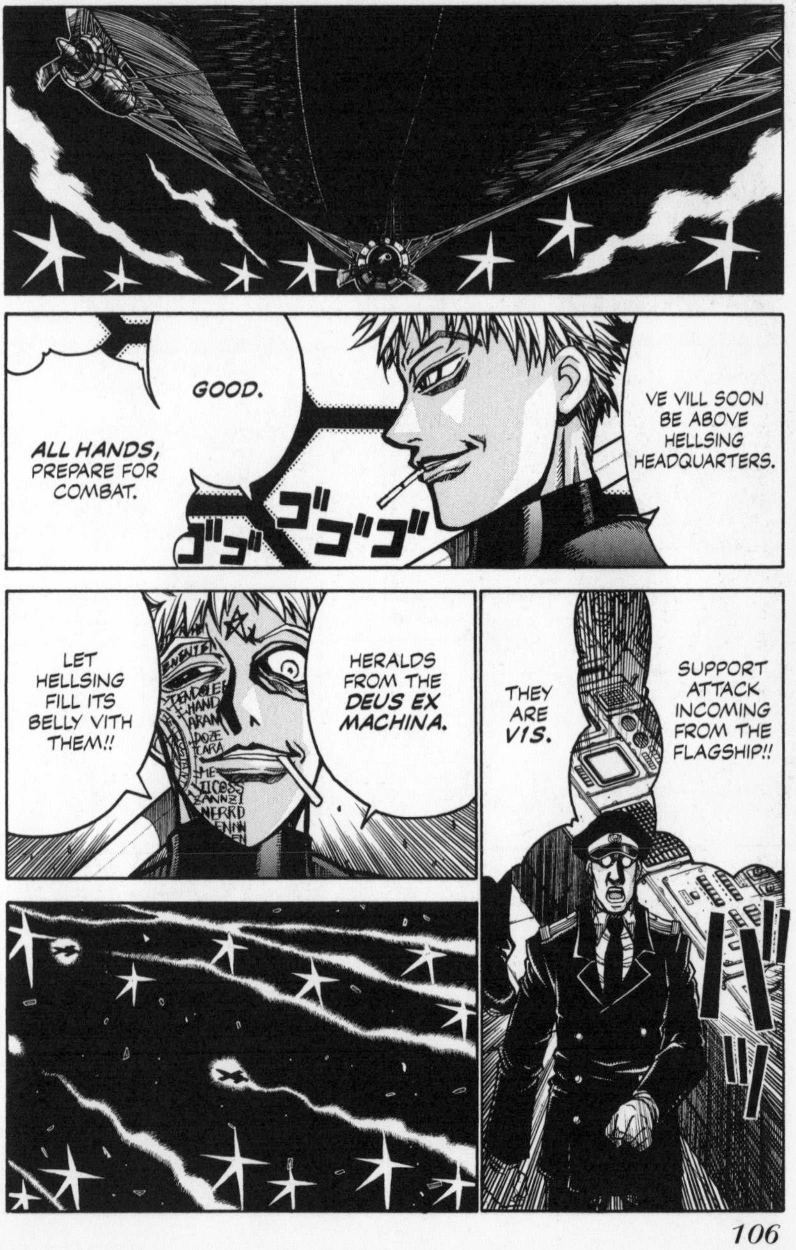
VE VILL SOON BE ABOVE HELLSING HEADQUARTERS.
GOOD.
ALL HANDS, PREPARE FOR COMBAT.
SUPPORT ATTACK INCOMING FROM THE FLAGSHIP!!
THEY ARE V1S.
HERALDS FROM THE DEUS EX MACHINA.
LET HELLSING FILL ITS BELLY VITH THEM!!

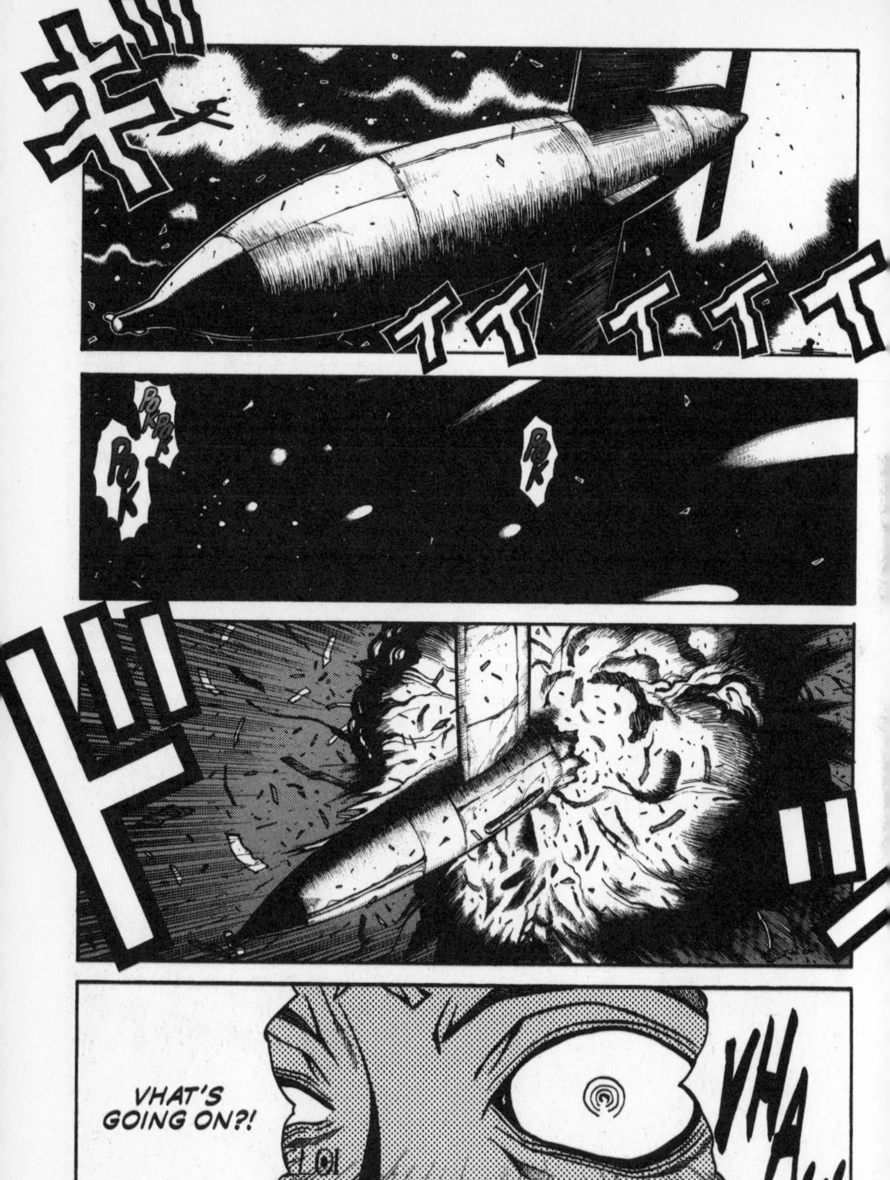
POK
POK POK POK
VHA...
VHAT'S GOING ON?!

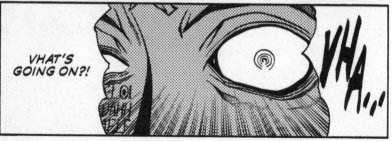

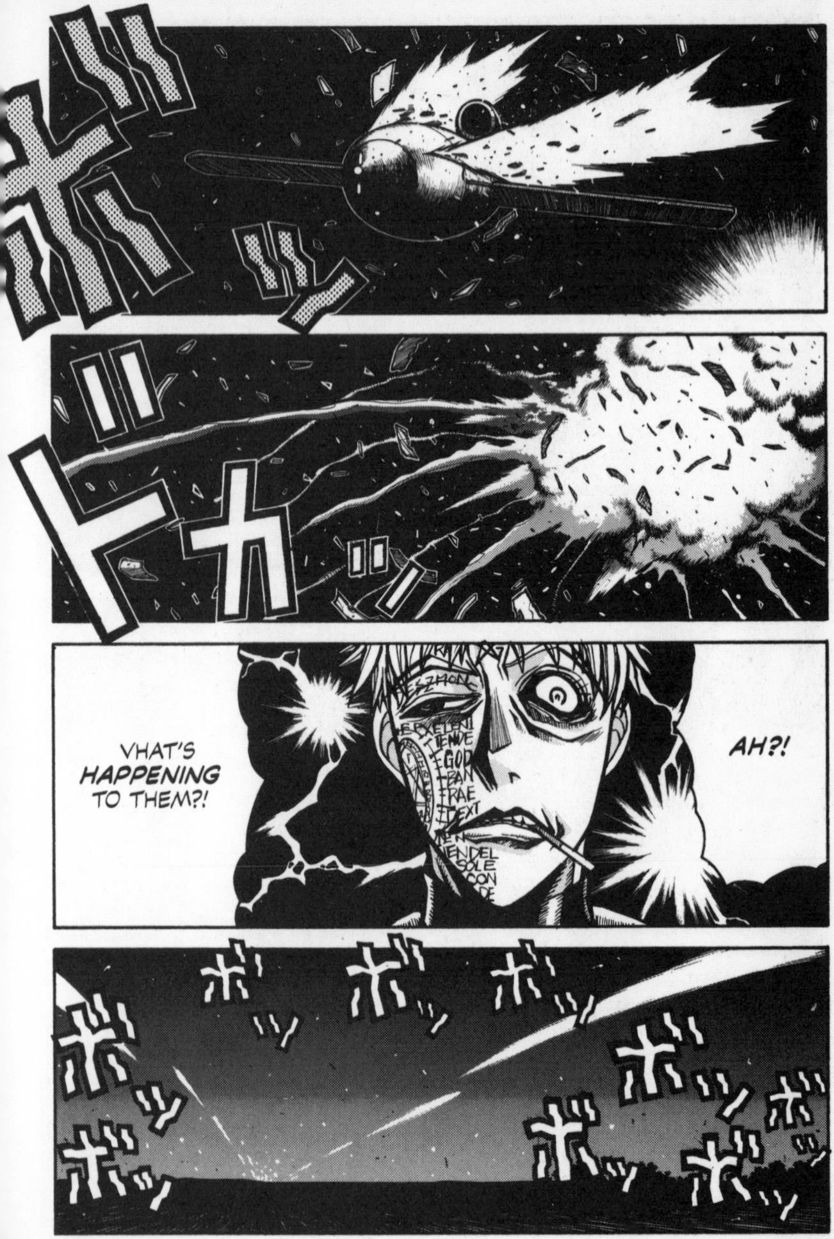
ボッ
ドカッ
AH?!
VHAT'S
HAPPENING
TO THEM?!
ボッボッボッ
ボッボッボッ

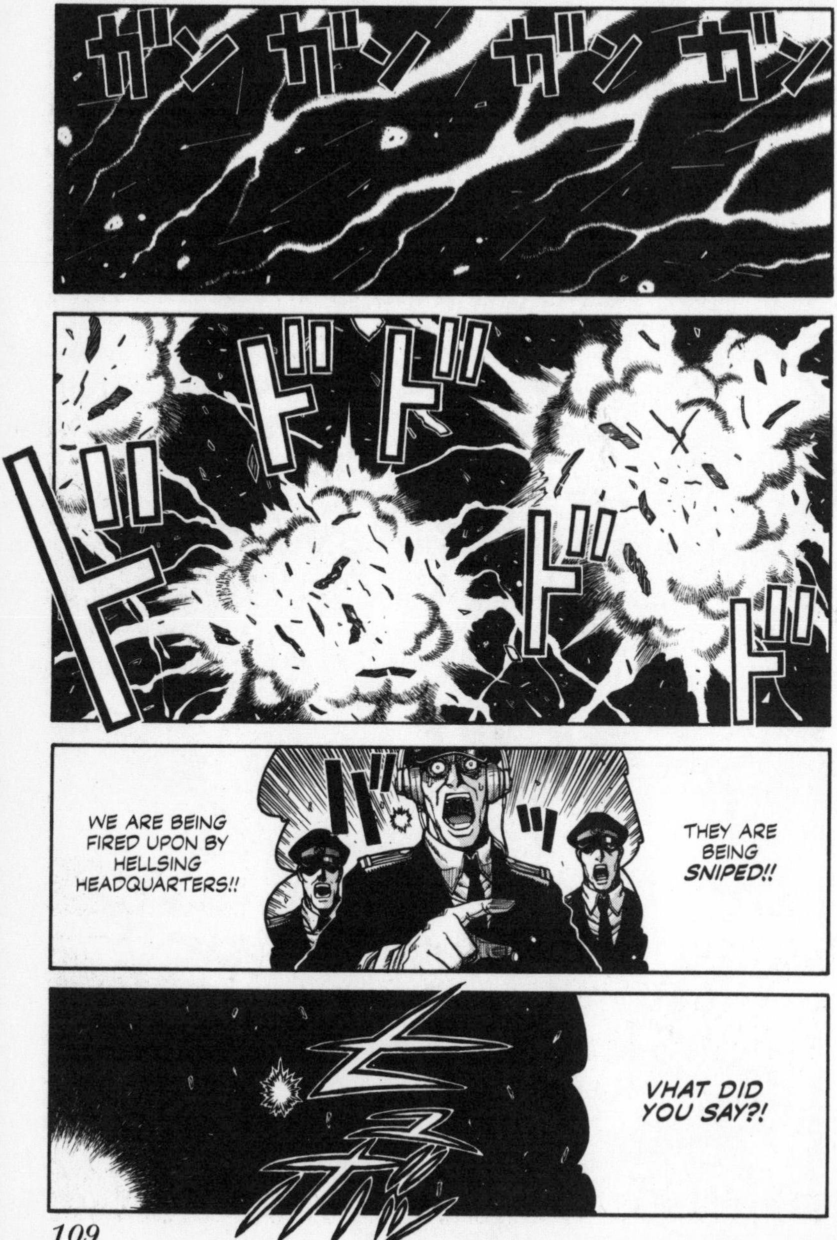
ガン ガン ガン ガン
ドドドドドド
THEY ARE BEING SNIPED!!
バッ
WE ARE BEING FIRED UPON BY HELLSING HEADQUARTERS!!
VHAT DID YOU SAY?!

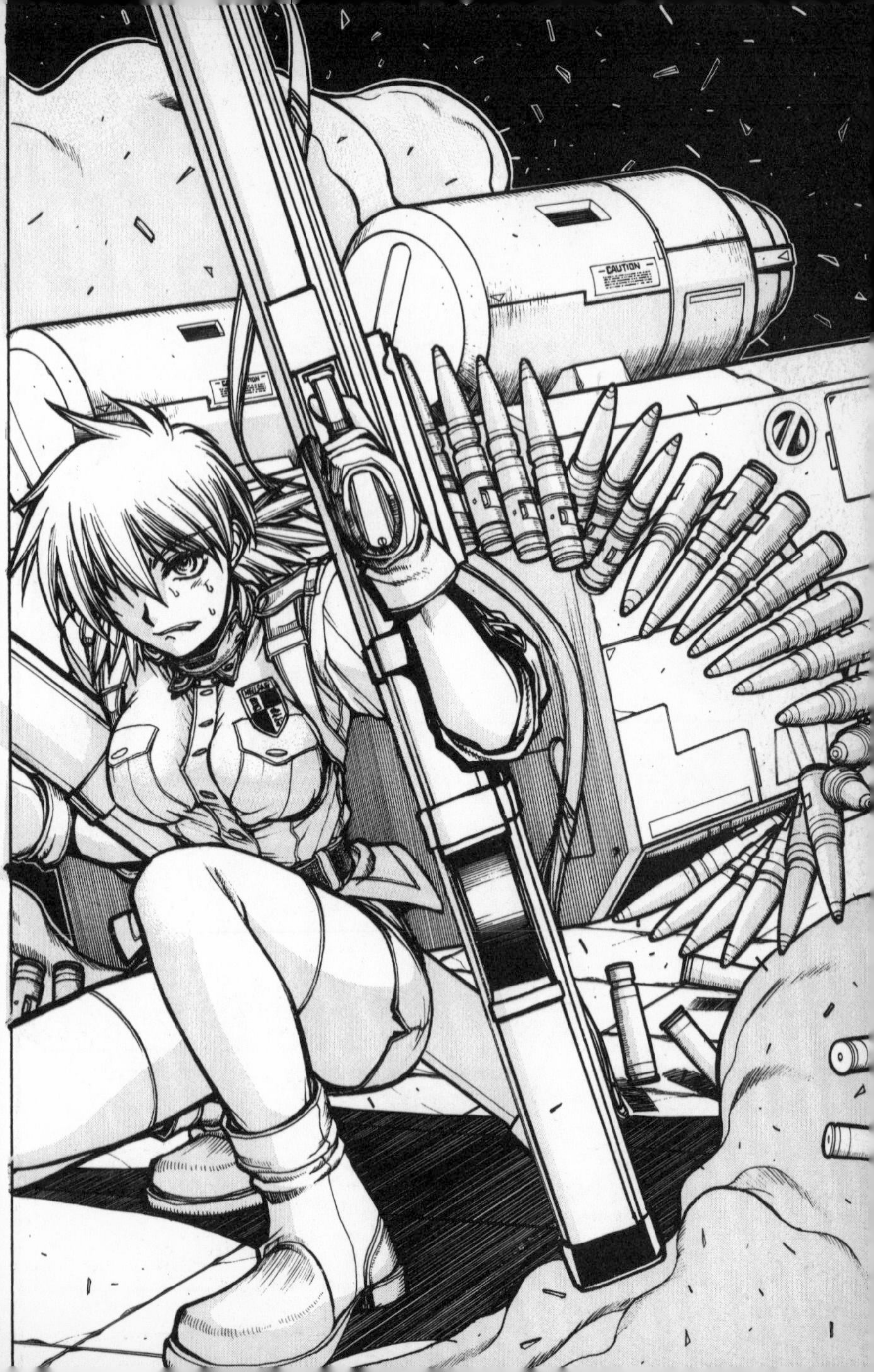
CAUTION

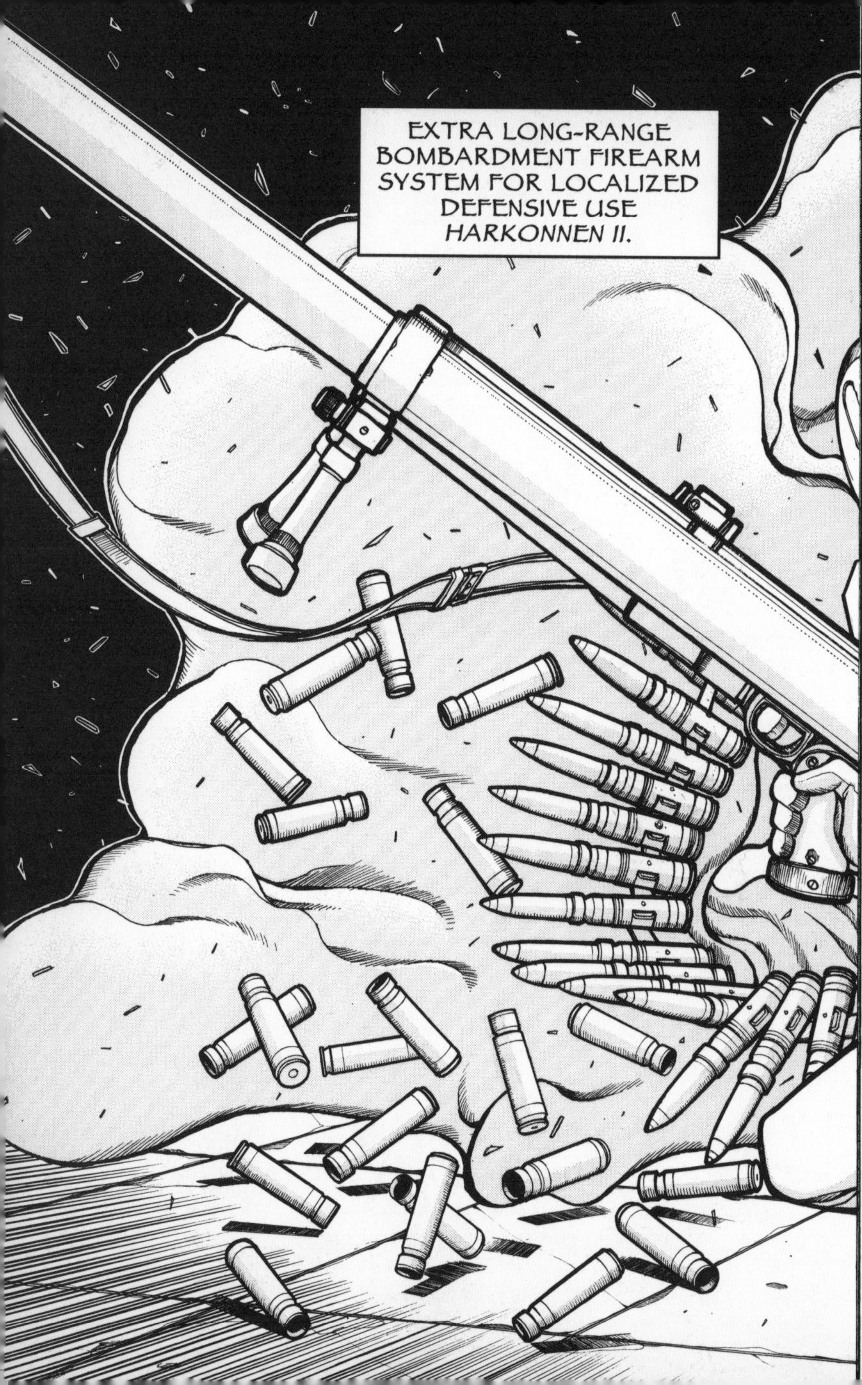
EXTRA LONG-RANGE BOMBARDMENT FIREARM SYSTEM FOR LOCALIZED DEFENSIVE USE HARKONNEN II.

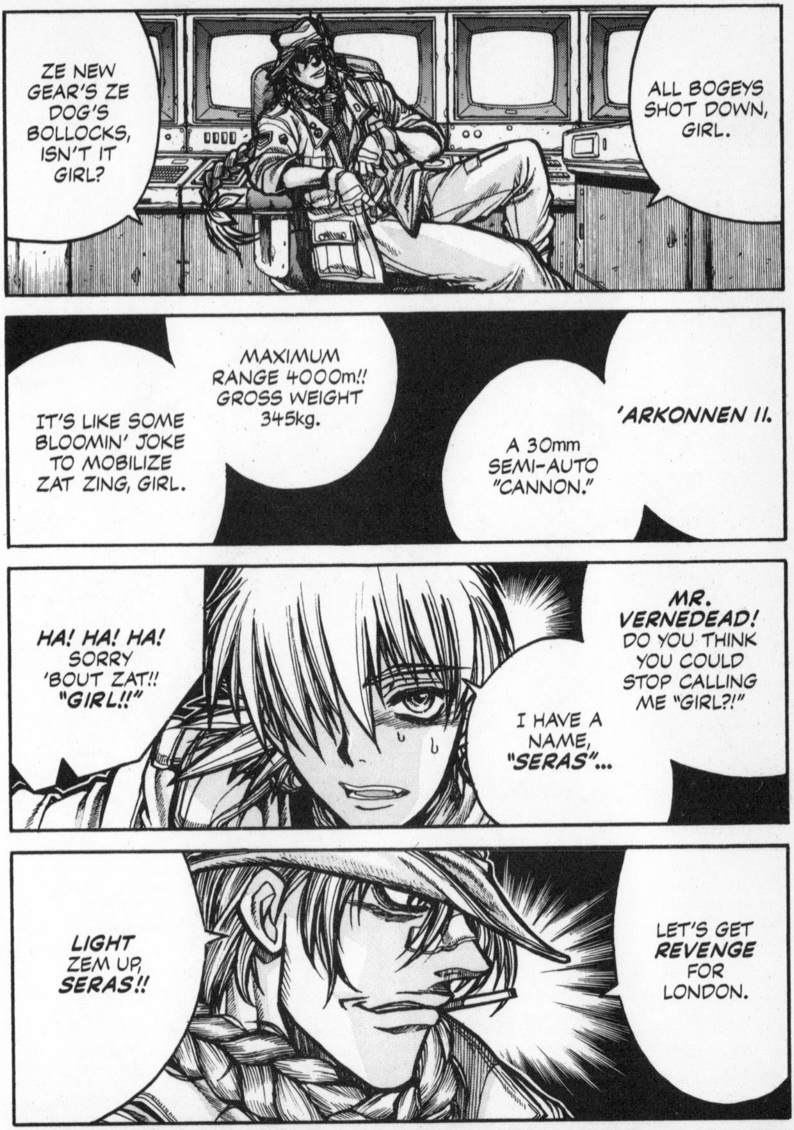
ALL BOGEYS SHOT DOWN, GIRL.
ZE NEW GEAR'S ZE DOG'S BOLLOCKS, ISN'T IT GIRL?
'ARKONNEN II.
A 30mm SEMI-AUTO "CANNON."
MAXIMUM RANGE 4000m!! GROSS WEIGHT 345kg.
IT'S LIKE SOME BLOOMIN' JOKE TO MOBILIZE ZAT ZING, GIRL.
MR. VERNEDEAD! DO YOU THINK YOU COULD STOP CALLING ME "GIRL?!"
I HAVE A NAME, "SERAS"...
HA! HA! HA! SORRY 'BOUT ZAT!! "GIRL!!"
LET'S GET REVENGE FOR LONDON.
LIGHT ZEM UP, SERAS!!

TO BE CONTINUED

ORDER 6 / END

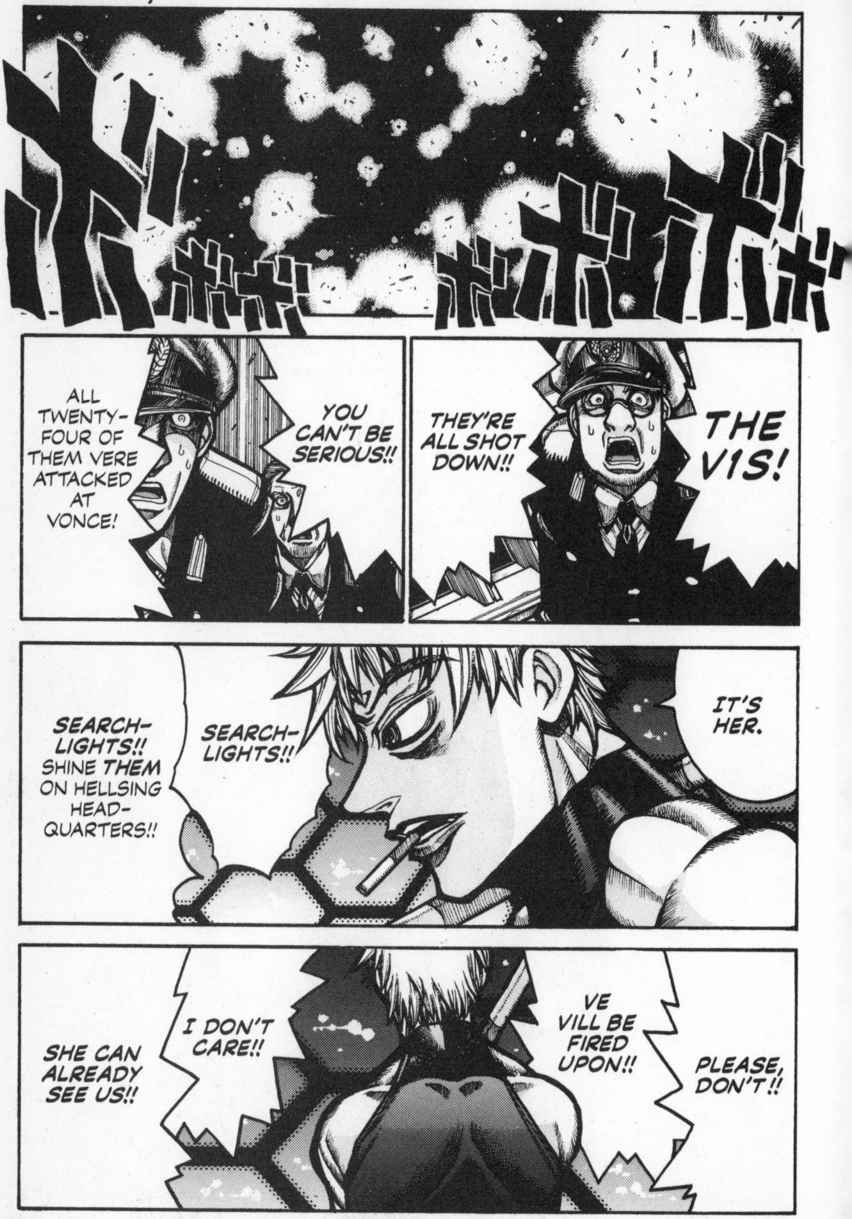
THE V1S!
THEY'RE ALL SHOT DOWN!!
YOU CAN'T BE SERIOUS!!
ALL TWENTY-FOUR OF THEM VERE ATTACKED AT VONCE!
IT'S HER.
SEARCH-LIGHTS!!
SEARCH-LIGHTS!! SHINE THEM ON HELLSING HEAD-QUARTERS!!
PLEASE, DON'T!!
VE VILL BE FIRED UPON!!
I DON'T CARE!!
SHE CAN ALREADY SEE US!!

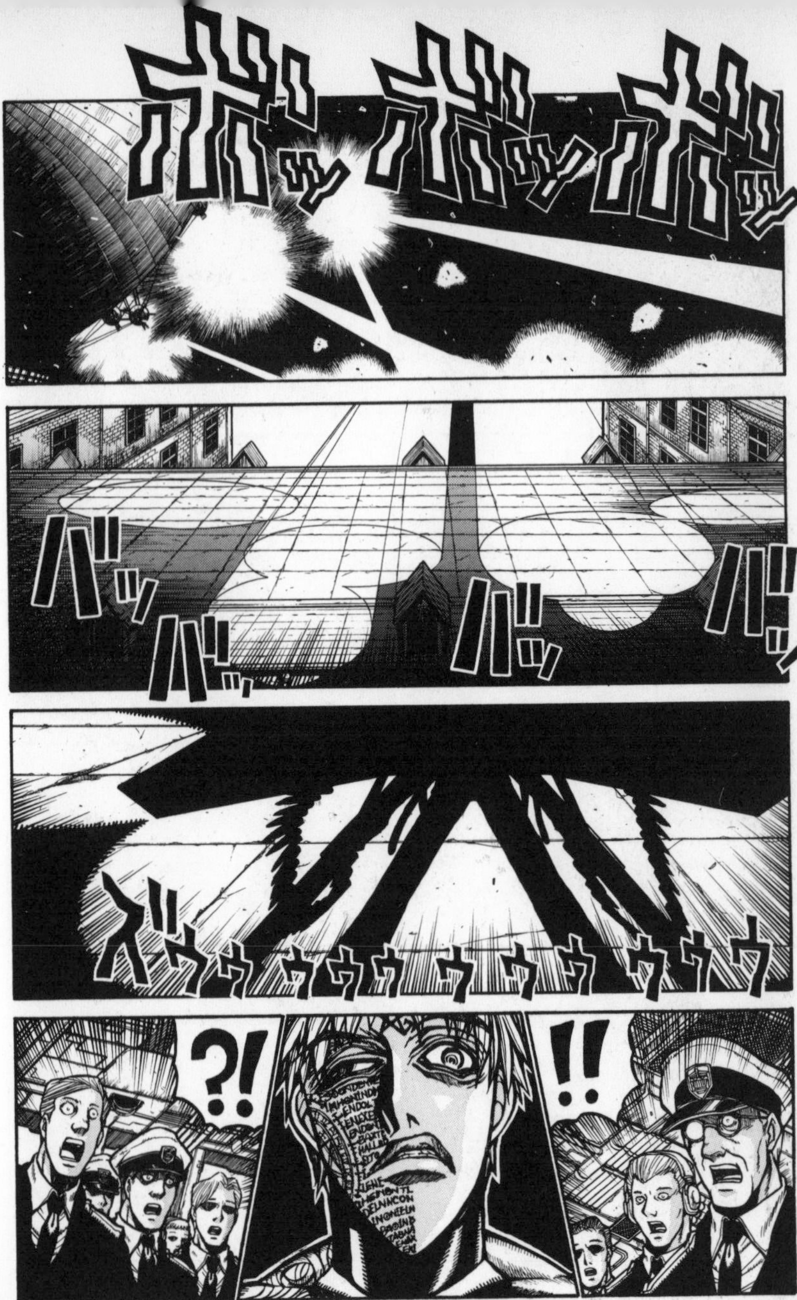
バッ
バッ
バッ
バッ
ズウウウウウウウウウ
!!
?!

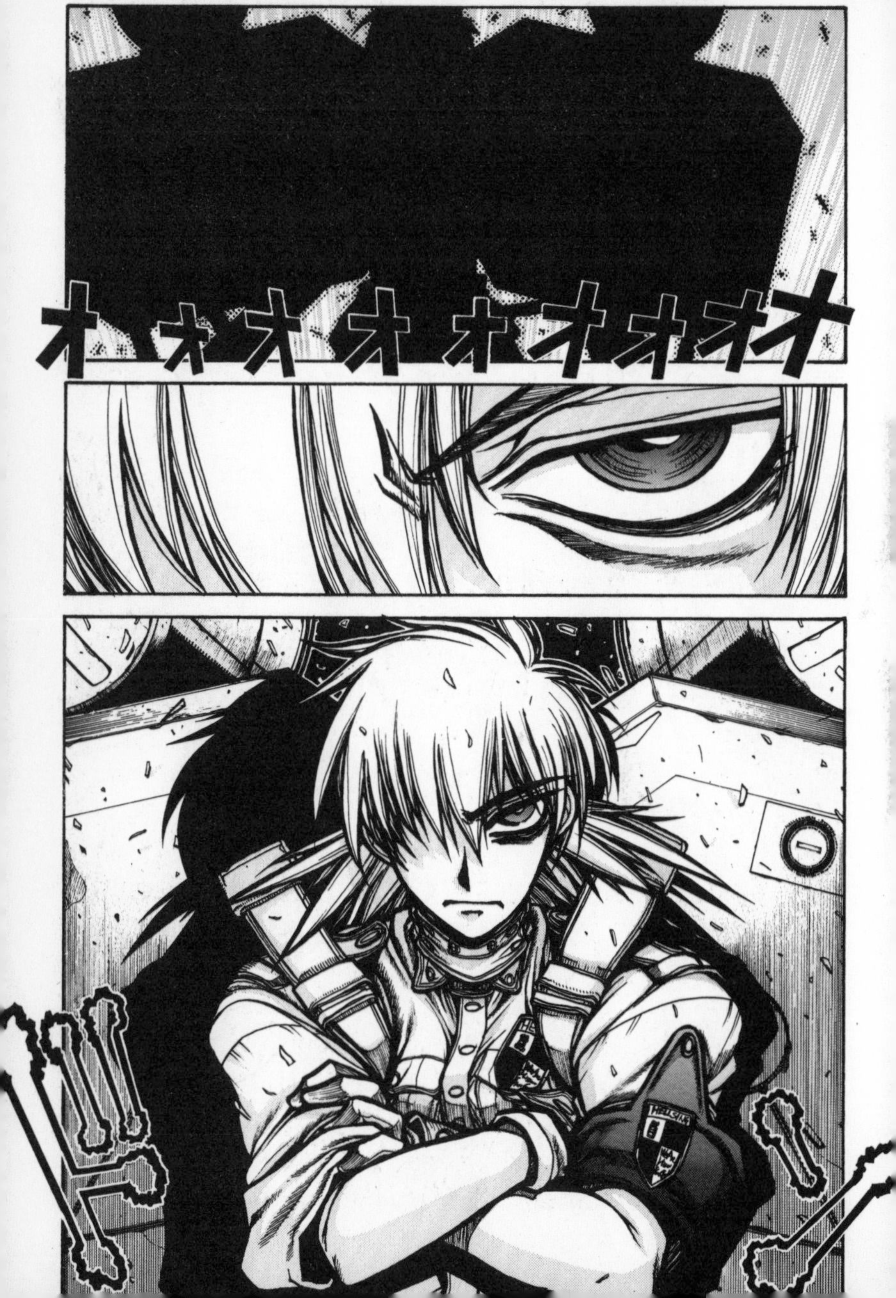
オォオオォオオオオ

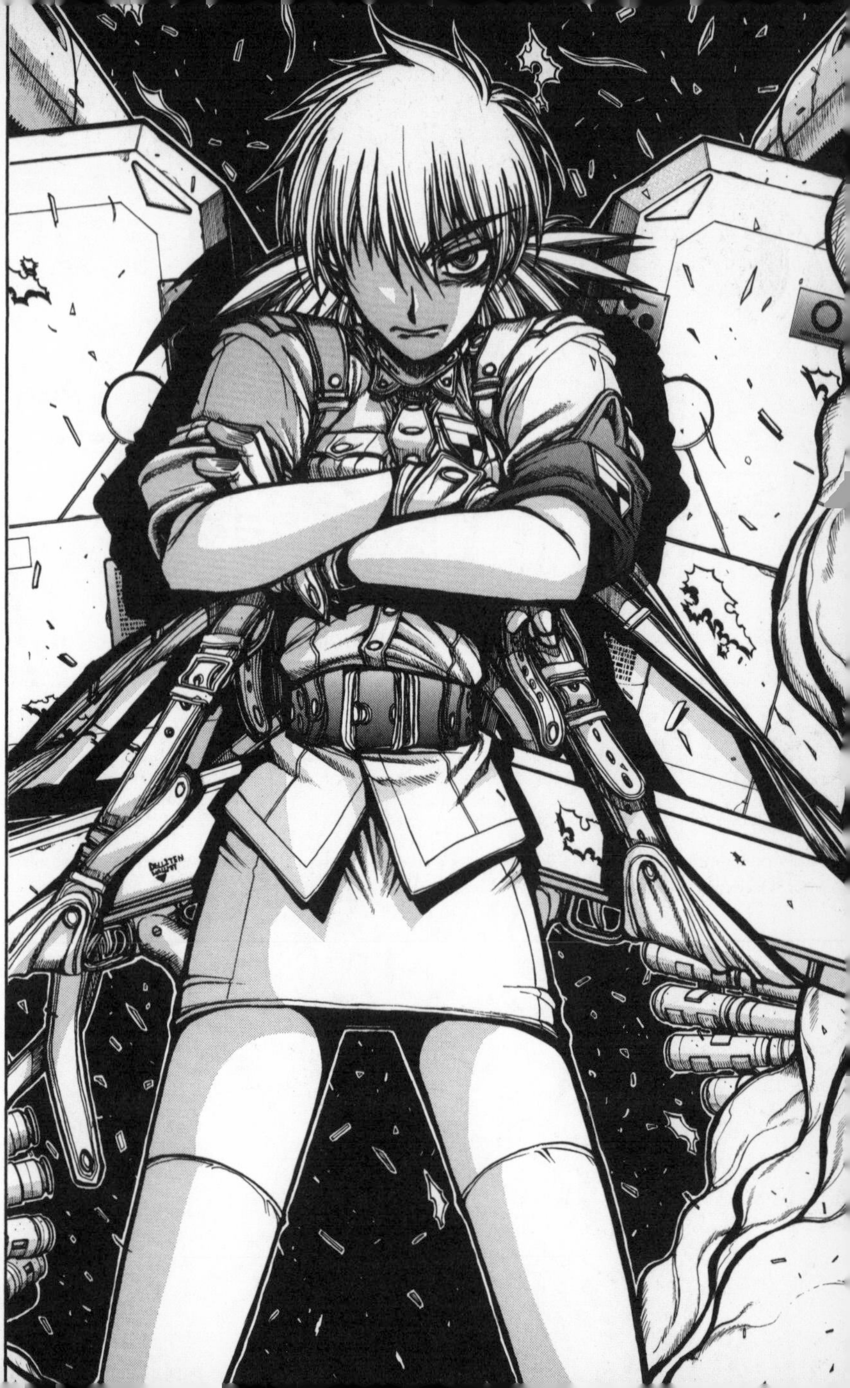

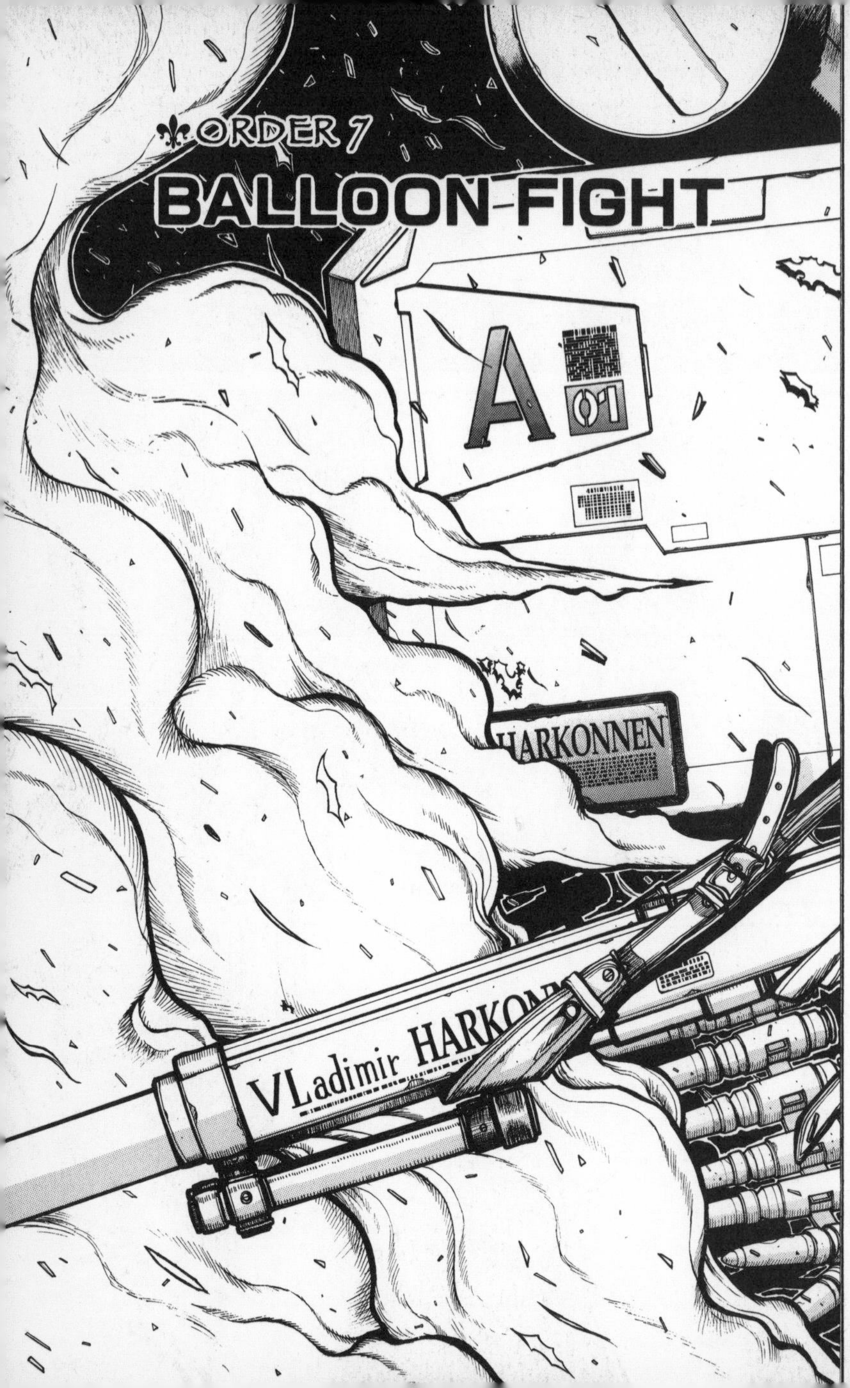
ORDER 7
BALLOON FIGHT
A 01
HARKONNEN
VLadimir HARKON

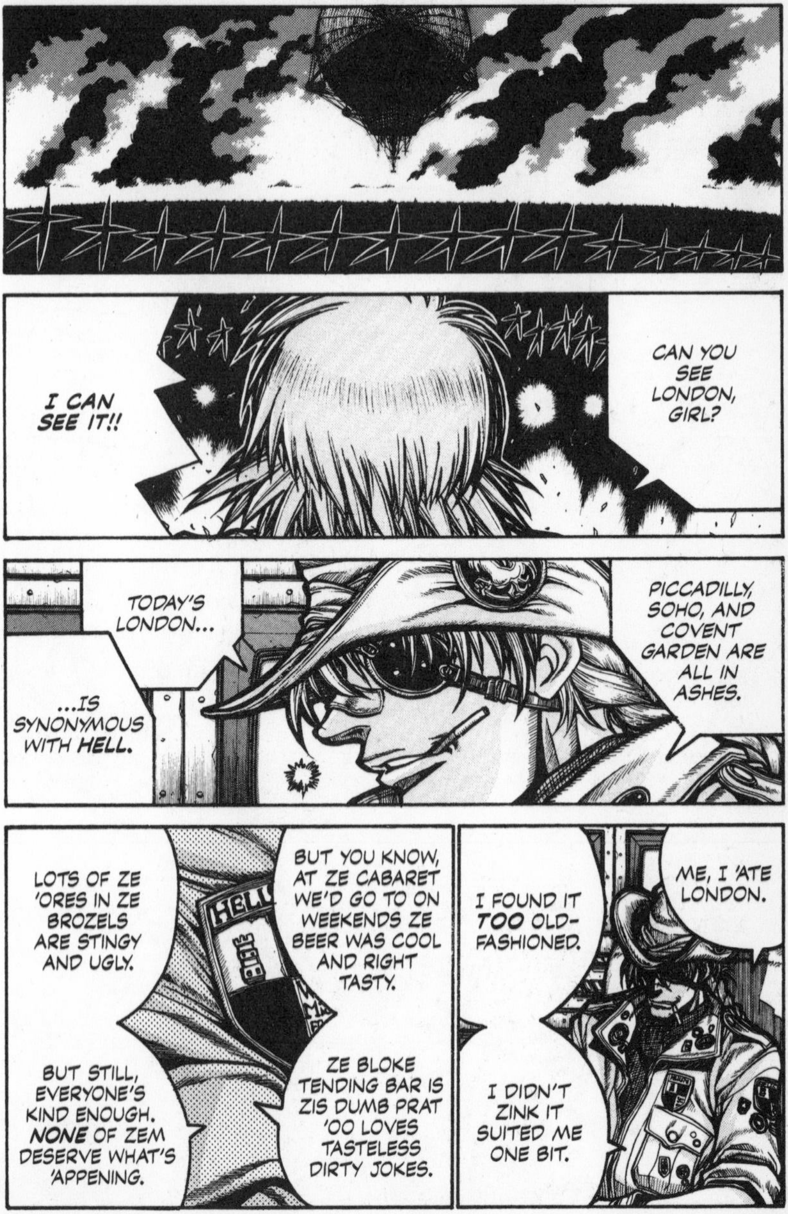
CAN YOU SEE LONDON, GIRL?
I CAN SEE IT!!
PICCADILLY, SOHO, AND COVENT GARDEN ARE ALL IN ASHES.
TODAY'S LONDON...
...IS SYNONYMOUS WITH HELL.
ME, I 'ATE LONDON.
I FOUND IT TOO OLD-FASHIONED.
I DIDN'T ZINK IT SUITED ME ONE BIT.
BUT YOU KNOW, AT ZE CABARET WE'D GO TO ON WEEKENDS ZE BEER WAS COOL AND RIGHT TASTY.
LOTS OF ZE 'ORES IN ZE BROZELS ARE STINGY AND UGLY.
ZE BLOKE TENDING BAR IS ZIS DUMB PRAT 'OO LOVES TASTELESS DIRTY JOKES.
BUT STILL, EVERYONE'S KIND ENOUGH. NONE OF ZEM DESERVE WHAT'S 'APPENING.

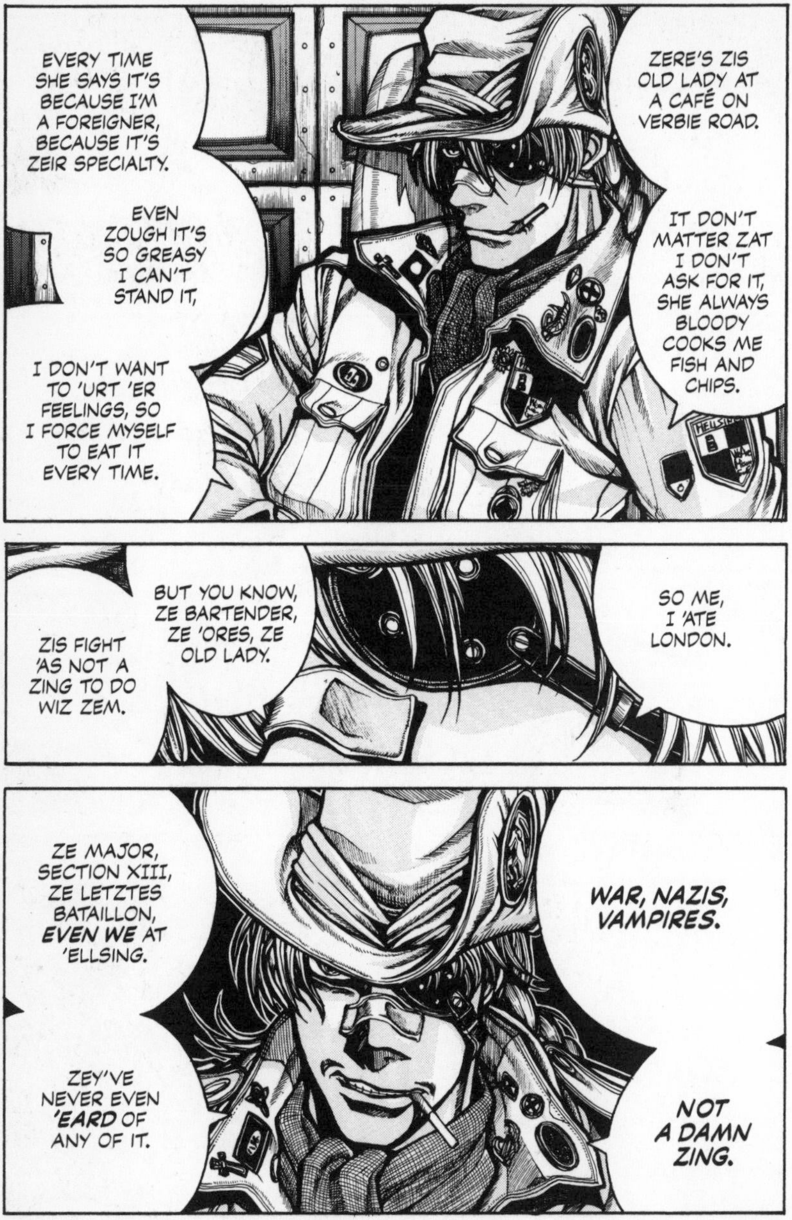
ZERE'S ZIS OLD LADY AT A CAFÉ ON VERBIE ROAD.
IT DON'T MATTER ZAT I DON'T ASK FOR IT, SHE ALWAYS BLOODY COOKS ME FISH AND CHIPS.
EVERY TIME SHE SAYS IT'S BECAUSE I'M A FOREIGNER, BECAUSE IT'S ZEIR SPECIALTY.
EVEN ZOUGH IT'S SO GREASY I CAN'T STAND IT,
I DON'T WANT TO 'URT 'ER FEELINGS, SO I FORCE MYSELF TO EAT IT EVERY TIME.
SO ME, I 'ATE LONDON.
BUT YOU KNOW, ZE BARTENDER, ZE 'ORES, ZE OLD LADY.
ZIS FIGHT 'AS NOT A ZING TO DO WIZ ZEM.
WAR, NAZIS, VAMPIRES.
ZE MAJOR, SECTION XIII, ZE LETZTES BATAILLON, ***EVEN WE*** AT 'ELLSING.
ZEY'VE NEVER EVEN ***'EARD*** OF ANY OF IT.
NOT A DAMN ZING.

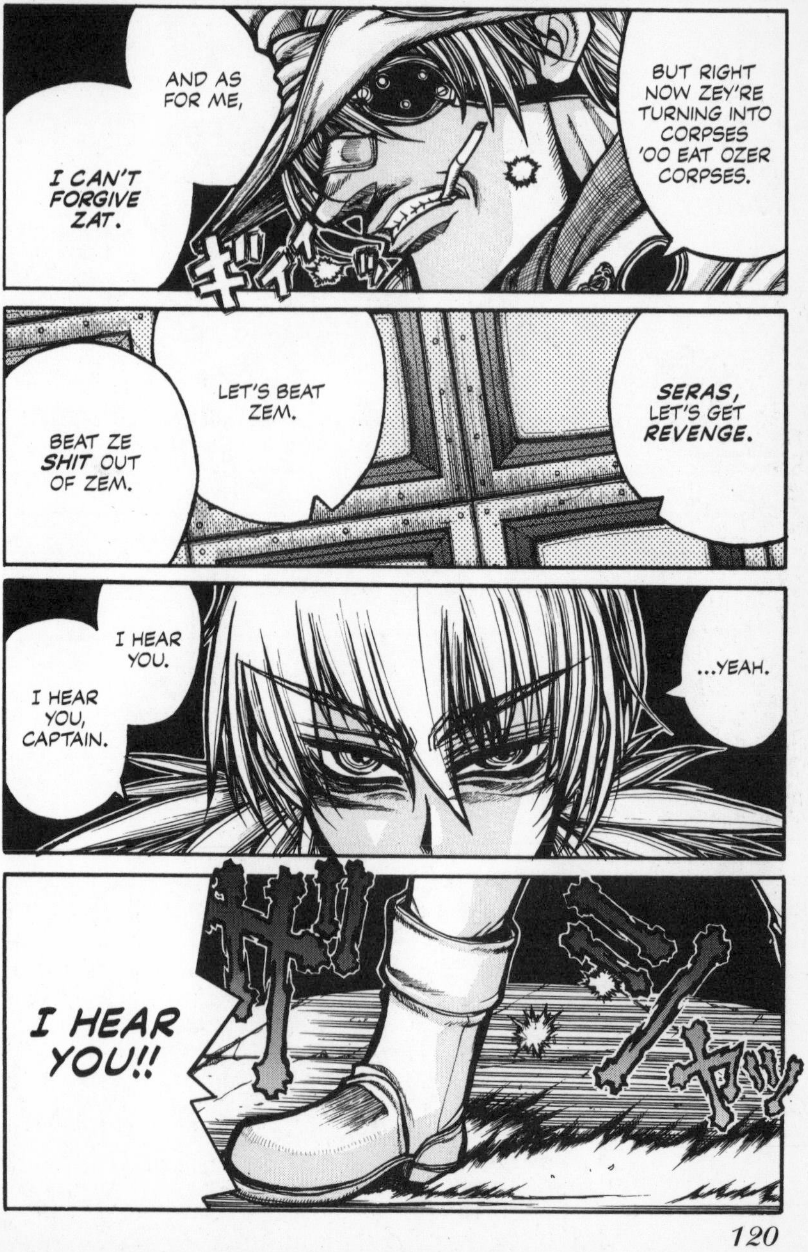
BUT RIGHT NOW ZEY'RE TURNING INTO CORPSES 'OO EAT OZER CORPSES.
AND AS FOR ME,
I CAN'T FORGIVE ZAT.
SERAS, LET'S GET REVENGE.
LET'S BEAT ZEM.
BEAT ZE SHIT OUT OF ZEM.
...YEAH.
I HEAR YOU.
I HEAR YOU, CAPTAIN.
I HEAR YOU!!

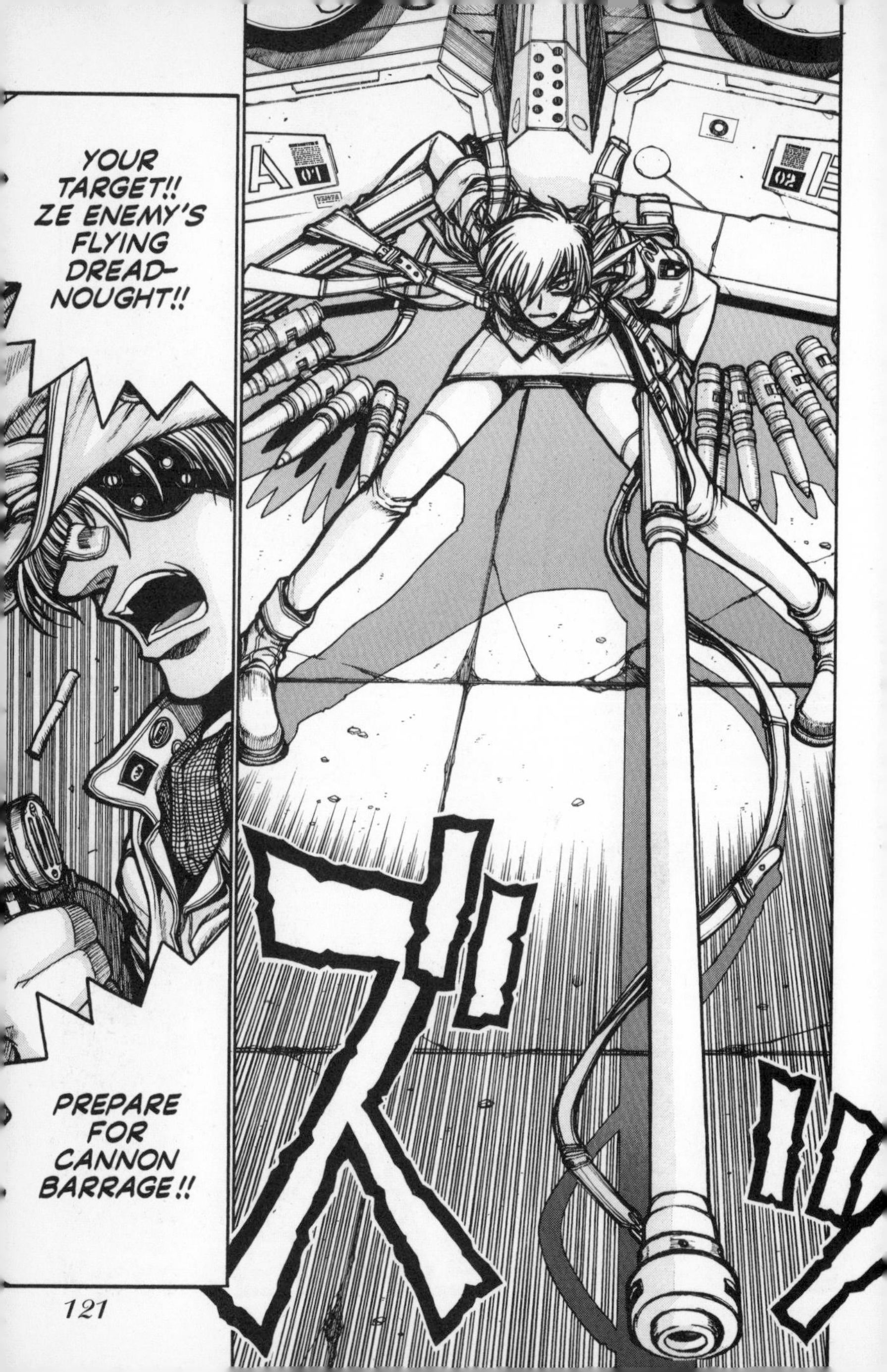
YOUR TARGET!! ZE ENEMY'S FLYING DREAD-NOUGHT!!
PREPARE FOR CANNON BARRAGE!!

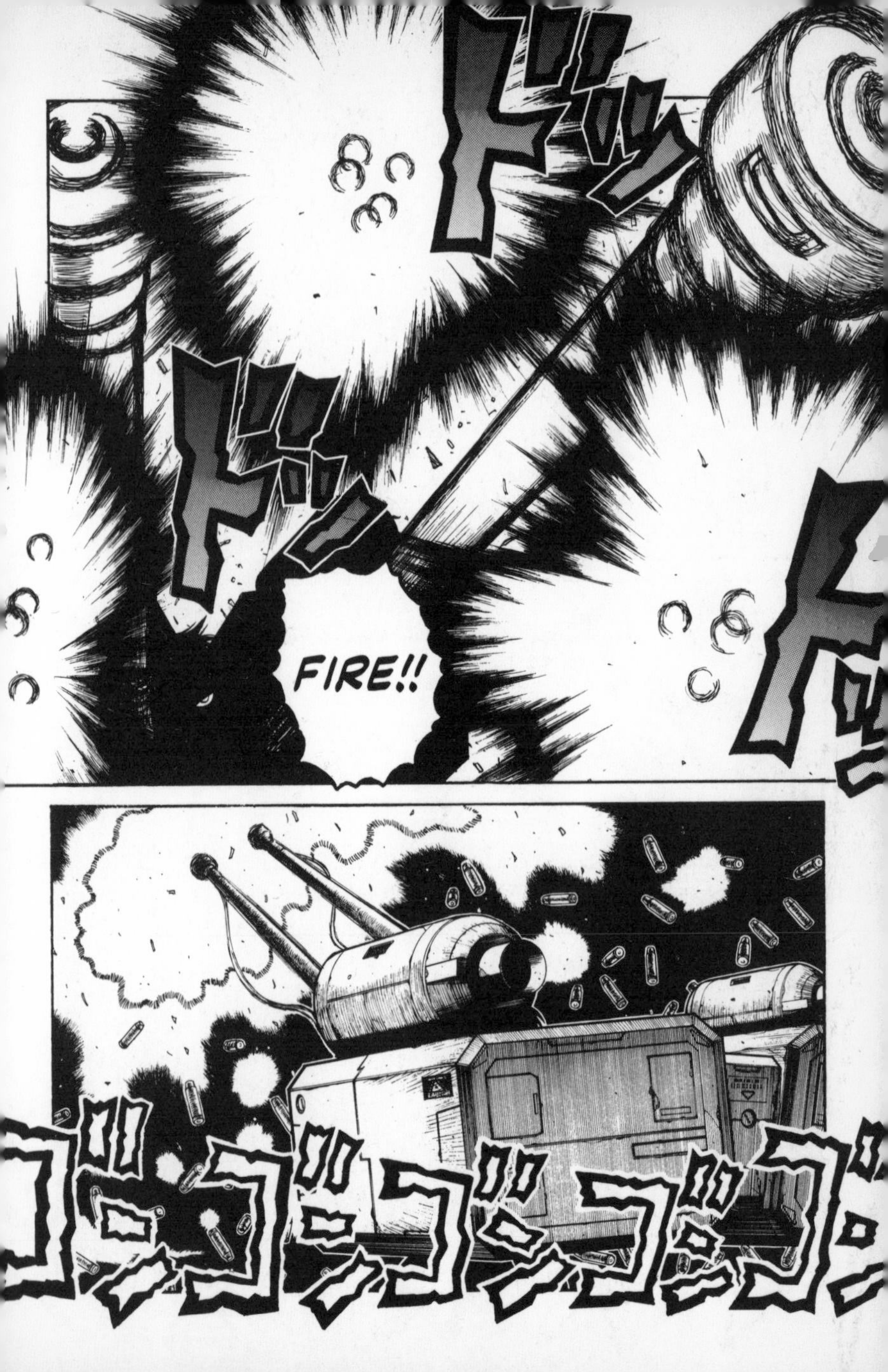
FIRE!!

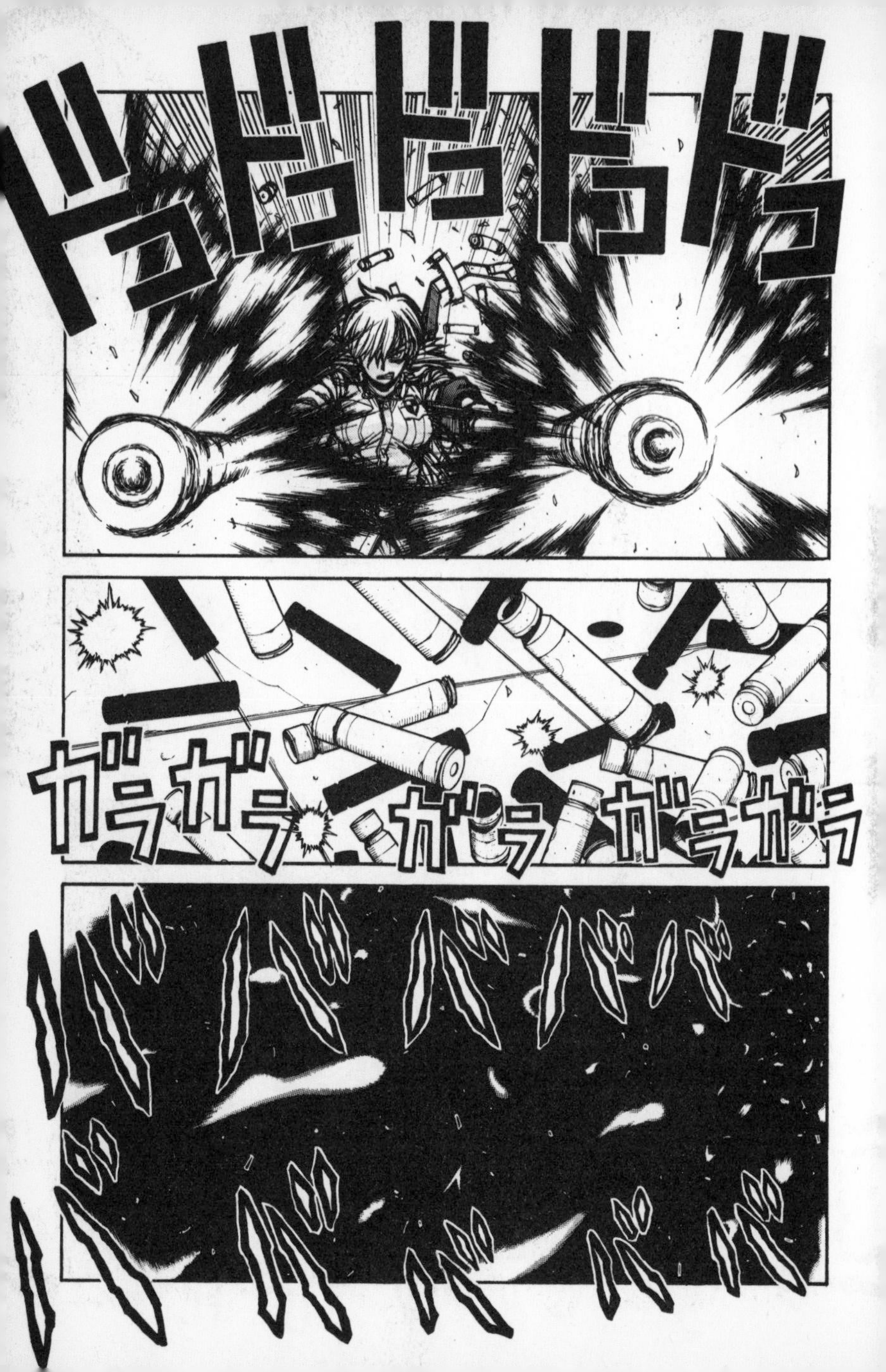
ドゥドゥドゥドゥ
ガラガラガラガラガラ
バババババ
バババババ

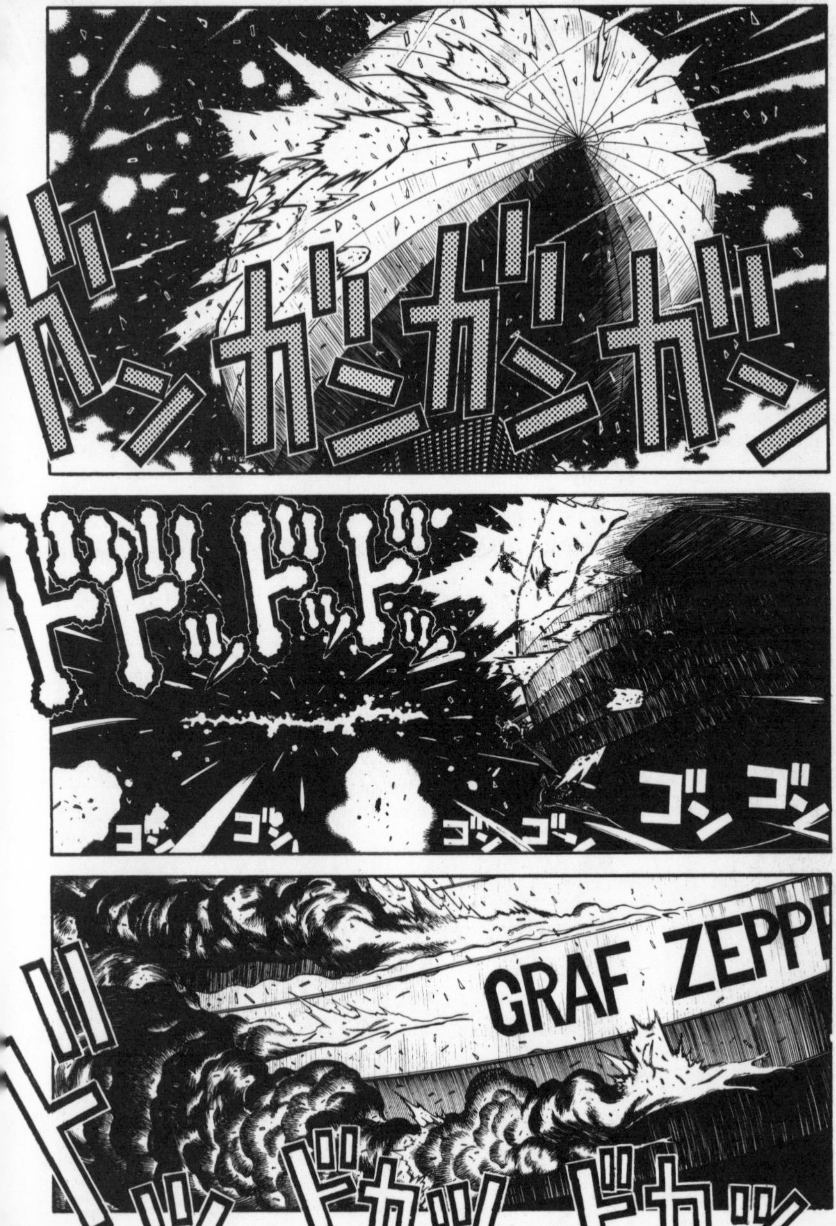
ガッ
ガンガンガン
ドドドドドド
ゴンゴン
ゴンゴン
ゴンゴン
GRAF ZEPP
ドッ
ドカッ
ドカッ

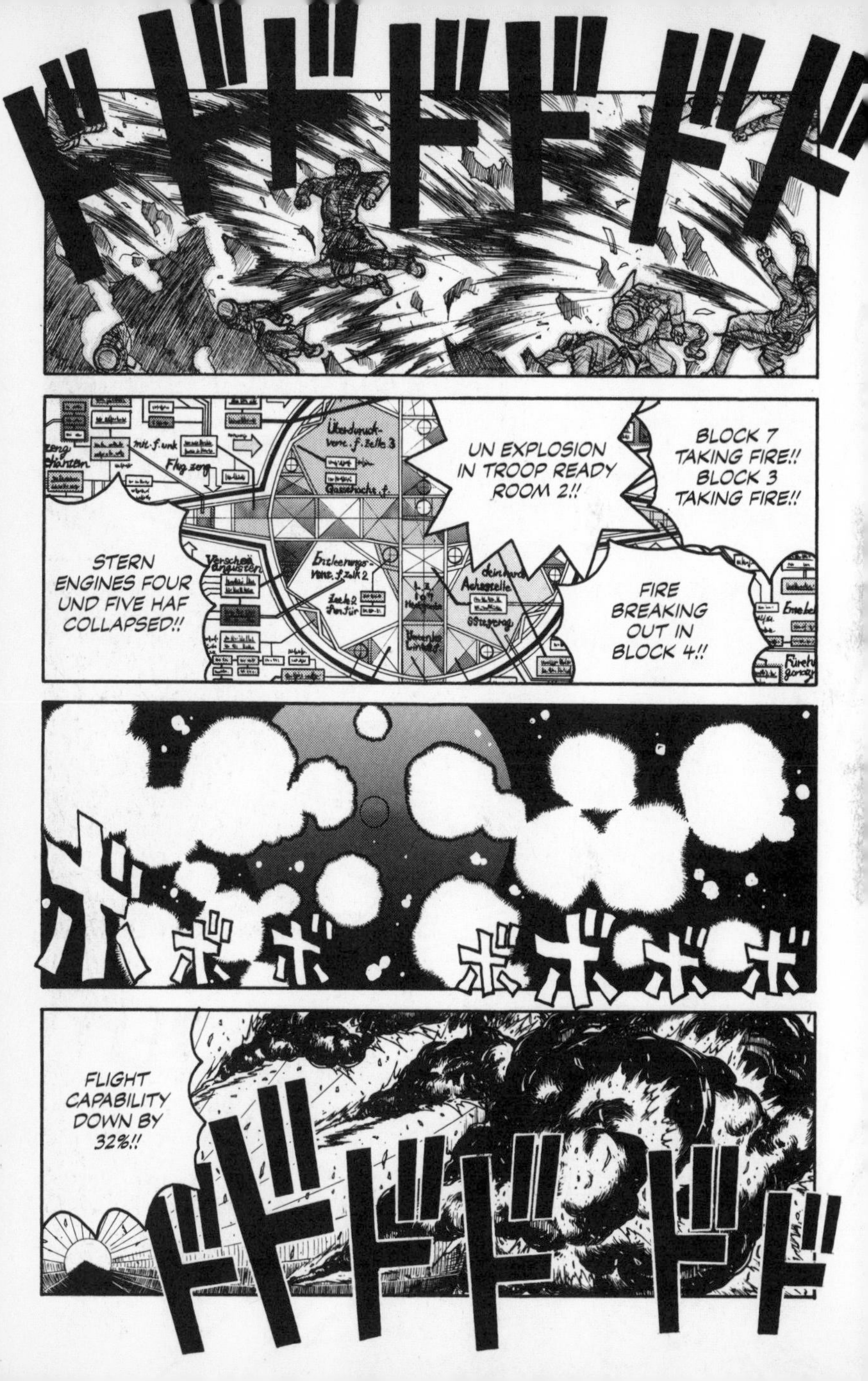
BLOCK 7 TAKING FIRE!! BLOCK 3 TAKING FIRE!!
UN EXPLOSION IN TROOP READY ROOM 2!!
FIRE BREAKING OUT IN BLOCK 4!!
STERN ENGINES FOUR UND FIVE HAF COLLAPSED!!
FLIGHT CAPABILITY DOWN BY 32%!!

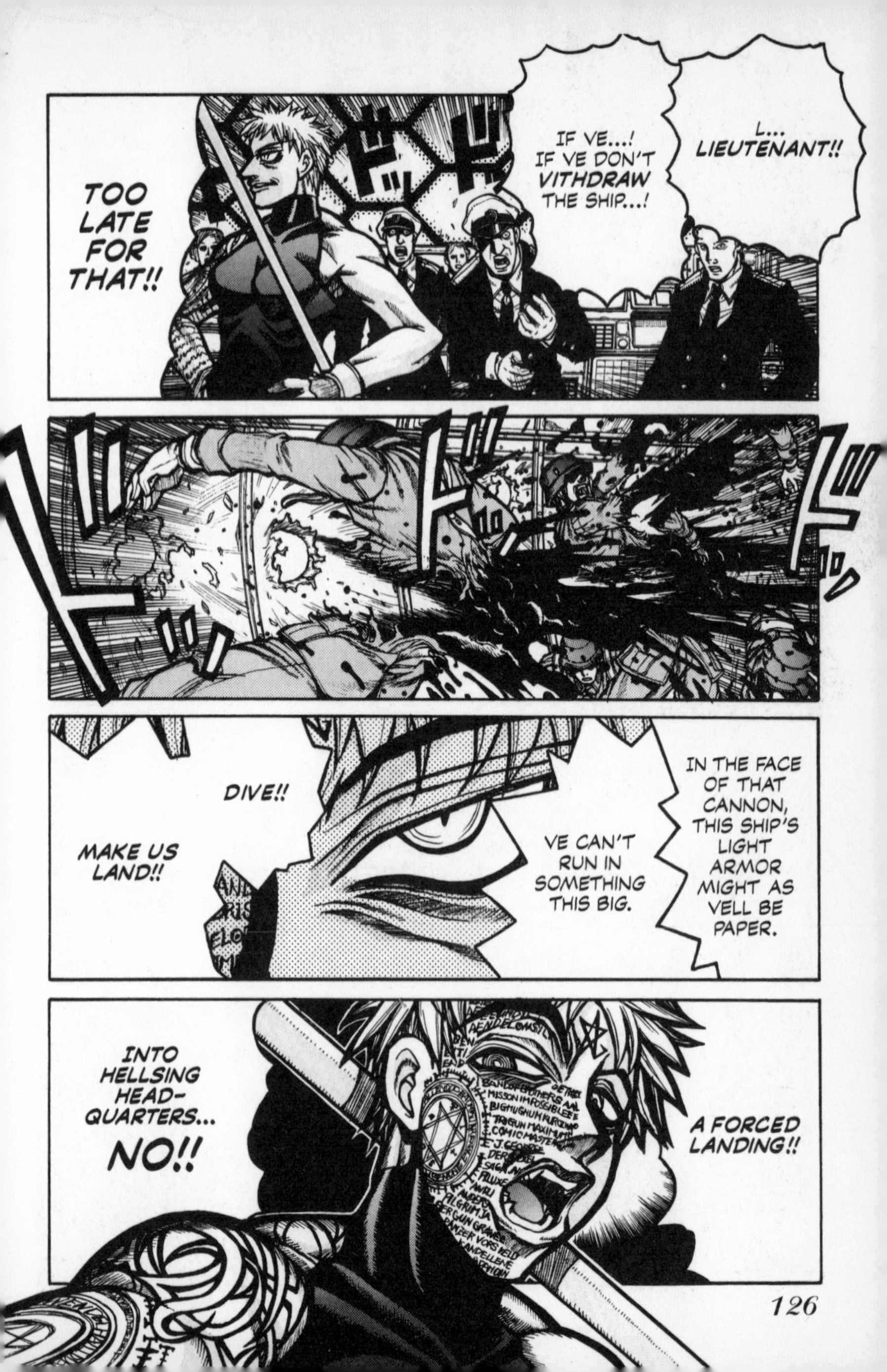
L... LIEUTENANT!!
IF VE...! IF VE DON'T VITHDRAW THE SHIP...!
TOO LATE FOR THAT!!
IN THE FACE OF THAT CANNON, THIS SHIP'S LIGHT ARMOR MIGHT AS VELL BE PAPER.
VE CAN'T RUN IN SOMETHING THIS BIG.
DIVE!!
MAKE US LAND!!
A FORCED LANDING!!
INTO HELLSING HEAD-QUARTERS... NO!!

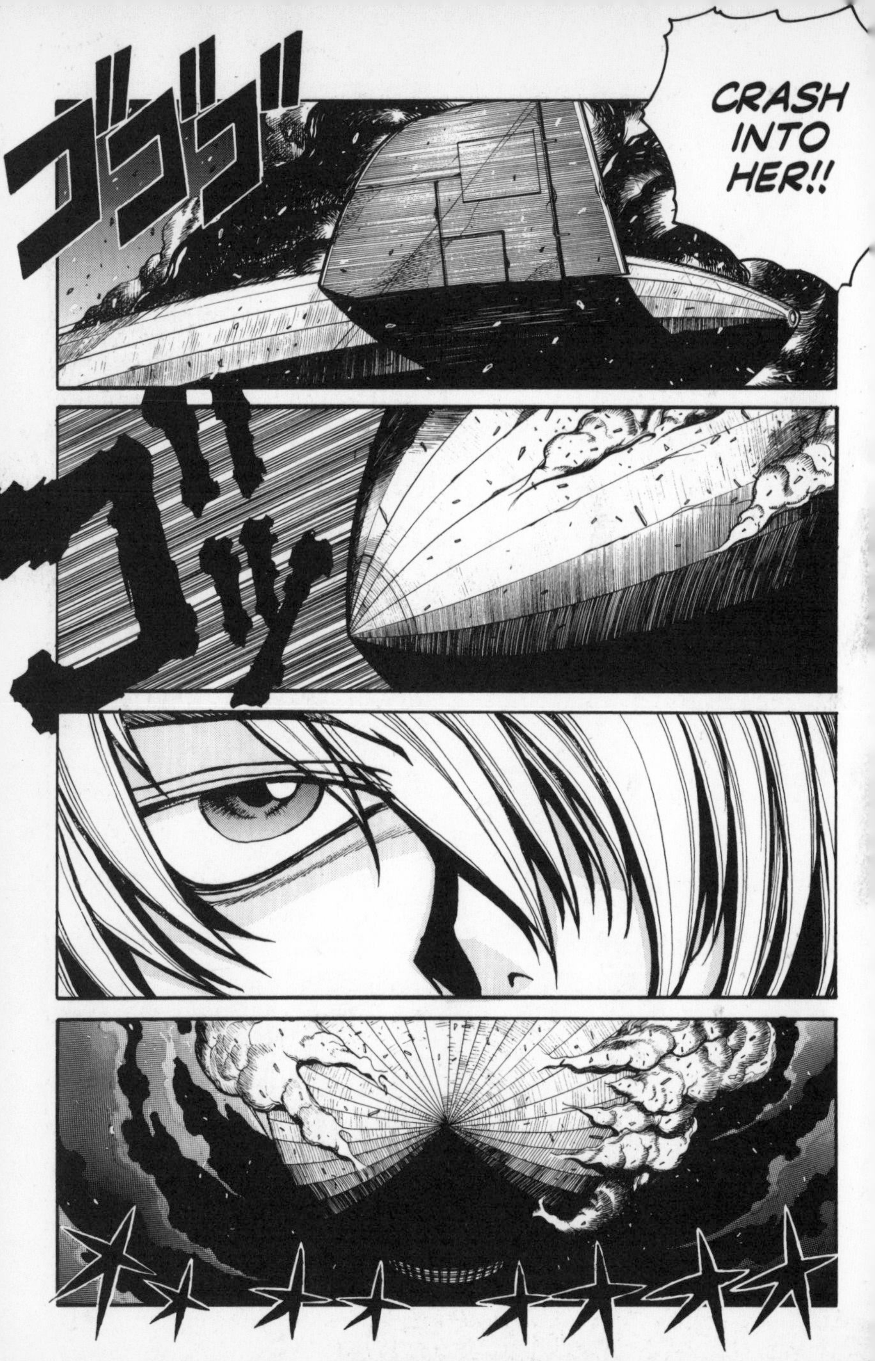
CRASH INTO HER!!
ゴゴゴ
ゴッ

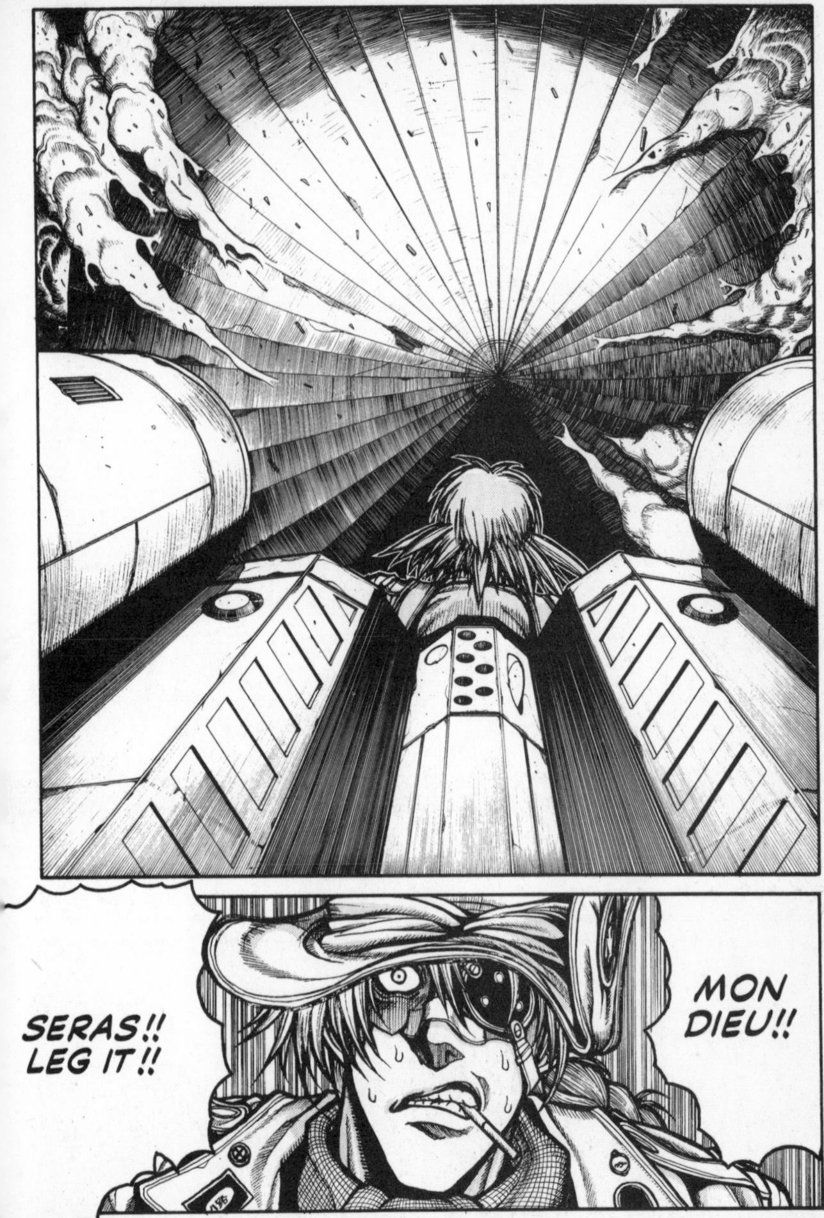
MON DIEU!!
SERAS!! LEG IT!!

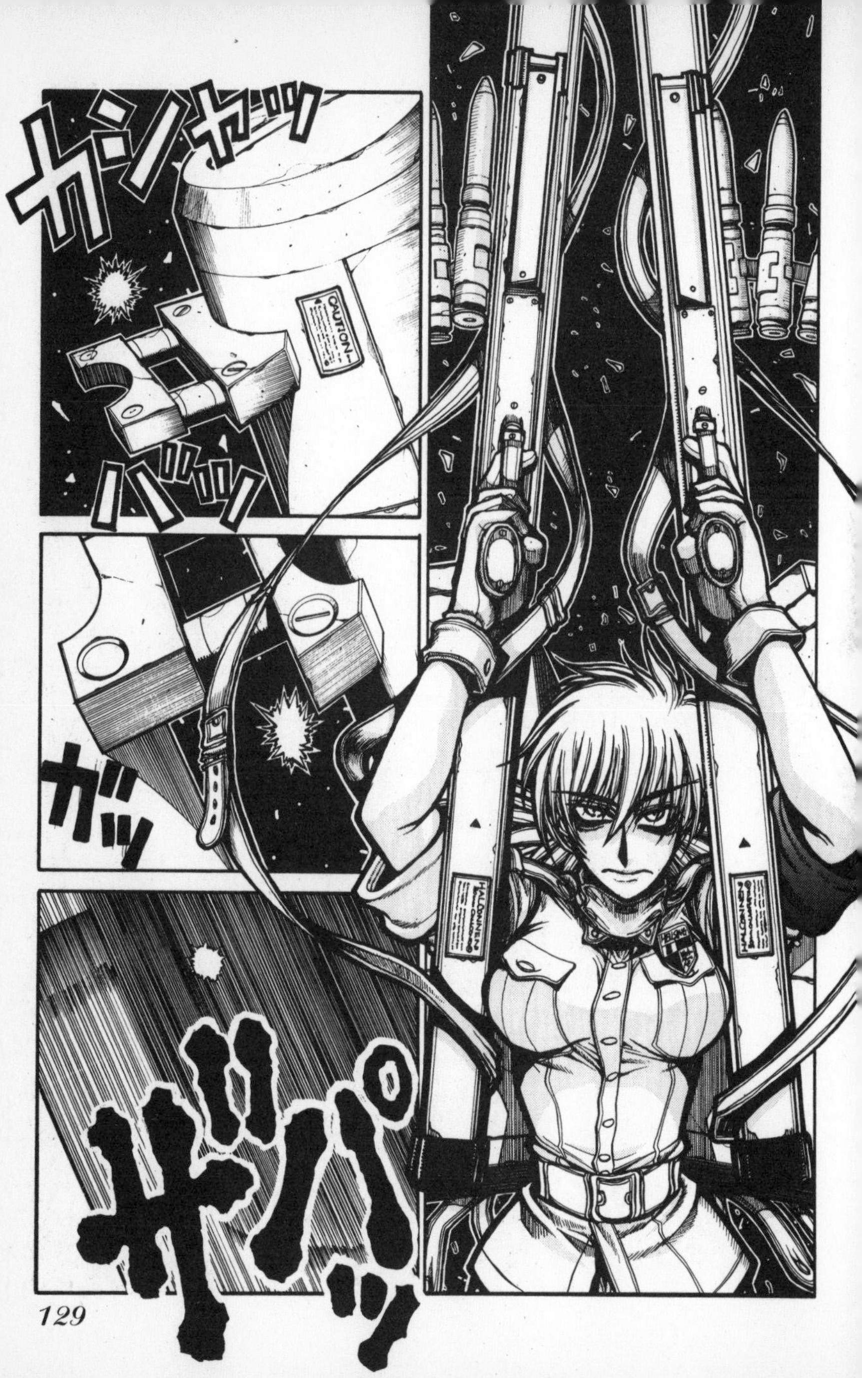
ガシャーッ
CAUTION
ガッ
ザパッ

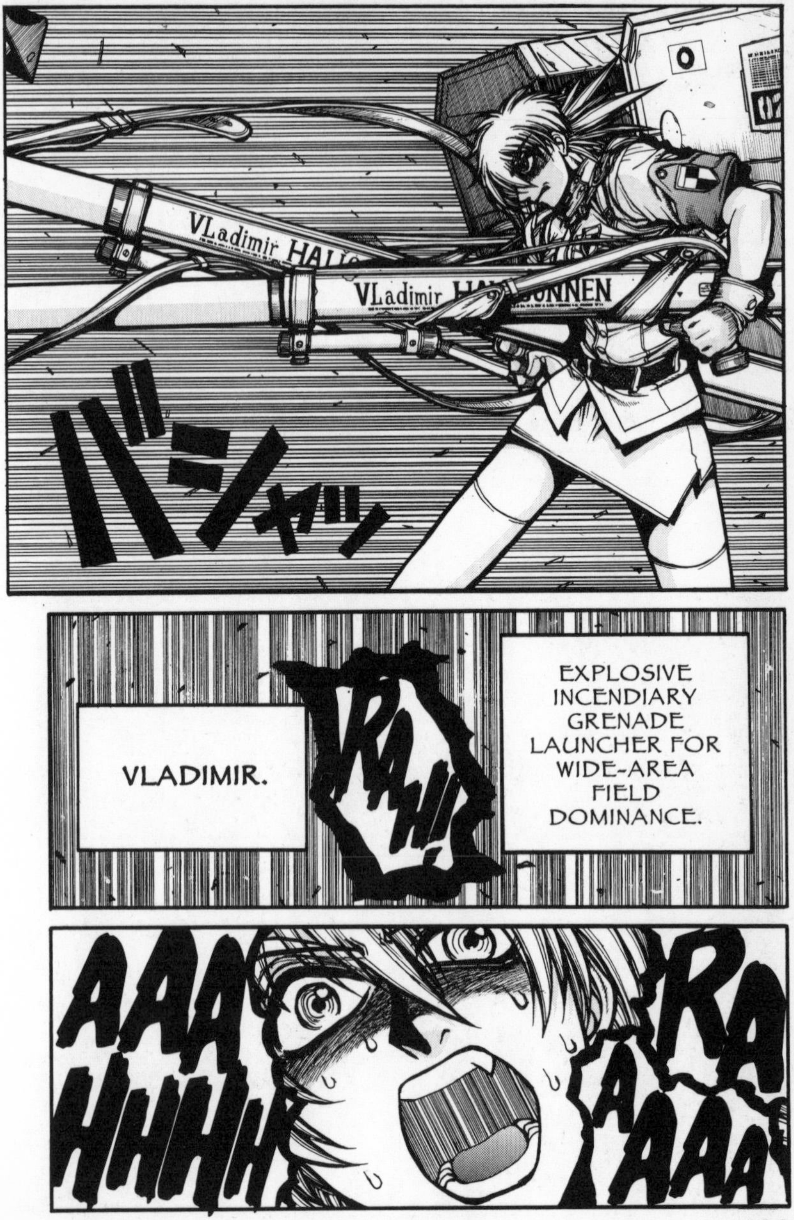
VLadimir HAL
VLadimir
バシャッ
EXPLOSIVE INCENDIARY GRENADE LAUNCHER FOR WIDE-AREA FIELD DOMINANCE.
VRAW!
VLADIMIR.
RAAAAAA
AAAHHHHH

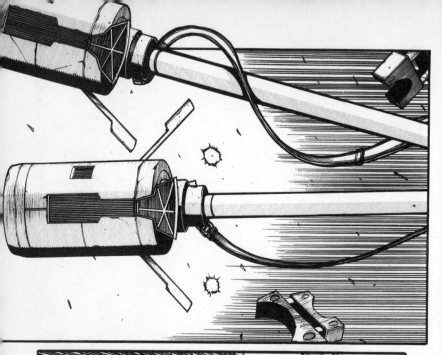

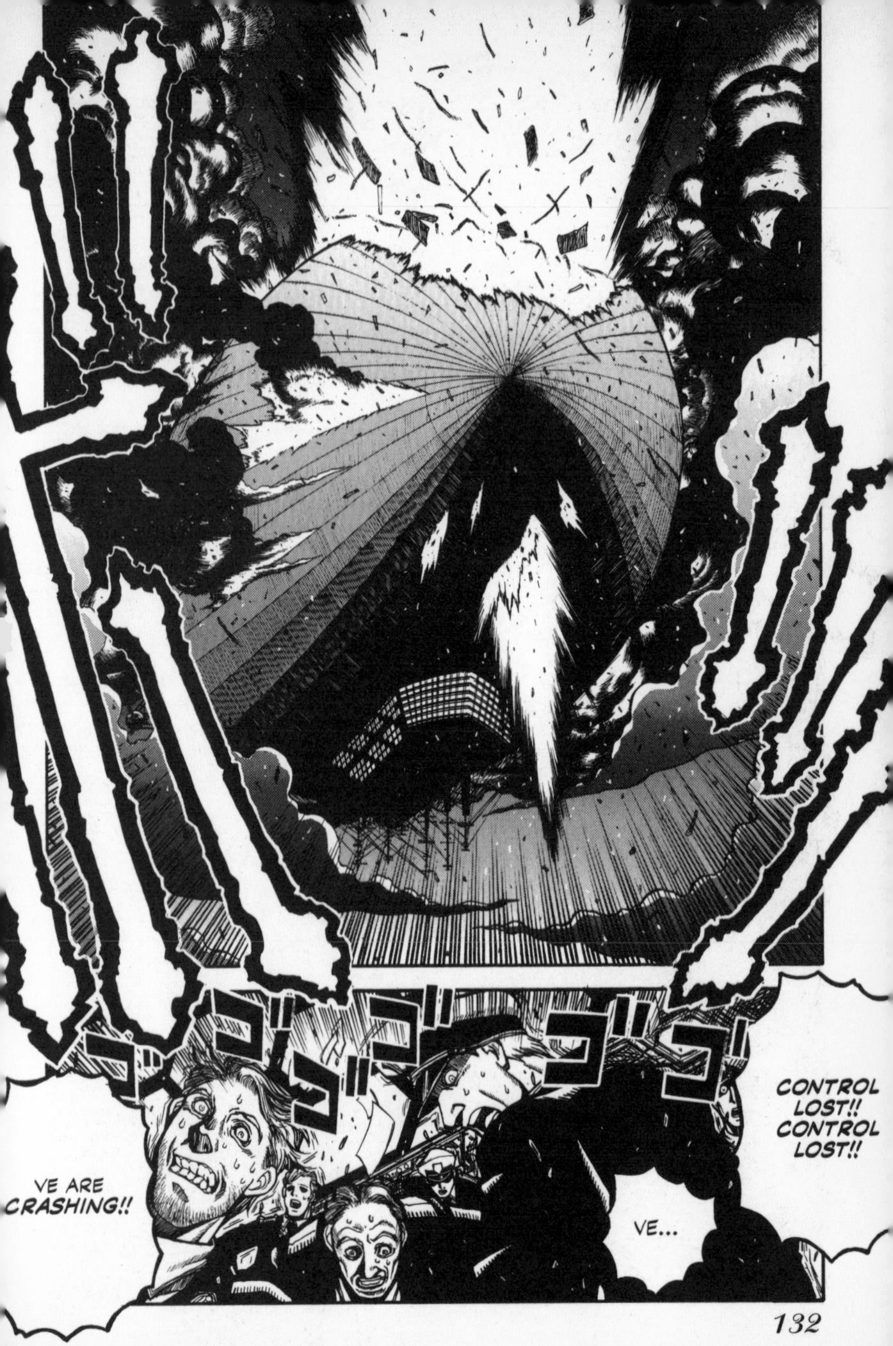
CONTROL LOST!! CONTROL LOST!!
VE...
VE ARE CRASHING!!

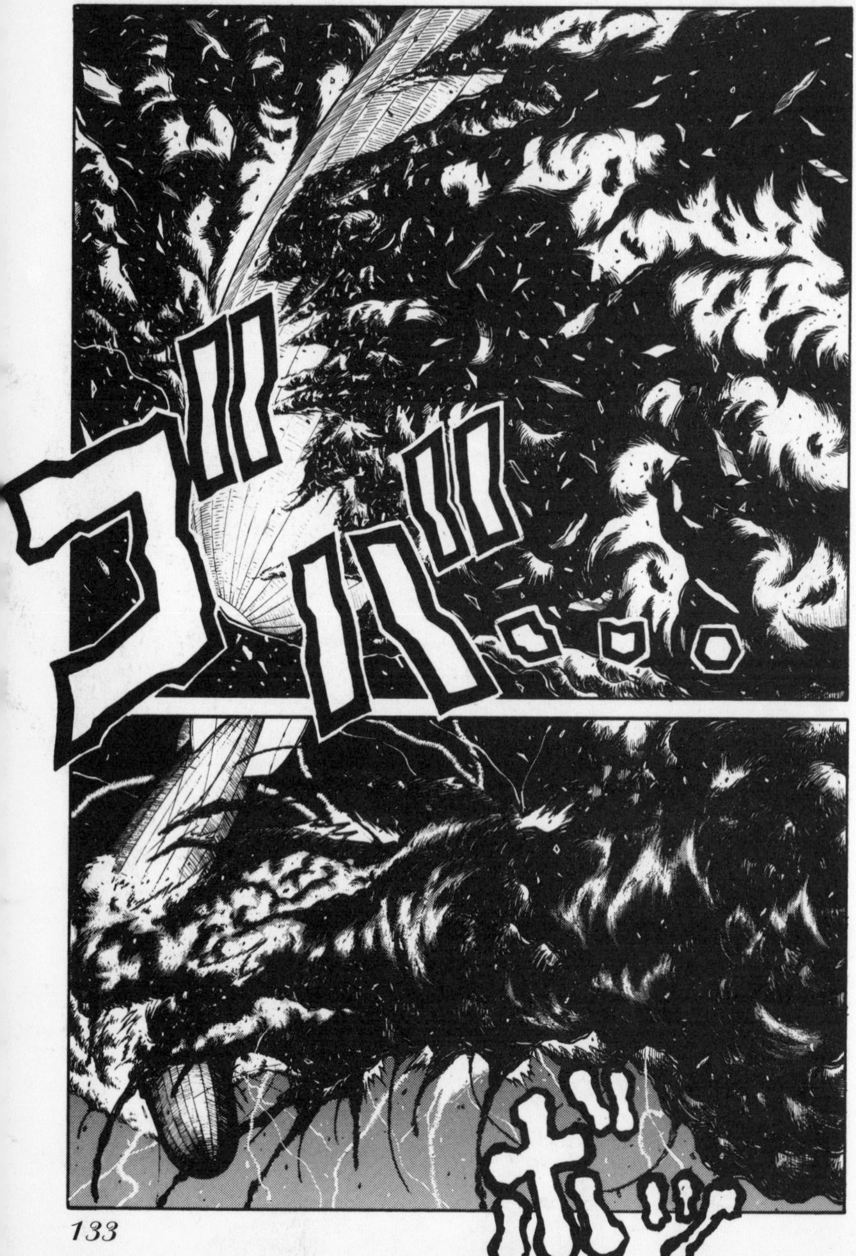
ゴバ。。。
ボッ

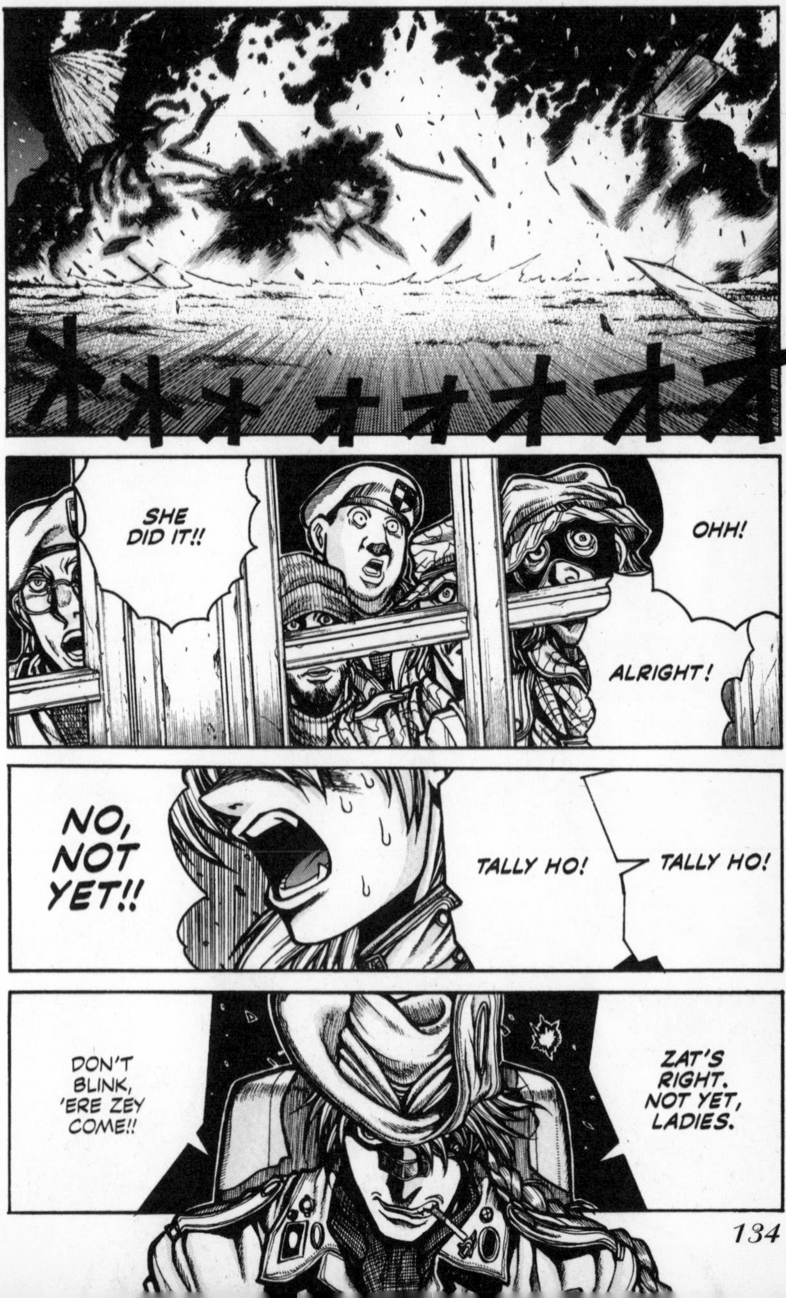
オオオオオオオ
OHH!
SHE DID IT!!
ALRIGHT!
TALLY HO!
TALLY HO!
NO, NOT YET!!
ZAT'S RIGHT. NOT YET, LADIES.
DON'T BLINK, 'ERE ZEY COME!!

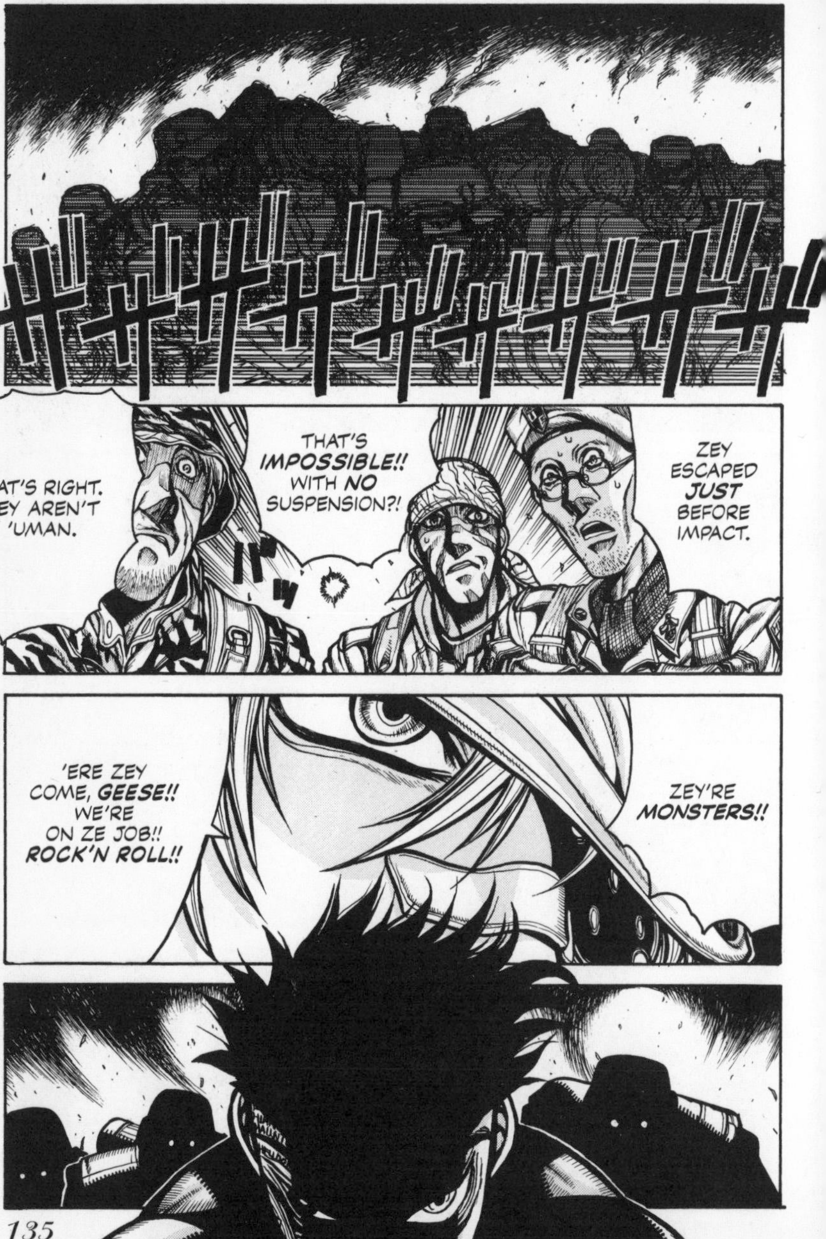
ZEY ESCAPED JUST BEFORE IMPACT.
THAT'S IMPOSSIBLE!! WITH NO SUSPENSION?!
ZAT'S RIGHT. ZEY AREN'T 'UMAN.
ZEY'RE MONSTERS!!
'ERE ZEY COME, GEESE!! WE'RE ON ZE JOB!! ROCK'N ROLL!!

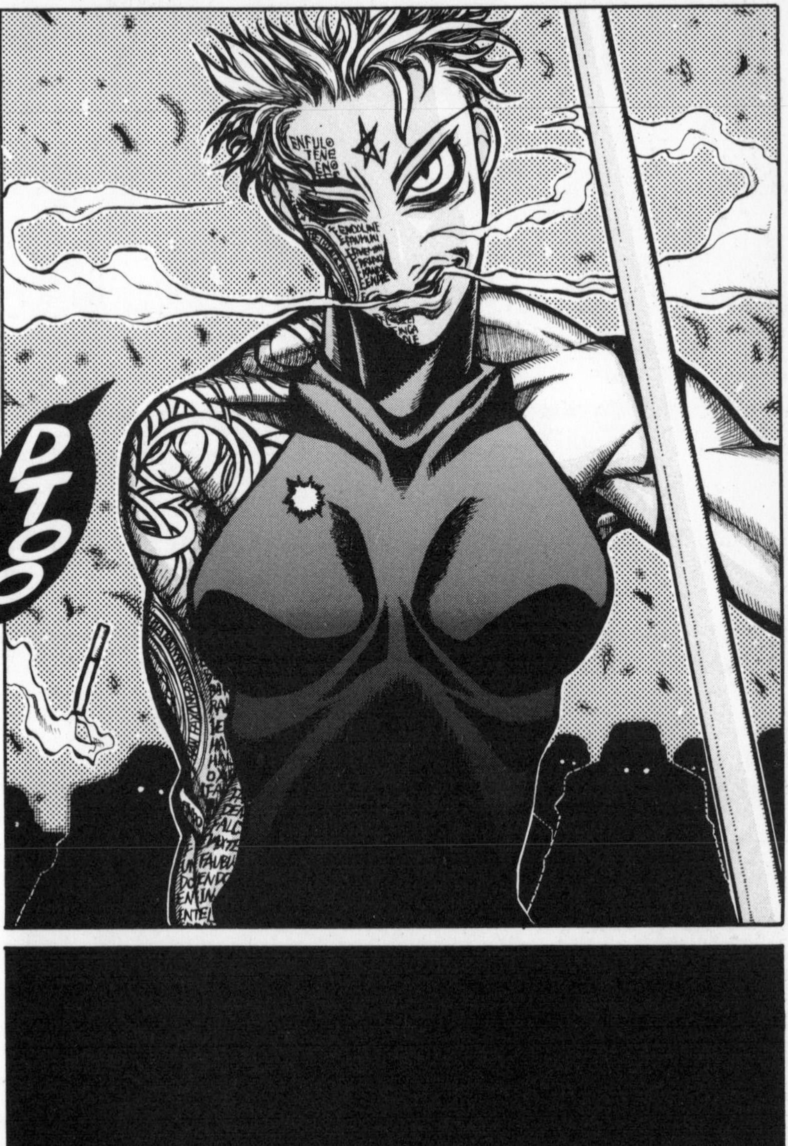
PTOO
TO BE CONTINUED

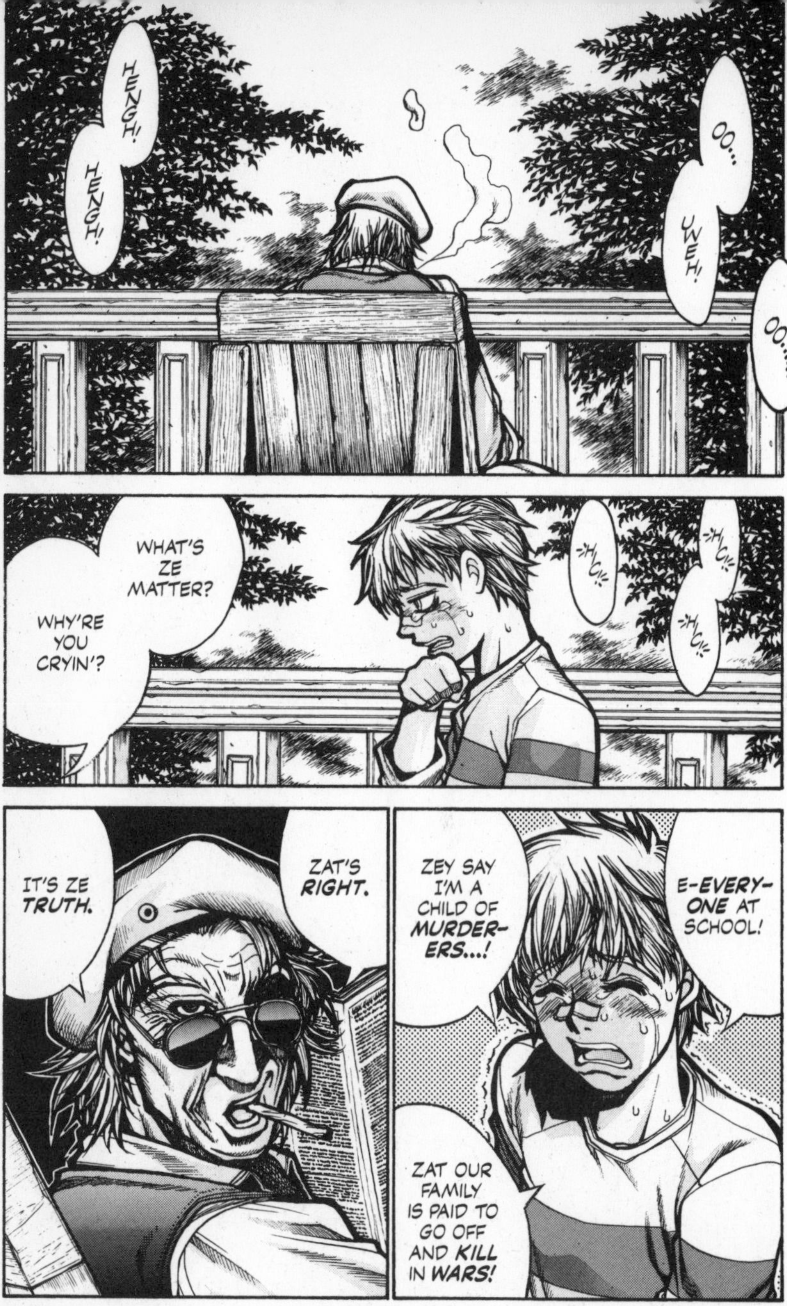
OO...
UWEH!
OO......
HENGH! HENGH!
-HIC!-
-HIC!-
-HIC!-
WHAT'S ZE MATTER?
WHY'RE YOU CRYIN'?
E-EVERYONE AT SCHOOL!
ZEY SAY I'M A CHILD OF MURDERERS...!
ZAT OUR FAMILY IS PAID TO GO OFF AND KILL IN WARS!
ZAT'S RIGHT.
IT'S ZE TRUTH.

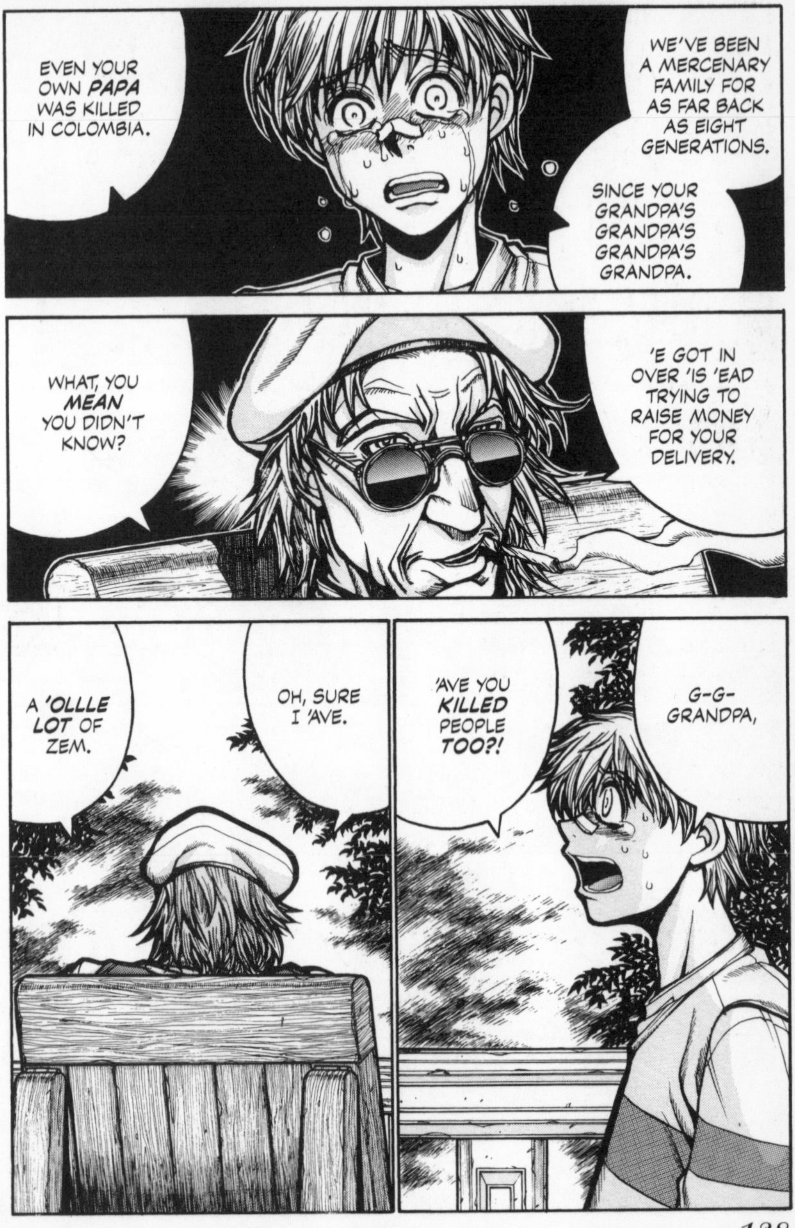
WE'VE BEEN A MERCENARY FAMILY FOR AS FAR BACK AS EIGHT GENERATIONS.
SINCE YOUR GRANDPA'S GRANDPA'S GRANDPA'S GRANDPA.
EVEN YOUR OWN PAPA WAS KILLED IN COLOMBIA.
'E GOT IN OVER 'IS 'EAD TRYING TO RAISE MONEY FOR YOUR DELIVERY.
WHAT, YOU MEAN YOU DIDN'T KNOW?
G-G-GRANDPA,
'AVE YOU KILLED PEOPLE TOO?!
OH, SURE I 'AVE.
A 'OLLLE LOT OF ZEM.

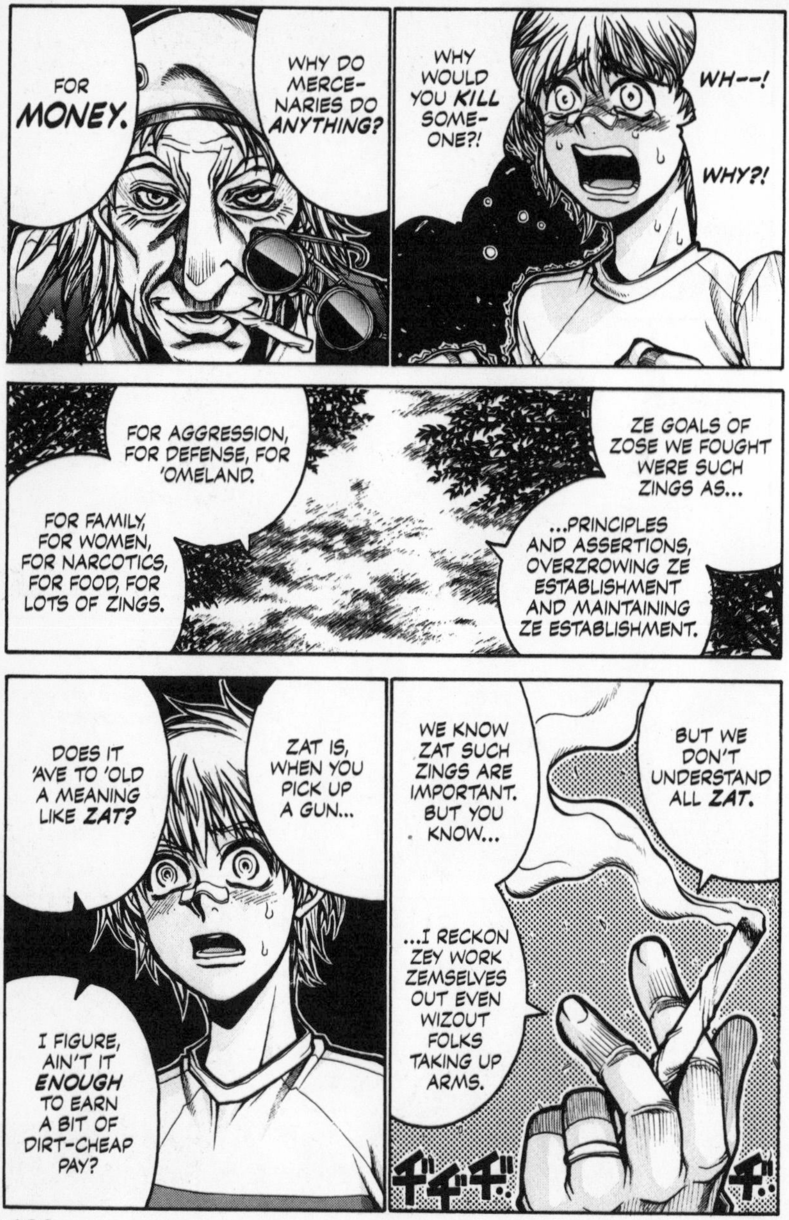
WH--!
WHY WOULD YOU KILL SOMEONE?!
WHY?!
WHY DO MERCENARIES DO ANYTHING?
FOR MONEY.
ZE GOALS OF ZOSE WE FOUGHT WERE SUCH ZINGS AS...
...PRINCIPLES AND ASSERTIONS, OVERZROWING ZE ESTABLISHMENT AND MAINTAINING ZE ESTABLISHMENT.
FOR AGGRESSION, FOR DEFENSE, FOR 'OMELAND.
FOR FAMILY, FOR WOMEN, FOR NARCOTICS, FOR FOOD, FOR LOTS OF ZINGS.
BUT WE DON'T UNDERSTAND ALL ZAT.
WE KNOW ZAT SUCH ZINGS ARE IMPORTANT. BUT YOU KNOW...
...I RECKON ZEY WORK ZEMSELVES OUT EVEN WIZOUT FOLKS TAKING UP ARMS.
ギ
ギギギ
ZAT IS, WHEN YOU PICK UP A GUN...
DOES IT 'AVE TO 'OLD A MEANING LIKE ZAT?
I FIGURE, AIN'T IT ENOUGH TO EARN A BIT OF DIRT-CHEAP PAY?

ON ZE OZER HAND, A *DIRT-CHEAP PIECE OF SHIT* REWARD IS ENOUGH FOR US TO STAKE OUR LIVES ON.

FOR DIRT-CHEAP PAY WE RUN 'ERE AND ZERE TO BATTLEFIELDS ALL OVER ZE WORLD.

FOR DIRT-CHEAP WE KILL AND ARE KILLED.

AND IT'S NOT LIKE ANYONE TOLD US TO DO IT, WE *CHOOSE* TO.

ON ZE BATTLE-FIELD, DIRT-CHEAP IS MORE IMPORTANT ZAN YOUR OWN LIFE OR SOMEONE ELSE'S.

YOU COULD SAY OUR FAMILY LINEAGE IS ZE REAL SCUM OF ZE EARTH.

I'M SORRY, BUT MAYBE GETTING PICKED ON AT SCHOOL CAN'T BE 'ELPED.

NO, ZEN AGAIN PER'APS ZE TIME WILL COME WHEN YOU UNDERSTAND.

'EY, AFTER ALL,

YOU'RE *OUR* GRANDKID.

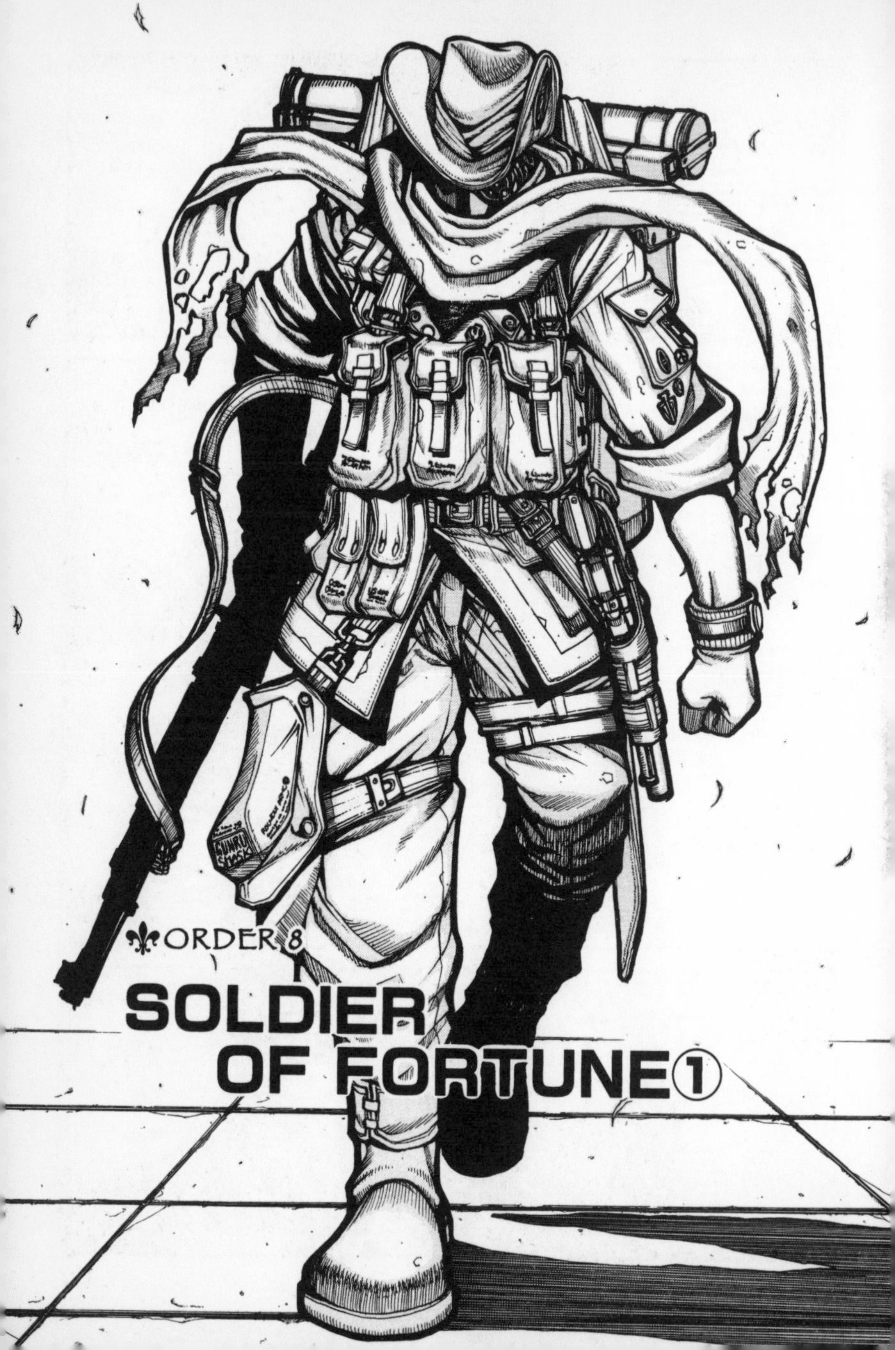
ORDER 8
SOLDIER OF FORTUNE①

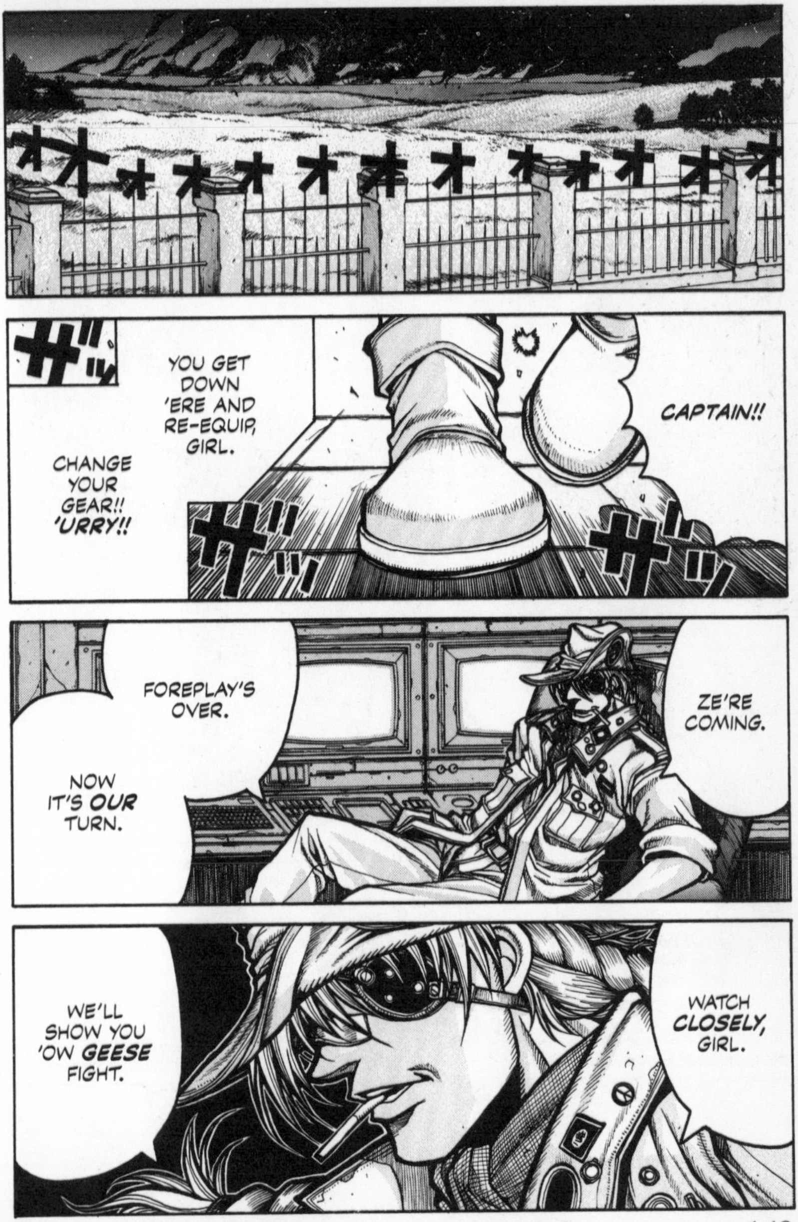
CAPTAIN!!
YOU GET DOWN 'ERE AND RE-EQUIP, GIRL.
CHANGE YOUR GEAR!! 'URRY!!
ZE'RE COMING.
FOREPLAY'S OVER.
NOW IT'S OUR TURN.
WATCH CLOSELY, GIRL.
WE'LL SHOW YOU 'OW GEESE FIGHT.

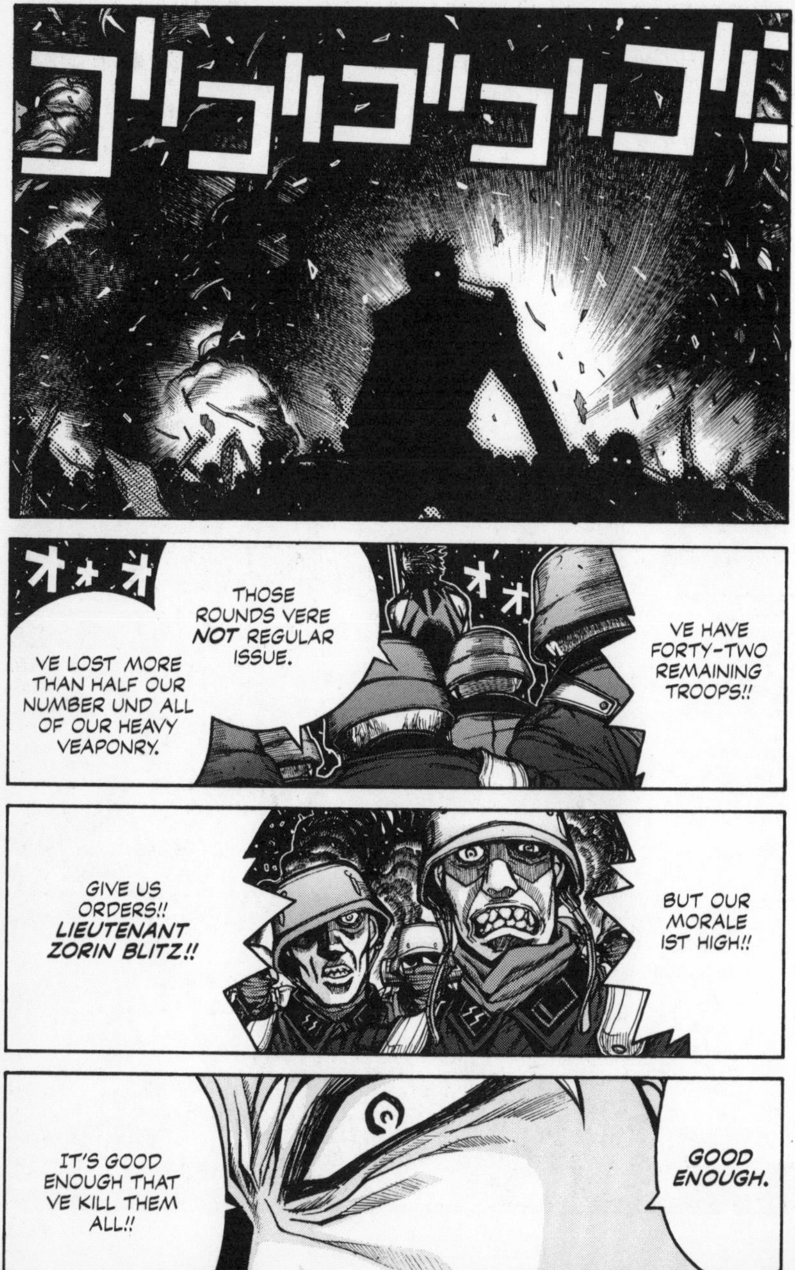
ゴリゴリゴリゴリ
オオ
VE HAVE FORTY-TWO REMAINING TROOPS!!
THOSE ROUNDS VERE **NOT** REGULAR ISSUE.
VE LOST MORE THAN HALF OUR NUMBER UND ALL OF OUR HEAVY VEAPONRY.
オォオ
BUT OUR MORALE IST HIGH!!
GIVE US ORDERS!! ***LIEUTENANT ZORIN BLITZ!!***
GOOD ENOUGH.
IT'S GOOD ENOUGH THAT VE KILL THEM ALL!!

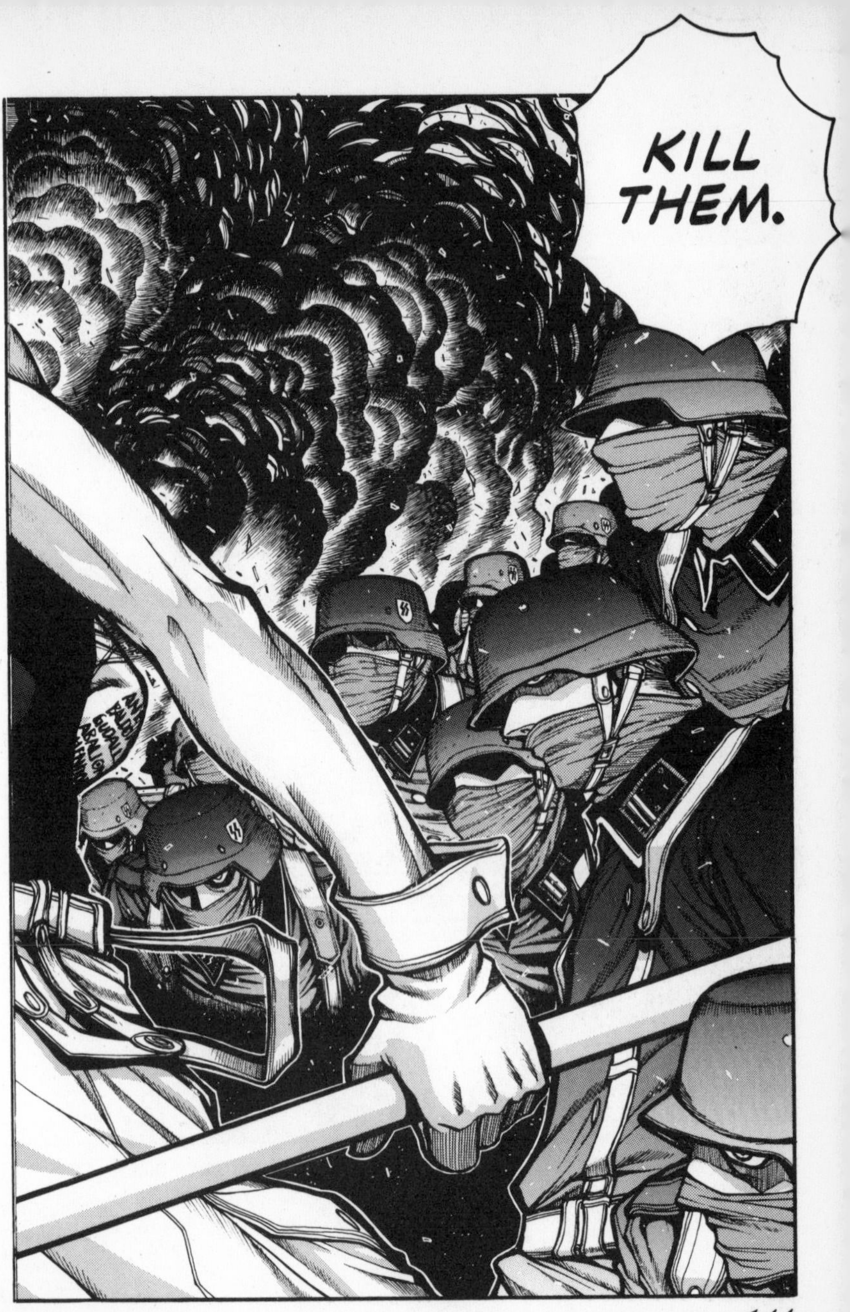
KILL THEM.

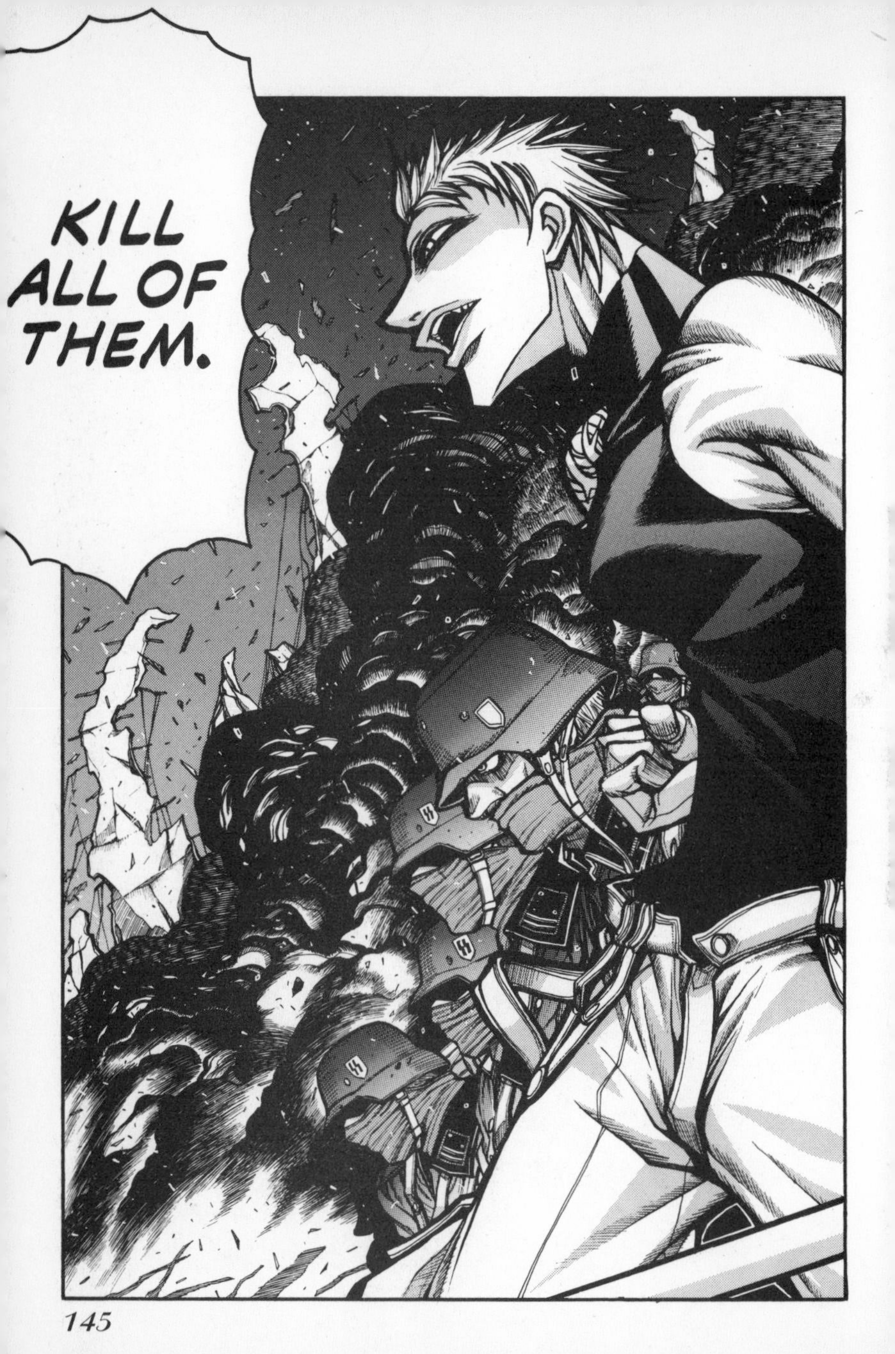
KILL ALL OF THEM.

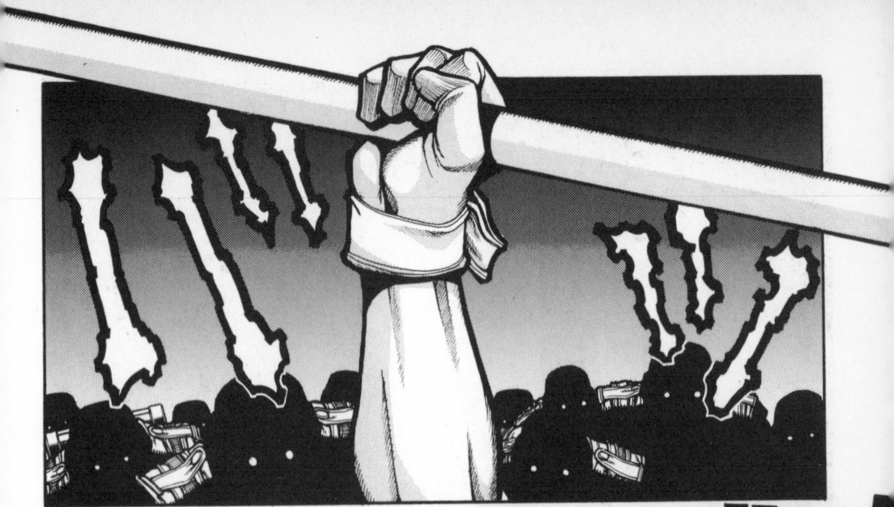

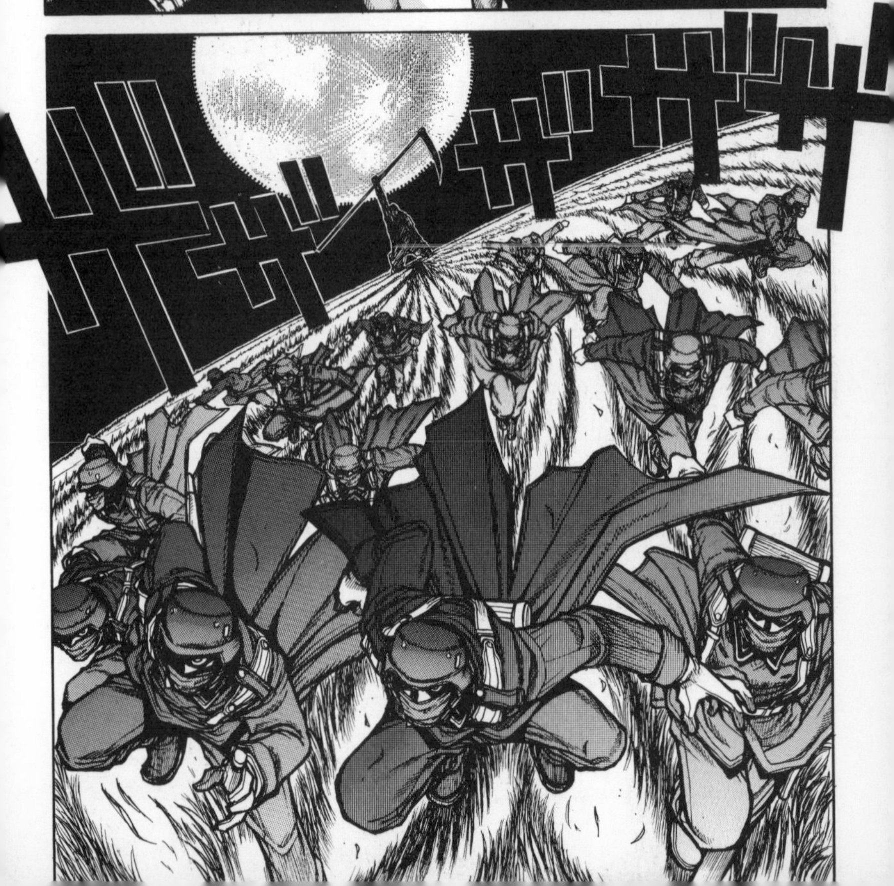

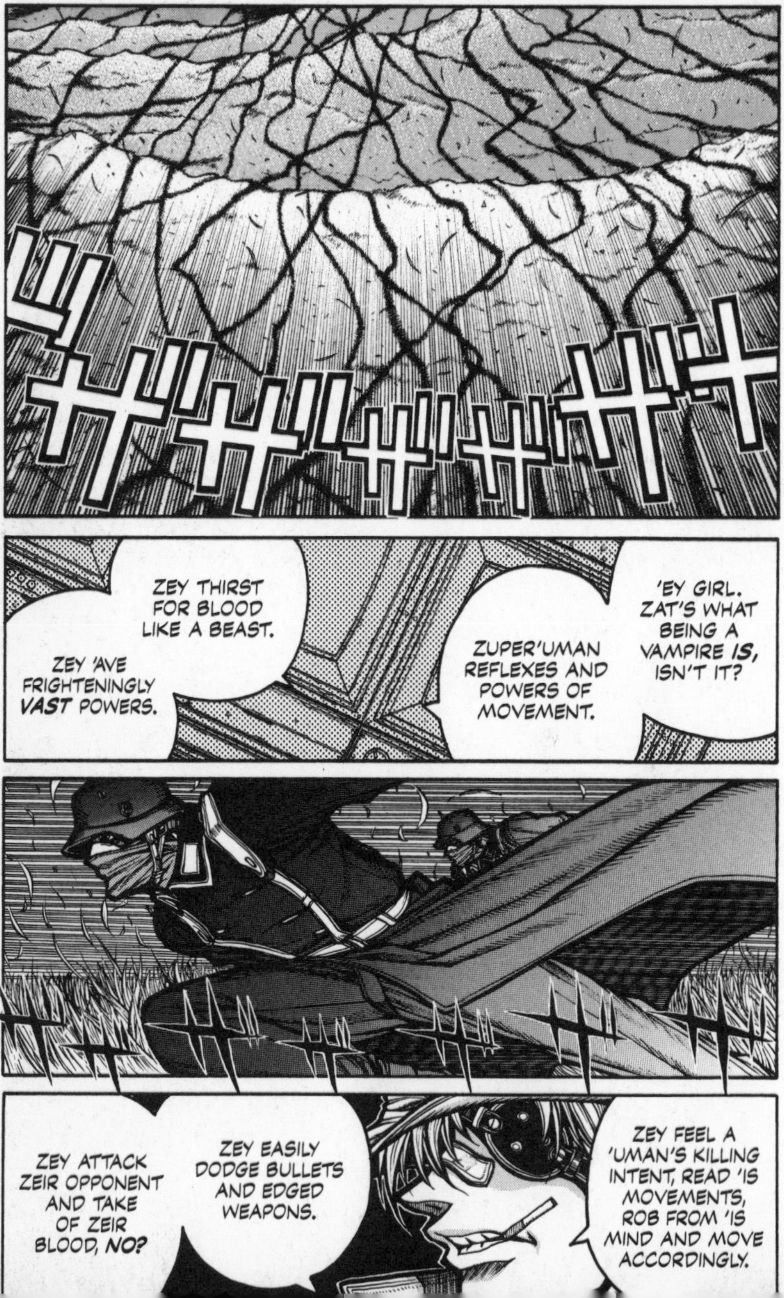
'EY GIRL. ZAT'S WHAT BEING A VAMPIRE *IS*, ISN'T IT?
ZUPER'UMAN REFLEXES AND POWERS OF MOVEMENT.
ZEY THIRST FOR BLOOD LIKE A BEAST.
ZEY 'AVE FRIGHTENINGLY *VAST* POWERS.
ZEY FEEL A 'UMAN'S KILLING INTENT, READ 'IS MOVEMENTS, ROB FROM 'IS MIND AND MOVE ACCORDINGLY.
ZEY EASILY DODGE BULLETS AND EDGED WEAPONS.
ZEY ATTACK ZEIR OPPONENT AND TAKE OF ZEIR BLOOD, *NO?*

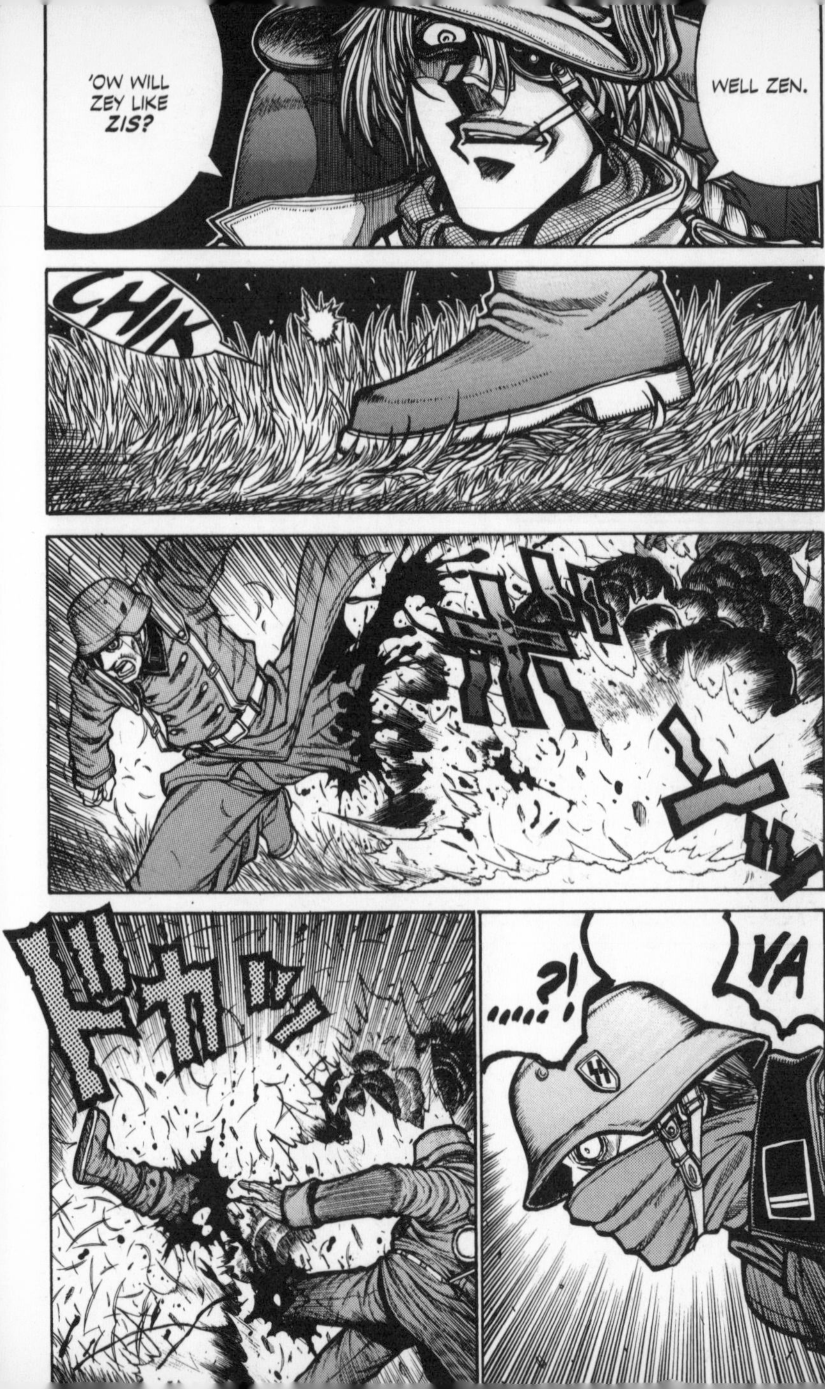
WELL ZEN.
'OW WILL ZEY LIKE ZIS?
CHIK
VA
.....?!

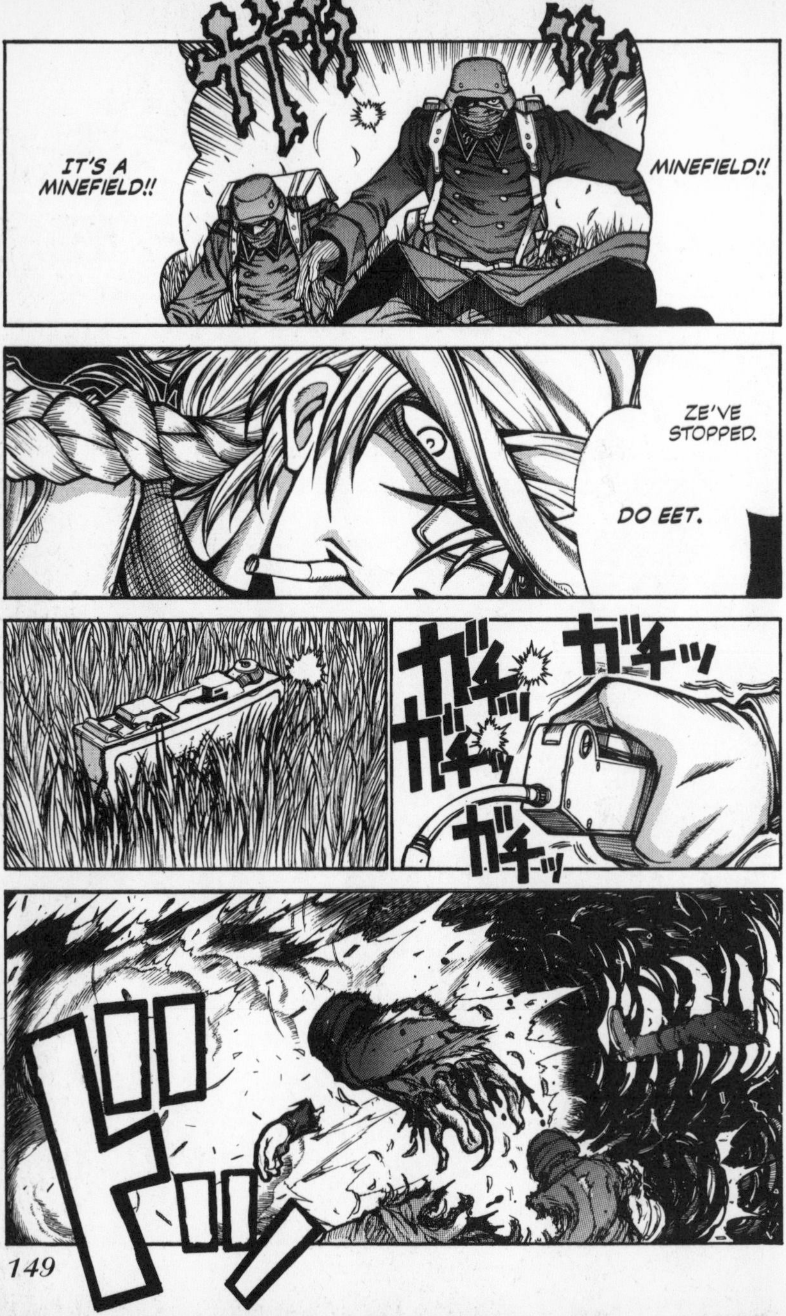
MINEFIELD!!
IT'S A MINEFIELD!!
ZE'VE STOPPED.
DO EET.
ガチッ
ガチッ
ガチッ
ガチッ

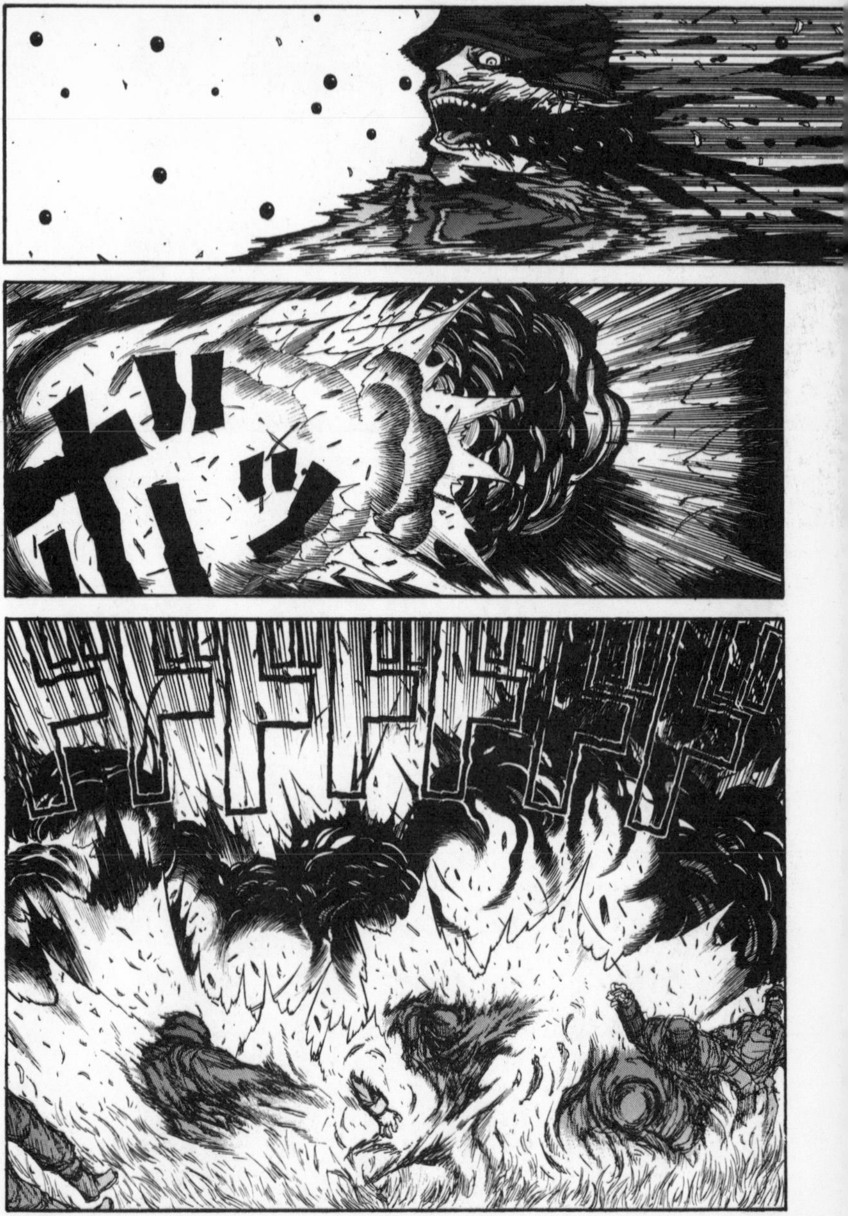
ボッ
ドドドドドドド

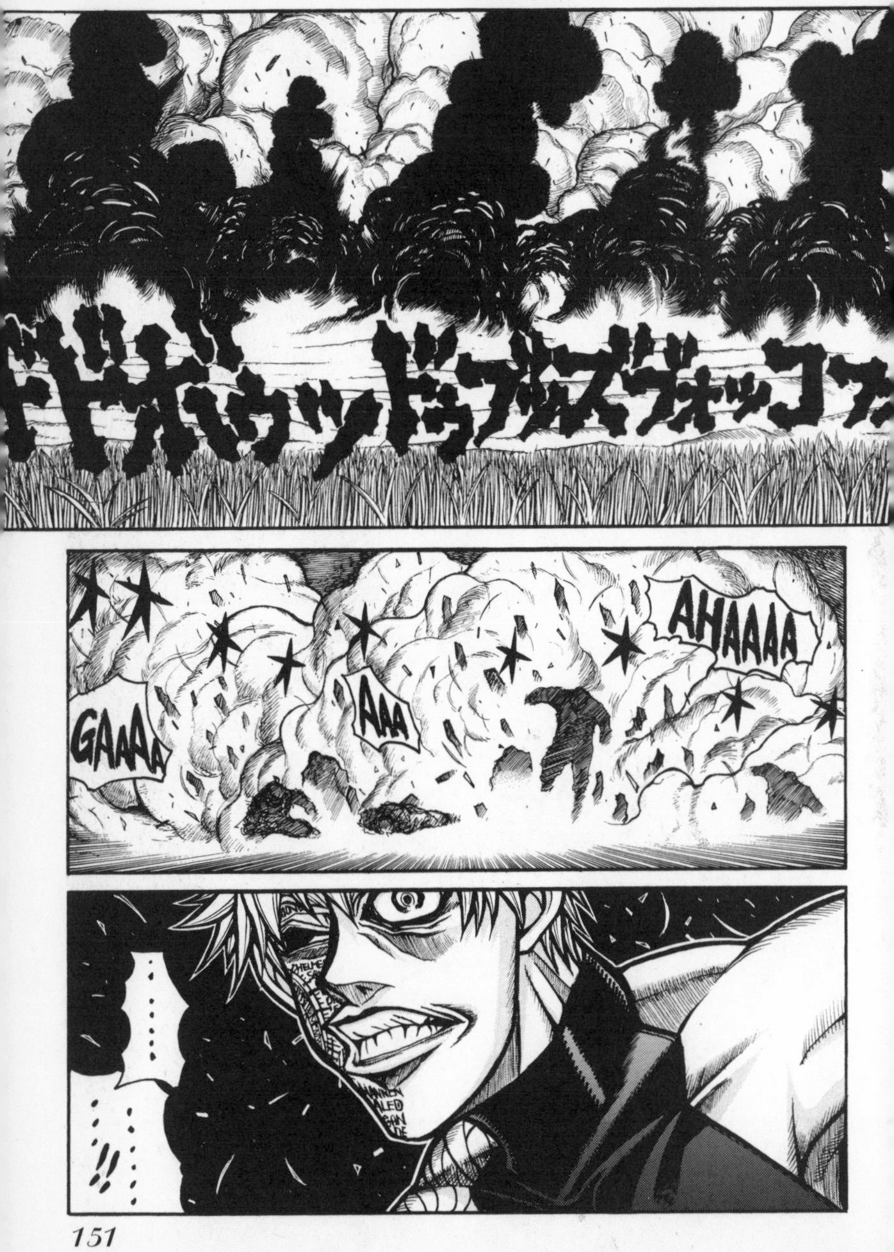
AHAAAA
AAA
GAAAA
……
……!!

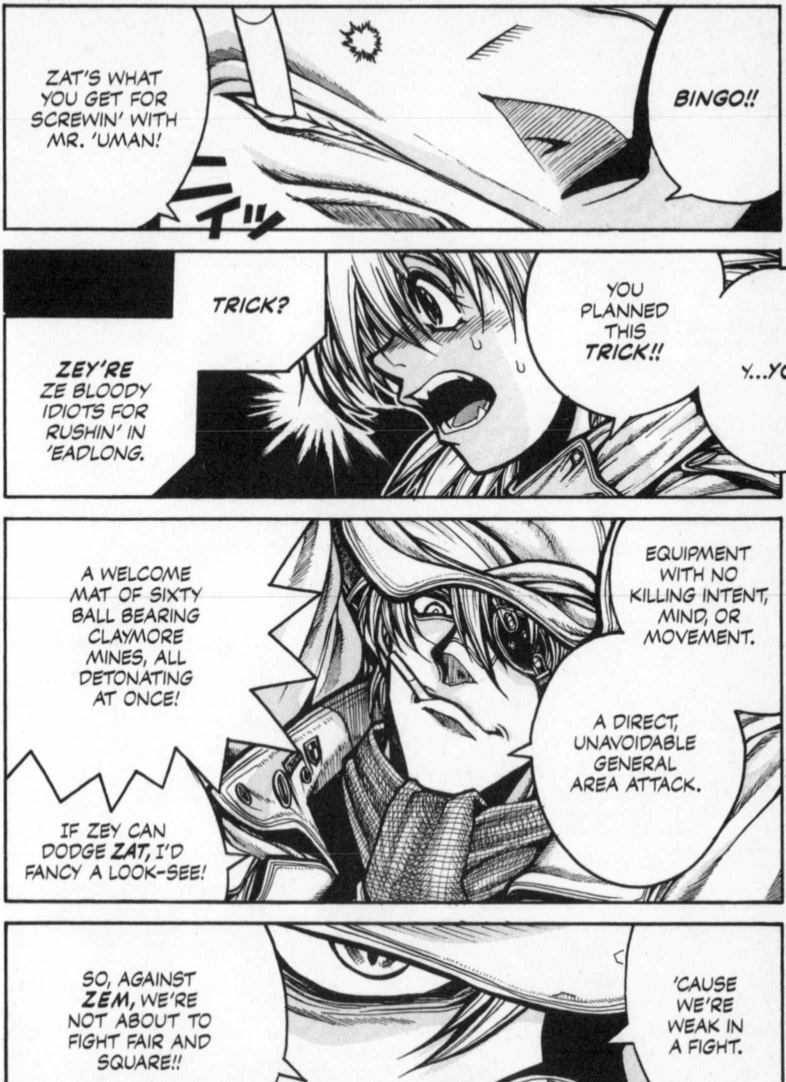
BINGO!!
ZAT'S WHAT YOU GET FOR SCREWIN' WITH MR. 'UMAN!
Y...YOU!
YOU PLANNED THIS TRICK!!
TRICK?
ZEY'RE ZE BLOODY IDIOTS FOR RUSHIN' IN 'EADLONG.
EQUIPMENT WITH NO KILLING INTENT, MIND, OR MOVEMENT.
A DIRECT, UNAVOIDABLE GENERAL AREA ATTACK.
A WELCOME MAT OF SIXTY BALL BEARING CLAYMORE MINES, ALL DETONATING AT ONCE!
IF ZEY CAN DODGE ZAT, I'D FANCY A LOOK-SEE!
'CAUSE WE'RE WEAK IN A FIGHT.
SO, AGAINST ZEM, WE'RE NOT ABOUT TO FIGHT FAIR AND SQUARE!!

TO BE CONTINUED

ORDER 8 / END

ORDER 9

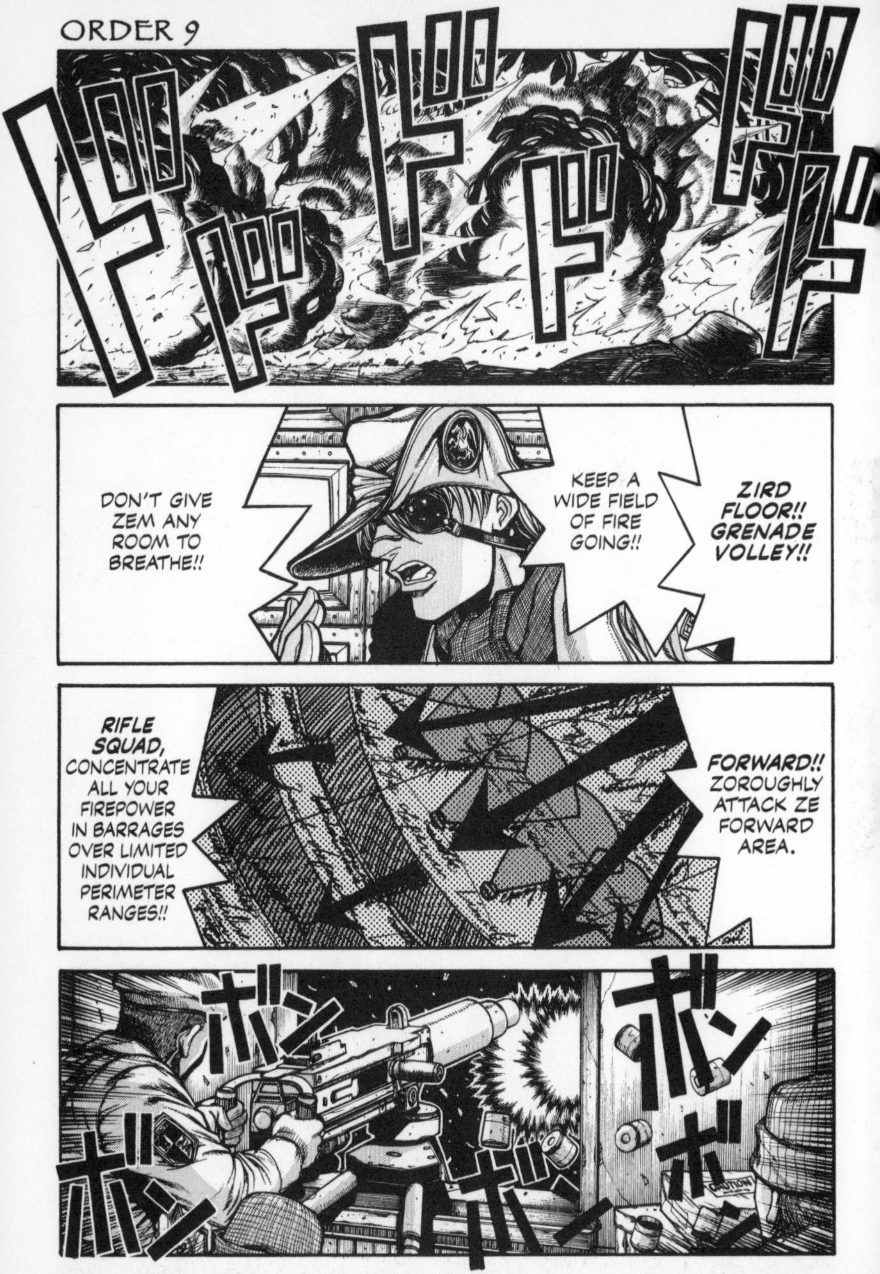
ドドドドドドド
ZIRD FLOOR!! GRENADE VOLLEY!!
KEEP A WIDE FIELD OF FIRE GOING!!
DON'T GIVE ZEM ANY ROOM TO BREATHE!!
FORWARD!! ZOROUGHLY ATTACK ZE FORWARD AREA.
RIFLE SQUAD, CONCENTRATE ALL YOUR FIREPOWER IN BARRAGES OVER LIMITED INDIVIDUAL PERIMETER RANGES!!
ボン
ボン
ボン
ボン
ボン

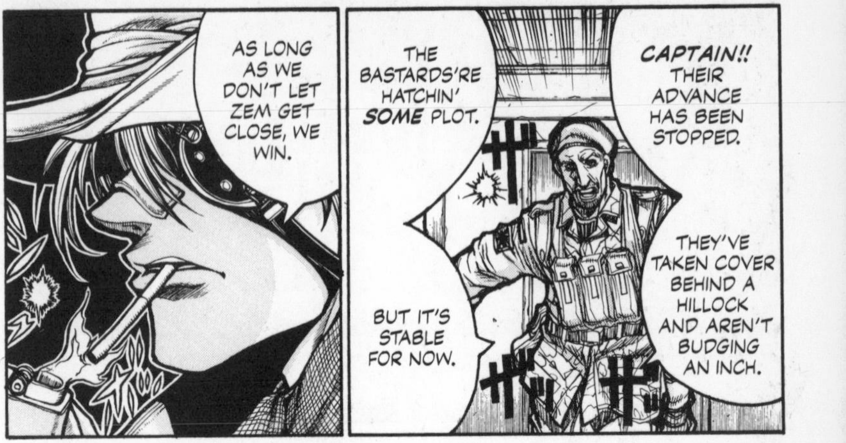
CAPTAIN!! THEIR ADVANCE HAS BEEN STOPPED.
THEY'VE TAKEN COVER BEHIND A HILLOCK AND AREN'T BUDGING AN INCH.
THE BASTARDS'RE HATCHIN' SOME PLOT.
BUT IT'S STABLE FOR NOW.
AS LONG AS WE DON'T LET ZEM GET CLOSE, WE WIN.

⚜ORDER 9

SOLDIER OF FORTUNE②

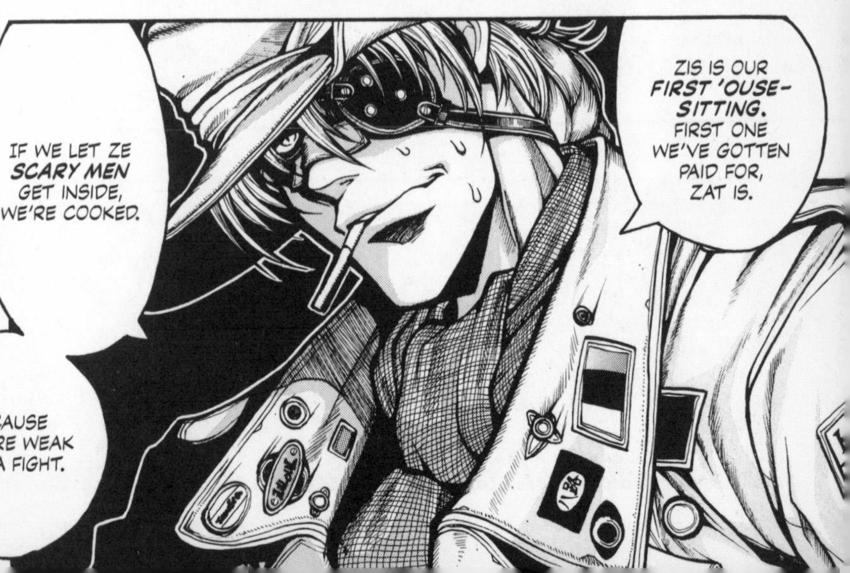
ZIS IS OUR FIRST 'OUSE-SITTING. FIRST ONE WE'VE GOTTEN PAID FOR, ZAT IS.
IF WE LET ZE SCARY MEN GET INSIDE, WE'RE COOKED.
'CAUSE WE'RE WEAK IN A FIGHT.

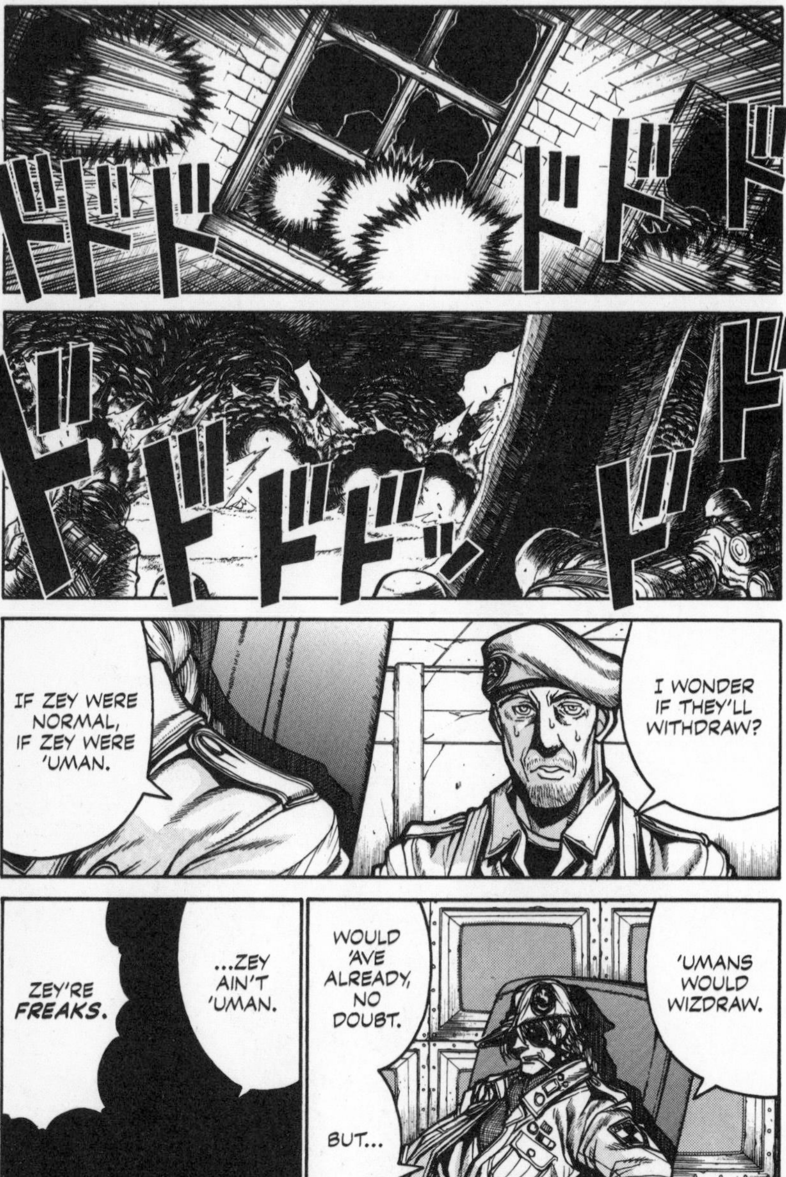
ドドド
ドドド
ドドド
ドドドドド
I WONDER IF THEY'LL WITHDRAW?
IF ZEY WERE NORMAL, IF ZEY WERE 'UMAN.
'UMANS WOULD WIZDRAW.
WOULD 'AVE ALREADY, NO DOUBT.
BUT...
...ZEY AIN'T 'UMAN.
ZEY'RE **FREAKS**.

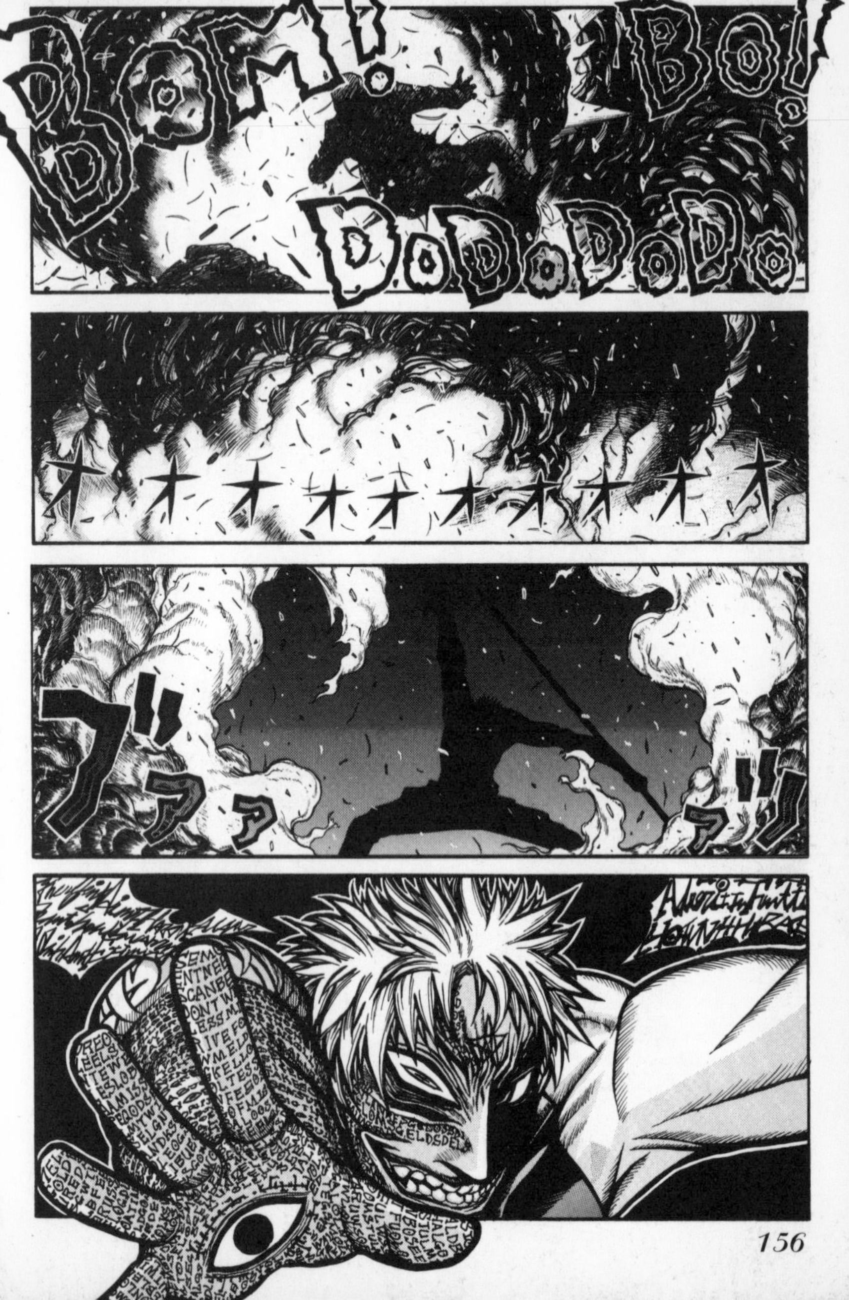
BO!
BOOM!
DODODODODO
オォォォォォォォォォ
ブァァ
ブァ

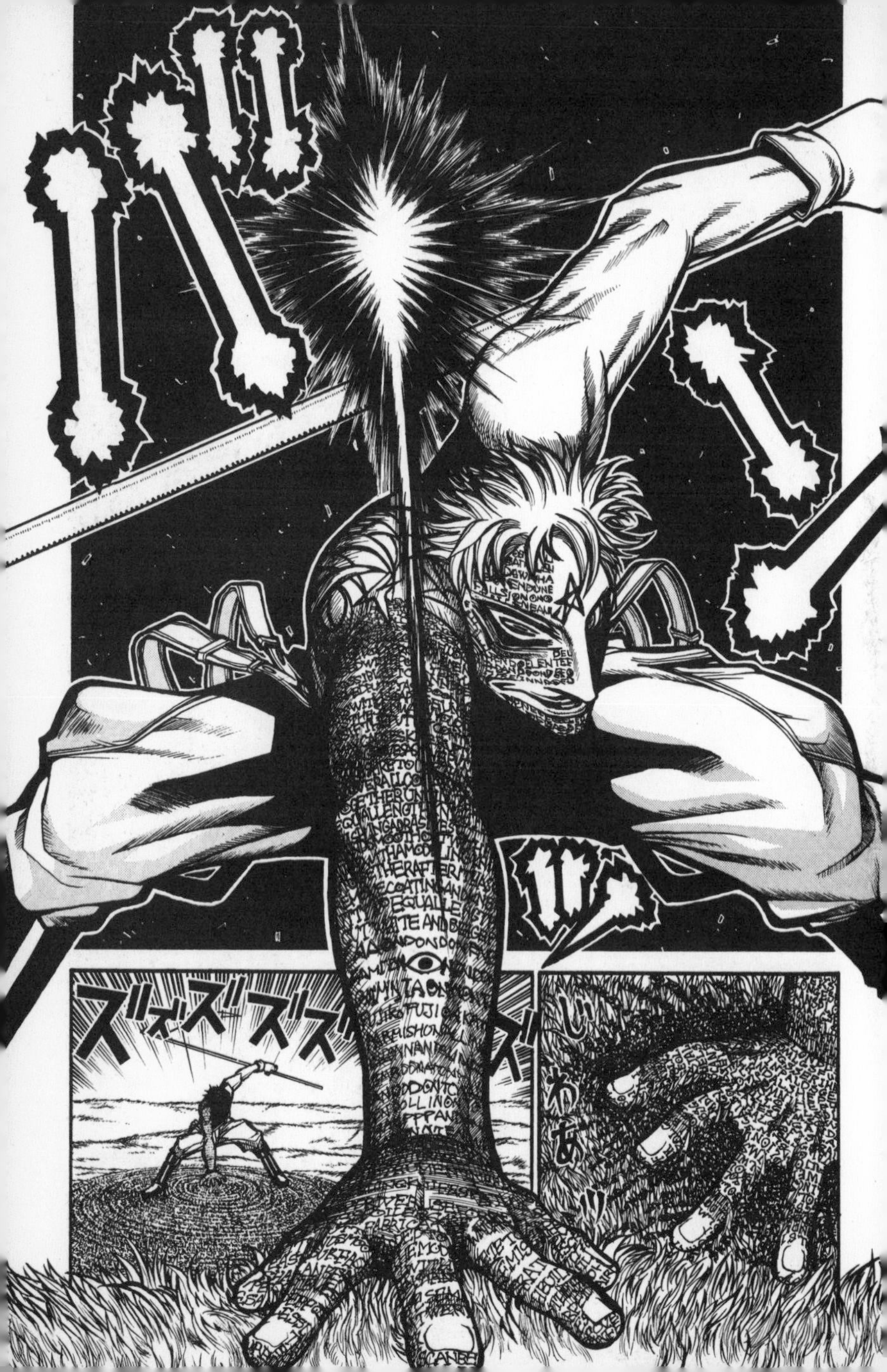
じわぁ
ズォズズズズ

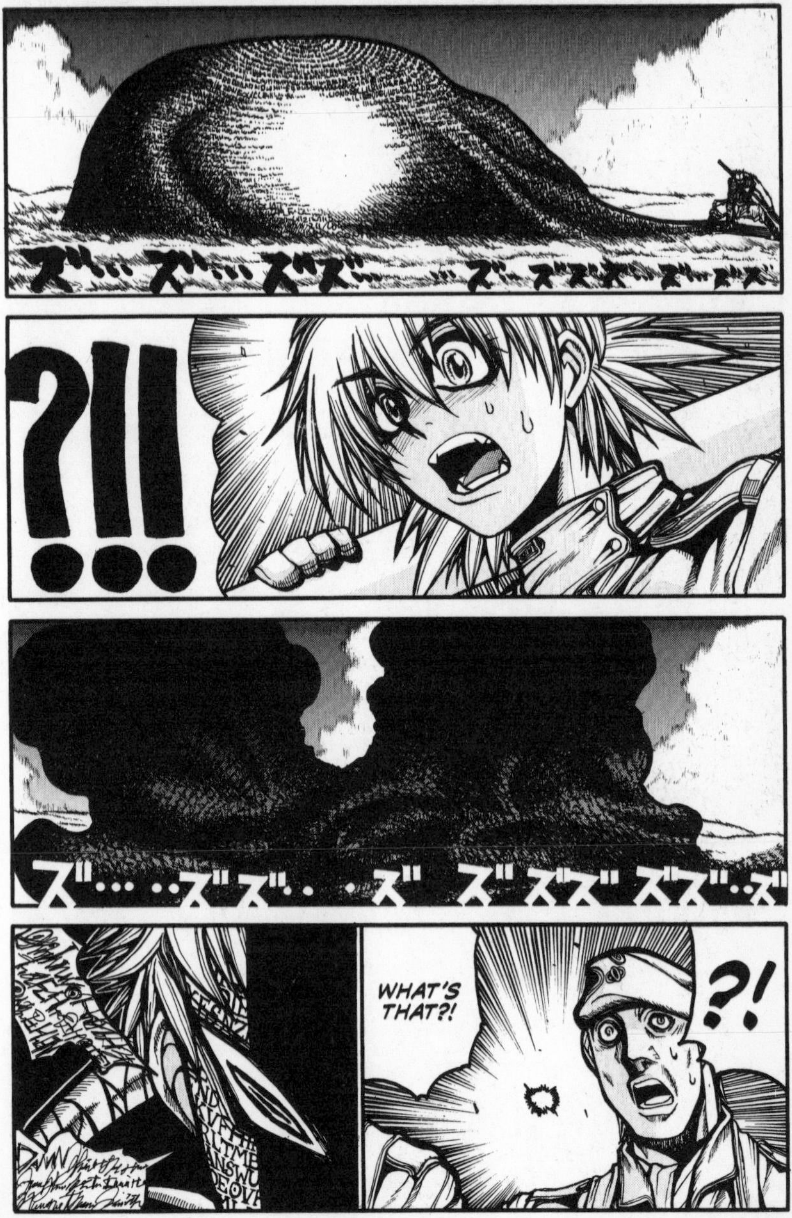
ズ… ズ… ズズ… ズ… ズズズ…ズ…ズズ
?!!
ズ… …ズズ… …ズ ズズズ ズズ…ズ
WHAT'S THAT?!
?!

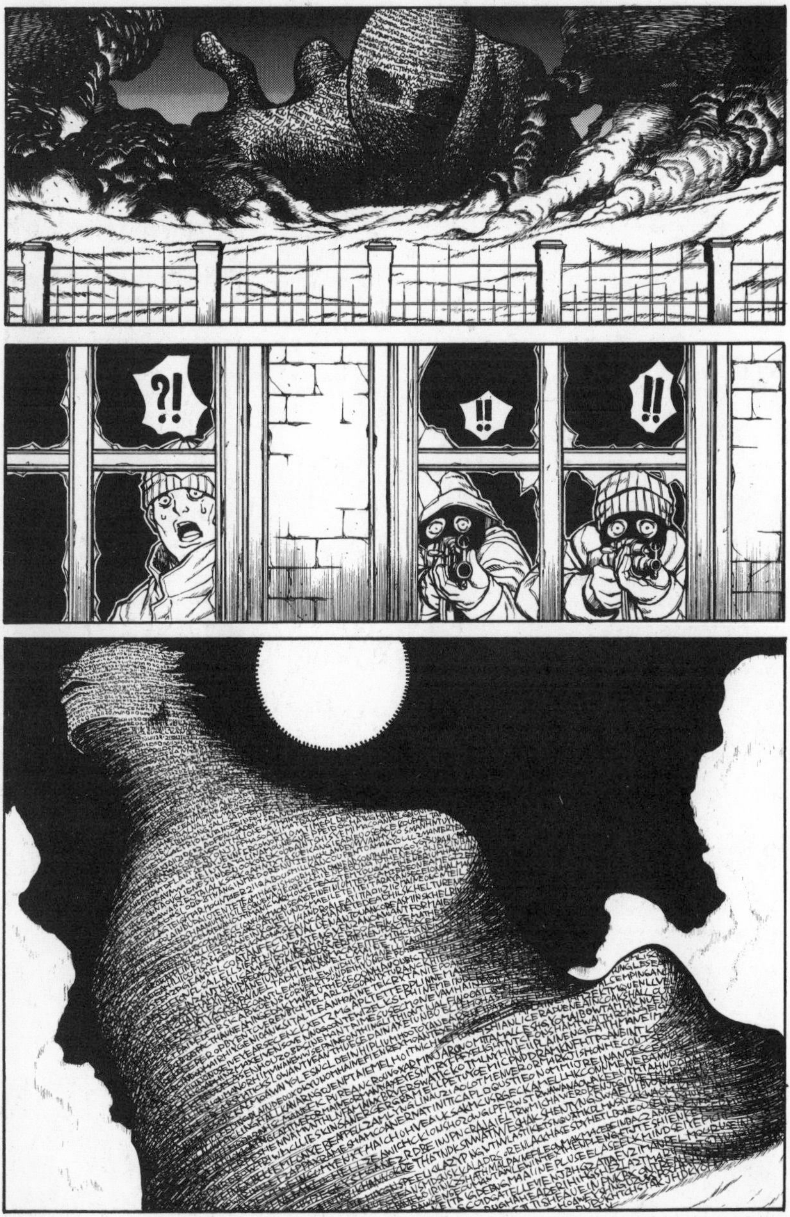
!!
!!
?!

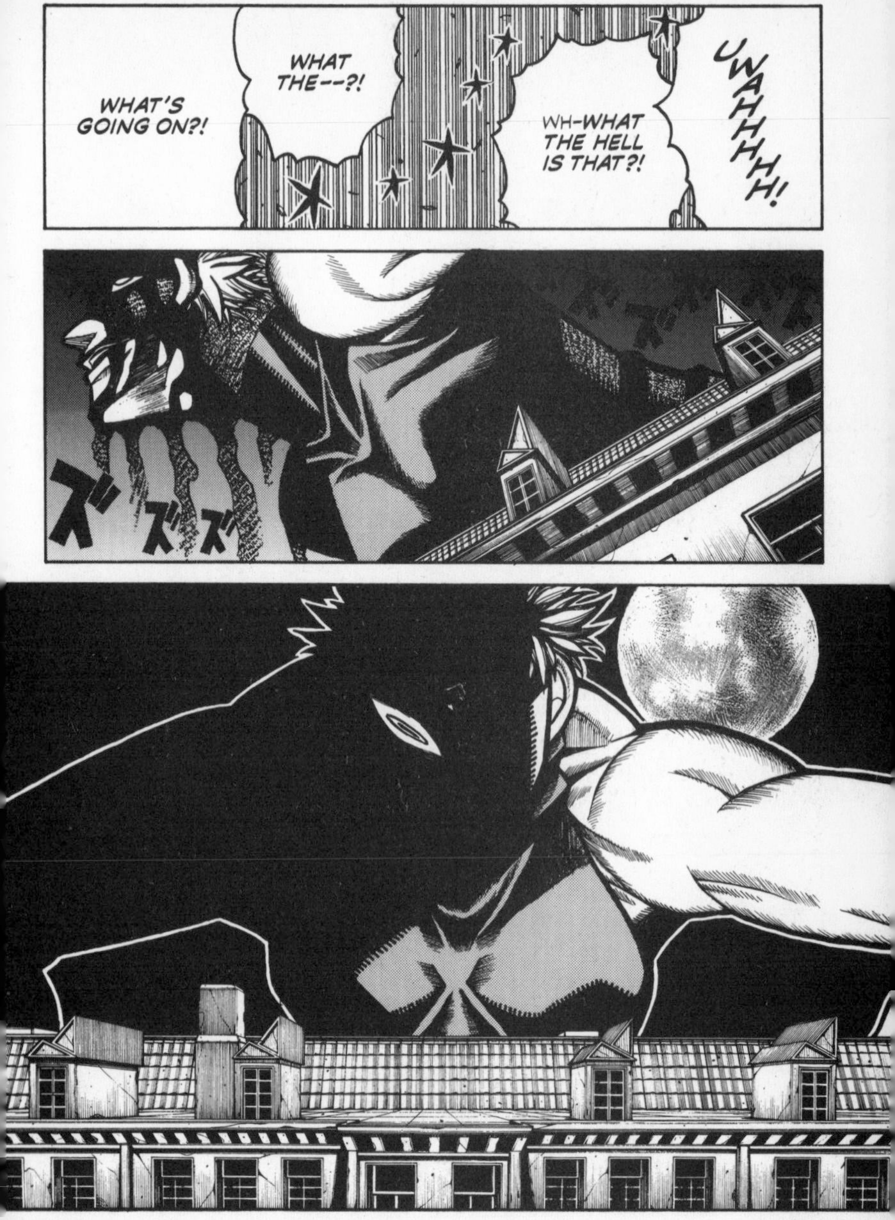
UWAHHHHH!
WH-WHAT THE HELL IS THAT?!
WHAT THE--?!
WHAT'S GOING ON?!
ズズズ

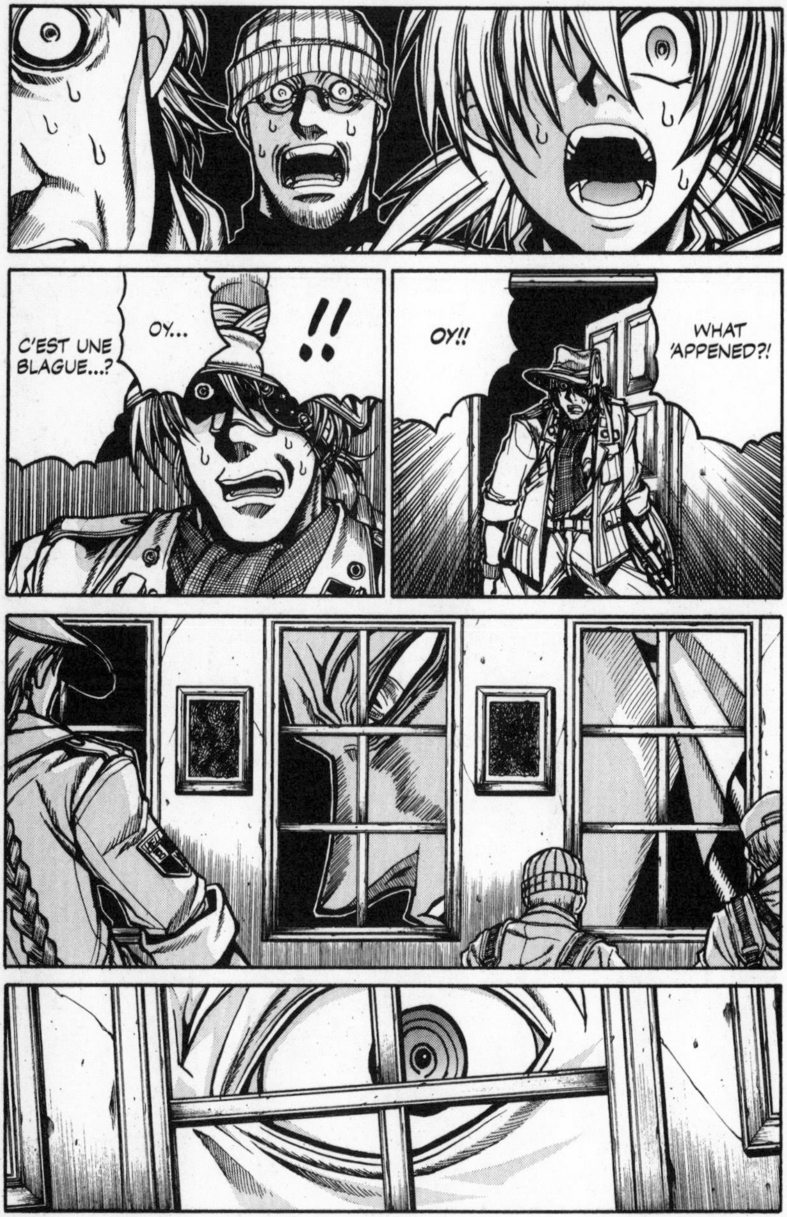
WHAT 'APPENED?!
OY!!
!!
OY...
C'EST UNE BLAGUE...?

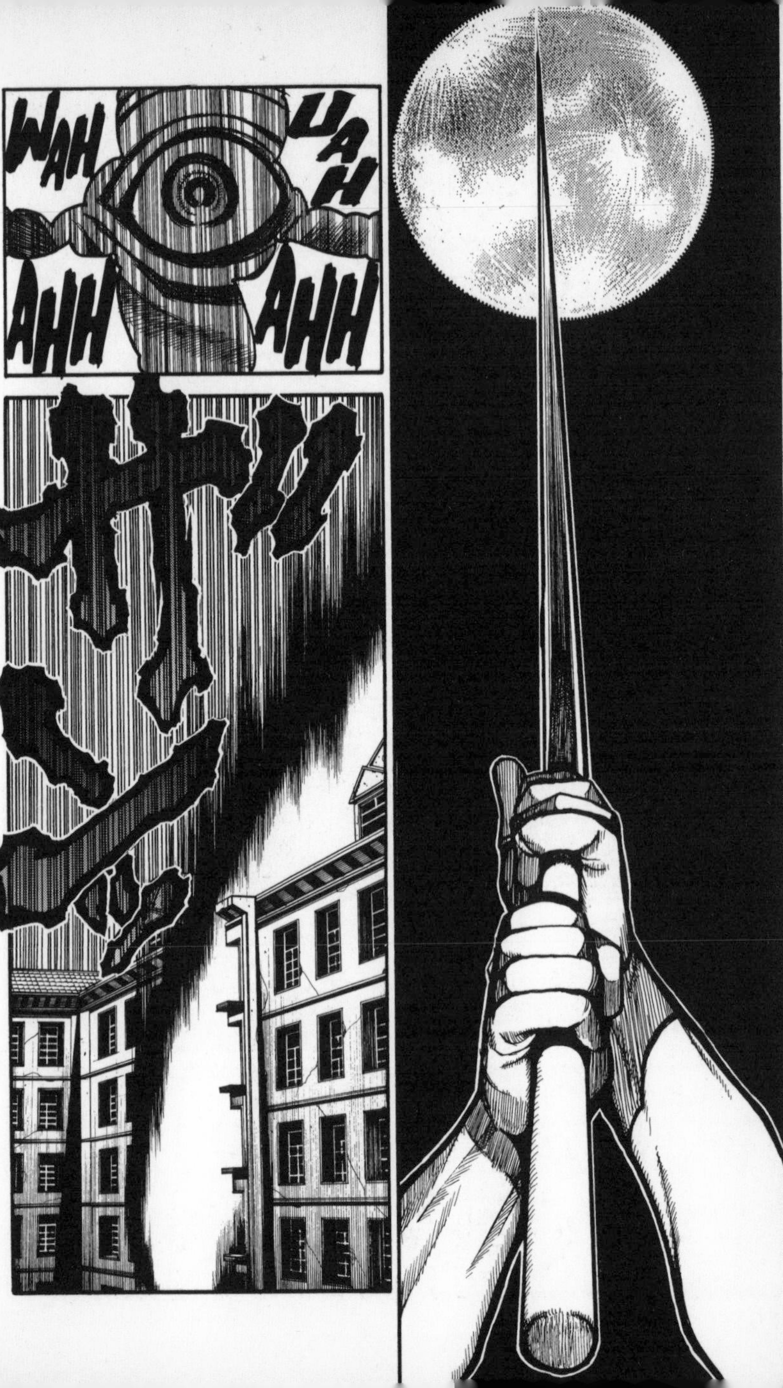
UAH
WAH
AHH
AHH

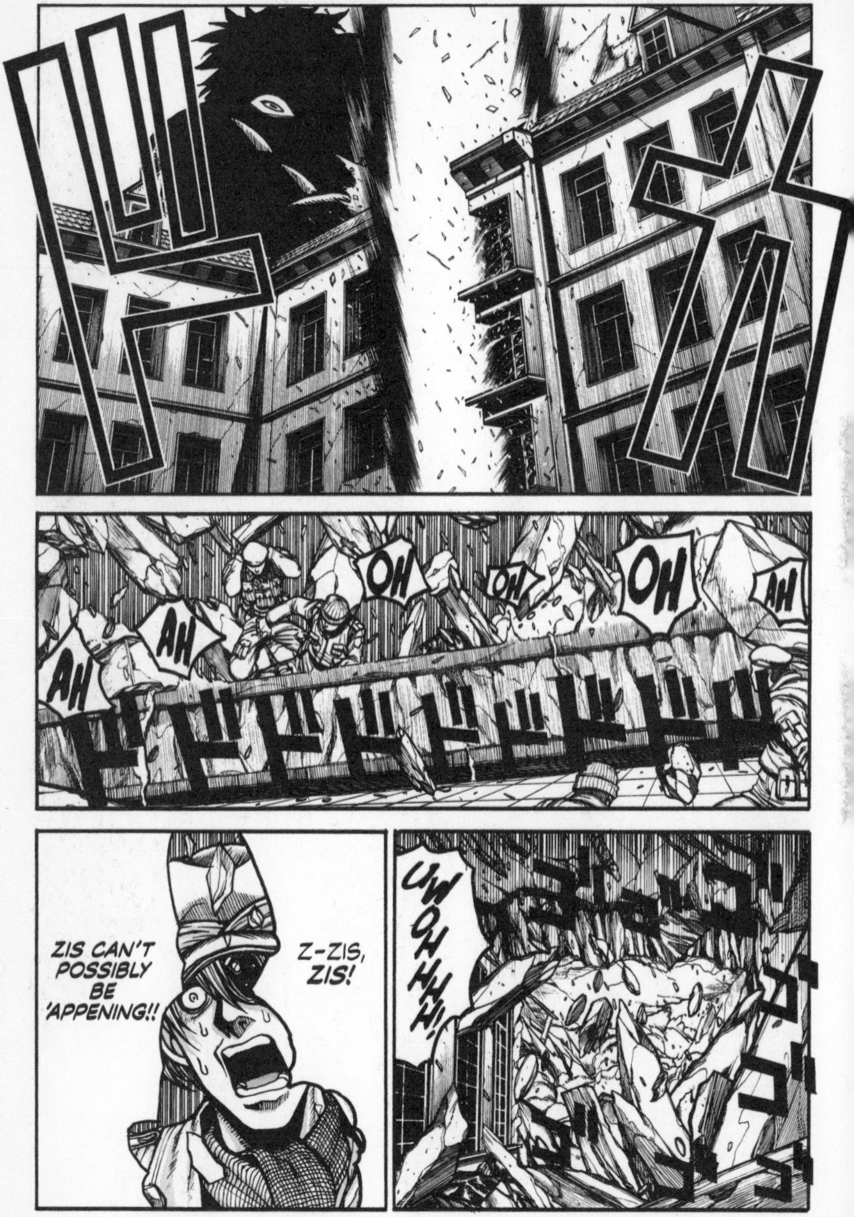
AH
OH
OH
OH
AH
AH
AH
UWOHHHH!!
Z-ZIS, ZIS!
ZIS CAN'T POSSIBLY BE 'APPENING!!

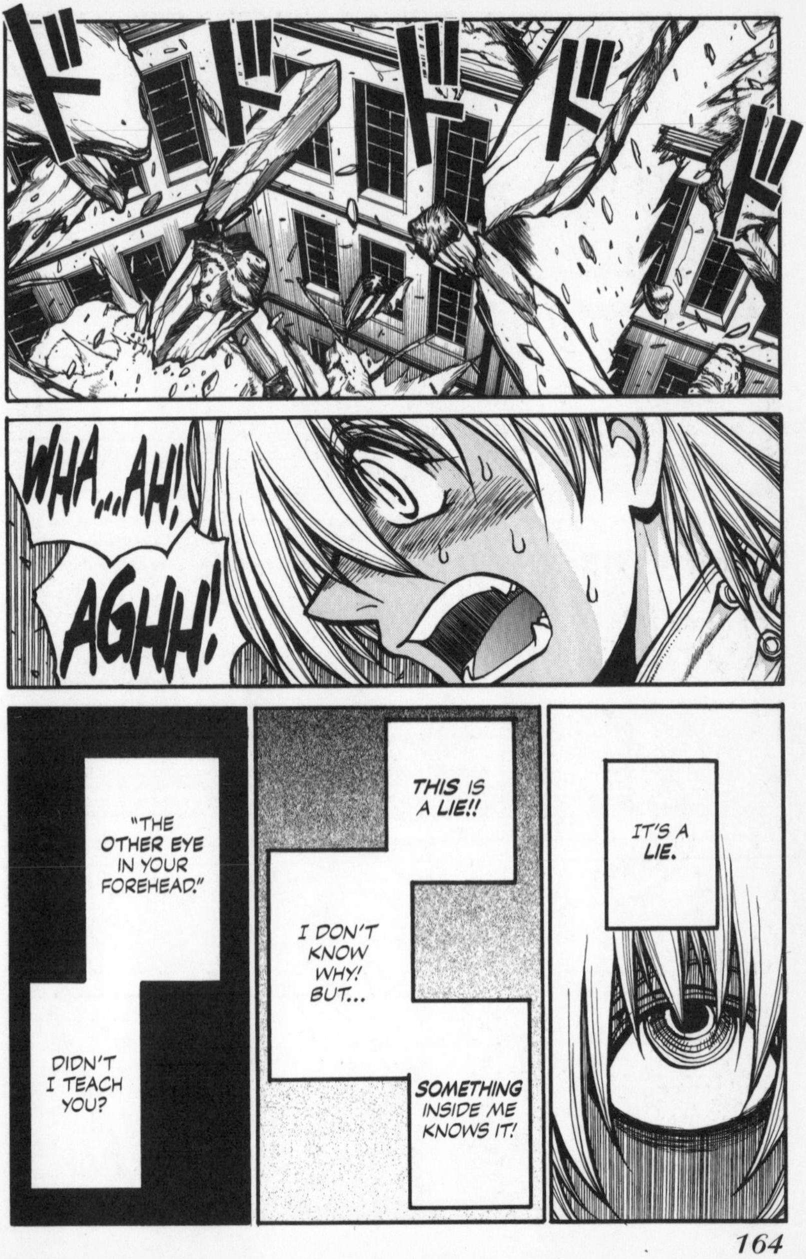
ドドドドド
WHA...AH!
AGHH!
IT'S A LIE.
THIS IS A LIE!!
I DON'T KNOW WHY! BUT...
SOMETHING INSIDE ME KNOWS IT!
"THE OTHER EYE IN YOUR FOREHEAD."
DIDN'T I TEACH YOU?

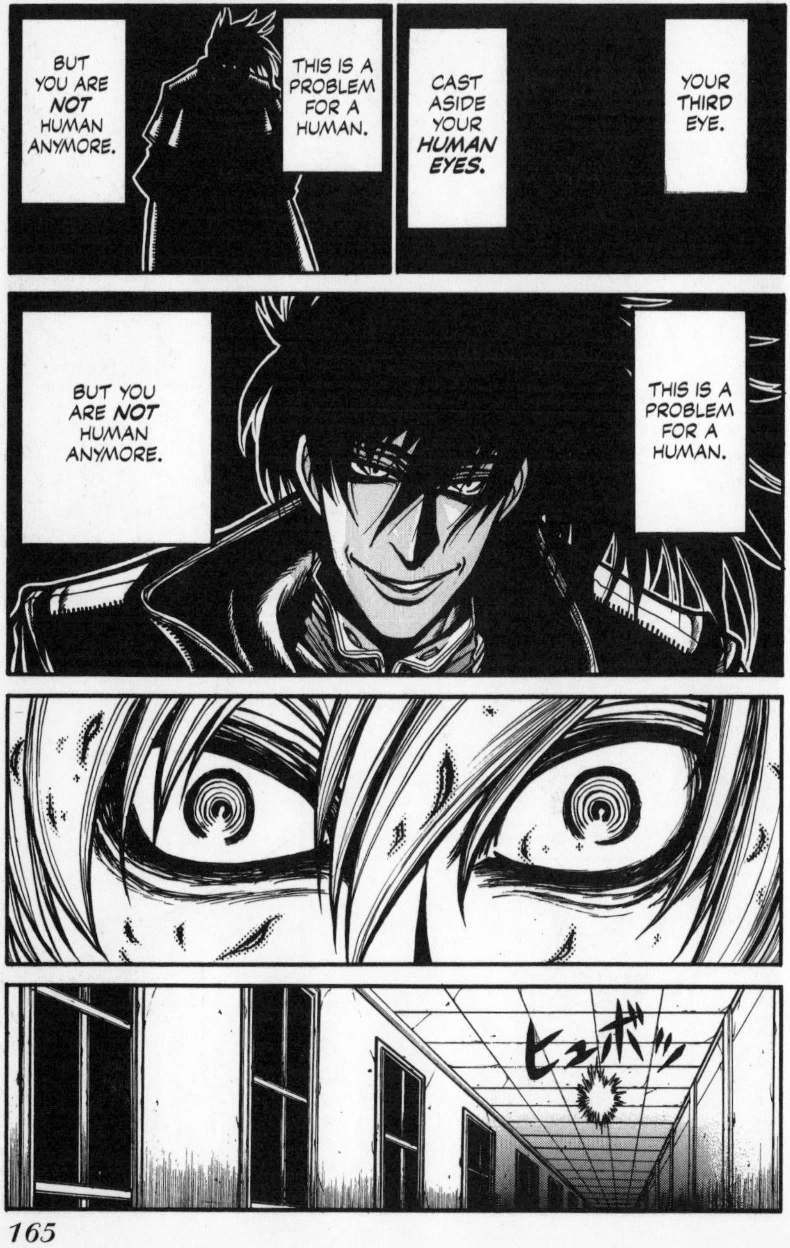
YOUR THIRD EYE.
CAST ASIDE YOUR *HUMAN EYES.*
THIS IS A PROBLEM FOR A HUMAN.
BUT YOU ARE *NOT* HUMAN ANYMORE.
THIS IS A PROBLEM FOR A HUMAN.
BUT YOU ARE *NOT* HUMAN ANYMORE.
ヒュボッ

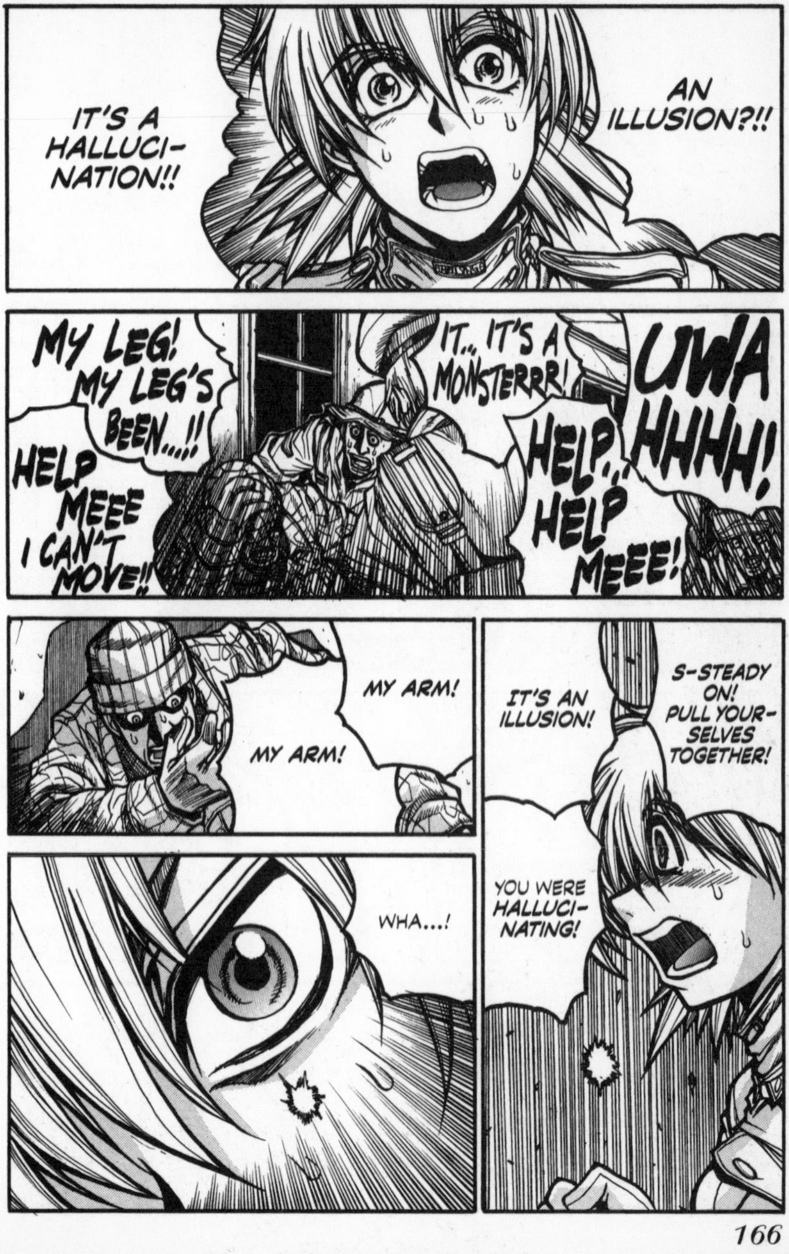
AN ILLUSION?!!
IT'S A HALLUCINATION!!
UWAHHHH!
HELP... HELP MEEE!
IT.., IT'S A MONSTERRR!
MY LEG! MY LEG'S BEEN...!!
HELP MEEE I CAN'T MOVE!!
S-STEADY ON! PULL YOURSELVES TOGETHER!
IT'S AN ILLUSION!
YOU WERE HALLUCINATING!
MY ARM!
MY ARM!
WHA...!

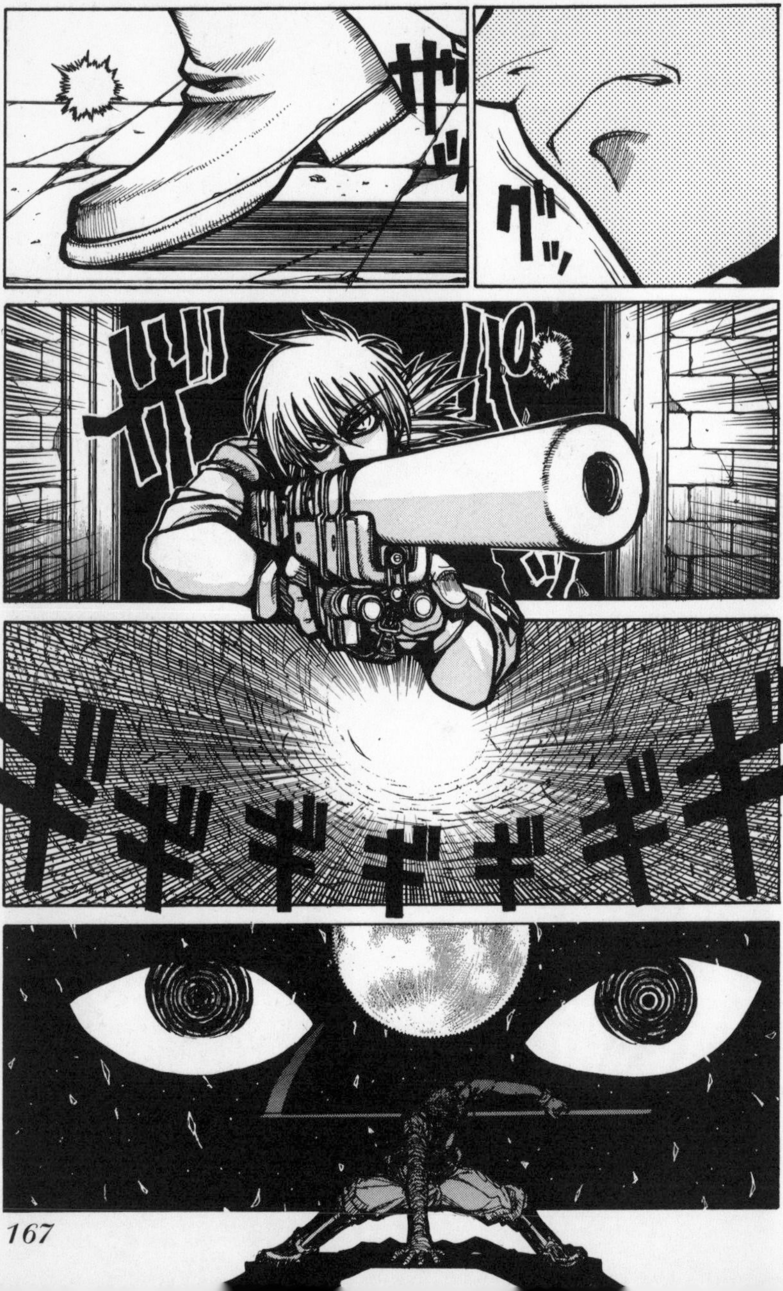
グッ
ザッ
パッ
ガッ
ギギギギギギギ

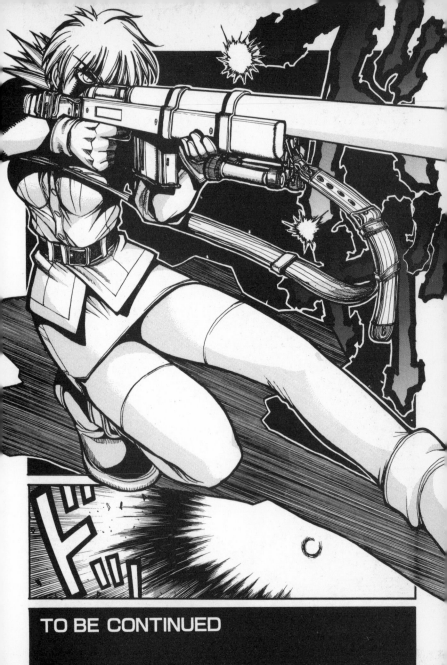

TO BE CONTINUED

ORDER 9 / END

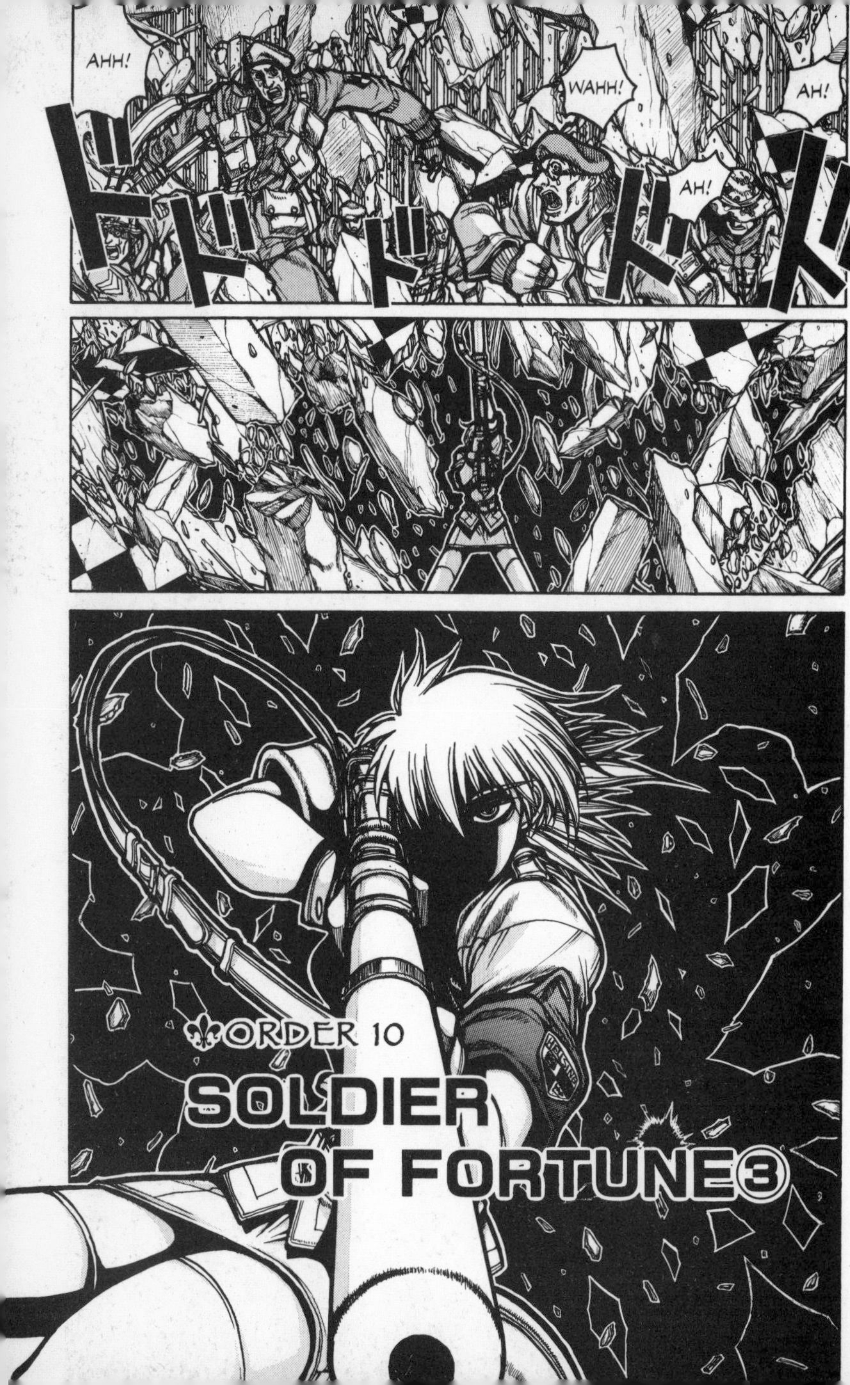
AH!
WAHH!
AH!
AHH!
ORDER 10
SOLDIER
OF FORTUNE 3

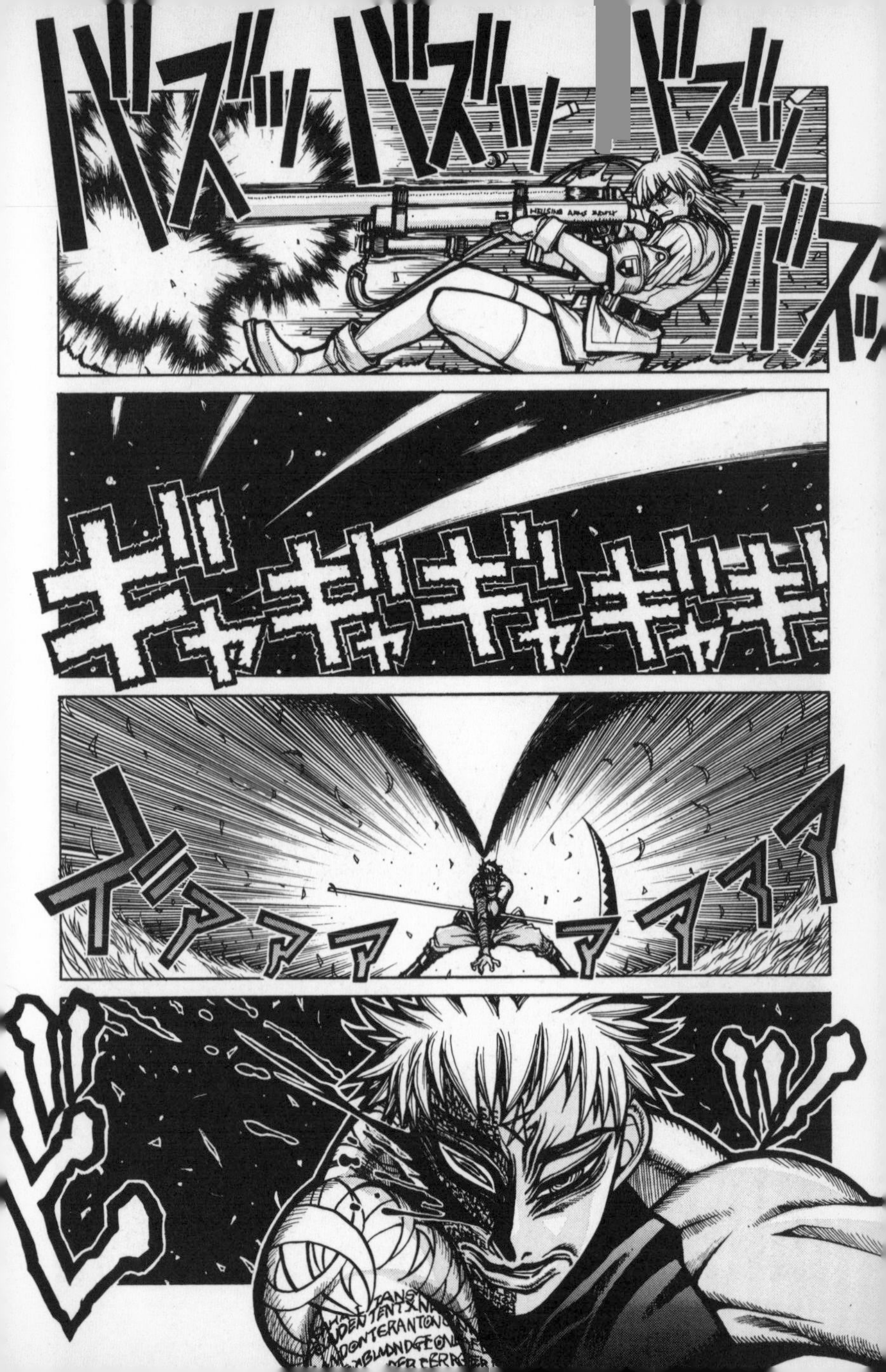
バズッ
バズッ
バズッ
バズッ
ギャギャギャギャギ
イァァァァアアア
ビッ

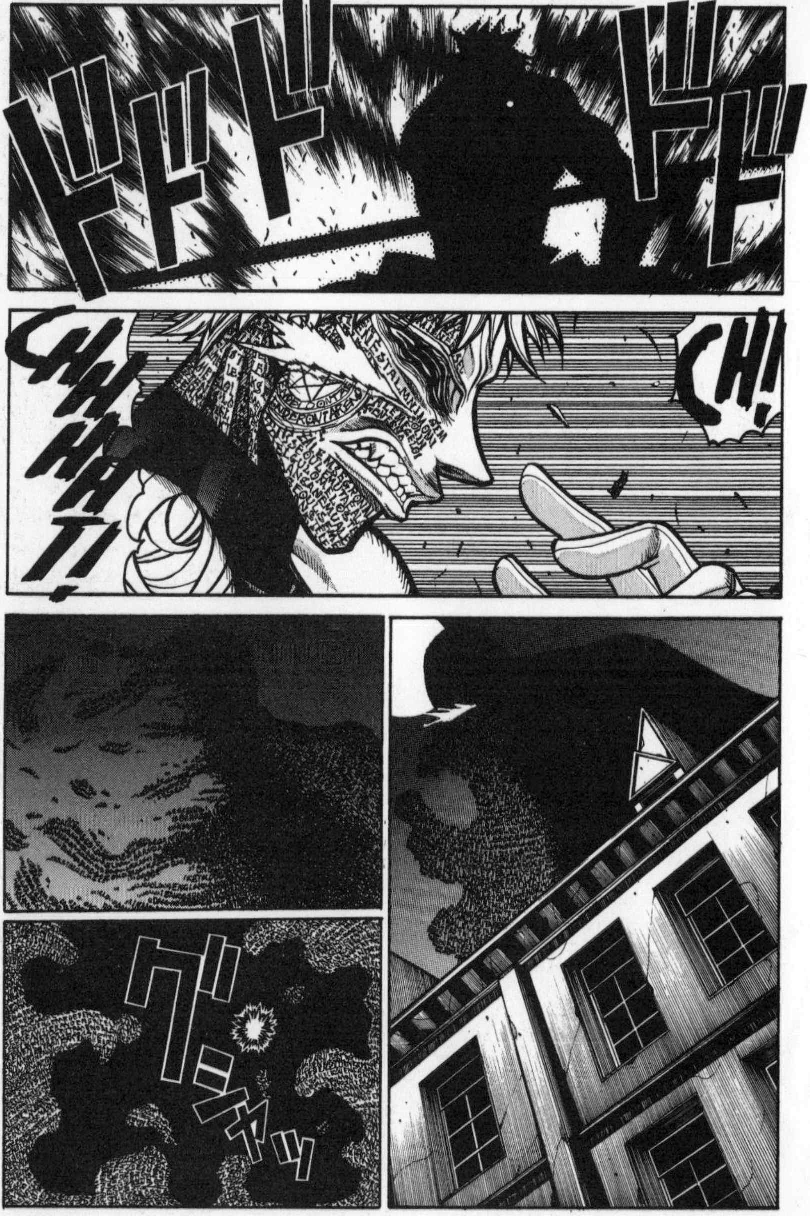
ドド
ドドド
CH!!
CHHAATT!
グニャッ

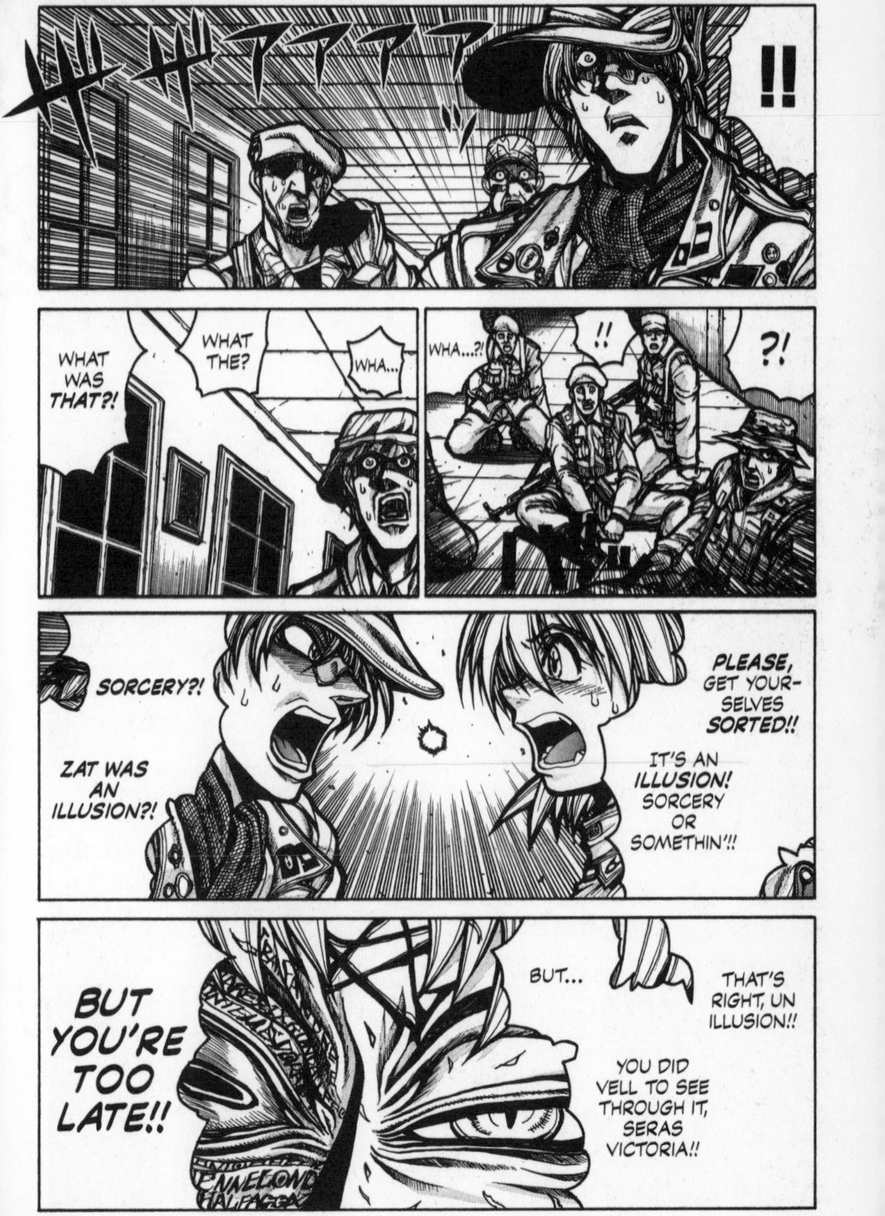
ザザアアアア
!!
?!
!!
WHA...?!
WHA...
WHAT THE?
WHAT WAS THAT?!
PLEASE, GET YOUR-SELVES SORTED!!
IT'S AN ILLUSION! SORCERY OR SOMETHIN'!!
SORCERY?!
ZAT WAS AN ILLUSION?!
THAT'S RIGHT, UN ILLUSION!!
BUT...
YOU DID VELL TO SEE THROUGH IT, SERAS VICTORIA!!
BUT YOU'RE TOO LATE!!

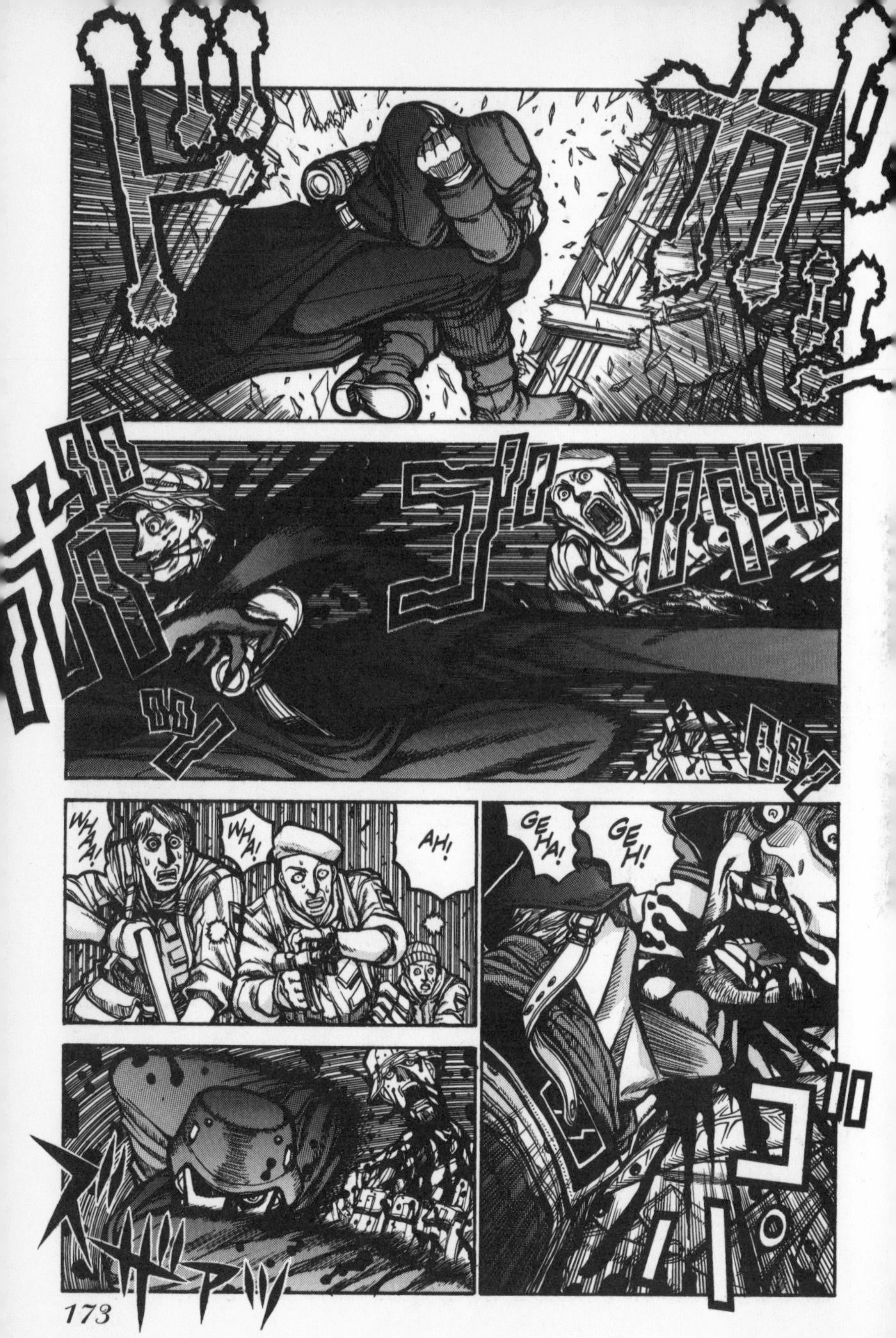
GEH!
GEHA!
AH!
WHA!
WHAA!

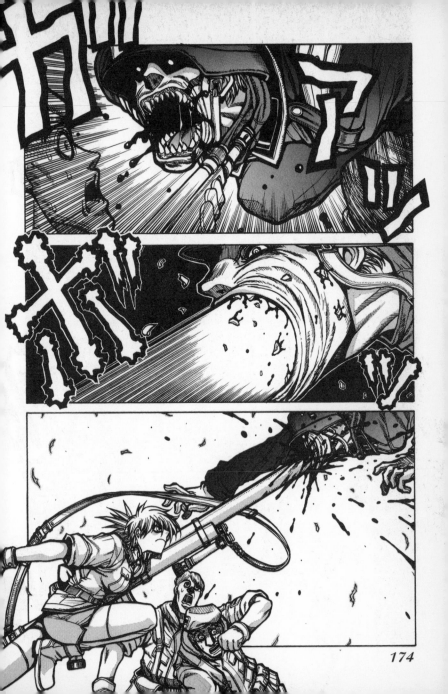

174

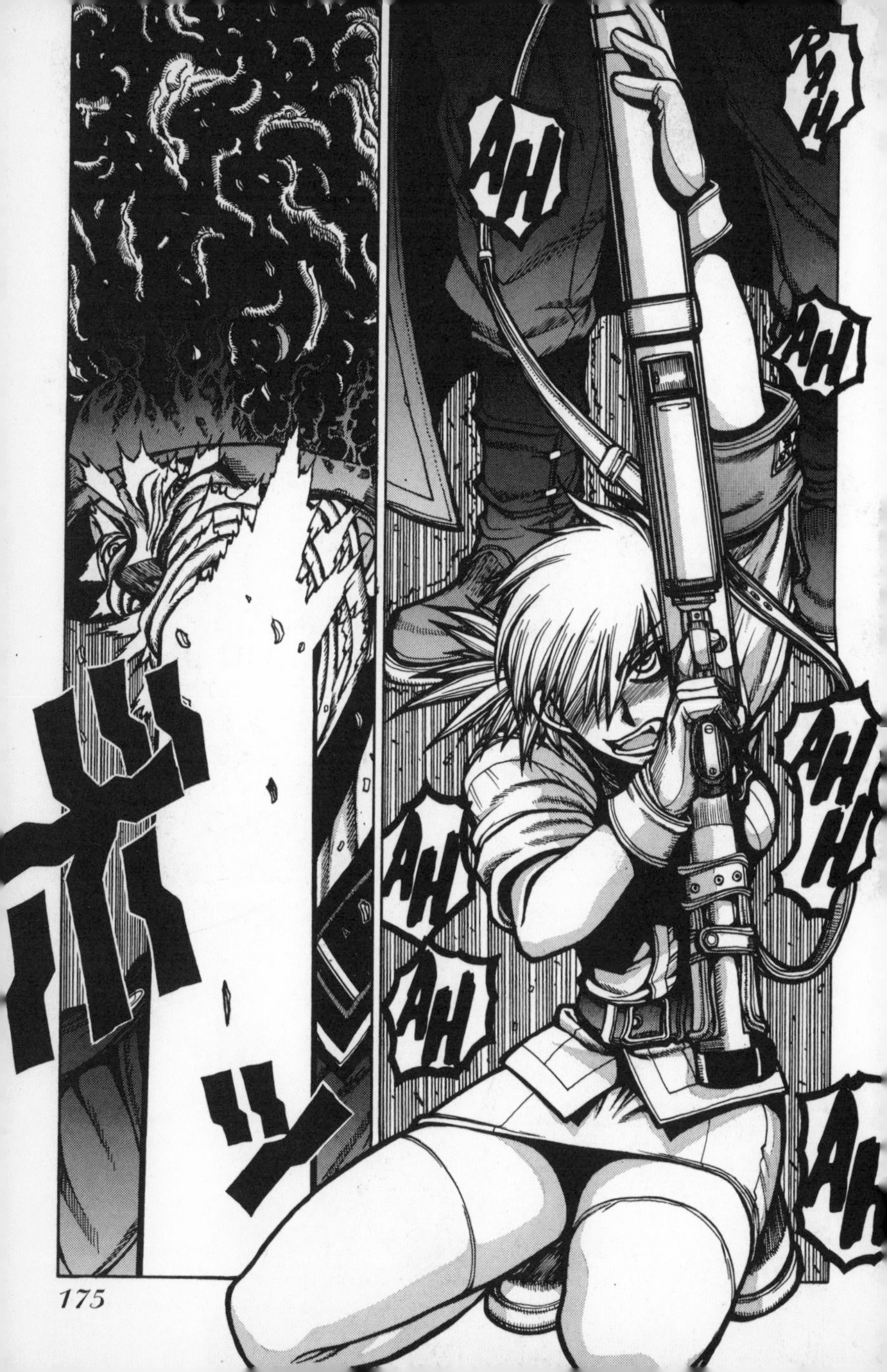
RAAH
AH
AH
AHH
AH
AH
AAH

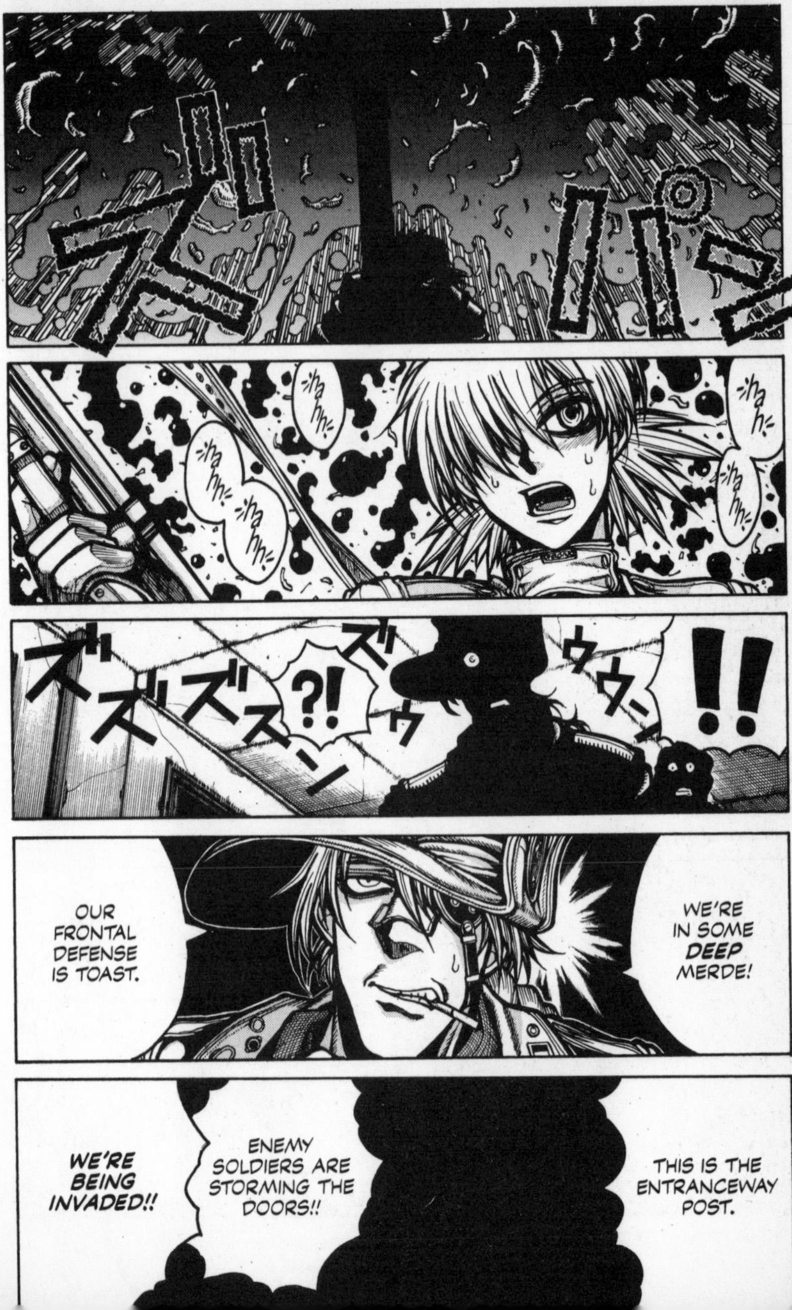
hah
hahh
hahh
hahh
hahh
?!
!!
WE'RE IN SOME *DEEP* MERDE!
OUR FRONTAL DEFENSE IS TOAST.
THIS IS THE ENTRANCEWAY POST.
ENEMY SOLDIERS ARE STORMING THE DOORS!!
WE'RE BEING INVADED!!

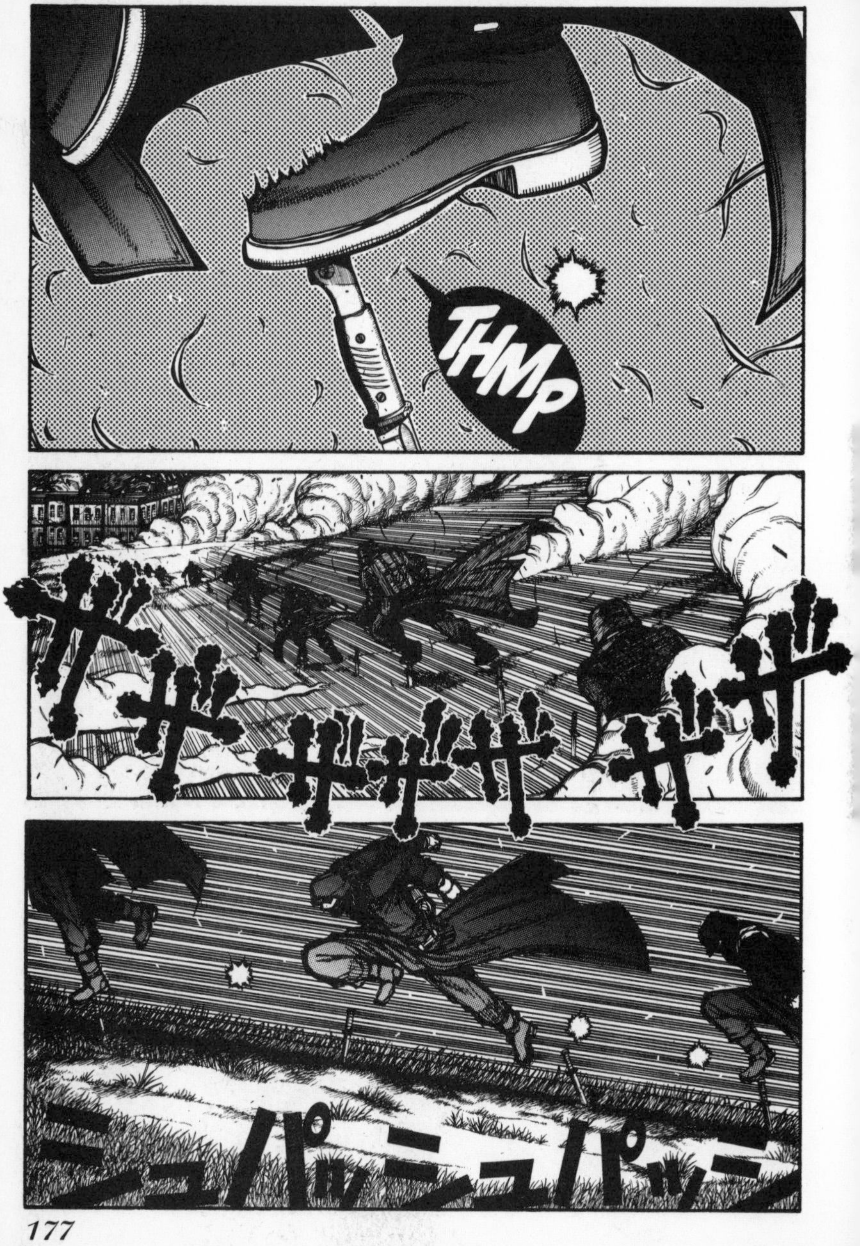
THMP

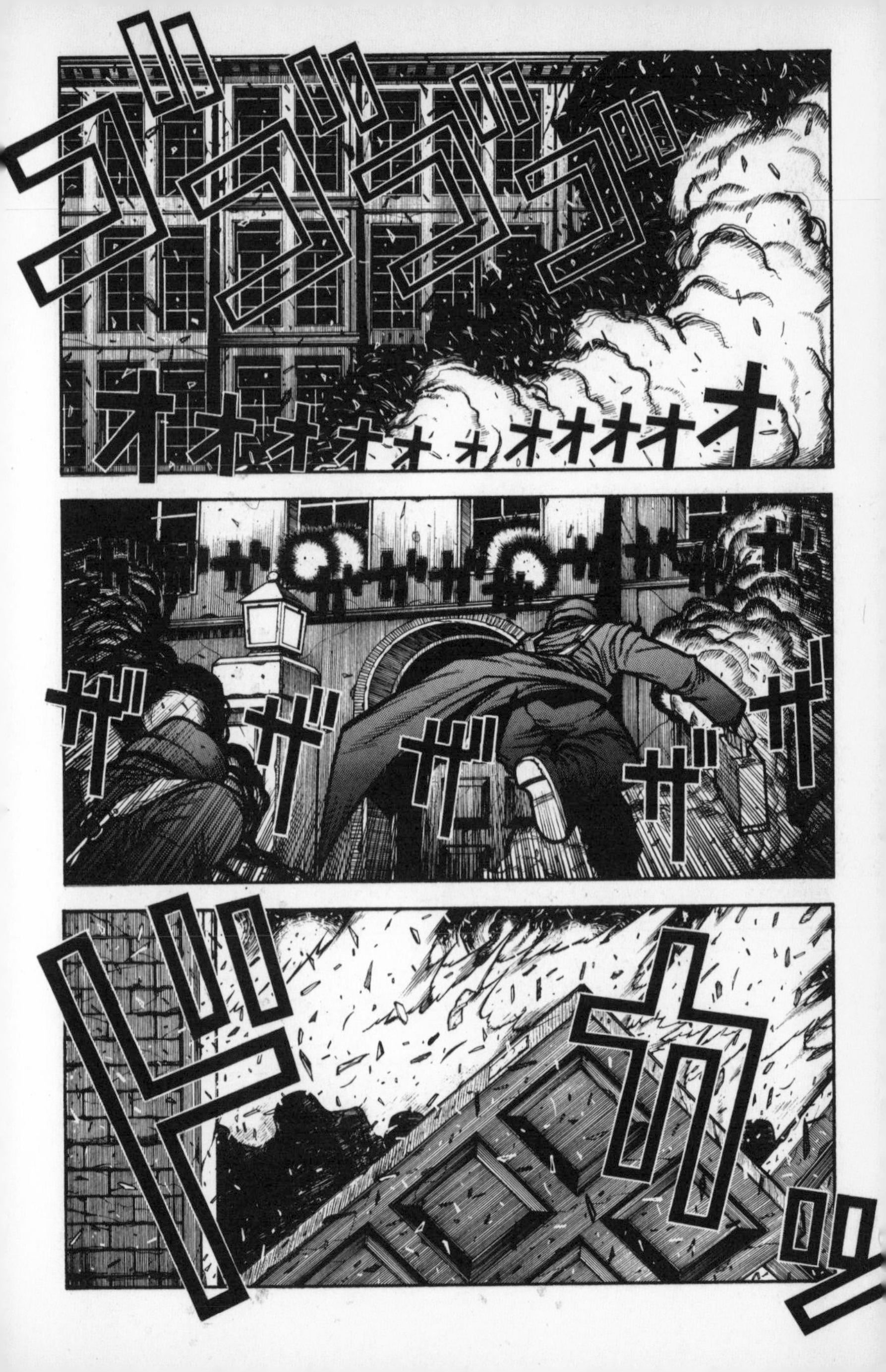
ゴゴゴゴ
オオオオオォォオオオオオオ
ザザザザザ

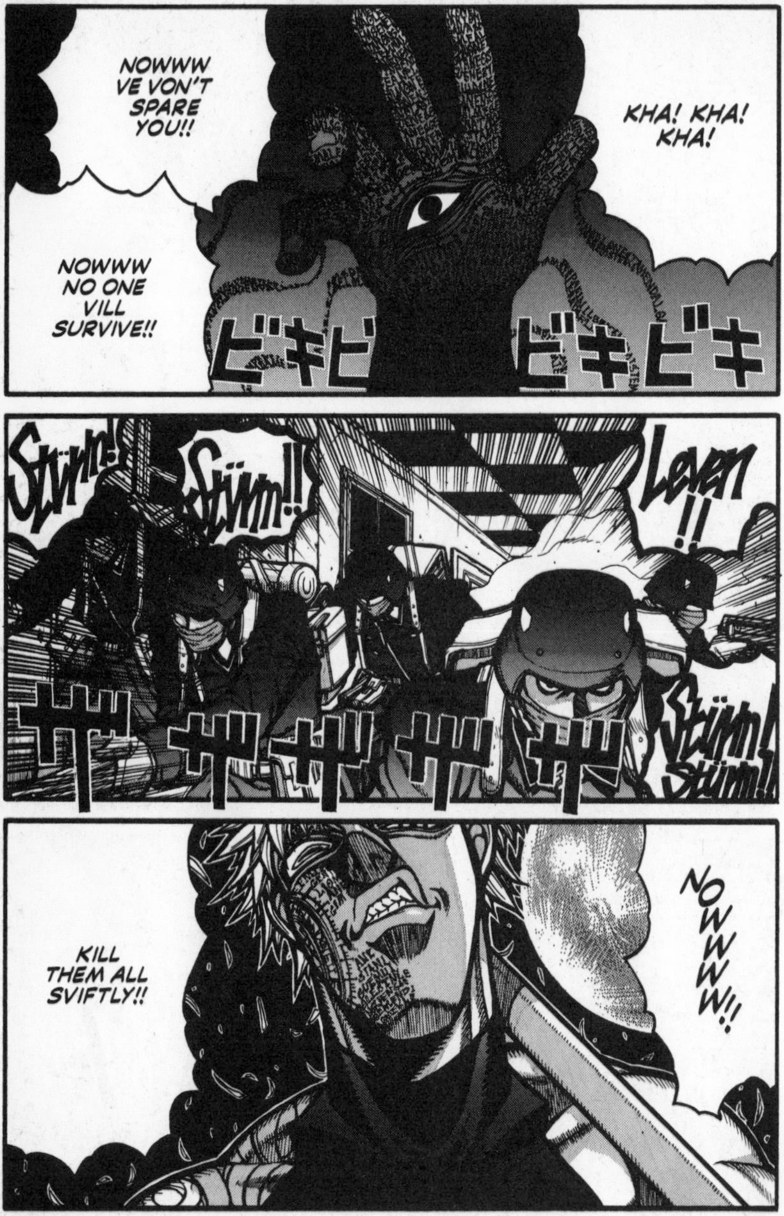
KHA! KHA! KHA!
NOWWW VE VON'T SPARE YOU!!
NOWWW NO ONE VILL SURVIVE!!
ビキビキ
ビキビ
Leven!!
Stürm!! Stürm!!
Stürm!!
Stürm!!
ザザザザザザ
NOWWWW!!
KILL THEM ALL SVIFTLY!!

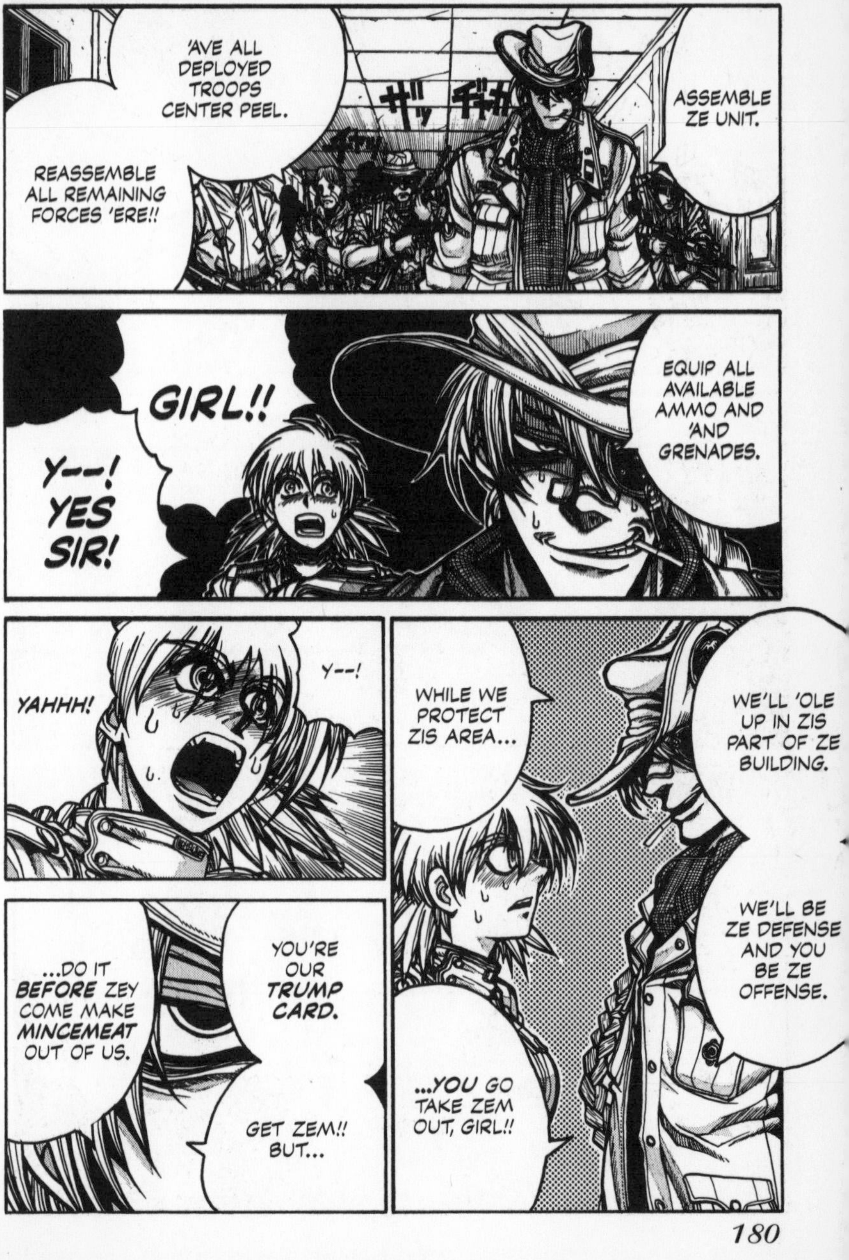
ASSEMBLE ZE UNIT.
'AVE ALL DEPLOYED TROOPS CENTER PEEL.
REASSEMBLE ALL REMAINING FORCES 'ERE!!
EQUIP ALL AVAILABLE AMMO AND 'AND GRENADES.
GIRL!!
Y--! YES SIR!
WE'LL 'OLE UP IN ZIS PART OF ZE BUILDING.
WHILE WE PROTECT ZIS AREA...
WE'LL BE ZE DEFENSE AND YOU BE ZE OFFENSE.
...*YOU* GO TAKE ZEM OUT, GIRL!!
Y--!
YAHHH!
YOU'RE OUR *TRUMP CARD.*
GET ZEM!! BUT...
...DO IT *BEFORE* ZEY COME MAKE *MINCEMEAT* OUT OF US.

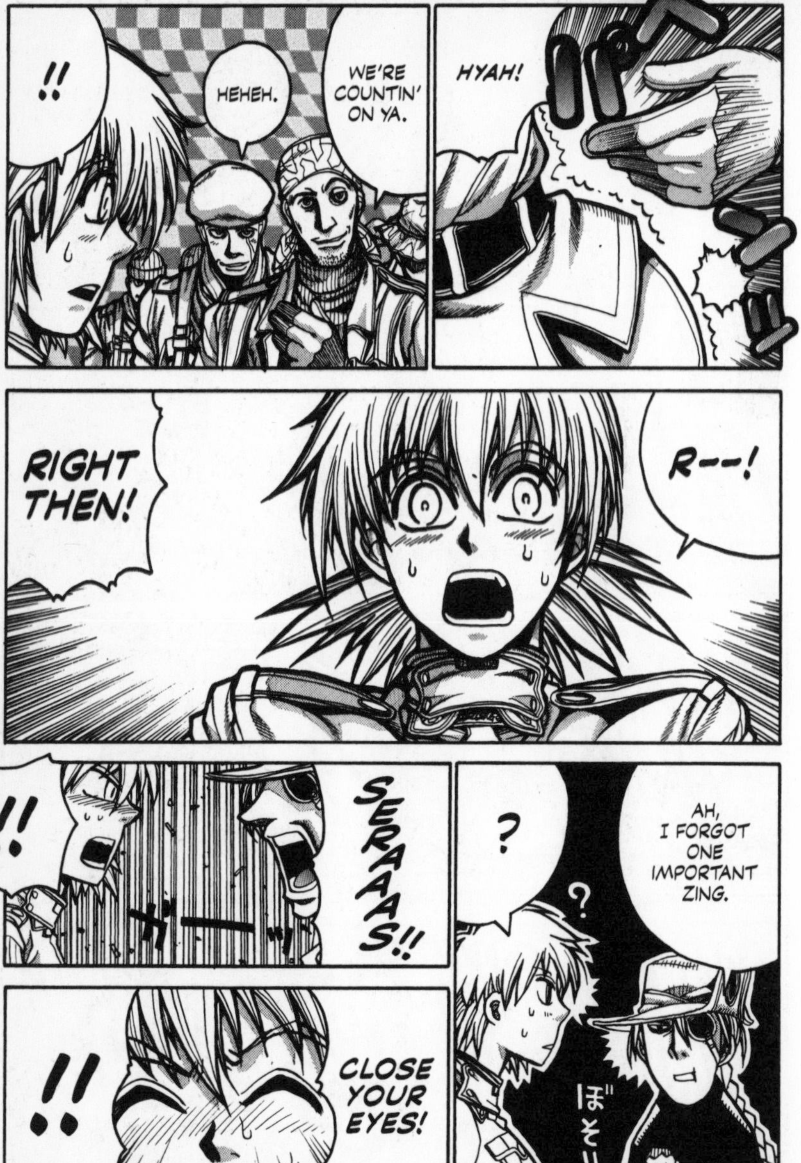
HYAH!
WE'RE COUNTIN' ON YA.
HEHEH.
!!
R--!
RIGHT THEN!
AH, I FORGOT ONE IMPORTANT ZING.
?
?
ぼそり
SERAAAS!!
!!
CLOSE YOUR EYES!
!!

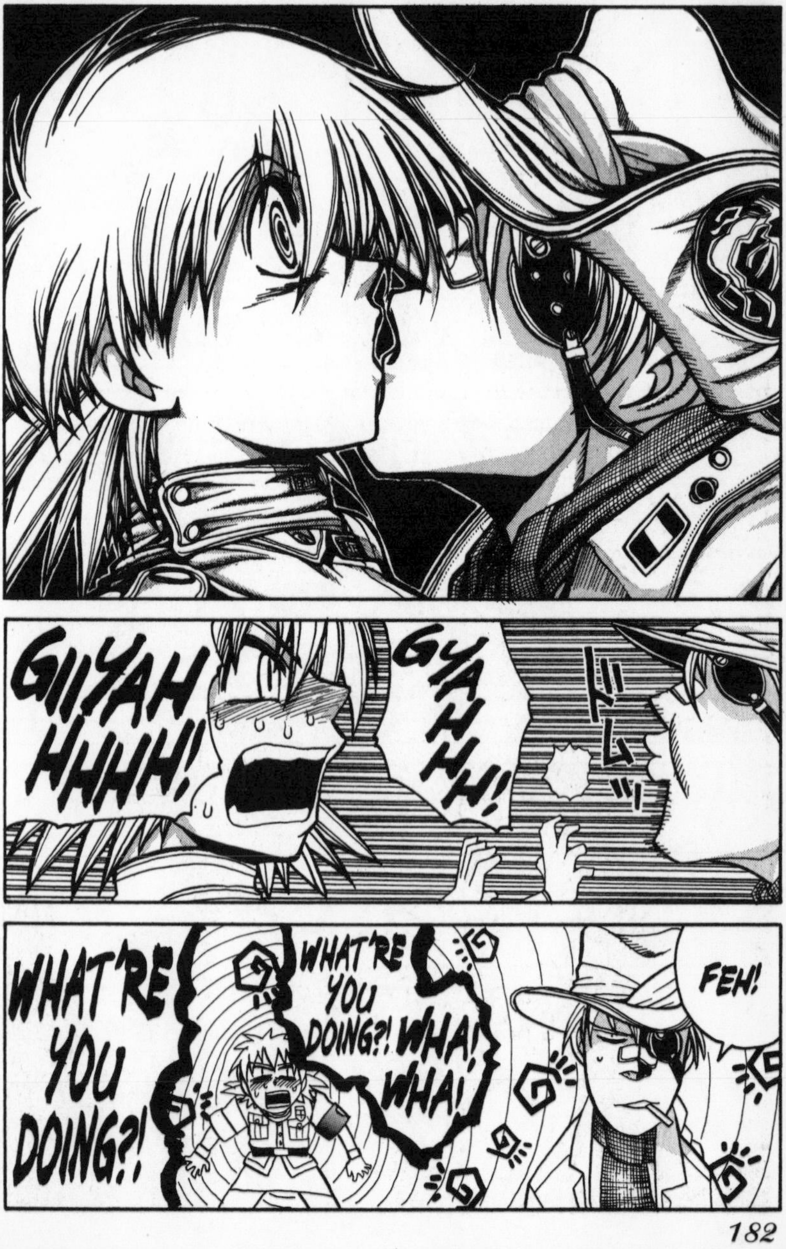
GYAHHHH!
GIIYAH HHHH!
FEH!
WHAT'RE YOU DOING?! WHA! WHA!
WHAT'RE YOU DOING?!

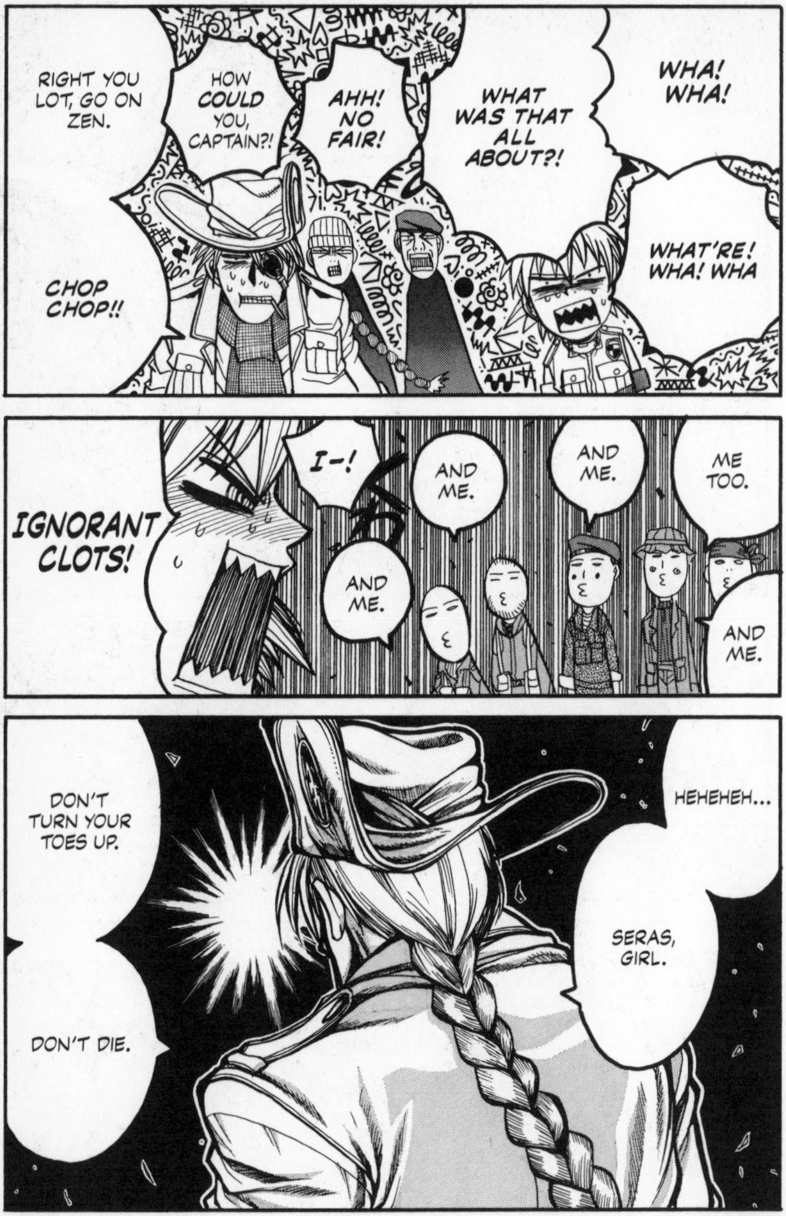
WHA! WHA!
WHAT'RE! WHA! WHA
WHAT WAS THAT ALL ABOUT?!
AHH! NO FAIR!
HOW COULD YOU, CAPTAIN?!
RIGHT YOU LOT, GO ON ZEN.
CHOP CHOP!!
ME TOO.
AND ME.
AND ME.
AND ME.
AND ME.
I-!
IGNORANT CLOTS!
HEHEHEH...
SERAS, GIRL.
DON'T TURN YOUR TOES UP.
DON'T DIE.

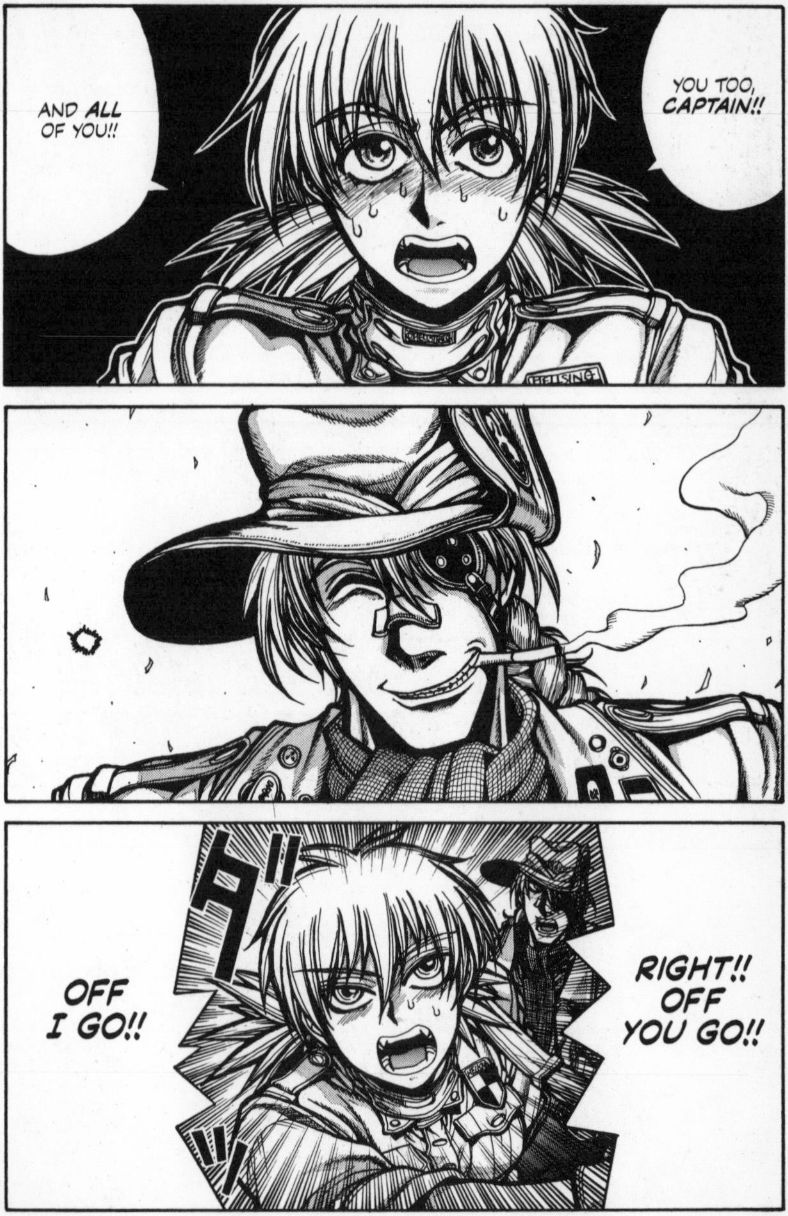
YOU TOO, CAPTAIN!!
AND ALL OF YOU!!
RIGHT!! OFF YOU GO!!
OFF I GO!!

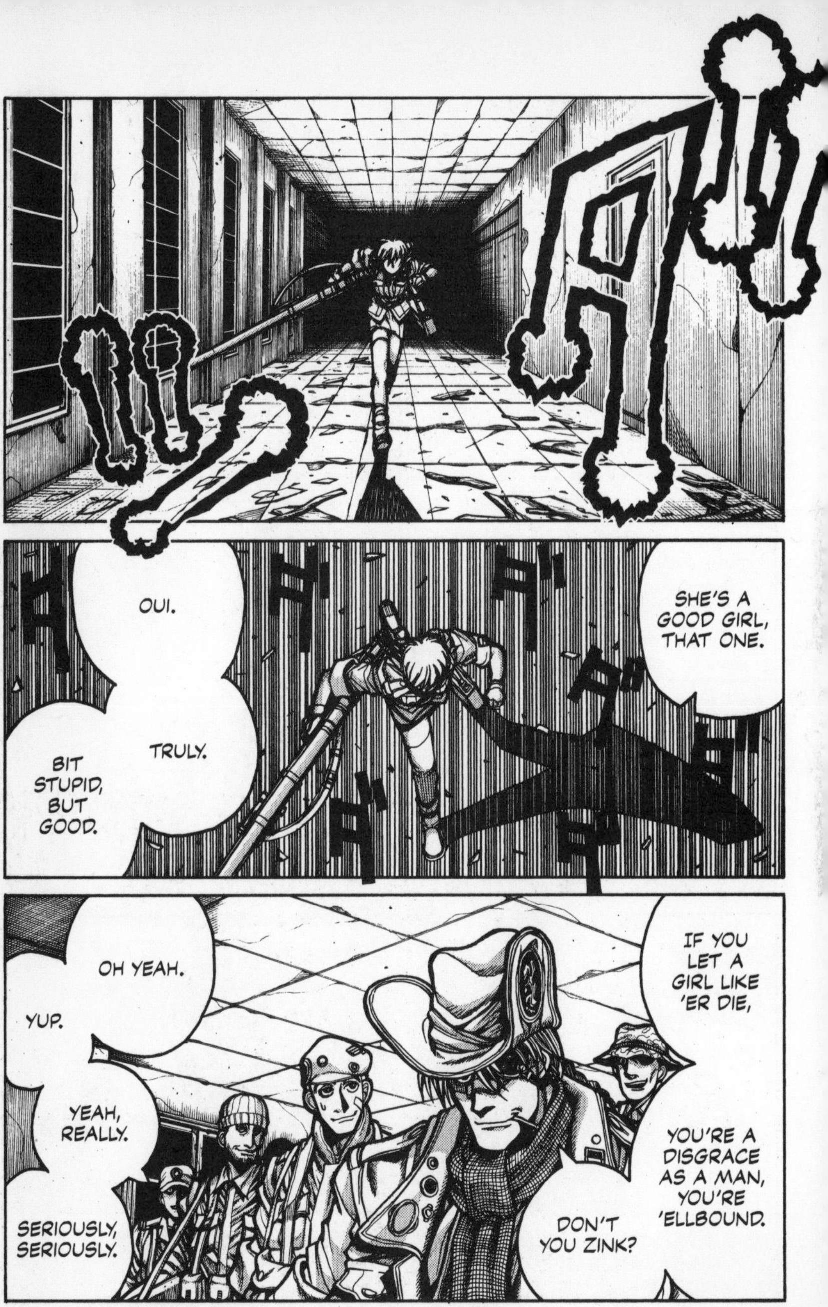
SHE'S A GOOD GIRL, THAT ONE.
OUI.
TRULY.
BIT STUPID, BUT GOOD.
IF YOU LET A GIRL LIKE 'ER DIE,
YOU'RE A DISGRACE AS A MAN, YOU'RE 'ELLBOUND.
DON'T YOU ZINK?
OH YEAH.
YUP.
YEAH, REALLY.
SERIOUSLY, SERIOUSLY.

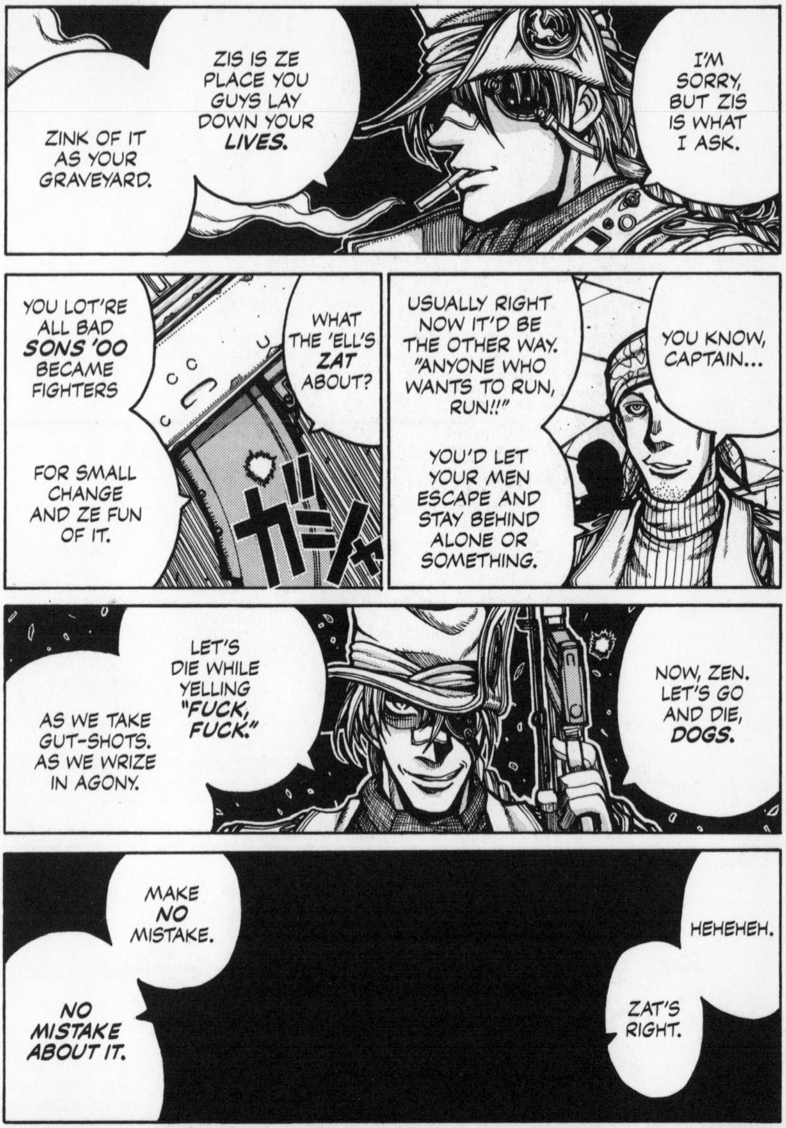
I'M SORRY, BUT ZIS IS WHAT I ASK.
ZIS IS ZE PLACE YOU GUYS LAY DOWN YOUR **LIVES.**
ZINK OF IT AS YOUR GRAVEYARD.
YOU KNOW, CAPTAIN...
USUALLY RIGHT NOW IT'D BE THE OTHER WAY. "ANYONE WHO WANTS TO RUN, RUN!!"
YOU'D LET YOUR MEN ESCAPE AND STAY BEHIND ALONE OR SOMETHING.
WHAT THE 'ELL'S **ZAT** ABOUT?
YOU LOT'RE ALL BAD **SONS 'OO** BECAME FIGHTERS
FOR SMALL CHANGE AND ZE FUN OF IT.
ガシャ
NOW, ZEN. LET'S GO AND DIE, **DOGS.**
LET'S DIE WHILE YELLING **"FUCK, FUCK."**
AS WE TAKE GUT-SHOTS. AS WE WRIZE IN AGONY.
HEHEHEH.
ZAT'S RIGHT.
MAKE **NO** MISTAKE.
NO MISTAKE ABOUT IT.

KOHTA HIRANO

I Billion Yen.

Kohta Hirano, so happy about
this volume going on sale that
he's changed into Sarah and
tries to pass it off on Fujita at
an exorbitant price for the
gallery fake.
(Shot to death 3 seconds later)

Hailing from Adachi Ward, Tokyo

Hobbies
+Being obnoxious, beating off

Favorite ER
+When Doctor Carter got hooked on drugs

Favorite Fukamichi ranker
+Sniper Karate

Favorite Mika Doi
+Sakiyama
*Note: Mika Doi does the voice for the
character Sakiyama in Air Master.

- Oh wow! That stinks! (surprised by my own fart.) Greetings. It is me. Little Ol' me. And here's another manga volume after nine months. You know, that makes two volumes in one year. Oh my. Surprising. (pfbt!)

- Anyway, it's the bomb. It's as awesome as taking a dump and a piss at the same time, and it feels so good you just swoon right there in the bathroom.

- Even so, a lot has happened over the course of nine months. Heads of broccoli went from 120 yen to 280, then fell to 150 yen. Nothing else really happened.

- Once again there's too much space left over.

- As there's too much space left over, I'm going to sing a song. Again.

"Okoi's song" -Basilisk folk song-

Haaaaa! Boobs, boobs, sun goes down on uuuus. ♪♫
Okoi's boobs, boobs, booby-boobs (booooobs)
I suck on Okoi's boobs, she sucks on my dick. (boobies!)
Sucking, sucked, I go down, she goes down, sun goes
  down on uuuus.
Then we go off on a journey for Nirvanaaaa,
  me and Okoi.
Before I knew it we were in Hanahata. ♫♪
Not Hanabatake, Hanahata. In Adachi Ward.
And we lived there many long years. About 100 of them.
In elegance.

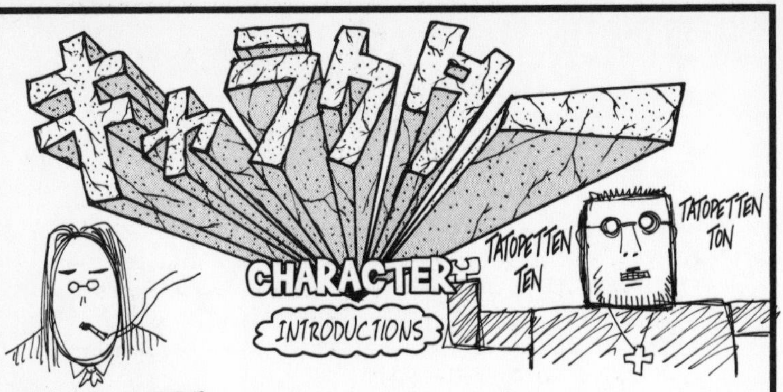
CHARACTER
INTRODUCTIONS
TATOPETTEN TEN
TATOPETTEN TON

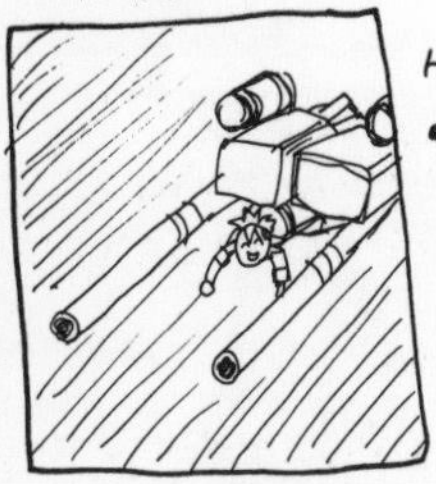

Harkonnen 2 Vladimir alias Urakonnen

- It actually has a beam weapon-nullifying I-Field attached, but the generator was busted up by Gato's claw arm and destroyed. That's just too bad, isn't it?
- Drawing it was a pain so it got ditched quickly.
- Now that I think about it I went overboard. Sorry about that.

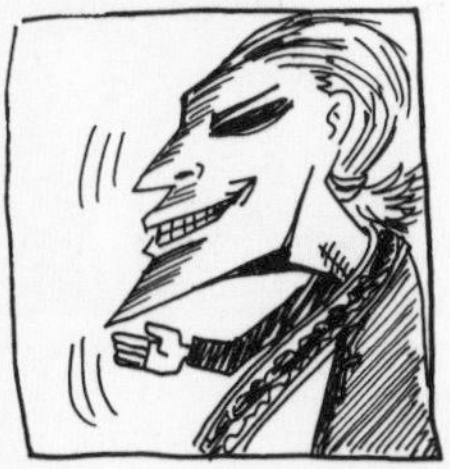

Maxwell Archbisop Version alias Baldy

- Gooo gooo Max-wellll
- Flyyy flyyy Grandizerrr
- When I first thought him up, he really wasn't this type of character at all...
- He's got the shadow of death.
- Anal-retentive

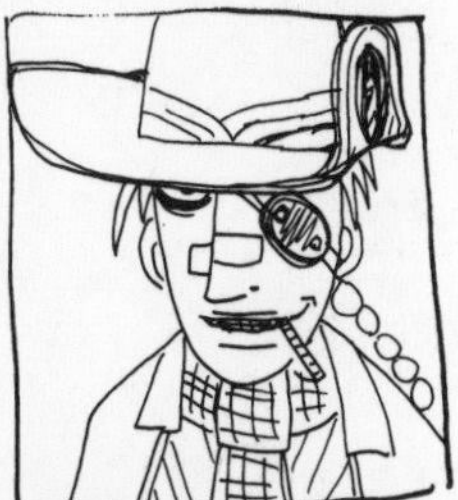

Captain Vernedead alias Kissing Fiend

- Armed with **Colt Single Action Army.**
- An erotic mercenary straight from my adult manga days.
- Loves boobs. He's French after all.
- Bonjour. mon ami. Les nénés.
- He's got the shadow of death.

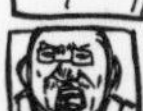

Yoshio Yamamori alias founding head of the Tenmasa Corporation
"Hey hey, nice ass! Where ya from, girlie? Woops."
After changing the Hiroshima Yamamori gang into a political organization (the Tenmasa Corporation), he handed over the position of chairman.

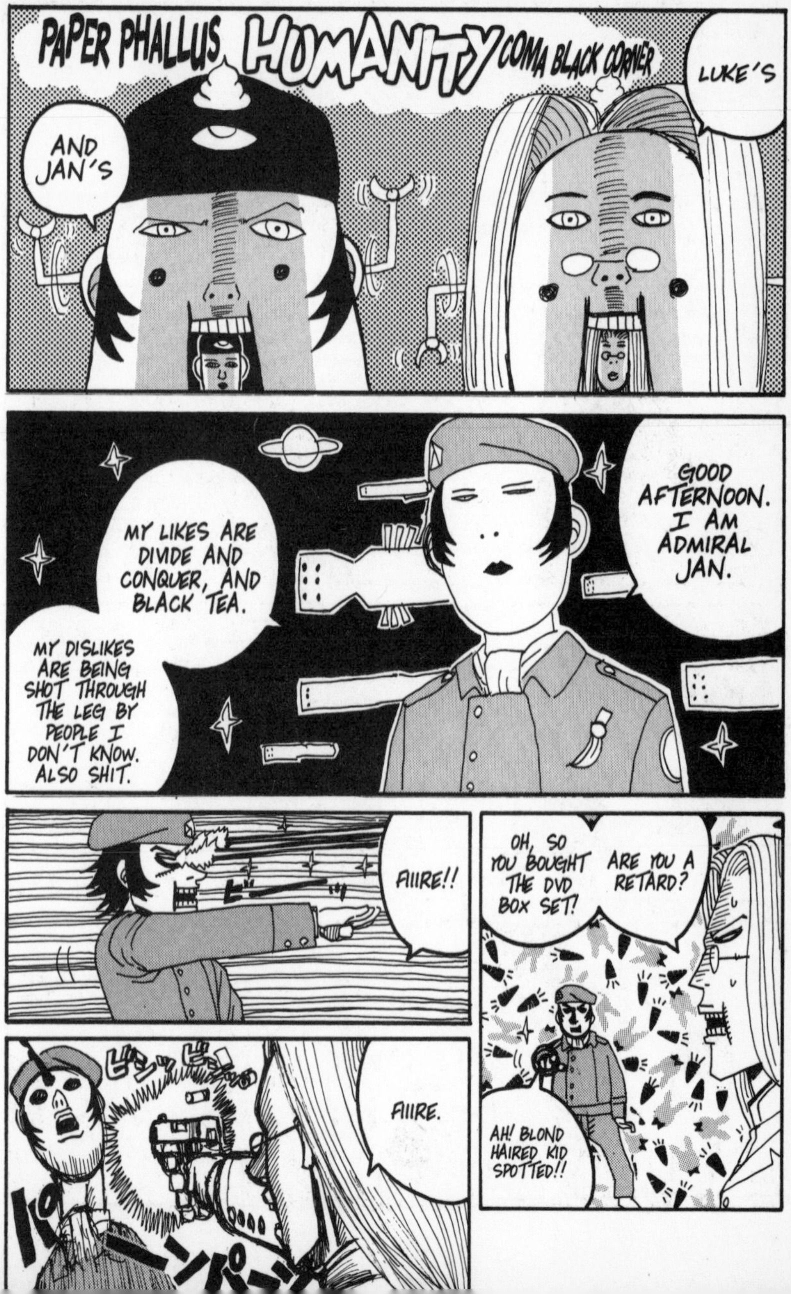
PAPER PHALLUS HUMANITY COMA BLACK CORNER
LUKE'S
AND JAN'S
GOOD AFTERNOON. I AM ADMIRAL JAN.
MY LIKES ARE DIVIDE AND CONQUER, AND BLACK TEA.
MY DISLIKES ARE BEING SHOT THROUGH THE LEG BY PEOPLE I DON'T KNOW. ALSO SHIT.
ARE YOU A RETARD?
OH, SO YOU BOUGHT THE DVD BOX SET!
AH! BLOND HAIRED KID SPOTTED!!
FIIIRE!!
FIIIRE.

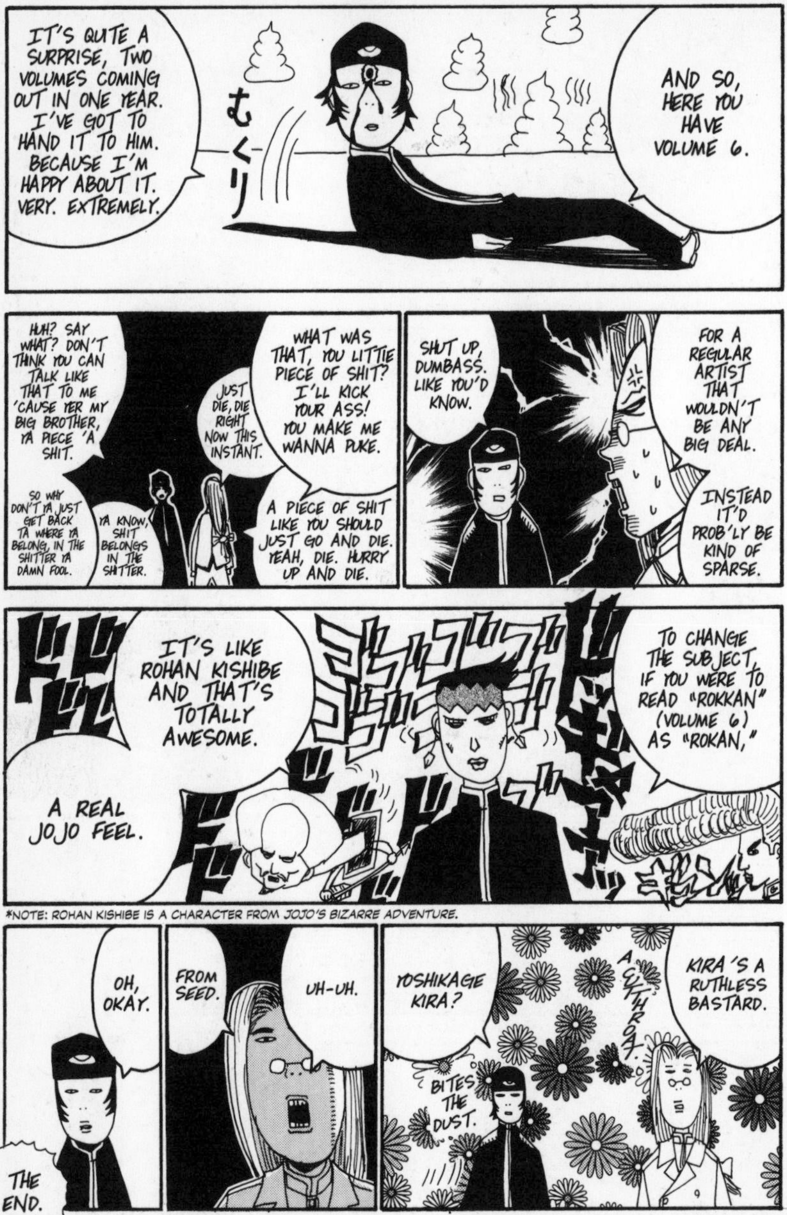
AND SO, HERE YOU HAVE VOLUME 6.
IT'S QUITE A SURPRISE, TWO VOLUMES COMING OUT IN ONE YEAR. I'VE GOT TO HAND IT TO HIM. BECAUSE I'M HAPPY ABOUT IT. VERY. EXTREMELY.
むくり
FOR A REGULAR ARTIST THAT WOULDN'T BE ANY BIG DEAL.
INSTEAD IT'D PROB'LY BE KIND OF SPARSE.
SHUT UP, DUMBASS. LIKE YOU'D KNOW.
WHAT WAS THAT, YOU LITTIE PIECE OF SHIT? I'LL KICK YOUR ASS! YOU MAKE ME WANNA PUKE.
JUST DIE, DIE RIGHT NOW THIS INSTANT.
HUH? SAY WHAT? DON'T THINK YOU CAN TALK LIKE THAT TO ME 'CAUSE YER MY BIG BROTHER, YA PIECE 'A SHIT.
A PIECE OF SHIT LIKE YOU SHOULD JUST GO AND DIE. YEAH, DIE. HURRY UP AND DIE.
YA KNOW, SHIT BELONGS IN THE SHITTER.
SO WHY DON'T YA JUST GET BACK TA WHERE YA BELONG, IN THE SHITTER YA DAMN FOOL.
TO CHANGE THE SUBJECT, IF YOU WERE TO READ "ROKKAN" (VOLUME 6) AS "ROKAN,"
IT'S LIKE ROHAN KISHIBE AND THAT'S TOTALLY AWESOME.
A REAL JOJO FEEL.
KIRA'S A RUTHLESS BASTARD.
YOSHIKAGE KIRA?
BITES THE DUST.
UH-UH.
FROM SEED.
OH, OKAY.
THE END.

*NOTE: ROHAN KISHIBE IS A CHARACTER FROM JOJO'S BIZARRE ADVENTURE.

STOP

This is the back of the book!

This manga collection is translated into English but oriented in right-to-left reading format at the creator's request, maintaining the artwork's visual orientation as originally published in Japan. If you've never read manga in this way before, take a look at the diagram below to give yourself an idea of how to go about it. Basically, you'll be starting in the upper right corner and will read each balloon and panel moving right to left. It may take some getting used to, but you should get the hang of it very quickly. Have fun!

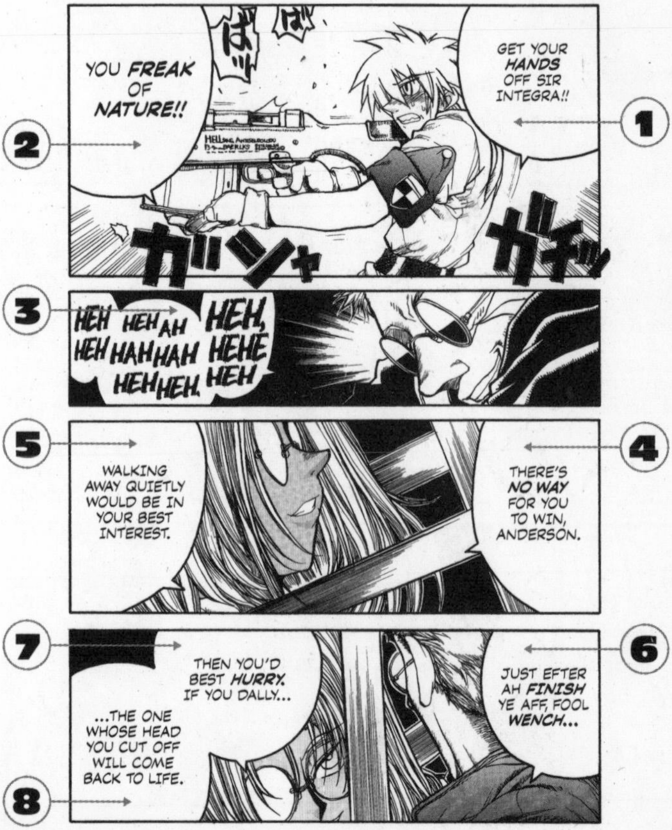
1
GET YOUR HANDS OFF SIR INTEGRA!!
2
YOU FREAK OF NATURE!!
3
HEH, HEHE HEH
AH HAH HEH.
HEH HAH HEH
HEH HEH
4
THERE'S NO WAY FOR YOU TO WIN, ANDERSON.
5
WALKING AWAY QUIETLY WOULD BE IN YOUR BEST INTEREST.
6
JUST EFTER AH FINISH YE AFF, FOOL WENCH...
7
THEN YOU'D BEST HURRY. IF YOU DALLY...
8
...THE ONE WHOSE HEAD YOU CUT OFF WILL COME BACK TO LIFE.